Matt's Boys
of Wattle Creek

Olwyn Harris

Unless otherwise stated Scriptures quoted here are from the King James Version (Authorised version). First published in 1611. Quoted from the KJV Classic Reference Bible, copyright 1983 by the Zondervan Corporation.

A special thank you goes to Cedric and Joan Cook for allowing "Sandy Knowe" to be featured on the cover. The property has been owned by them since 1968 and is believed to have been built prior to 1870 as an inn which had a wine and butcher shop. It is also known locally as the Strahley house.

Published by: Helen Brown
Cover Art: In Your Eyes Photography (Jennifer Maybury)
Cover Design & Publishing Facilitator: Wendy Wood
Technical support end eBook conversion: Ridge Wilkins

For more copies contact the Helen Brown at:
Glenburnie Homestead
212 Glenburnie Road
ROB ROY NSW 2360
Mobile: 0422 577 663
Email: hbrown19561@gmail.com

Dedication: to my boys, Dean and Steven...
and your father, Trevor, who has shared the journey
with me.
May every good plan and vision God has for you come
to be...

Table of Contents

Prologue

Matt lashed Josie's chair to the back of the cart. He tightened the ropes and checked them again. He stepped back as a light trap rattled past, splashing up mud from the street onto his trousers. "Jump up son. We have a good way to go today."

Little Nathaniel stood resolutely beside his dad; his five-year-old hands stuck firmly in his pockets like his father. "No Daddy. Mummy and the baby need to ride more."

Matt ruffled his hair. "That's my boy… looking out for your mother. I'll need you to hop up later though, just to keep an eye on them for me. Is that okay? Tonight, we pick up the saddle horses, so tomorrow we can ride."

He beamed. His scrubbed face glowing with pride. Matt walked to the front. "Ready? We are all set!" Josie returned his look with determination, and smoothed the small blanket that coved her baby's little arms. The trip loomed large and uncertain. This was daunting, this start to their new life, away from everything that had been familiar for their family. She glanced at Toby sitting beside her, his chubby legs swinging over the edge of the seat.

Matt reached up and gave his wife's hand a reassuring squeeze. "Tobias, you help with your baby brother now. Mummy might need some help if Malachi is restless." Toby's wide eyes nodded seriously. He didn't say anything; his legs continued to swing. "Well, let's make a start. Nat, come here; we are going to pray." Nat scampered to his father's side and held onto his strong hand, as his voice spoke clearly over the sounds of the street. "Heavenly Father, we commit our trip and new life to you as we set out. I ask Father, for your protection and your blessing over our family, not only for this trip but also for our new life on the farm at Wattle Creek. I pray today – as I do every day, especially for my boys, that they will grow strong in Your ways, with hearts completely devoted to You. That their friendships, and families to come, will be as blessed as I am with my Josie and my boys. This I ask in Jesus' Name, Amen."

Then Matt walked resolutely to the harness horses and grabbed the halter, clicking his tongue. The cart wheels slowly turning as they started moving, slowly walking from one life... into another.

Part 1

The Baker's Daughter

Acknowledgment:
Many thanks to Mr John Stark for chatting to me about his
Bakery days

"Dear Tobias,

I sit here and watch you in your crib. Your little screwed up face is so expressive even as you nap. I wonder what dreams you are having that make you smile and sigh in your sleep. You look so contented and I wish I could always protect you against the painful reality of a world that is not always kind. But that is not a realistic prayer for a father to pray. I would rather pray wisdom, and strength, and courage for my son... so that no matter what life throws at him, he will be a man who will stand strong, and tall – daring to be innovative and a challenger of the way things are. I asked God for a character study... someone to pattern my prayers for you... and I thought of Solomon: a man of wisdom, a leader who leant on the strength of God to undertake the mission God had on his life. And while he remained humble and focused on the things of God, his nation and the people in his care, prospered and were blessed.

So, Tobias... I would pray that you would be a Solomon... but that you would learn from his mistakes, and stay close to the heart of God with integrity. Don't be lured away by the excesses of this world. What potential lies in your tiny hands that clasp so trustingly onto my rough fingers? The day will come when my hand is not here for you to hang onto... so son, hang on tight to the hand of God, stay close to his chest so that you can always hear his heartbeat. Never let Him go.

~ your devoted Father, always..."

1.

The routine was so automatic that it required no thought at all. It was as if the lamp lit itself voluntarily in the early morning, lighting up the dough that had stood and proved all night in the long dough trough that stood in the centre of the bakery floor. The large wooden tables standing along the wall held floured sacks lined up, set for the dough to be sectioned and thrown. Everything stood in readiness for the clock to turn five. The Bakery Inspector could spring a visit and impose a fine for breaking the five o'clock law: no bakery was to operate before five o'clock in the morning. Here there was no room for the luxury of budgeting fines, or escape hatches and lock-down drills like some of the larger bakeries.

Belle lifted her floured hand to her face to hook a stray hair behind her ear and went to tend the oven fire. She stared at the clock and sighed. He didn't even show this morning. She knew exactly how long was needed for the ovens to be hot for the risen dough and she could wait no longer. She grimaced at the dwindled wood chutes, and knew she could not afford the time to fill them herself. But again… she would have to. Her father had worked solo all his bakery years. She again shook her head in disappointment: if only she had that same capacity. This was such physical work. She loaded some of the remaining logs of river oak into the firebox. Surely, he would come any moment… this wood burnt hot and fast – right for bakery ovens, but not good for tardy workers.

She washed the soot off her hands and proceeded back to the heavy wooden benches scrubbed to a polished finish. She cut the dough through with the metal scraper. She paused and leant over the wooden yeast troughs, her tired body aching with an unnatural heaviness. Her father had done the work of three bakers. That was before he had even created his mixing machine. She stared at it standing abandoned in the corner. One week. Life had changed so dramatically in one week.

She heard her young helper rattling at the door, taking off his boots for his indoor shop shoes. "Terry! Hurry up with that wood! I've started the ovens but they are starting to fade. Come on – you're way late this morning. We'll never be able to deliver on time!"

She thought she heard a mumbled "Sorry", but doubted very seriously he understood the implications of her plight. She needed support now, not someone who would take advantage of her predicament. Belle didn't look up. She needed to focus. She had been intending to try extra dough this morning, but she was glad she hadn't. It would not do to compromise the quality of the loaves she produced.

As she started into the rhythmic kneading, the knots in her shoulders began to uncoil. Round and over, turn and fold; round and over, turn and fold. She thumped it into the floured bag and went onto the next... round and over, turn and fold; round and over, turn and fold. She was relieved to get to this part of the early morning routine. It gave her thinking time. Time to strategise. She needed to absorb all the things that had happened.

It would be an understatement to say she had been stunned by what the last week had thrown at her. Another stroke! Another one, when her father's progress had been so remarkable. What a blessing their little town had a hospital – well, everyone called it the hospital. It was a small two-ward private establishment that was well serviced because their town was fortunate enough to have a permanent doctor. Just when they were planning to bring her dad home in a few days to finish recuperating, another vicious attack had left him completely paralysed.

He could not talk. He stared through Belle as she held his clammy, limp hand. Belle's heart ripped apart. These hands carried her as a child; they had done the work of mother *and* father; lifted and lugged more loaves of bread than this little community could count. He single-handedly established their business. Her father had always said it was "their" business – never just his. Now those muscles refused to work and distorted his aging, handsome features. An occasional tear leaked uncontrollably from his unfocused eyes. Although they were still that famous iron-steel blue, the glint had faded into an unrecognisable watery marsh. The colour of his eyes had earned him a name for being a hard businessman. But to Belle - his only family, those same steel-blue eyes had been symbolic of his solid, unbending dependability. Now they could not even see.

Belle pounded the dough as anger throbbed into her hands. Round and over, turn and fold; round and over, turn and fold. She was not going to let every thing that her father had built turn into powder before her eyes. She could almost see it spinning into reverse. This morning she had woken with a nightmare freshly imprinted on her soul. When she went to open the oven, the loaves had not baked. They had unmixed themselves and the flour had swirled away into a draught when she pulled open the oven door… leaving nothing. Nothing at all… except the hot oven tins that burnt her hand and clattered loudly as they fell to the hard stone floor, jolting her awake.

Belle blinked violently as she pounded again on the dough under the heel of her hands. Even her arms, strong from years of bakery work, ached from the tension she felt knotting up in her slight body once more. She went straight on to throw the batch of brown dough and to start over. There was no way she could compete with the demand that her dad's mixing machine had created… but at least she could hang on to the reduced orders from her father's customers who had heard of his tragedy. Without exception, every customer had left a note or concocted some sort of excuse as to why their orders no longer needed to be so large.

"The kids have gone over to Gran's for a few days… could we just have a single loaf this week?"

"Doc's put Blake on a diet, but we couldn't do without at least one of your loaves…"

"Your bread is our favourite, but my boys have a hankering after old fashioned damper just now. One loaf today and one on Thursday should do…"

Every time Belle noted their request in her order book, her heart acknowledged their selfless desire to help her retain her dignity and sustain the business in a manageable form until her father got better. She knew there were a lot of bread-tins being dusted off at home and quietly put back into service.

She heard Terry cutting the wood in rhythm with her kneading and she almost felt the pressure in her brow release. Finally! She hoped her persistence in trying to find reliable help had been rewarded. Although she did concede he was probably not the least bit remorseful over being late once more. Terry had been coming for nine weeks. He was as reliable as a jittery cricket on a burning log. Belle would have told him not to bother coming in a thousand times, but she did not have many options. Her ability to pay full wages was limited and she absolutely refused to alter her father's policy of full day's pay for a full day's work. The fact that Terry didn't offer a full days work helped her put a good face on unreliable help. Gone were the days when the bakery produced three or four hundred loaves a week. It was all history since her dad became ill.

Belle started the round of weighing and shaping the dough into the dark baker's tins. Flour smeared across her forehead and streaked her dark hair. "I'm just about done here! Can you check the oven? Terry!" She glanced over to the wall to see his back disappear out the door. She sighed impatiently. Why in the world did she sacrifice so much to pay his wage? The ovens at least should be covered! She finished shaping the last loaf and went to check it for herself. To her amazement the wood box was comfortably full and freshly loaded, and the wide mouth of the firebox full of red-hot coals. With relief she tested the heat of the oven by tossing a handful of flour onto the floor of the wide stone bakers' oven. The flour smoked slowly, showing that it was ready for baking. The first of the rounded, blanched loaves were set to slide the tins into place on the long oar-like peels. She started at the back and systematically lined up the tins until the floor of the oven was stacked with baker's tins and the sweet smell of baking bread.

As she was taking the first tins from the oven and slid them onto the cooling racks, she heard Terry putting on his boots at the door. Belle smiled as she checked the clock and called out her thanks. It was agreed he would stay until the ovens were finished with. This was the first time in ages that he had actually made the distance. They may not be so late this morning after all, even if she still had to hitch the delivery cart. But when she went to the stable, to her surprise, old Bronza was already harnessed and quietly eating from a nosebag. All she needed to do was load the deliveries into the bakery cart.

Belle climbed into the seat, quietly clicked her tongue and flicked the reigns. For years it was the morning ride through the town with her Dad that was the reward for a morning's work well done. Like a morning sparrow they watched households stir into their daily routine. Bronza snorted lazily and slowly ambled his way to the start of the run, his heavy hooves puffed up dust on the streets. The daybreak sun streamed sleepily through the trees and shone gold on his tarnished coppery coat, that morning phenomenon that gave him his name: Bronza.

Today, she barely noticed the enchantment of dew on the little window boxes with hardy geraniums spilling out over the sills of the cottages. Her thoughts swirled around at a fever pitch pace. By the time Bronza turned into the back lane that led to the stable and shed at the rear of the shop, Belle forced herself to start tuning her mind to the rest of the day. Her original expectation was that Terry would manage the shop until she returned from the deliveries. During the morning she would still have a chance to catch up with household chores as she kept an ear out of the tinkling of the bell by the door for any customers that would drop by. It was a fairly routine sort of business. By half eight o'clock most of the mothers had bagged their kid's lunches and were ready to tackle other morning routines. Very few customers would come in without pre-ordering their loaves. The bread register was as predicable as Christmas.

Yes, the morning had gone smoothly. It had to be a sign that things were getting better. Surely Doctor Wallace would tell her today when she could bring her father home.

But Doc Wallace would not commit to a time line for her father's recovery... that morning, or the next week. Every morning the Doc gently told her it was a waiting game: hard work and waiting. There was nothing else they could do. Every morning she went to see him with the hope that today there would be some improvement.

For the first time in ages she felt the bakery work was manageable. This morning she had confidently attempted larger doughs, and handled them easily. Belle felt victorious over that milestone. No matter how long it took, she would hang on. Bronza plodded into the stable yard, returning from the deliveries and Belle felt a stab of guilt for being so harsh with Terry. With just a little extra time he had settled in remarkably well. How she appreciated him getting to his duties with no fuss. No longer did she have to prompt and cajole. The fact he kept out of her way and honoured her space in her crisis was another point in his favour. As she unhitched Bronza from the cart, she heard Terry preparing to go off into his day. Grabbing a remaining loaf from the breadbasket on the seat she ran out of the stable into the morning light.

"Wait! Terry, I wanted to thank you..." He was mounting his saddle horse, his hat down over his eyes. She handed him the bread, her voice taking on a starched school-marm' tone. She didn't mean to be condescending, but his perpetual stupidity seemed to always make her feel older than her nineteen years.

"Terry, you haven't been taking your loaves home, so I've delivered them to your Mum this week. Could you give this extra loaf to your mother?" Now she felt awkward. "And... Terry...." She cleared her throat. "I... arhh, I wanted to thank you. You have worked really hard this last week... your help has been good and I really appreciate it."

"Ah-huh," he mumbled. "I scrubbed the benches and floor..."

As he turned the horse to leave, even in the distress that flooded her life, Belle had to look twice. He paused momentarily and decided to continue, gently nudging his horse to go. But before he could move far, Belle whirled past and grabbed the bridle forcefully; the horse flung its head back in surprise, so the rider's brimmed hat went toppling to the ground. She had suddenly remembered: young Terry only rode a dilapidated pushbike.

The rider's shoulders slumped momentarily, as if he was bracing himself for the barrage that he knew would be forthcoming, but he stayed in his saddle.

"Toby Lawson? Is that you?"

There was a pause. "Uhuh…" came the mumbled reply.

"Toby! What do you think you're doing? I don't want people coming around and giving out charity!"

His eyes flashed so brightly it was a wonder Belle did not see the sparks fly. He squeezed his lids shut, trying to dissipate the anger that her arrogance ignited. Why! Why didn't he just ride off and leave her to it? He knew she would go under without help… well, why shouldn't she, if she was so hell-bent on destruction?

He sighed as a thousand thoughts assaulted his mind. He knew why. Damn it! He kicked himself. It was sloppy of him not to keep the standard of his work at a Terry-all-time-low. This wasn't at all what he had planned. Still, he had to somehow make his assistance acceptable. He'd been so sure he could continue running on anonymity. But now he was exposed, he had to change tack. Slowly… ever so slowly, he rolled his shoulders and eased the tension out of his frame. His head sagged forward, and he feigned shame. He slowly climbed down from his saddle stumbling clumsily as his foot touched the ground. "Sorry Belle…" He scraped his foot retardedly.

"Sorry Belle?" Belle blinked as she heard his toneless response.

"Toby - are you okay?" This was not the Tobias that she knew. The restless stance and the way he spoke… it

20

sounded so… simple… but not in the pure, uncomplicated way. Even the way he said her name… it was nothing. He could have easily been saying "wheelbarrow".

"Belle… I've gotta go… Nat will be cross…" His voice trailed off… listless and colourless… almost anxious.

"Cross?" Now she was concerned. Never, in all the years they waged war at school, did he ever say anything so overworked. Suddenly Belle burst out laughing. "Okay," she conceded, "You really had me going! You can cut it out now!"

But he didn't smile. He stood, stooped and hopeless…like a burning wick that had been pinched out and left smouldering.

"I gotta go… Nat will be cross… I gotta help with the brandin' today…"

She stared at him in disbelief. "Toby – what's got into you? What happened?"

It seemed he was getting agitated. "Nothin'. I gotta go… Nat will be…"

"Yes, yes… I know… he will be cross. I just…" She stopped and shook her head still hanging onto the reigns. He stumbled to his horse. "Wait! Where's Terry?"

"I dunno… maybe home…" he slowly admitted. The statement was totally beguiling.

The effect on Belle was bewildering. Her mind was already fogged with fatigue and grief over her dad, now this? Did life have any more blows to slug at her and knock the air out of her lungs? Her face contorted as she struggled for control. She spoke slowly… "Come on Toby. Why did you come here if you don't know? You must know," Belle pressed impatiently.

He hung his head at an exaggerated angle. He wished now that he could have stayed anonymous; he had for over a week. Every day was another notch in his belt. Belle – the ice child, his aggressive opponent, had finally let him help her; all be it – unknowingly. For some egotistical reason, that did nothing to dampen the edge of victory. But suddenly it didn't seem so clever. He would have eagerly walked away if he could. He slowly shrugged his shoulders and in the process committed himself even deeper. He *was* bound, so he was here to stay, at least until he wasn't needed or the crisis abated, either of which didn't look like they were going to happen any time soon. Slowly he drawled out his reply. "I dunno... I come to chop the wood since Terry hurt his arm bad. Doc Wallace said..."

Belle went quiet. This too was bizarre. "Doc Wallace sent you? Terry hurt his arm?"

"I gotta go... Nat will be..."

Her mind grappled with the memory of last night's mixing of the doughs. She had impatiently waited for Terry to lift the flour bags into the trough, and had continued all night with her own thoughts. But it hadn't been Terry who had spent such a long time in the flour room tidying and setting mice traps. "Does Nat know you helped me last night?" she asked, suddenly feeling she was collaborating in a crime scene. She was abetting truancy and breaking a curfew.

"Doc Wallace said it was okay..."

"Alright Toby, go straight home. Thank you for helping. I'll get to the bottom of this. Just give this to your

Mother… okay?" The tinkling bell of the shop door, forced her hand from the halter and she returned to the shop so she could serve her morning customers.

2.

The sun rose higher and reflected tones of bronze-copper off Bronza's coat. Belle climbed up, settling in the seat of the cart as the last of the close deliveries around town were completed. Bronza would trudge from house to house on autopilot, as she ran into the house yards and placed loaves into waiting bread-baskets.

Each household had their own quirky little spot for the bread. Mrs Hollis has her basket on top of the ice-box on the side verandah. Mrs Craddick only wanted one loaf delivered and always came into the shop later to pick up two more. The Jameson household had a basket inside their mailbox by the gate – an enormous structure that mirrored the style of the main residence and was more like an elaborate house itself than a mailbox. Belle sometimes wondered if swaggies spend a night's boarding in their mailbox… blessing the family for the best night's shelter they had had in a while.

It is the privilege of those few early morning delivery services to know every household's routine: the baker, the milkman and the ice deliveries. They all knew who woke early. Some were stirring when Bronza trudged past their gate and a few households were late risers, cloaked in sleepy silence awaiting their fresh bread and milk deliveries before they started their day with any seriousness. It was considered something of a moral failing to be a late riser in Wattle Creek.

Much to Bronza's consternation, Belle did the deliveries in a different order this morning. The very last delivery she pulled up outside Terry's ramshackle home with the remaining loaves of bread in her basket. A grubby two-year old without a nappy, was playing with a flea bitten dog near the step. His face lit up when he saw the Bakery Cart.

"Mumma! Mumma! Bed-cart! Bed-cart! Yummy!" He toddled towards the cart and fell over the dog chewing on a large shank bone. Belle quickly went to set the lad up on his legs but the dog snarled, baring its gums. Belle carefully backed off.

"Hi Hermie... would you tell your Mummy I've brought some bread for you?" He toddled away squealing in anticipation. The dog and Belle carefully eyed each other at a distance.

Mrs Levin emerged at the door. Even in the morning, her dress was crushed and soiled. She anxiously smoothed her hair, and wiped her hands on the tatted apron that bulged just a little too much. Surely, she was not pregnant again? Belle never remembered seeing Doris when she was not pregnant or didn't have a baby attached to her hip. It somehow made her seem much stouter than she actually was. Doris lifted little Hermie and hitched him onto her hip. "My Miss Belle, you are a sight for sore eyes. Come in, come in."

Belle was not intending to stay. Levin's lived on the wrong side of the railway tracks... but the look on this woman's face made her think that perhaps there was at least one soul on this earth whose plight was less fortunate than her own. Belle pointed to the dog barring her way; its teeth exposing another guttural growl. Doris picked up a stray boot by the door and flung it at his head. He went hurtling around the corner with a yelp.

Belle collected the bread from the cart and came inside. There was a string of kids that pounced on the basket. Mrs Levin shouted out rough instructions. "Fanny – you make sure all them kids share now! Ya'll hear?" Fanny was the eldest daughter – a strip of a girl of about ten, yet she supervised the herd of siblings with expert adeptness. She tore open a fresh tin-loaf and divided it among them.

Each grubby hand stuffed what was given to them in their mouth, protesting it wasn't fair through full mouths because their portion was hardly enough. "I don't think my portion is fair either," thought Belle to herself.

"Terry ain't here just now," said Mrs Levin as she swept aside the debris on the table and cleared a chair for her to sit on. "I must say I have mighty appreciated the bread Miss. That's right charitable of you... with Terry not being able to work now."

"You're welcome Mrs Levin. I have..."

"Oh, Miss Belle - we're hardly much different in age really. Just call me Doris. It sounds much more friendly like."

However, familiar is not what Belle was hoping for. "Well, Doris..." Yep - that was awkward. She made herself push on. "I really wanted to say that I have appreciated Terry's help so much. Since my father's illness he has been a great benefit to me." She tried not to sound condescending, but somehow it seemed she always sounded a little snootier than she intended. The last time she visited was to offer Terry the job. "How long do you suppose he won't be able to work?"

"Well Belle… see, just by using our first names - that is much more akin to company. Just like ladies visiting. Don't get to visit much now days. Anyway…" Her face turned away in a heavy, disappointed sigh. She had completely forgotten the question.

"Doris? How long will Terry be off work?"

"Oh… not sure. Doc Wallace said that Terry's arm will take weeks, maybe months… it was a right nasty break." She poured some water from the kettle over the fire into a chipped enamel mug and plonked it on the table in front of her. Belle ignored it, until she realised that Mrs Levin sat down beside her with a similar cup. She really was being offered "tea".

"He *broke* his arm?" gasped Belle. Oh, this was much worse than she thought.

"Yeah," sighed Mrs Levin. With the prospect of a sympathetic ear - a soul mate who was experiencing her own family crisis, Doris was pleased to give copious details. "The pain was right agonising. Should-a heard him scream when Doc had to yank it…"

Belle winced visibly and cut her short with a question. "How did it happen Mrs Levin… Doris? It sounds very bad…"

"You know these young lads… more brawn than brains." She smiled proudly. Belle didn't feel the need to point out that Terry Levin was generally not known in the district for either brawn or brains. Normally she would not have been at all disappointed had he been unable to stay on. But now, it seemed like she was being dealt yet another low blow. She nodded and tried not to look at the mug sitting in front of her as two flies buzzed frantically on the rim.

Mrs Levin continued, starved of another woman to talk to in her world of brute men and babies. "Him's sparring down at the pub... O' course he was tough then, but damn cried like a newborn in his sleep - he did - all night. Just set the old man on edge somethin' awful, til I went and took him to the Doc. The ol' man just up and left... and hasn't come back... not that I mind when he's like that. Just better he's ain't here. The first few days were the worst. Hardly slept a wink he did. My Terry's..."

Belle was distracted, watching out of the corner of her eye little Hermie picking up some long dead critter, dissecting it limb by limb, and carefully taste testing each piece. Momentarily she looked up. "I beg your pardon, Mrs...Doris, how long did you say?"

"Oh, you know. Sleep means nothing to my Terry. Working his job at your Pa's Bakehouse and all, set his hours all skewed anyhow. A week without sleep from a busted arm is not goin' to bother him none."

"A week? He won't be able to sleep for a week?"

Mrs Levin soothed her. "Oh no. He's fine now. Slept like a baby last night – or the night before anyhow. Don't rightly remembering seeing him last night now I think about it."

Belle blinked. "Doris, when did you say Terry hurt his arm?"

"Well, it must have been Wednesday last ... those hoodlums at the Tavern just set upon him. Completely un-provi-cated. The Constable can't find nothin'..."

"This was three days ago?"

"Oh no, more than that: last Wednesday... like over a week. I know... time just flies, doesn't it? Been busy with the little ones I have. That's why I appreciate the bread you send round to us Miss, especially with the ol' man walking out like he does, and your father being in the ward too. You know, and I don't want to speak out of turn, but when I see the way you opened your heart to my Terry and been helping us in our need – me thinks you are an angel from Heaven." She paused. "You wouldn't be sweet on my Terry, would you love?"

Belle looked up in surprise. "Terry? Oh. Nooo... probably not. He's... what... fourteen... fifteen? I think I would be 'spinster-hag' rating for your young man Mrs Levin. No.. no... He needs some one a little more..." She was tempted to say "nursery school", but restrained. Suddenly, at nineteen, she felt fossilised.

"He's getting so tall... and you never know. Seen some mighty unusual partnering in these parts. Take me and George. Who would have thought?"

Belle stood up. Yes, who would have thought? "Well I need to go and see Dr Wallace. My father..." She was not going to mention that for the first time in a long time, her father was not going to be the main reason for her call to the Doctor. She felt like her mind was unravelling, and panic threatened her sanity. She quickly took a couple of breaths. "Could you tell Terry I send my regards. And when he gets better enough to chop wood again, ask him come and see me. Thanks for the tea Mrs Levin... ah, Doris. It was nice to visit."

"Well, you come back again. Soon."

3.

Belle had thought everything had been going so well! But the reality was Terry had been out of action for over a week! That meant Tobias had not just come as a substitute worker for one night as she had supposed. He had been chopping her wood, and lugging flour, night and morning... since... when? How could she not notice? He had been so quiet, reserved... diligent... so un-Terry-Levin like. So un-Tobias-Lawson like!

The picture of their little one room school came unheeded into her mind. Mr Hewitt sat looking over his rimless glasses from the teacher's desk. Tobias Lawson always sat in the same row on the other side of the room. Their competition was fierce. And the fact that he always pipped her at the post, in every test, and every activity, left her resenting his presence violently. She despised him. Her whole purpose for being at school had fixed on trying to thwart every attempt he made to humiliate her. Her performance improved, but even now she had to concede she never quite succeeded. Tobias Lawson was a blessed golden child that everything he touched turned precious. Never had she had any reason to rethink her view. Until now. The only accounting for this complete selfless character change was his tragic accident.

Alice Dampier stepped out from behind the counter of Mrs Craddick's store and swept aside her fashionable blue skirt to let her employer pass. As she did Mrs Craddick dumped a wad of hand crocheted doilies in her hand. "Alice – add these to the display…" Mrs Craddick rarely said please… and never shortened her name to 'Ali' like the rest of Wattle Creek. But Ali was not one to take on other people's smallness. She smiled and hummed a little tune as she re-sorted the doilies on the counter and added the new ones. Her blonde hair was stacked prettily on the top of her head and there was a rather becoming flush to her smooth, fresh complexion.

The shop doorbell tinkled and she paused, turning around curiously to see who was there. Her green eyes betrayed a trace of disappointment as she watched a stooped customer come in and start browsing. It was Mrs Nancy Hollis – a widow who partnered Mrs Craddick in caretaking the emotional health of every resident in Wattle Creek. Nancy and Mrs Craddick didn't always see eye to eye, but when it came to diagnosing strife there was not a more willing duo.

Ali called a cheery hello to Mrs Hollis and resumed humming her way through the next pile of linen tea towels. "My dear Alice – you are a picture of happiness this morning," said Nancy significantly, as she blinked through her small round glasses. Here was another who always used her full name. It made Ali feel that she was on the verge of getting a spanking. Her Dad used her name like that when she was a girl. Mrs Hollis continued to stare at her. "You look like you are nesting my dear… is there a lucky young gentleman on the scene?"

Ali was one of those guileless girls who were incapable of being devious. She lived as transparent as glass and expected the same of everybody else. Life was very uncomplicated for Ali. Even the nasties of social narrow-mindedness had not calloused her open heart. "Mrs Hollis, it is not my place to be anticipating the efforts of eligible gentlemen. It would hardly be seemly, don't you think?" Evasion was her only escape. She giggled in an attempt to avoid further discussion and Nancy Hollis looked thwarted. In truth Nancy was thinking it was a shame that such a beauty didn't have more ability. That would provide endless courting competition to keep the social news vibrant. It had all been a little flat in Wattle Creek of late.

Belle found catching up with Ali, as elusive as harnessing butterflies. Ali was everybody's friend and no one's foe. For Belle survival mode had kicked in, and it never occurred to her that a few moments with a friend might do more for her longevity than throwing more dough to make extra loaves of bread. On top of this, her dad remained silent and unresponsive. Did he hear her half whispered explanations of the business? Perhaps he was as frustrated as she was, locked in a body that was unable to communicate.

Once she thought it would be different, to be free from all the demands her father made. She had no idea that the other part of that freedom would be so tough: making decisions and wondering if her reasoning was okay; never being sure if her Dad would agree… or worrying whether it mattered if he didn't. She didn't have Sam Kane's experience, or his decisive spirit. He was a hard act to follow. Would she forever be walking along the worn trail that he had trod before her? Perhaps this was her destiny, and she would never forge her own track.

Belle pulled up outside the Doctor's residence. She was desperate for someone to confide in and lingered by the path as Mrs Wallace weaved her way through her garden. The way she planted her beds was far too busy and way too random for Belle's liking. Gardening seemed such menial labour for a Doctor's wife, and she couldn't understand the enormous attraction this garden had for Mrs Wallace. It was just odd. Roses grew next to broccoli... spinach in amongst the marigolds. It was the most peculiar garden in the district, and although the status of Doctor's wife gave a smattering of licence to eccentricity, it still was a source of many local raised eyebrows.

Mrs Wallace was watering her climbers with a can as Belle opened the gate.

"Good morning Belle," she smiled graciously. "How is your Dad doing?" It irritated Belle sometimes, how this lady could be so sweet and so concerned, knowing full well that she probably knew more about how her father was doing than she did.

But Mrs Wallace was a gracious lady and Belle could never bring herself to be tart in return. So, she smiled and said, "I'm not sure... I am hoping Dr Wallace has more news."

Mrs Wallace nodded, as she always did, as if this was a most remarkable initiative and said, "You are such a great support to your Dad, Belle. He is very blessed. Dr Wallace is having tea in his library... just go on in and knock. He'll be pleased to see you." And in spite of herself, Belle felt she had been given a little puff of air, to help her through the day without sinking.

Dr Wallace looked up from his paper as Belle tentatively tapped on the door jam. It was beyond Belle how he never seemed to find his patients an intrusion. She knew that the seriousness of her father's condition gave her special privileges. He smiled and waved Belle to a chair. "Good morning my dear. I take it that the residents of Wattle Creek are enjoying their oven fresh loaves already? Tea?" Without waiting for a reply he reached for the spare cup and poured from the cosy-covered pot on a tray at his elbow.

Belle closed her eyes and silently reprimanded herself. She had given away all her bread to Mrs Levin, and forgot to save her usual loaf for Dr and Mrs Wallace. It was one thing she could give in return. She felt like an idiot. "Dr Wallace…"

"A-hum…" He pointed to the paper and commented on the editorial column. "They are getting all stirred up about the plans for a stage theatre. People are always so very opinionated about how they play. What they don't realise is that entertainment is not just play… it is business… bigger business than most would like to admit."

"Dr Wallace, I wanted to ask you about Toby Lawson."

He quickly looked up over his reading glasses. "Didn't he show up?" He knew of course, that he must have shown, for his name to even come up in conversation.

"Yes, yes he did. I just didn't know that Terry had broken his arm until this morning. I feel quite silly that Toby's been helping for over a whole week and I didn't realise."

"Oh, I wouldn't be too concerned. You have a lot on your mind. I don't think it would worry Tobias much."

Belle felt miffed that he had missed the whole point. Why did people think they had the right to organise her life? If he had suggested this remarkably clever plan – why didn't he tell her? Especially in the light of Toby's problems?

"But Dr Wallace – that is just it. I didn't realise Tobias... has, umm... is... well, you know... damaged."

Dr Wallace looked into her face for clues. "Damaged?"

"The way he talked and never even looked at me... and he keeps mumbling about making his family "cross". What happened to him?"

Dr Wallace paused and carefully removed his glasses. "Hmmm." He seemed to be gathering his thoughts and sipped the tea in his cup. He put it down again. It was stone cold. "You know that any information I have as Tobias's doctor, I cannot talk about. Have you been unhappy with his help?" Then as an afterthought he added, "He wasn't aggressive, was he?"

"No, no! Not at all. That's just it. We used to fight all the time. It is like he can't anymore. Dr Wallace... it is really sad. He was so clever. He always got top of our class. Everyone thought he was going to be a doctor like you."

"Well, you would know more than most that things don't always go according to plan. If Tobias is happy to help out... then perhaps that is enough for now. Just let him do what he can. Is this alright?"

"I guess... I just didn't know. I hadn't heard anything. How can I not know something like this... in a place like Wattle Creek?"

"About Terry or Tobias?"

"Both!"

"Well, people are loyal... even if they get a bit nosey. They probably didn't want to add worry to worry." He quickly changed the topic. "About your Dad, he slept well last night." Belle's eyes immediately brightened. She clung to every minor improvement as a sign that things were miraculously going back to normal. So instead of hearing her Dad had a settled night, she heard that he slept soundly, like he used to when he was healthy, and would probably be coming home soon.

Dr Wallace read her misplaced optimism like a second editorial. "You know this does not mean he will be discharged soon... it just means 'he slept well'."

The rest of the weekend was a complete disaster in Belle's eyes. The shop was always closed on Sunday and she spent every waking moment by her father's side.

"Daddy?" Belle started to speak but she choked on the words she so desperately wanted to say. His glazed eyes stared unfocused beyond the ceiling and drool seeped from his sagging lip. Creeping on her was the realisation that life had turned an irreversible corner of change. She shivered in the revelation.

"Daddy, I love you... really..." she whispered, tears welling in her eyes.

She tried not to notice the stark white sheets and the sterile metal beds lined up along the ward. Their knobbly metal frames reminded her of gnarled arthritic hands that were clutching their occupants against their will and keeping them prisoners. Other patients openly stared their sympathy. Her father had been an inventive man, a man who was busy and energetic. This seemed too cruel, and her whole being was tormented with the pain of losing him. Overlaying that was the agony of seeing him in this state of living death – the cold, hard, colourless infirmary sucking the remaining warmth from his soul.

It was a relief to wake up in the dark early Monday morning knowing that she had already had a trough full of dough that she had mixed the night before and she had to go back to work. She wondered if Toby would come. She didn't have the heart to send him away if he really was willing to chop the oven wood. Perhaps it was all he could do now. It was bizarre that Tobias Lawson was chopping her wood. But at the same time, in a way, it was a relief. No one else would ever accept the insulting wages she offered sixteen-year-old Terry for a little woodcutting, and she couldn't do it all by herself. What were her choices? She had no plan. She was drained of any creative thought. She desperately hoped he would come and dreaded it at the same time. She tried to justify every mean and malicious thought she had towards him. It seemed he held no ill will towards her. Perhaps he was not able to remember how they used to go at each other all bluster and thump. Why had Doc Wallace asked if he had been aggressive? He seemed benign enough… tragically so.

At exactly half-four o'clock she heard him banging and thumping at the door. It was not long before she heard the persistent chopping of wood and the chutes being bashed and loaded in an impatient, rough tumble way. At least that was something. The automatic routine took over and Belle threw herself into cutting and throwing the dough. If Toby would do this… she could do her part. Even if this was to be the last round of loaves from this bakery, they were going to be her best.

As the final tins slid into the ovens on the long-handled peels, Belle turned to see Toby standing near the door. His head hung low, his feet restless. "Am going now. Nat and Mal are mustering the big cows."

Belle raised her eyebrows. "Big cows?"

"Yeah. Mal reckons he's got a new way of telling which cows are ready for market. I think we could just get the big ones."

Belle laughed at that. "I reckon you are right – simple does not always mean unintelligent." She caught herself and held her breath. Why had she said that?

Something jammed in Toby's throat. At moments like these… when, in an unguarded moment, it seemed life stood still, he really wondered how this charade was going to pan out. He desperately didn't want to care.

As he turned to go, she suddenly found her tongue. "Toby? Thanks for your help. Be careful mustering." And the tears in her eyes masked the flicker of a snide smirk that crossed his lips as he quickly turned and left.

4.

This morning after the deliveries, instead of turning up the street for her early morning visit to Dr Wallace, she made her way out to the Lawson farm. Toby's mother was in the vege-garden when Belle pulled Bronza to a halt. Belle took a deep breath. "Good morning Mrs Lawson…" Her voice trailed off. Belle realised that directness was probably the best approach, but she lacked courage. Once her voice had faded, she barely could find it again. Mrs Lawson emitted efficiency-vibes wherever she went. It was hard for Belle to get to the point.

The lady looked up from her spinach and tomato plants that were lined up in military ranks. Belle was struck by the contrast it made to Mrs Wallace's garden. Mrs Lawson removed her gloves, quickly scanning the situation, taking everything in. "Good morning Belle… finished your rounds already?"

"Yes. The run is shorter these days…"

"Well, if that be the case Belle, you probably have a moment for tea. Come in while I brew us a fresh pot. Take a seat on the verandah, and I'll wash my hands. It'll just be us. The boys are out mustering. I don't expect them 'til dinner."

Belle sighed from relief. The last person she wanted was to see Toby. She sat down on the verandah and looked out at Mrs Lawson's broad beans climbing over the picket fence. Yet she wasn't thinking about beans: another debate replayed like a theatre play in her mind. This was a schoolroom exercise that Mr Hewitt had concocted to give a form of legality to their sparring. And just for a twist he gave out the topic: "My opponent is the more intelligent." The class was in an uproar that simmered to snickering, as they were given three minutes to present their argument. Belle stood to her feet delighted and presented her position with such conviction that everyone had been totally caught unawares. "My fellow class mates, in conclusion I do not hesitate to present my case. I have shown my opponent is an intelligent individual, and I have given an account of the string of awards and achievements to his name as evidence for this position. Should he win this debate – I have proved the account I have presented in demonstrating that one of his virtues is articulate reasoning – he will be judged to be the more intelligent: therefore, I am correct – therefore I win. If the esteemed adjudicators favour my presentation… I win again. This is a debate I cannot lose. Surely, that in itself, demonstrates without a shadow of a doubt who is, in reality - the more intelligent. Ladies and gentlemen, I challenge you to judge."

Tears sprang to her eyes. She couldn't even remember what Toby had said that day. She guessed he was probably not too convincing because the victory was so sweet. Her hands twisted her driving gloves into a ball, and then meticulously smoothed them out. She folded over the fingers into the palm of the glove and then carefully unfolded them. Finally, Mrs Lawson brought out a tea tray. "So, tell me Belle, how is your Father?"

Belle sighed again. How do you describe something that is too awful for words? "He's sleeping a lot. Doc Wallace is not saying how long until he can come home." Belle made no attempt to drink the tea that was poured. Tea seemed so trivial in the light of all the things that had taken place. One thought kept coming to Belle: Josephine Lawson was a woman who had survived.

When Josie's husband had been killed in an accident clearing land, she had three small boys and a farm. Tobias had been only six. Dozens of prophets of doom had predicted her fleeing back to the city, or falling into destitution, but she had proved them wrong. Josie had a stubborn tilt to her chin. Now her smooth skin was starting to crease from years of hard work and difficult decision-making, but she still held it high with determined confidence - or was it arrogance? Belle could not be sure. She did not know, but whatever that quality was, there was just enough of it, to make people look at this woman twice. This prevailing woman had stamina. Survival was what Belle needed to do.

"Mrs Lawson, you know Toby has been helping me at the Bakehouse?"

She looked at Belle and sort of nodded. "Yes, he told me - but I don't know that I really believed him. It has been an observation of mine that Kane's are not keen on outsiders."

Belle felt pricked. "Dad encouraged a strong sense of family that is all. It is the way he was... I mean... is!"

"Of course dear," said Josie, but although the words should have sounded gentle, Belle felt that they held a rebuke. Mrs Lawson raised her eyebrows a tad and studied the few tea-leaves in the bottom of her cup as she swirled it around. It was a habitual motion – nothing more meaningful, other than it reminded her that the tea strainer had a tiny hole in the gauze. She suppressed a caustic remark.

Every overture she had made towards Sam Kane, a handsome widower, in her younger, more needy days had fallen by the wayside. Attractive and well established, even if not quite well-to-do, Josie was not considered a bad prospect in those years when she needed an honourable man to father her three sons. But Sam Kane had locked Josie outside on an emotional verandah... always courteous, but never close. The realisation that Sam would never consider her family an option, had resolved in her heart that her own sons would always have each other. Family loyalty was something that she would cultivate in her own. Her experience with Sam Kane made it difficult for Josie not to dump his daughter in the same barrel and slam the lid shut.

She stared at the dregs in the bottom of her cup again and cautiously reminded herself that she was once as needy as this little girl sitting opposite her. She also remembered blue-eyed Sam. She would see what Belle wanted. She just would not show all her cards. Transparency with Kanes did not pay.

Belle took a breath. "Toby has been coming since Terry broke his arm. I didn't realise... honestly... so, I haven't been paying him. I have brought the money that is owed him for the work he has done. I have really appreciated his help."

"I'm not sure how you could not realise."

Belle shrugged. How could she explain? She couldn't even shed light on that herself. "I bought the money that I owe him. I am sorry that it is late."

"Why don't you just give it to him yourself? You needn't have come all the way out here. You said yourself he has gone to the bakery every night and morning."

"I just wanted you to know that I wasn't withholding what is due him. I would never take advantage of him. I honestly didn't know about Terry's arm, or Toby's accident."

Instantly Mrs Lawson sat upright. "Accident?" Tobias had come in a little later than usual from the Bakery, and she couldn't understand his insistence on being there. But, all in all, he had seemed fine when they had saddled up for the muster this morning. There was no possibility Belle had seen him since.

Belle's heart was strained beyond her limits. Her eyes filled and spilt over. "I had no idea Mrs Lawson! If I had known about the accident, I would have come and visited him. I know we have not been great friends, but I am not so callous that I would not have come had I known! Please believe me," she pleaded in distress.

Josie nodded and covered her hand of imaginary cards. "There, there. What seems to be your greatest concern?"

"Well, Toby of course! He was so clever! I hated that he was so intelligent, but I had no idea that I would miss that at all. When he talks, he seems so flat... two-dimensional... slow... vacant... that's it... vacant. The lights are on but...." She stopped mid sentence, mortified. Finally, she lamely finished. "We always had such energetic debates."

Again, Josie raised her eyebrows. She had seen their competition in action. To call it "energetic debating" was white-washing straight-out armed combat. "Are you worried you cannot fight with him anymore?" she suggested with an ironic smile.

"Oh Mrs Lawson, I never meant it that way! I was the only one who would stand up to him. He could always make the most illogical argument seem plausible and it didn't seem right he should get away with it all the time." She paled as she realised what she had said. "Oh Mrs Lawson – I am sorry. I meant no disrespect. Honestly. It's just that it is such a shock."

"I know what you mean," Josie quietly surmised.

Finally, Belle burst into tears. "I had no idea!" she groaned over and over. And if Josie thought that it would be a good idea to enlighten her regarding the mental status of her middle son, she decided that the distress that the girl was suffering would impede her ability to absorb the truth. It would be best to let her settle down first. She patted her shoulder as Belle flung herself into her arms and sobbed and sobbed.

5.

She could sense the clock hands turn to half past four o'clock and she held her breath until she heard the familiar scraping of boots near the door, and the rhythmic chopping of wood outside. In the busy routine, they just did what needed to be done to get the loaves in the oven and baked. The morning aroma of baking bread spread over the town like the sweet chime of a mantle clock, predictable and comforting. But Belle was not thinking about that. She scrubbed down the benches furiously, trying to swallow the most unexplainable anger that burned within her throat. She hated that nothing ever stayed the same. Toby was the enemy. It was unfair that he would confuse her equilibrium by an accident that he wouldn't talk about. He silently greased the warm empty baker's tins with lard from the butcher's shop ready for tomorrow. It was like throwing fuel on the fire in her chest. He had no right to change!

Just before she left to start the delivery round, Toby scraped his foot awkwardly, nervous to be finished. Making conversation was not what he wanted. "Nat's branding some weaners today." He rushed on. He'd had enough. Whatever the pay-offs, working at Kane's bakery was not worth the menial, brainless, repetitive tasks that were expected of him. Tobias turned away and went back to a safe topic: the farm. "I gotta help and…" He had been practicing this speech all day. "Miss Belle?"

Belle looked up at him then. "Oh come on Toby – we have known each other forever. Belle is all you need to call me."

He shuffled, and continued with a rush without addressing her by name. "Umm – when ya find another fella to come chopping your wood, I won't come anymore, because you won't be needing me then."

Belle did not stop pushing the hard-bristled scrubbing brush along the bench. This time she couldn't look up. "Did your Mother tell you to say that?" she asked abruptly.

The retort that flew to his lips seemed a little too articulate… so he stumbled over his words. "No," he said in a wounded, defensive voice that had just enough lisp for effect. "No, I said that all by my's-self!" And he felt every bit like an angry six-year-old with a point to make.

"Fine! That suits me fine!" Belle did not turn around as he left and slammed the door behind him. She smiled harshly to herself. It was almost like old times.

Joe Golders shook his head. "I'm mighty pleased that you would be offering my boy labouring money, but the truth is Miss Belle, I can't afford the time out it would mean for any of my boys. We have early starts and deliveries ourselves to make. Have you tried old Bate's grandson?"

Belle tried to smile and keep her voice light. "Yes – I tried him and the Peters' and the new people over the back of Henry's place… and Redding's and Phil Pollock, and those two on the other side of the creek."

"Looks like you just about covered it then," the farmer lifted his hat and swiped his brow with his arm. "Oh, unless you tried them Lawson boys. They'd work mighty fine if you could get one of 'em. The youngest could be interested in the extra pocket money, they were over here the other day looking at one of my bulls."

Belle made one last effort not to show her disappointment. "Joe - thanks for your help. I'm sure the right person will be just around the corner."

He looked at her and was not fooled. "That's the spirit. Sam has every right to be proud of you – the way you are handling things so mightily. He did well with you Belle. That he did." Of all the things he could have said… this was the thing that Belle yearned to hear most of all: that her Dad would be proud. She swallowed the lump in her throat and hurried back to Bronza's cart.

She knew Toby's younger brother Malachi, would not be interested as Joe suggested. There was absolutely no point offering one Lawson work over another. Toby was part of their family too. Besides, he would be the one who would need the work – especially in his condition.

So, why wouldn't she talk with Toby about it? He was uncomfortable to be around. That was true – but surely that was because of who Tobias had been – not who he is now. It seemed like such a ludicrously simple solution, but how could it work? Even in thinking it – she answered her own question. Perhaps it could work, because Toby was altered: irrevocably, tragically changed.

Yes, she decided, she would offer the arrangement to him. She had already worked with Toby nearly a month without having her life desperately interfered with. She could do it again. She would continue to pay the money to him until Terry Levin could come back. It would help her hang on.

Belle reminded herself of a little saying her Dad would often quote when loading the cart: "Good bread and hard work – that's all it is my girl!" he would say. "It ain't Medical Science... and virtually fool-proof."

"If it's so fool proof, why do I find it so difficult!" She spat the words out in disgust. A sense of failure started to swell up, until it began to drag her under. Why did the baker's daughter always have an aura of failure about her? She shook her head as if trying to clear water from her ears and tried to convince herself once more that it was not so. The whole thing left a metallic taste in her mouth – in a bizarre way, like a bit and bridle. She wanted to be able to make her own choices – not be led along by things outside her control.

When she returned from the deliveries, Toby was finishing getting some loaves for a customer. Just before he left to go home, Belle handed him a glass of milk poured fresh from the dairy jug that had just been delivered. "Toby, I want to offer you this job until Terry gets better." Toby took the glass of milk and stared at it. He hated milk. "It's okay," Belle coached, "You can drink that. It is good for you." Toby grimaced. She sounded like his mother... about sixteen years ago! He swallowed hard on a mouthful and left an exaggerated milk moustache on his top lip, and then smeared it all across his sleeve. To save going through all that again he accidentally knocked over the glass, and then busied himself sopping up the mess.

"You want me to stay on? Why? It was just for a little bit and then you'd be okay! You don't want me here."

"Toby!" Belle cried out. His child like candour mortified her. "That is not true!" She had to say it – but she knew that the thin veneer of politeness did not fool him. She quickly reminded herself that Tobias was different now. Once he would have just said it to get a reaction. Now he was like a child, a six-year-old who loudly tells her mother in the haberdashery shop that the lady behind the counter looks like a witch because she has a wart on her chin. "But what is true, is that Terry cannot do the chores I need done here. There is no one else available. I tried really hard to get someone... anyone." She swallowed hard and cringed at the grovelling. It did not come easily. "I would like it if you stayed to help. I'm sorry."

"You're sorry?"

"No! Yes. What I mean is that I need you to do the work. But you sounded reluctant – like you didn't want to. That is all."

"You *want* me to help you?" He couldn't resist hearing the words from her lips.

"Yes Toby. I need your help." There – she said it. Even she could appreciate the irony of her saying this to Tobias Lawson. Belle closed her eyes. "Toby? Do you remember going to school with me?"

A large grin spread across his face. "Belle was feisty!" he said in a teasing tone.

"You do remember!" Belle was amazed. "What do you remember most?"

"The Lolly Jar on Mr Hewitt's desk."

"They were for the little ones. Why would you remember that?"

"Cause I never got one. I only wanted *one*." This time he smeared his nose on the other sleeve, and sniffed. Belle's lip curled instinctively in revulsion. She was just about to chide him, but then looked away and calmed the agitation that was eating her up. She took a deep breath.

"I could give you a lolly if you stayed to help me. I would pay you like I paid Terry. But I could get some boiled lollies from Mrs Craddick's store as well. Would you like that?"

"Oh yes! I like the red and white ones best."

When Belle went to Mrs Craddick's store two weeks running to buy sweets, her friend Ali, serving behind the counter just had to ask about her sudden fascination with red and white boiled lollies.

"No reason in particular. Someone I know likes them – that is all."

Ali laughed. "Older or younger than twelve years old?"

Belle shook her head and rolled her eyes. "Okay. Older."

"Hmmm. The only adults in this town partial to red and white boileds, are old Mr Lang, Wallaby Joe, Evan Hewitt and Tobias Lawson. Mabes, why would you be buying Mr Lang sweets?"

"I'm not. Oh, come on Ali – I just have a hankering after sugar. My taste buds need sweetening up."

"You're lying through your teeth… and you know I'm right. Fair enough – you have a secret." She raised her eyebrows knowingly.

"Ali – give it up. There is no secret."

"Hmmm…" she conceded unconvincingly. "Never mind… I have some secrets of my own!" Just then Mrs Craddick appeared to serve a waiting customer and looked significantly in her direction. She didn't have to say anything. She quickly grabbed Belle by the arm and whispered, "Mabes – I am coming over when I finish work. I'll bring dinner and feed you up. You look like you've been through a famine. We will talk then. I've got to get back to the customers."

For the first time Belle could ever remember she didn't want to get together with Ali. There was no secret – but she would make so much more of Toby working for her than there was, especially since his accident. She just didn't need this now.

At a little after half past-six o'clock the door bell tinkled as Ali hustled in with a radiant smile and the most fabulous smelling casserole. She swept into the back of the Bakery, spread a cloth and utensils on the table with the flourish of a magician. She took Belle's hand and led her to the table, flicking a serviette into her lap with the finesse of a maître-d'. Belle tiredly submitted to her attentions… but raised her hand in protest at the liberal helping of casserole she started to ladle onto her plate. She ate and then sat on the lounge as Ali brought her a delicious coffee and a red and white boiled lolly on the saucer. "Normally one would have chocolate fudge with coffee for a special secret – but knowing your hankering after boiled sugar of late…"

Belle smiled sheepishly. "You win… I *do* prefer fudge." Ali was never one to let sleeping dogs lie and Belle knew now she would have to explain the whole thing. Instead Ali produced a delicious square of fudge and placed it on her saucer with a curtsy!

"Oh Ali – you're a saint! You know me too well. This is such a special treat!" However, to Belle's surprise, Ali was happy to have that victory clocked in her favour and let it alone, for the urgency of the moment was on revealing her own secret.

"Now – are you ready?" Belle nodded and feigned anticipation – but honestly, she didn't have much curiosity about Ali's secret. She thought she should feel a tad guilty about that, but she knew it would not be anything very thrilling. Ali's dramatic secrets usually consisted of a new hair-do, scarf or hat. Occasionally it involved a new recipe, or discovering some fantastic product for the shop.

Ali stood up for dramatic effect. "I have been asked to go courting – by Jimmy Golders!" She did a pirouette around the room and then turned glowing – her headscarf loosened and thrown over her face in a bridal veil. "We are going to the Friday Night dance again next week!"

"Again?" Belle stared at her friend. She could not be serious! Every childhood vow to stay friends forever – and never to let boys get in the way came rushing back. Once they had even sealed it in spit down behind the town hall. Belle watched astounded as she continued with the bridal procession around the room. Her intentions were very clear. "Has he given you a ring?" demanded Belle finally.

"No – of course not silly. We have to wait six months at least… Mum says that six months courting is the absolute minimum. But we both know this is for real and Jimmy is okay with that. Oh Mabes – I had no idea that this is what being in love was like!"

"Ali! I believe you are absolutely in earnest!" sighed Belle in despair. "How can you be serious? You've known Jimmy your whole life. How can you suddenly be in love with him? That is irrational! It makes no sense at all."

Ali stopped still and stared at her friend. "Mabes – I don't believe you just said that. Why can it be so impossible that someone like Jimmy would love me? It's because his family's got money and I'm just a dairyman's daughter!"

"Ali! You know that's got nothing to do with it! I know his family's well regarded and Jimmy's considered a good enough catch. He's even good looking – I guess." She sighed. "Fair enough…he's just all round 'good'…" It sounded like an insult.

Ali dazzled triumphantly with an "I told you so!" look.

"Still, if you ask me, he's not good *enough*…" It had to be said. It was not Belle's fault that she had this incurable honesty-bone. She refused to be silent when the truth was going begging.

"Well I'm not asking! How can you doubt this is wonderful news? We love each other!"

"I just don't get how you can be non-committal one moment and devoted the next. What changed? We said we would be business-women. Besides I thought Betsy Jameson had her hooks into him."

Ali smiled with a mature worldly-wise gaze. "Betsy! Pooh! Jimmy said Betsy has never meant anything to him."

"As he would…" muttered Belle cynically.

"Jimmy started coming to the shop to buy things… anything… gifts for his Mum, his sister, his dog… his dad. He always waited for me to serve him. If Mrs Craddick came to serve him, he'd suddenly change his mind and need more time to choose until I was able to serve him. He even bought red and white boiled lollies once cause he couldn't think of anything else! And then one day – just out of the blue – he asked if I would go to the Friday dance with him. We danced all night and then when he walked me home, he asked if he could come calling… even though he'd been calling at the shop for ages! It was soooo romantic. And then he went and saw Dad… that is the sort of man he is: very… very, well… nice."

"Nice?" Belle cringed. Nice was not the way you described the man of your dreams. It was like admitting you sucked your thumb at night… weak and insipid. She gritted her teeth and smiled.

Ali lowered her eyes from the ethereal glow that hovered around her in a love-haze, and stared at Belle.

"Mabes – you're my best friend. Why aren't you happy for me? It's been killing me I haven't been able to tell you. Everyone else knows anyhow: we've been to three dances now."

"Three!"

"Yeah. With your Dad being sick and all, it just never seemed a good time to tell you. The boiled lollies gave you away though. No one buys lollies in the middle of a trauma… they are far too trifling. It told me things were getting better! That's why when you came back the second week, I knew I could tell you! So now I have!"

Belle blinked her eyes. She had no idea that Ali could be so brain dead. It was like every ounce of sense evaporated as soon as the irresistibly *nice* Jimmy Golders had lifted his hat toward her. She stood up and went and gave her friend a hug. "Congratulations Ali. I'm sure you and Jimmy will be very happy." She hoped it sounded more sincere than it felt in her heart.

"Oh Mabes, I knew you would come round! This is just delicious! Well I know you start your doughs soon, so I'll leave you to it. Don't forget to eat – you look half starved!" she called as she swirled out the door.

"Thanks Ali - you were always one for compliments," sighed Belle as she shut the door and flipped over the "Open for Custom" sign hanging in the glass panel. This was another blow. She was riding a runaway horse – out of control – twisting and turning… with no destination in sight, and at great risk of being dumped in the dust at any moment. She could not believe the betrayal that she felt in her heart over the Ali's confession. She grabbed a drink of water and went and lay down on her bed. She turned into her pillow and cried. Her one relief was that the secret of the boiled lollies remained intact.

6.

Josie wordlessly served her sons their evening meal. She was unusually quiet as she listened to them discuss the business of the day and their planning for the morrow, carrying on with their typically energetic banter. When Matthew was alive, she had always insisted that business was not a table-topic. She often wished the same pattern could be followed still, and hold farm-talk at bay until the meal was over. However, when they were younger – the practical structure of the days around schoolwork and farm chores, had cemented this practice into their family. Mealtimes were never silent and never comprised of social chit-chat. They discussed with gusto the issues at hand. Living the farm meant the most consistently pressing topics revolved around its workings.

As brothers they had had their share of spats… but more than anything else they were mates – they had grown *up* as play mates and grown *into* work mates. Nat and Mal in particular had a rather interesting working relationship. Malachi, as the younger brother, had to fight to have his voice heard. Those times had not uncommonly ended with a split lip or bloody nose. Now they understood how each other operated, but it was more out of necessity that they had learnt to meet each other half way. Tobias on the other hand, rarely bothered to include himself in the agony of farming decisions. He would present the logic of the business decision, and then leave them to process the data. His brothers never made a conscious choice to exclude him; he just wasn't passionate enough to lose blood over it. In his eyes, there were bigger wars to fight.

Tonight, as he did every evening, Nat sat at the dinner table with a makeshift pad made of cut up brown paper and a clothes peg. He was vigorously working calculations with a pencil to prove a point in progress. Finally, the boys filled their coffee mugs, and Nat grabbed his notes to adjourn to the living room. Josie cleared her throat. "Tobias – could you help with the dishes tonight please?"

He looked suitably disgusted and his brothers sniggered like seven-year olds. "Toby's in trouble!" they chanted, as they thumped his arm good-naturedly and grabbed a biscuit from the barrel on the way out. They had plenty of work and the sooner they were out of the way, the sooner Tobias would be tortured and released. Helping with the dishes meant that their mother required some one-on-one talk time: another family tradition – one that was not jealously sought after.

Josie stacked the dishes in regimental rows of dishes and cups, according to size. Tobias sighed and picked up the tea towel. His mother never had any qualms about her boys helping in the kitchen doing "female" duties. She was very conscious that at a very early age her young men had to be suitably independent to fend for themselves in a world that was ruthless for the unskilled – in every sphere of life.

"How is the Bakehouse work going?" Josie paused to pour hot water from the kettle she had taken off the wood stove and lathered soap from a bar into the water.

"Alright", he conceded.

"Belle came for morning tea the other day…" Josie handed him a plate. She had been thinking about this all week. She had very few clues on how to address her concerns.

"That's sweet," Tobias smiled at the thought of Belle and his mother cosily having 'tea'. The idea was completely foreign. He unenthusiastically wiped his way around the edge of the plate.

"Yes – it was." She paused. "Tobias – the girl seems to be of the opinion you have lost your mind."

"Oh," he said without further elaboration. Josie looked at him quickly. Now she was certain something was a foot.

"I cannot comprehend how the dux of the district school is suddenly seen in the eyes of his noblest competitor as a complete dimwit! Care to explain that?"

"Mum I would hardly say her competition was noble, and surprising as it may seem, the idea of her considering me a nitwit is not new."

"Tobias – this moronic notion is not a product of indiscriminate loathing. She honestly thinks you have no faculties left. She says you are "*damaged*"!"

Suddenly the plate that he was wiping was in danger of having its blue and white pattern scrubbed from its surface. "Really? That convincing?" He smiled in conceited victory!

"Tobias! To what end? The girl is so positive you had some sort of accident. What did you tell her?"

"Nothing – honestly Mum… I have never told her anything. She has just made a series of assumptions… and I have never had cause to contradict her."

"Tobias – are you doing the right thing? This seems a tad callous... she is very exposed at the moment, given her father's situation."

"Callous? No way. This means I am no threat. She lets me help. Quite *simple* really." He smiled at his pun. Josie ignored it.

"This is the bit I don't get. It makes no sense that you feel so beholden to this girl. You have no obligation to her or her father."

"The only obligation I feel, Mother, is to myself. Believe me – if there was another way, I'd find it. At the moment, this is what I have to do."

"Tobias, do you think your father would approve?"

"Oh, Mum that is absurd! You make him out to be some sort of super-conscience that is ever present. Well – he is not! I have no idea if he would approve or not!" Even though he kept the volume low, the tension in his voice gave it a shrill tone. He was sick of his widow-mother's guilt trips she used when she was running out of options.

Josie studied the suds as she washed the prongs of the table forks very carefully. Toby was her puzzle. He was the one who at times reminded her of a fish out of water, flopping around on the riverbank trying to breath outside his environment. He didn't fit like Nat and Malachi, even with all their rivalry. Her mother's heart was at loss to know what to do.

"Oh Mum! You didn't let on did you?"

The mortification on his face, made Josie raise her eyebrows. The mystery was bewildering. "No, no – relax. I didn't know what you were up to that's all. Mind you, I still don't."

"Mum, please… for now, you have to let me do this. You absolutely have to. If she finds out, I'm dead. Please, it won't be for long I'm sure. Just until she is out of the woods. I need to…"

"But son…"

"Promise me Mum. This is really important."

"Very well. But I will not lie. I guess however, like yourself, I can omit clarification if necessary. You just be careful. She is formidable, even if she is young."

"Yeah, well. So am I." And they finished the dishes in silence.

Word got around that Tobias Lawson was working at the bakery. There were many raised eyebrows and people were keen to get his perspective on the shop and Sam Kane's progress… or lack of it.

Even customers began to broach the subject of Belle's hired help. Mrs Craddick was the first. She never was one for beating around the bush. "Heard you have the Lawson boy helping you Belle. It ain't going to be interfering too much with his book learning is it?"

Belle laughed. Book learning? Goodness. People went to great lengths to white wash reality. "No, I don't think so Mrs Craddick. Toby will only ever do as much as he can, and I won't push him."

She nodded sagely. "Good of you to be so understanding. He's going to be needing the money. You *are* paying him his wages Belle, and not taking advantage of his good nature?"

"Mrs Craddick! Of course! How could you say that?" She wrapped her order of bread in brown paper and Mrs Craddick left. After that there were a myriad of little comments and innuendoes made. Belle always responded in the same way, and there was always reference to Toby's books.

The next morning Belle asked Toby about it. "Why does everyone around town connect you with books?"

"I like books. Doc Wallace has lots of books. He lets me look at them. Some have pictures." Toby shuffled, hung his head restlessly and intently watched for her reaction in his peripheral vision. But she didn't have one. It seemed perfectly natural to her that he would have a morbid fascination with looking at graphic and detailed dissected diagrams in medical books. All boys liked gory pictures.

7.

Ali came in with a glorious smile, waving a collection of good-sized envelopes around her head like a banner. "I have an invitation – a very important invitation… for you!" she exclaimed as she danced from the door to the table and back again. "There's going to be a party! A very big party - for the biggest event of the year! Jimmy says that money is no object! I can invite all my special friends!" Belle suspected that the definition of 'special friends' included anyone Ali had engaged in a conversation during the last 5 years… so all-encompassing was her happiness.

"Oh, by the way," she said coming and thrusting her hand under Belle's nose, unsuccessfully trying to sound nonchalant, "there is a ring! Look at this baby!" The cluster sparkled and glittered in its white gold setting as she flashed it towards the light. "I have never seen gravel look so appealing. Jimmy has had this *forever* … and I didn't even know! Isn't it gorgeous? It's official Mabes – we're engaged! He asked Dad… so we don't have to wait until the end of next century after all!" And she danced off again prattling on about dressmaking arrangements, and Reverend Bernard's pre-marital lectures, and who was doing what, and when.

Belle couldn't help but laugh at her contagious delight. If being in love was like this, then it was understandable why it was such a sought-after condition. Even she had never seen the normally upbeat Ali so buoyant and bubbly. It really did seem she would float away on the euphoria. Ali quickly returned and placed the envelope on the mantle. "Almost forgot to leave this with you. Bring anyone you want," she said magnanimously as she bounced off to share the same special and exclusive invitation to the next person she met.

Belle readied to prepare the risen doughs in the trough, and looked up when the familiar early morning rattle at the door came at half-four. It was not Toby who stood there with his yard boots on, but his brother Malachi. "Mal? Is Toby okay? He's not sick is he?" She felt a stab of concern.

"Nah Belle – he's fine. He asked me to fill in for the next couple of days. Told me to tell you he had to go to the Big-Smoke for some tests. He'll be back next Friday. I'll come until then."

"Tests? What for?" She already knew what they would be for.

"Medical tests – that's what he said."

She paused a moment, at a loss as to how to appropriately respond to a brother's tragic news. She knew from experience that medical investigations were costly and often times inconclusive. "Well, I hope you all get the answers you are looking for. Remind me to give you the loaves for your mother before you go home." She hurried into the morning baking routine and tried not to think too much about her own father's subjection to pointless diagnostic procedures.

Belle hummed under her breath as she scrubbed down the last section of bench. Toby came in and stood by the warm ovens stamping his feet and blowing on his fingers against the frosty morning air. She had poured him a warm mug of milk, and cut a thick slice of bread hot from the oven. "Toby, why don't you sit down and have something to eat?" Toby hesitated. "It's okay Toby. We made such good time this morning. I don't have to start the deliveries for a while yet." It was good to have him back.

Toby screwed up his face as he scraped out the chair. Belle studied his slouched frame and smiled. He never looked at her. Sometimes Belle just wanted to grab his face and force him to make eye contact. "Toby? Are you okay? You've worked hard. Don't tell me you don't like my bread after all this time?" she said with a laugh.

"I don't like milk," he said finally as he pushed the mug away. Pretending could only go so far.

"It's good for you..." Toby said nothing. Belle was uncertain as to how to continue. "Really? Well, would you like... um... a cup of tea?" He nodded. Belle put the cup on the table. "I've already put milk and sugar in it. Don't burn yourself," she said helpfully. It was weak... and tepid. He almost laughed. This offering presented no danger of scalding him. He realised that the hope of warming up, even just a little, with a hot cuppa, had been a tad ambitious. He ate the bread happily though. That was something. Belle could make a first-rate loaf of bread and it always tasted better first thing in the morning, straight from the ovens.

Belle sat down opposite him with her own steamy cup of tea. She tucked her knee comfortably up under her chin and wrapped her hands around her warm mug. "I missed you while you were away. Mal is great, but..." she confided, "the way we get through our mornings is really something! We've had a couple of extra orders this week yet we are finishing earlier. What a team we make!" She laughed out of the pure elation of that small victory. Wins were rare. Toby tried to pin point the last time he heard Belle laugh. He thought that it was a little unnatural, forced almost, but oh, how amazing it sounded.

He quickly looked at Belle as she picked up a slice of bread and nibbled the corner, chuckling away with delight. "I bet no one thought that we could do this you know! But not only that – we have excelled. See this..." She leant over and showed Toby the slice of bread in her hand. "This texture, and see how the colour is even across the crust. Dad would call this loaf: 'good taste and class'. It is a science with Dad – how to make the best loaves. I remember when he first told me that his apprentices were introducing unnecessary variables into the process. That was when he decided to start working on his bread machine. I must have been about seven."

Yeah. Toby remembered that: seven or eight. It was about a year after his Dad was killed. He had come into the Bakery one day and Mr Kane had offered to show him an important invention that would change baking forever. He took him out the back and unveiled the work in progress. He'd come in once a week when Belle was out – at her piano lessons, and worked with him on the mixing machine. The time they had spent on that machine was sacred. They had made a pact about "scientific bread business". Toby had not thought about that for a long time. He was kinda surprised that even Belle didn't know.

Belle sat for ages and chatted about the shop, and her customers. She wasn't really talking to Toby... she had sort of slipped into an audible musing. A couple of smart remarks automatically came to Toby's mind – totally unprompted. It was instinct with him. He had countered and fought with Belle for too many years to suddenly be able to listen without wanting to comment – no matter what she was saying. But to say anything would blow his cover, so he sat on his tongue, unable to insert just one witty retort. All that was left was to listen...

"Mrs Craddick came in today. She is so obsessed with 'her Alice' being engaged, it was all she could talk about. She told me that she knew this six months ago... and she didn't even comment on her order! How's that? Perhaps we should encourage Ali to have a really long engagement. It will be so much better for our customer relations!"

Each morning, before the deliveries started, Toby came in and suffered through one of Belle's weak, milky, tepid cups of tea. He happily devoured a good number of slices of bread. In his silence Toby became increasingly captivated. He had never seen Belle talk about the small things, personal things. This was completely new to him. He allowed himself to chortle now and then as he listened. It became a mission – to hear more, to understand more. One morning, as he sat absorbed, it occurred to him that he had always been on guard; ready to counter with the next parry in their verbal jousting. Here, now, in the cool, early mornings – there was no need for attacks and thrusts – armour was removed, no defences were in place. It shocked him a little that he was enjoying the transparency that it allowed… the trust that it showed… the person it revealed.

He always kept his head down. He could not risk an encounter with full, clear eye contact. But he couldn't help but to watch her with fascination from under his brow. This morning he noticed in the early morning light, a smear of flour on her cheek and he watched how the light played with the shadows on her face. Why had he never noticed she was attractive?

Oh boy! That observation shocked him – he needed to take a step outside himself and determine how his perceptions could be so remarkably altered. As he chopped and loaded wood boxes during the week he had plenty to think. Belle obviously had not changed the skin she was in. Her situation had not changed much at all. She still was the same Belle who irritated and challenged him for years. The cold chill of the morning gave the air a solid crisp sound as his axe rang through the neighbourhood and echoed around the streets. A dog yapped at a cat that skedaddled up over a paling fence. He placed another slab on the chopping block, and attacked it forcefully with the block-splitter.

Belle had always been his arch-enemy: the competitor who threatened to take him out and destroy him. He smiled to himself remembering the ingenious guerrilla tactics they engaged: he had smuggled the carpet snake into her school desk, and there was the time she had managed to enlist him into Shakespearian tights as Romeo just so that she could hear him say those ridiculous lines to her on the balcony to win a two bob bet with Ali. He tipped his head as he counted the times that they both got into trouble and Belle never resorted to name fixing or blame, but as a matter of pride stood up for anything that Mr Hewitt dealt out. He knew that she had saved the seat of his pants from a lot of standing-up time.

He had an addictive need to engage her – positively or in spite, it didn't seem to matter. He never quite understood the power of this hate-love bond he had with her. The necessity to publicly loathe her had always been stronger than his incurable underpinning admiration.

Truly, he admitted, she was one who was adept at dealing with whatever life placed before her. If it came to that – Toby thought, perhaps Belle did have the upper hand. Had he been as diligent as he could - to put his hand to whatever plough was before him? He had felt for a long time, that the opportunity to be a professional in his chosen field had been ripped out from under him. He had given up – because if he could not fulfil that ambition, then would he be nothing at all.

By the time he had refilled the wood boxes and tidied up outside, his competition with Belle was drained of its energy. The fight for survival by being the last man standing was now a savage, barbaric game and he wanted out. *All very deep insights*, he thought wryly, *for a brain-damaged woodchopper.* He stamped the moist wet fragments of muddy grass off his boots at the door and undid his laces, removing them to come inside.

He found Belle well behind in her routine. She was pacing and thumping in frustration at the kneading bench. Toby washed his hands in the cold well water he had brought inside in the wooden bucket, and came and stood beside Belle.

He picked up a lump of bread dough. "Belle's not feeling so good..." he observed simply. He went to work, his tall, strong frame kneading quickly into rhythm. "Is Belle's Dad okay?" he ventured after a while.

Again, she grunted. "Yep – Dad's the same." She thumped and thudded the dough with the heel of her hand. "Damn it Toby – Mr Jameson – Betsy's father, came in today: to sell up the bakery! It's not even his! He says that Dad put a mortgage on it and that the payments are now too far in arrears. He's going to *make* me sell. I had no idea! He never came before this to say what was happening. It's been months and months since Dad was admitted. He's been circling out there like a blood-crazed dingo. I can't budget and manage something I have no information about... and mind you, he had no intention of giving me the heads up about this. He wants the bakery, just like he's taken the pub and the general store and every other place in town that isn't nailed in blood to the owner's heart. Well, I've got news for him! This place *is* nailed in blood – to my Dad... and come hell or high water, it is going to be here for Dad when he gets out. He has to have this store to come home to. There has been too much history and sweat gone into this little place. Unimpressive on the outside... big on the inside... that's what this bakery is!"

Toby's mind went into overdrive. He couldn't help but recognise that this was a way out, an escape. No bakery, no Belle, no contract to fulfil... he would be free of it. Belle would be too. She'd be released with sufficient money to support her dad, pay his medicals... and to pursue whatever she wanted with the remaining years of her gifted life.

But almost as the thoughts formed in his head, he heard what Belle was saying; not just the words that she was speaking, but also the heart behind it. *This shop is his life. If I can keep the shop going, Dad will be able to come home. I must keep it going.* Tobias looked at Belle with new respect. Everything he had suspected was confirmed. The shop was her father's life-line. She was saving her father in the only way she understood, by sustaining his shop. She'd fight to the death if she were forced to sell. Tobias guessed that she was probably very misled: that no matter how hard she tried, or how well the shop did, he may never come home.

He also was aware of what some of the town's folk had been saying: that a daughter's place is by her father's bed. Why should the girl be so entrapped in mercenary gain while her father so desperately needed her? The town had supported her in the crisis: Tobias had to give them that. But the new set-back in her father's health had only delayed the inevitable scourges of moralising that would come. He knew that as time went on, she would not be the heroine battling a war-front, but a deserter who was the very reason for the battle being lost. He quietly took a breath. Yeah, he agreed on the inside, this little shop was important to her Dad. But he didn't think the shop was his link to getting better – Belle was…

He wondered then, whether it was significant to Belle whether it was a bakery or a piggery or a millinery store that her father had owned. Tobias didn't think so. The bakehouse was her father's: that was all that mattered. She would never opt out because it was an easy – even logical, solution. What was important - was what it meant to her father. Toby had to acknowledge that there was something quite noble in her dogged persistence in the face of such news.

"I'm not going to sell. I can't. I won't. I'll pay out the debt. I have to. That's all there is to it."

Toby shuffled the dough in his hands. "How?" he asked simply.

"We'll take on more orders. Work longer. I have to start somewhere."

"How much is it?" he asked innocently, hoping that Belle was distracted enough to not notice the specifics of the question. She named the amount... and then her lip quivered in anger. "Belle could use Toby's money. That would help," he offered.

"Toby – I have to pay *you*." Her frown deepened, and she thumped the dough again. "What is it with you? For some reason the whole town is in on this Belle-Toby audit... checking up that I am being fair to you and your precious books. I have never done anything to suggest that I wouldn't be upfront."

Toby said nothing for a while. He focused on the bread-dough in his hands to give him some time to consider. It had to sound simple... "Belle could pay without money. With something Toby likes."

She looked at him and softened her frown just a little. Toby became engrossed in the dough in front of him. "You really want to help. That is so sweet Toby. I really appreciate it. Thank you."

He wasn't going to let the conversation stop there. He had to keep her talking about it. "Toby likes boiled lollies," he suggested helpfully.

She laughed, releasing the tension in her throat momentarily. "Toby – there is no point me spending all your wages on lollies and giving them to you. Your mother wouldn't appreciate it and I would have no extra money left anyway!"

Toby smiled to himself. That was a suitably stupid red herring.

"Something else then."

"Like what…"

"I know!" he exclaimed with brainwave excitement, "Toby becomes Belle's partner!"

"Partner? Toby – how are you going to be a partner? This is a business… not building blocks."

"I chop wood good. Miss Belle said so." She admitted it was so. "Every time I chop good wood, Miss Belle pays me with a partner tick. When I get enough ticks… I get a share in the partnering. I know 'cause Nat and Malachi have ticks so that it is fair for who does the work."

"Are you serious? They have a tick chart?"

"They don't fight so much," he said significantly.

"Then what?" Belle couldn't see it. What would be gained? She covered her face with her hands, flour rubbed up into her hair as she lent her elbows forward on the bench. She was suddenly so overwhelmed. All the progress and success she had so recently felt was illusion – fairy floss on a stick that was caught in a shower of rain. She could see it melting into nothing, with no substance to say that it had ever existed.

"Then you have money to give Mr Jameson… and the extra orders… and we fix Mr Kane's mixing machine… and Belle gets to keep her Dad's shop for when he gets home."

Tears that she had never cried suddenly came. They surged from a deep untapped well, and the pressure from the wounded source caused a geyser of colossal proportions to erupt from a small slit in her damaged defences. She leant over and pressed into his shoulder as she sobbed as if her heart would break. He quietly stood there, stiff as a board. All he wanted was to gather her in his strong axe-hardened arms, protect her, make her pain go away... but he didn't dare. Finally, the tempest eased. Her body relaxed and she gave him a hug. That was even more difficult. He could smell her hair, and the lingering baking smell of wood-smoke and oven fresh loaves. It was too much. He stiffened again and Belle sensed his discomfort. She dropped her arms and stepped away with an awkward apology. He almost ran from the kitchen and he avoided getting close to her after that.

It seemed that the ghost of Belle haunted Tobias. Little things. Everywhere he looked there was evidence of her. Unrelated, unconnected things, random things: like a hat walking down the street on the head of some unknown lady, or the tread of a cart-horse that looked nothing at all like Bronza. One day he was taking off his jacket on the porch at home when he felt something in his pocket. It was a red and white boiled lolly covered in pocket fluff. He stared at it in the palm of his hand for a long time.

He felt besieged. Fresh emotions assaulted him that did not align with how he viewed his relationship with Belle Kane. Finally, he laughed and shook his head in amazement. After all the years of warring with Belle, in the end she had won. The most hilarious thing of all was that she didn't even know that she had struck the fatal blow. His eyes smiled as he drew out a white flag in surrender. Victory was hers and the thing that shocked him most of all, was that nothing could have pleased him more. Mabel was her full name. Belle. May-Belle... he rolled the sound of her name over in his mind, and it sounded so sweet. He went inside whistling and washed off the red and white lolly. He placed it in a jar and stood it on his desk.

8.

Toby stayed and helped finish off chores in the morning. They had canvassed more work, and without much difficulty the orders had started to rise again. His challenge was to get Belle to release the mixing machine into his care to see if he could do some repair and maintenance. He started taking the cover off and dusting it down with great respect. He had two motives. The first was to get Belle looking at the machine again, remembering what it could do. The second was, that as he made the appearance of respectfully dusting it off, he was tracing the mechanics of it, reminding himself how it operated. He was very impressed with the simplicity of the engineering. Mr Kane was a very clever man.

Belle stared around the Bakery that her father loved so much. Her eyes rested on the uncovered contraption in the corner as Toby traced the lines of the machine with his cloth, caressing it. Belle was brooding. "The mixing machine: if only it was still working, we could make more loaves."

Finally! Tobias had been waiting for her to make a mention of it. He was running out of ways to scatter his not so subtle seeds of suggestion. "Miss Belle, I could look at it for you!"

"Oh no – I don't think so. It is Dad's invention. No one would know where to start on it."

"It maybe stopped 'cause of something easy."

"Maybe once, but since..." she paused. Tobias sometimes seemed to forget that things had changed for him.

75

"The machine was Dad's special creation – like a baby. Toby – what if something happened so that it could never be fixed?"

Tobias grimaced. "Belle is his baby – not the machine!" This was not just a broken bread dough machine – it was a shrine. All it needed was candles! It would never make bread while it was that way. He turned away more than a little disappointed, and allowed himself the liberty of a pout.

"Toby…" Suddenly in the quiet of the dawn, and the stillness of the shop and wafting of hot baking bread, reality swarmed in to sting, and its bite was almost paralysing. She stared at him as if she was trying to remember why he was here. Tobias shrugged. He was not getting through. He stood up and went to the oven. He slid open the metal sliding door and the smell of baked bread enveloped the room in fresh wave. He took down the long bread peel from the rack and pulled out the tins, unstacking them onto the cooling trays.

How he wished he could just say that he went to Doctor Wallace's every morning he wasn't needed for a major job at the farm and studied. How he wished he could say that his motive for coming to the bakery was no longer just to fulfil a commitment to Doc Wallace.

After Terry broke his arm the Doctor had asked him to come in and see him. They had a long talk. Doc Wallace asked him about his shelved plans to become a doctor. The financial burden required in going away to study medicine had meant that Tobias had to realistically put his dream aside. The Doctor talked to him about the dedication and commitment his profession demanded, to be there for people, even if it was inconvenient and undesirable. He talked about long hours and sleepless hours on duty. He talked about the satisfaction and influence, and as he spoke, Tobias' dream was resuscitated.

They struck a deal. If Tobias could demonstrate he had what it took, the Doctor would sponsor him through college and med-school. His test: to help Belle for as long as she needed or until the end of next year – which ever came first. In the meantime, he could come and study in the back room during the day whenever he was able. It was a private arrangement. If he told anyone, it was made null and void. He said it was the principle of the "left hand" – whatever that was. If Tobias wanted out, he need only give Belle two weeks' notice that he would not be able to continue at the Bakehouse.

Toby had made those moves to get out. He was convinced that nothing was worth the condescension that his retarded work at the bakery demanded, or the long hours. He gave Belle the opportunity to find someone else so he could leave. As thick-skinned as he was – he knew she was in a jam and fully appreciated that the Doctor struck the deal as much for her, as it was for him. When Belle hadn't been able to find a replacement, she had unwittingly locked him into fulfilling an unknown contract, like running a marathon; and he had pushed through the pain-barrier. Now it felt like he was on the other side, heading for the finish line. It didn't seem so hard anymore.

What did seem hard... was the pretence.

9.

The routine was numbing. Fatigue was Belle's constant companion. Dr Wallace was concerned that his patient's daughter would soon become his next admission. "Belle, is there a way that you can take some time off? My dear you are quite exhausted." Belle stared at him. There was nothing she would love more. But it was impossible. Suggesting it was just another demand. "Can't Toby do more to relieve your load?"

"No," she responded quickly.

"I see him periodically – would you like me to suggest it?"

Belle tried to focus. "He's already doing much more. I'm not sure he could."

"So, you wouldn't mind – if he would, or could?"

"I suppose not – I just don't see…"

"Is he doing this job well?"

"Well, I guess so," she said reluctantly. Admitting that Toby, in his impaired state, was working out better than anyone else she had managed to employ did not reflect well on her ability to engage suitable people.

"Guess so? There have been problems?"

"He has been very reliable actually. More than any of the others I have had."

"Belle – it is not unreasonable for a manager to gradually introduce new tasks, if your worker is showing aptitude."

She stared at him some more. "Manager? I guess I am." She gave a tired smile. The thought was new to her. The doctor had a way of making normal routine stuff sound like art. Although it made sense, being a manager didn't feel at all as prestigious as it sounded. However,…she *was* managing: that at least was a good thing. "Doctor Wallace, would you mind seeing Toby about this? Just to be sure." She had no idea how far reaching his condition was.

"You know Belle – you might be surprised. Tobias is doing quite well." He sighed. There was something about Belle's dark hair and serious corn-flower blue eyes that tugged strongly at his heart. He felt more protective towards her than being her father's medico warranted. Toby was another one: a protégé with potential. It was a tenuous balancing act that he was playing. "I tell you what, next time Toby comes in I'll ask how it is going."

There was something else. "Doctor Wallace, about Dad…" Belle paused before blurting her question. "Is there any hope? This is going on so long! How much longer?"

The question – the crystal ball question. The number of times it was asked by anxious family members, the Doctor sort of hoped he would get used to it. He never did. "Belle, I usually don't give a definite prognosis, because it seems to cut short people's expectations. The human body is remarkable in its fight to be whole… and I am open to those miracles happening. However, when you see these sorts of things over the years, there is a definite pattern that develops. It can be very predictable. It is a dilemma I have never quite reconciled. Will we continue to work hard, and wait to see how it goes? Or, do you want me to share the probable outcome? It may not be what you want to hear."

"Oh Doc… I just want to know. It feels like you are holding out on me."

"Perhaps I am. Perhaps I am holding out for a miracle too…" He paused and sighed softly. "Belle, I have never seen anyone affected by a severe stroke like your father's, return to their normal life. I'm not saying it can't happen. I'm saying I have never seen it."

"What have you seen?" Her voice trembled. Nothing could be worse. Surely.

"I think you know. Usually another stroke."

"But he's already had another one."

"Yes…"

"And…"

"If he had another stroke of the same intensity, I wouldn't expect him to live through it…"

The cold hard words thudded through her. Her whole life was in the process of having rocks thrown at it – like a formal Roman execution, progressively and systematically being destroyed. Her breaths came in deep, gasping whoops. The room began to spin, and the doctor's concerned face started towards her from across the room in an eerie swirl of brown and white, like a smudged sepia photograph.

Belle woke up in a bed surrounded by wooden framed dividers covered with starched white cloth. A small lamp shed a dim flickering light onto the material creating a creepy shadow-play in the gloom. In between the dividers she could see curtains further over that looked as if they had been made from converted bed-sheets. Hospital: that hospital carbolic smell. The lamp on the stand beside her bed had not been recently trimmed. It was night time. Had she fallen asleep at her Father's bedside?

She sat bolt upright trying to remember! Her head thumped and she clutched her chest. It seemed a knife stabbed her chest every time she moved. She gasped and struggled out of bed. She was making her way to the door when she was accosted by the night-nurse thumping her way around the ward like an aggravated apparition. She had seen this nurse on her father's ward, but Belle had forgotten her name because in her mind she always referred to her as the Ward-Hun. "Get back into bed! You're not goin' nowhere Miss Kane: doctor's orders," she whispered harshly.

Belle stared at the intense ferocity on the woman's hard features. Her nurse's veil bobbed like a fishing float in a whirlpool. In a moment, Belle summed up the remote probability of winning a logical argument with someone who used the phrase "Doctor's orders" as punctuation.

Belle leant forward and gasped as another knife stabbed her chest. "Sister, what's the time?" she asked vaguely. It was time to start work soon. She had to get back to the shop. Belle put on her most pathetic voice. "Sister, I need to see my father. Please…"

The woman's lips were pursed together in a very unimpressed line. "He's sleeping. His condition has not changed in weeks."

Thanks for that, thought Belle dryly. "I just need to see him. I didn't get in to visit yesterday." She paused. "What happened to me?" She looked bewildered at her hospital gown that hung unflatteringly on her body like a flour sack – only with a little less finesse than one would expect from the average bagged bushel of baker's-grade flour.

"You collapsed at the doctor's rooms. Hit your head and broke a rib when you fell. The doctor was not near enough to catch you. You are confined to bed-rest. Doctor's orders." She was talking in dot-points. Belle sighed. Her diversion had travelled full circle back to "Doctor's orders". Her chances of getting to see her father, out of sight of the nurse and home to the bakery had again diminished to zero.

Suddenly there was a loud clang from the end of the ward and a frail voice called out. The Ward-Hun muttered under her breath, and flung a command at Belle. She stood watching her return to the curtained cubical before she stomped off to rescue the bedpan. Belle quickly stuffed pillows under the covers in an immature attempt to delay detection. Even she had to admit it was not very convincing, still, as she blew out the bed lamp, she hoped that the shadows were deep enough to conceal her movement. Belle felt like an escaped prisoner as she painfully slid out the door and made her way back to the bakery, keeping to the darkness.

Belle stood leaning on the benches in the gloom. Nothing was done. Everything remained cold and clean, scrubbed from the mornings work from the day before. Tears rolled down her cheeks. This time it was too much. This time she had been unable to rally to join the battle. The pain in her body peaked and ebbed in relentless waves. She leaned over and grabbed a bucket and was sick. She screamed as pain overwhelmed her. Clammy perspiration beaded over her body – making the hospital gown cling. She shivered. The cold floor of her father's bakery shimmered – like it was at melting point – turning to fluid and she would drown in it at any moment.

The familiar stirring at the door roused her. How long had she been there, braced solid against the bench? She could not move.

"Belle? What happened? Belle!" Toby was standing beside her as she started to fade.

She tried to protect him, like a child. He would not know what to do. "It's okay. I'm okay…" and then the small lamp he was holding went black.

She roused in her own bed. The lamp in her room glowed yellow. She could hear her Dad moving about. She smiled before she faded back into sleep. Everything was okay.

Her eyes flickered open again. The lamp was out and the curtains in her room were drawn holding back the daylight. She tried to sit up, but pain pinned her to the sheets. She looked over at the strong frame of her father standing by her wash-stand. "Dad? What time is it? The deliveries…"

Tobias turned around. "It's me Belle, Tobias. Your Dad's not here…"

"Toby! What are you doing here? Where's Dad?

"Belle – your Dad had a stroke. He's been in hospital a while now. Have a drink." He held a glass to her lips and supported her head. "Now, rest and everything will come back to you. I'm sure. Doc's been to see you. He'll come back later, after his rounds."

It seemed completely normal that Toby would be there in her bedroom, holding her head and offering a drink. She nodded her drowsy thanks... and drifted off.

Suddenly her eyes flew open. She stared wide-eyed at Tobias as he stood by the window. She clutched her sheet up under her chin and tried not to think of the ridiculous gown she had on. No one should ever have to see a living person in this primitive one-size-fits-all attire. She didn't even think it was a suitable shroud for a dead person – if it came to that. Yes, she remembered... sort of. But something was missing – something was not adding up.

She went over in her mind flashes of the freeze-frames of what she remembered. She remembered her Dad – taking him to hospital, Terry chopping wood. She stopped and rewound. Terry broke his arm and when Toby arrives he is taken to the doctors. No... that was not right... That didn't even make sense.

Toby...

Her head throbbed and she rubbed her forehead restlessly. Why? She just wanted the pain in her chest to go away. And she didn't seem to notice that the pain that she was referring to was not from the stabbing of her fractured rib. She stirred restlessly and closed her eyes against the reality of her life.

Toby turned around and watched his patient. Never could he have believed he would feel so completely unprepared and useless. This was not what medicine was about. It was about creating options, more control, more influence, changing outcomes. He quietly cursed himself for the foolish pretence he had so persistently created. It was a candid moment as he vowed to make amends. He was aware of a crushing breathlessness in his spirit. It was a sensation totally new to him. Doc Wallace had stood by her bed in the lamp-light and said that Toby had done everything right and that all she needed was rest. Rest! How could he tie Belle Kane to a bed without keeping her permanently comatose? Why wasn't there some chemical concoction that would stir her to health… real health – not just a drugged suppression of pain? There was a significant difference.

He sighed and quietly went and sat by her bed. He fiddled with a loose thread on the bedspread vacantly waiting for whatever one waits for when a loved one has been seen by a doctor and has been told that "time is the great healer". Toby vowed never to use that line. Time did nothing except chew up valuable moments.

It was a defining revelation. Life was so short… hanging by a tenuous thread. Didn't Reverend Bernard pray in Church on Sunday mornings one of the Psalms? How did it go? We should seek God to "teach us to number our days". He always went on to piously sermonise that Moses' prayer was one that was "worthy of us all." Reverend Bernard had a grey stock of hair that circled his balding head like a halo, one that Toby could not look at without thinking he must have done something incredibly wicked to have his halo slip so convincingly.

Toby had no great respect for the Reverend. He never seemed engaged in real life, but those words breathed a life of their own. He was acutely aware of his mortality… now… in the face of Belle, lying pale and weak, determined, stubborn, young… so vulnerable, on her bed. It was foolishness, but the words echoed relentlessly around his head. Toby got up and paced the room.

He stopped and looked at the books lined along a shelf, and picked up a Bible. Perhaps he could find that phrase. He opened the soft leather cover. The inscription in the front was a feminine scrolled hand.

"To my dearest Nell, may God bless you as He takes you on His journey of truth…"

~ with much affection, your mother.

"Eleanor Joyce Parker m. Samuel Roderick Kane 1879"

b.   14 July Mabel Joyce Kane 1884

The last two entries were rough and scratched.

b.   22 September Roderick George Kane 1887

d.   23 September Nell Kane 1887

Toby grimaced and shook his head: some journey of truth. He turned over the tissue thin pages, fragile and cream – like the translucent skin of a newborn. How could these pages of print simultaneously have such a diverse reputation for being the source of truth, or the vessel of hypocrisy, or the mark of blind ignorance… depending on your perspective?

"God – what is truth?" he whispered to himself, as he stared at a page. His eyes rested on the book of St John and followed words that Jesus was speaking: "'Every one that is of the truth heareth my voice.' Pilate saith unto him, "What is truth?"

He snapped the book shut. Freaky.

With an arrested sense of time he found the page again and continued to read. A number of times he backed up and kept reading. Jesus, this asserter of truth was taken away and killed. And still there were people who went to their grave declaring that he had not died in vain. Then there were the reports that his grave had given up its conquest… and he had been restored to life. Now Toby wanted to know why. With hours to fill beside Belle's bed before the nurse came in for her next visit, he sat and read.

It was the most peculiar journey. That part he could accept. He *was* being drawn along on a voyage that was taking him somewhere; his own journey of truth, and this bible was the map. Sometimes he felt so angry, so cheated, so sceptical, and so cynical that he would put the book aside in contempt. But again, he was drawn back into the story – the history. Why would they chronicle this? There was no doubt in his mind that this book was not fiction. That was never the issue with Toby. The issue was whether it mattered to him now. Was it just an interesting record, or could the events from the turn of the world's millenniums impact him now? Was truth that all-invasive?

He came across small passages that were underlined carefully in thin pencil. He tried to work out what it might have meant to the eyes of the original reader – probably Belle's mother Nell. What was it that she wanted to highlight in these passages? What did they mean? Mostly it was hard to fathom why they could be significant. Like, "*be not faithless, but believing*". Believe what? He read around the phrase for a long time, backtracking and going forwards, and still he couldn't quite get it. What was he to believe? The illusion or the truth? What was the truth?

In frustration he felt the whole thing was like the Cantonese recipe he had seen in his mother's cook-book, written out and given to her by a travelling Chinese hawker. It made absolutely no sense. It was like he needed a translator. Whoever said that the Bible was truth – had the brain cells of a mite. At least he could say he had given it a fair shot. He felt vindicated. He was not an unintelligent person. He was not going to walk blindly along on someone else's say so. "Just because" was not good enough. He was not going to commit his mind and his spirit to something that had no meaning or relevance now.

10.

Belle opened her eyes. She was rested and her eyes had a sleepy contented look, as if she had slept away all the pain and the anxiety. Toby looked at her. He wondered if he went to sleep for a week, would he also wake up believing that the world was a better place?

Belle sat up. "Toby – where is Doctor Wallace? I must talk with him."

Toby grinned. Belle was back. He was not unhappy to relinquish his vigil by her bedside. He could spend more time finishing the surprise he had been working on for her.

He was also relieved to be rid of the ridiculous 'Poor idiot - Helpless Maiden' scenario that he had concocted in a desperate moment. He was over it now. The deception increasingly drained him. Every lucid moment since Belle had collapsed in his arms, Toby had been absolutely determined to use normal language. If he used only sensible vocabulary, and answered every question intelligently, there could be no doubt in Belle's mind that Toby the woodchopper is the same Tobias that she went to school with, but with some significant changes.

He was pleasantly surprised how Belle took it. She didn't seem to want to make a fuss over the details of why he had felt he needed to use this ruse. One day he would explain his need to guarantee his right to help; but not now, not while she was so physically fragile. Belle was anything but helpless – when she was feeling herself. Granted, this last week - well, it was just an indication of how vulnerable any member of the human race was. Given the circumstances, he realised anyone can crumble. For the invincible, bullet proof Tobias – it was quite an accomplishment not to attribute her illness to some weakness of personal character. Some things just happen.

"Toby?" His eyes snapped back to Belle's tousled framed face.

"I need to see Doc Wallace." But as their eyes momentarily locked, Belle averted her gaze restlessly. "To-by," she said with distinct enunciation, and the condescension of talking to a small child. "Please find Doc-tor Wall-ace."

"But he'll be by after lunch. He comes twice every day."

"To-by," she said with exaggerated patience, "You don't understand, I need him *now*."

"It's already nearly Eleven. Even if I…"

"Toby, please don't be difficult!"

Toby shook his head in disbelief and then sighed, momentarily resigned. "Yes, Miss Belle,"

The relief in Belle's face was stark, as she gave him the most radiant smile.

"Oh, Toby, thank you so much," and she closed her eyes against the shuttered light.

Toby went downstairs into the shop. There was no way the Doc could come sooner even if he found him. He was probably on his way already. Tobias knelt on the ground before his project. In between working the bakery, he had consistently put untold effort into it while Belle was upstairs recuperating, but now he found it hard to focus. His eyes smarted with disappointment and the lump in his throat made it difficult to swallow. Belle had remembered nothing. She still was as convinced as ever that he was the impaired remanent of her school-day rival. How long he stayed there he could not be sure.

The Doctor had come and Toby took the opportunity to get out. Anywhere. His escapism felt childish, yet he was not sure he could hold on. But he needed to. He needed to prove himself to the Doctor. He needed to prove himself to Belle. How could two things that had seemed so aligned suddenly become so diabolically opposed? He walked randomly – and ended up sitting by the creek watching the dragonflies hover over the top of the water, darting across the surface on their urgent missions. Their hurry seemed to reflect the insistent tension in his belly.

The thing that shocked him most of all was the need for him to determine what was important. This became his urgent mission. Was the offer made by Doc Wallace the most important thing? Was there no other way he could fulfil his dream? Was it laying bare his soul to Belle, giving her the power to squash him like the brainless bug she thought he was? Was it finding out the truth and living towards that? Truth. There it was again. Truth… Integrity…

Integrity? Where did that come from? One thing he could say about the story he had read by Belle's bedside, was that Jesus had shown integrity. The man himself could not be faulted… and since he was the one that stated he was on the side of truth… perhaps there was something in it. It couldn't be any other way because if his integrity was faulty – it was all a lie… no truth.

Tobias remembered debating with Doc Wallace in the library, about the use of expensive procedures. "Some responsibility has to lay with the patients", Tobias argued. The Doc leant back on a bookcase and said, "Tobias, 'what ifs' are not helpful in managing the reality of some people's conditions. We can't select treatment options on the basis of why they have the disease in the first place. However, I do agree: the costs don't go away. Someone always has to pick up the tab."

That immediately confronted Tobias. "How can the choice of treatment always be chosen by the best outcome, whether the patient can pay or not? No one is going to realise that until they can see the expense… and pay the cost."

Doc Wallace agreed that in an ideal world, things would look different to reality, but before Tobias could gloat over his rational victory, the Doctor countered with his professional stance that in many cases he had opted for more costly choices because of the expected outcome. "Tobias, medicine is still about cure, more than any other one thing: prevention is not always chosen or possible. In fact, to discriminate treatment choices on that basis are exclusively in the Department of Divinity."

Funny that he should remember that conversation now. "Divinity". Doc Wallace was far too educated to seriously believe in a divine god. Surely it was just a turn of phrase. But perhaps not… he always went to church. Another question hung around the edges. If the doctor had chosen more expensive treatments, and someone always picked up the tab... then who paid?

Instinctively Tobias realised it was another example of the Doctor's "left hand" principle, a Jesus principle... one he had read in Belle's Bible: *"But when thou doest alms, let not thy left hand know what thy right hand doeth: That thine alms may be in secret: and thy Father which seeth in secret himself shall reward thee openly."*

Why would pleasing his idea of Divinity be so important to Dr Wallace? Was Jesus the embodiment of Divinity? Jesus said that was who he was. It was almost like the dawn getting lighter in the morning... a rapid illumination. But at the same time it created a conflict so intense that it felt as if he was being dragged apart by two powerful realities. He also knew that he had the authority to exercise a choice... and that the conflict would remain until he chose to put into effect that power. In this moment, it was in his control to cease the conflict. It would not be the only time he would need to make a choice, but a continuing process of choosing alternatives... a daily, moment-by-moment series of choices.

It was then he took a leap. He plunged in. "God, my understanding is pretty scratchy at the moment. But I feel compelled to make a decision – one way or the other. I've always considered that in turning towards You, I would be relinquishing my right to having solutions. But if you are honestly The Truth, your integrity will help me explore the questions and discover for myself more of the answers. I want to start this journey of Truth with You."

Just as he anticipated, the conflict ceased. And with the lack of conflict, a peace so surreal flooded the spaces left by it, and any doubt he had was washed away. He closed his eyes basking in this encounter with the Divine; the author of integrity. He knew that he knew, and it didn't matter just at this moment, that he didn't know how he knew.

11.

"Toby! What are you doing?" Belle screeched in horror as she looked up from the dough troughs. Toby had finished the tasks early and his hunched frame was focused on what was before him. He froze as she bounded over to him, yanking him backwards. "Toby stop! You have no right to touch this. You have no idea what damage you could do!" She caught him off balance and he toppled back. Immediately Belle was repentant – shocked by her own impulsive hostility. "Oh, Toby I'm sorry. I didn't mean... are you hurt?"

She knelt beside him and went to cradle him like a child. Tobias sat still, wanting her to soothe away the aching disappointment in his chest that had clung there for days. But he realised that while he perpetuated his own illusion it would remain just an illusion... and he could no longer tolerate that thought. It had to be real or not at all.

He gently placed his hands on her upper arms and moved her slight frame aside, like shuffling a delicate ornament on a shelf. He stood up tall and made every effort to look into her eyes. But she averted her gaze. "It is finished anyway. I was just checking," he said quietly.

"Finished?" she croaked, "Checking? What?"

He no longer lisped when he spoke. She could read into that anything she wanted. "I was checking your father's mixing machine. The boiler is working just fine. It runs off the oven fire. The steam engine just needs to be started. I'm sure it's fixed."

She stared at it – like a sacred thing; that breathed on its own.

"It was only a simple problem. You could have done it yourself," he said unapologetically.

"It's fixed?"

"Until you start it, we won't know for sure."

Belle took a deep breath and slowly exhaled. He could see an internal battle raging. The agony of waiting, unable to assist in the claiming of victory, was almost more than he could bear. She had to turn the switch herself. He knew that. He looked away, giving her the privacy to decide. She struggled to her feet, tiring quickly from her extended confinement in bed. "Toby – please come into the kitchen. I'm going to have a cup of tea."

Toby sighed. She was evading the inevitable. They needed to get it started. Time was not on their side. Belle went to the stove and lifted the lid peering at the water inside. Toby stepped over and took the kettle from her hand. "It's hot – don't burn yourself," she cautioned as he poured the steaming water over the leaves in the teapot. He dressed the pot with patch-worked cosy that was a gift from Ali and set it on the pot-stand. He turned it absently once to the right, and twice to the left.

"Your Mum does that," commented Belle as she sat and picked up an envelope on the table.

"Doc dropped that envelope in before he started on his rounds," said Toby as he poured two cups. Belle didn't even notice that he didn't milk and sugar his tea. She was staring at the envelope as if it was leprous, uncertain, her resolve wavering.

"Hmmm…" She cleared her throat.

Toby studied his mug. He waited for the tirade about messing with things that didn't belong to him; for touching sacred monuments without permission. After believing she had it all clear, reverting to the simple-child treatment was getting old very quickly. He sighed again. It was another test of his ability to persevere: this trial was one of his own making.

"Toby… I…" Again, Belle hesitated. It was tortuous seeing her like this.

Finally, Toby said, "Belle – just spit it out. You want to say it – so say it."

She swallowed hard and forged ahead. "When I asked to see Doctor Wallace so urgently last week, I needed his advice on an important matter. He has been more like a very good friend since my father got sick rather than just his doctor." Once she got started the words rolled more easily. "He helped me get some legal advice. You've done a pretty good job over the last ten days. That's the longest time since Dad started this shop nearly twenty-five years ago that a Kane hasn't been the baker. If you hadn't been here, it would have had to close, and I don't want that to happen. I have to make plans. That is what I wanted to talk to the Doctor about, since I can't ask Dad. Well if I could, the whole thing would not be necessary, I guess. So anyway, I did it. It's all drawn up by a lawyer…"

"Whoa Belle! What have you done? You're not selling, are you?"

"Selling? The Bakery? Don't be daft Toby!" She stopped, silent… kicking herself for being so insensitive. "Sorry. I just mean I wouldn't sell Dad's bakery. It's not mine to sell. Things are looking grim – I admit that. So, I took your idea instead…" she ploughed on – like wading through heavy mud. "…your idea about taking on a partner. Toby, I want you to be my business partner."

Toby choked on his tea and put down his mug. He turned and stared at her, stunned into silence. When he made no comment, she continued as if she had expected this response and had prepared and practiced this speech many times.

"You would draw as much of your allowance as you want – or put it back into the business. Doctor Wallace and I went and spoke to your mother."

"You told my mother about this – before running it by me?"

"It was your idea. You suggested it. Your mother had no objections. She even said that because of your age you could sign the papers yourself, and that it would be legal."

"She said that?"

"Yes. I just want you to understand what you would be signing. I've asked Doctor Wallace to go over it with you."

"Oh, I understand fine! You want to go into partnership with an imbecile Belle. Why would you want to do that?" He stood up and paced. This was not exactly what he was expecting. He couldn't go into a business arrangement with Belle thinking he was somehow mentally deficient. Oh, how he wished he could do the last months over. She misread his agitation… again.

"Toby – sit down. Please. I've asked Doctor Wallace to countersign everything – so it is fair. I won't take advantage of you. I need you, and I think that this is much fairer than the way things were."

"What did the Doctor say about this idea?"

"He said that you would have to make up your own mind of course, but he thought it would solve a number of problems. He was quite supportive."

"What if I want to leave?"

"Where would you go?"

"Belle – it doesn't matter where. I might want to leave… go to university. What then?"

She smiled indulgently. "We covered that – well, not university," she qualified, "but if you wanted out, I'll buy back your partnership portion… with interest of course, if I don't have the money on hand. Depends on when you'd want to go."

"But why Belle?" She didn't seem to notice that the whole conversation was carried on without one downcast look or any incoherent lisps. It made no difference.

"I've already told you Toby. I need a reliable partner. I won't discriminate against you in this opportunity because of what other people might think. You've worked harder that anyone I have ever had. That means a lot. And, just before, when you said you fixed Dad's machine – I guess I believed what your Mum said - that you were still quite clever with mechanical things. She said that she actually hasn't noticed any difference since…" Her voice trailed off.

Now Toby was enthralled. "Since…. when?"

"Well, you know…. since your accident. I tried to get your Mum to talk about it. She absolutely would not."

"Belle, I'm fine. There is nothing wrong with me." How much plainer could he be?

"I know. Your Mum said the same thing. You are both very brave."

Brave? That took the cake! He stood stock still, facing her.

"Belle, I won't do it."

"Doc Wallace said that you might not feel up to it, but I really want you to consider this Toby."

"Not up to it?" That was an interesting spin on things. For someone who was reluctant to bring up the topic, Toby acknowledged Belle had become very determined to have her own way. So, what was new? "It's got nothing to do with me not being 'up to it'. You don't understand what you are getting into. We will fight all the time."

"I think I'm used to that Toby. We've had our share of disagreements."

"Oh boy…" muttered Toby. "We haven't started yet." He picked up the envelope with the contracts. "I'll read these at home," he said abruptly, and left.

12.

Belle sat down on her bed exhausted. She was shocked that Toby had resisted the partnership, especially when it was his idea to start with! Every time she prompted him on it, he was evasive and said that things were working fine the way they were. But she wasn't making enough progress. The idea of a partner – the reliability of having someone who would put in the hours for a part ownership, seemed like the only way she could get the momentum she required, and the money to pay back the leech Jameson before he sold up on her. She had begged for time… and he had reluctantly considered that her situation allowed for a measure of leniency… but she was not sure how long she had. She had asked the solicitors, but they said until they were contacted by Jameson's solicitors they could not say.

Toby's simple notion had grown over the days when she slept, her exhausted mind struggling with the failure of keeping pace with the unrelenting demands of her Dad's small business. There was no room for weakness… yet she had shown enough weakness for it to slug her to the ground. Doctor Wallace had sat by her bed and talked – not about what her body needed, but about what the bakery needed, and in helping to process those solutions, her body was able to find the rest it needed.

She lay down hoping to close away the implications of Toby's refusal. But incessantly, Belle reviewed over and over the same internal conversations. Uncle George – her mother's brother, had not replied to her letter. Sure – the period of time had not been long since the letter was sent, but she could not wait for the almost certain curt and abusive response. Her Dad said that they never saw eye to eye since her Mum died after the birth of her baby brother. Restlessly her mind scanned the landscape for any other missed alternatives but all she could see was this partnership as the only path immediately available, unless, of course, her Dad miraculously got better. If he wondrously were able to come back to work at the bakery, all would be normal again. She sighed. No longer did she have the faith to hope against hope for the hopeless.

Now it all lay with Toby. What if, in his limited understanding, he did refuse? The irony that she was relying on his compliance was too bizarre to dwell on for very long. Toby. What else did he have? Why wouldn't he be grateful for this opportunity? Hadn't she given him a legitimate job? Her rage started to mount. It seemed that the few people in her life all had something to prove or to gain from her dilemma. Toby – had to prove his independence; Mrs Lawson – had her son to protect; the doctor – his patients; Ali – was desperate to ensure the social status of her engagement was not jeopardised by any distraction. When it came down to it, she could only think of one person who did not seem to have an agenda.

She found Mrs Wallace watering her garden. She enjoyed tending it herself even though they had a Chinese gardener. And occasionally Belle had seen Sarah, their housemaid in the garden, with hand-snips to trim off a little parsley and thyme for her cooking. They stood and made small talk as she filled up watering cans and went from bed to bed showering them with love. It was an act of pure affection. Belle found it quite awkward to watch the intimacy it involved. But her unease was not entirely due to watching the transparency of the gardener tending her precious plants. There was a contentment and dignity about her that did not seem natural... especially when her life appeared so small in comparison to her husband's role in Wattle Creek.

"Mrs Wallace, I was wondering," Belle paused. "Could we talk?"

Mrs Wallace did not even look up from the patch of cornflowers that were starting to bud, but intently finished watering every single plant, their tall stems bending over under the weight of the water droplets that gathered and ran over their leaves.

"It would be a delight Belle. Let me get my bonnet and we'll go for a walk." Belle smiled. Somehow this lady knew that fresh air and space was exactly what she needed.

Mrs Wallace removed her gloves and broad brimmed straw hat and went inside. Belle wandered around the garden for a moment. The garden was embarrassing; a rag-tag assortment of flower-beds and vege patches. Its unique approach was the most unexplainable thing in Wattle Creek. Everything else in Louise Wallace's life was beautiful and neat – artistic and precise. Even her manicured lawns at the back of the house in comparison seem more like what one would expect. And yet no one could see these from the street. Mrs Wallace was so devoted to this cottage garden. It was certainly not neglect that gave it the random, thrown-together look.

They walked for a while without talking – just absorbing the sunshine and quiet. Belle still felt weak from her confinement in bed, but even in her exhausted state, the seeping sluggishness did little to soothe Belle's turbulent mind. "Mrs Wallace? I... I wanted to ask you..." She said nothing for a while as they turned off the street and headed for the Common near the tree lined creek bed. Mrs Wallace said nothing. She just quietly stepped over the stones that started to appear in greater numbers down the middle of the track. "What I wanted to know was... how do you get someone to do something when you are not sure that they will."

Mrs Wallace waited a moment for some sort of explanation behind the question and when Belle didn't offer any, she smiled.

"Well Belle, in my experience: I have found that I *don't*."

"You *don't* ask... or you *don't* get them to do what you want?"

"Both *don'ts*. In fact - it is probably more of a "*can't*"..."

"Really? But people do things for you all the time. Remember when you got the whole town working on building the school playground one weekend? Dad said it was the most remarkable thing he'd seen in ages. We brought loaves of bread up for the lunch."

"They weren't doing it for me; they were doing it for the children. And they chose to do it. I could no more *make* them do something than swim the Pacific Ocean."

"But I need to get Toby to do something, and it was his idea to start with. But it seems that he's changed his mind."

"Ahhh." Now she understood.

"It is very important, and I'm afraid that he doesn't understand how essential it is. Not that I would expect him to, I guess. It's just so crucial to everything that's left."

"No doubt – if one approach does not work out – there is always another way."

"Not this time. It is the only way."

"Belle – whenever I've had situations like that, do you know what I find encouraging?"

"No idea." What about failure could be inspiring?

"There is an ancient saying that goes: "All things work together for good, for those who love God and work according to His purpose". Paul of Tarsus wrote that in a letter, to encourage some of his friends in Rome. What is remarkable was that he wrote it while he was in prison."

"Oh." It was kind of disappointing that she had to bring God into it, thought Belle. At least she didn't start quoting Bible Scriptures at her. She could cope with an excerpt from an ancient letter.

"Those words were not written lightly Belle. Paul knew what he was talking about. Even when things were going really badly for him, like being sent to prison for no good reason, he understood God had a bigger plan that he was part of. And he trusted that it was under control. But more than that: God could work it out for good."

They moved down toward the creek. Wattle trees generally did not grow along creeks, but here a long stony ridge ran above the gully that gave this community its name. The shrubby trees were starting to bud in small green-yellow clusters. Belle's spirit cringed, a fear seeping into her bones in a weird kind of panic. What would it be like if God had some sort of plan for her life? Or was the bakery her prison? She was spellbound by what Mrs Wallace was saying. Could there be a greater order to things than just the immediate solutions to her own pitiful cycles of nights and days? It would be hard not to love a god like that.

Mrs Wallace stepped around low branches that swung out over the bank along the creek. Some house cows were lying in the shade chewing their cud. "Another man, at about the same time, also wrote a letter. He said, 'Cast all your care upon Him because he cares for you.' He was a fisherman who knew about casting fishing nets. So, when he talks about the getting rid of cares, he understood that we have to be quite intentional about where we throw the net to get the best return."

"Casting a net of cares?" In a strange way the analogy made sense to her. She felt trapped in a net of cares.

"The only place he had the confidence to trust his most precious concerns is Jesus – God's son."

"I hardly think a fisherman would know anything over and beyond a good fillet!"

"He was one of the few close friends that Jesus had while he was teaching people about God. He became one of the greatest leaders of the church after Jesus left."

Belle felt defensive. This was not the way she had wanted the conversation to go. She just wanted to get Toby to sign the partnership papers. "How does this help me to get Toby to do what I need?"

Mrs Wallace smiled gently at the urgency of youth – it is the era of 'now'. She quietly sent a prayer for wisdom heavenward. "It probably won't help with Toby at all – because Toby has to make his own choices. But it may help you to understand that neither Toby, nor any other person on this planet, can be the resource in your life that only God is intended to be. We have to allow God to be God, and allow people to be people. It is easy to confuse the two."

"So, you think it is wrong to try and influence Toby to see things my way?"

"Not at all. But Belle, if I know you – you would have already put your case forward quite convincingly. Now you need to trust God with the outcome, and try not to hassle the man to do just what you want. He is an intelligent person. He will weigh all the issues for himself in considering your offer. If it doesn't work out – God will help carry your burden and assist you to find other solutions."

"Toby? Intelligent?" Belle tried not to grunt. Mrs Wallace was politely minimising his disability just like everyone else. Why don't they just say it as it is? "I don't need brains, just reliability. That is harder to find, than a doctor in Wattle Creek, it seems."

Mrs Wallace laughed. "You asked how I influence people towards an end? All I can do is put forward a case and trust the outcome to the One who does have influence. That One is God. It is what I did with the school playground. Trust, Belle – Trust."

"Trust? How can I know that I can trust God with my cares?"

"Trust is not 'trust' if there is a written guarantee. Some people call it 'faith'. There are no guarantees... just a confidence that grows with experience. But that is something that you have to try yourself. You can't live off my confidence because you have not had my experiences with God. Still, there are a number of good reasons to start your own journey of trust. Firstly, He is God – his shoulders are strong; and he understands our circumstances. The Bible says there is nothing that Jesus has not experienced and cannot identify with. But I think the most reasonable answer is that he loves us and he wants to help carry our burdens. Much like how the bullock wagons are yoked together... they share the burden so that together a greater amount of active work is done, more than ever could be done alone. Jesus said His 'yoke' is "easy" – fits comfortably."

Belle swallowed. Suddenly she felt very tired. Why would God want to share her burden? If He really loved her, why doesn't He take the burden away? Was there enough evidence that He could be trusted – in the face of all the tragedy that had met her family? She had bandied around the "God is love" debate with a number of people before, without ever resolving it satisfactorily. It doesn't seem to add up when you are living with heartache all the time.

Just then – looking at the serene woman walking by her side, it was the most tangible argument for trust she had ever been given. She desperately wanted to be able to quieten the turmoil in her soul. "Mrs Wallace, I know your daughter, Lois... died. Why do you still trust? Isn't that the greatest violation of trust?"

"Oh Belle..." Her lip quivered for a moment and Belle thought for a moment she had snapped the cord of her faith.

How transient religion can be in the face of the real facts of life. Mrs Wallace took a breath, her voice quiet. "You know, it never felt like God had violated anything. Oh, I was angry. Very angry. When I was through being angry, I became lost... so very sad. But the harsh reality is that sin and pain and death are part of this world. Harold sees evidence of this every day. We are not exempt from these experiences just because we love God who intended it to be good. In truth, I couldn't have got through losing Lois without Him... and being able to cast my care onto him... every minute of the day. I still struggle with it... perhaps I always will."

Belle was stunned. Could she really experience pain and love and trust simultaneously? Trust did not eradicate reality; but helped establish it? Belle reached up and wiped the tears on her cheeks. She didn't completely understand the pounding in her chest – she only knew that she desperately needed to start to grow that sort of trust. She wished she could transplant it into her own heart. "How? How do I start to trust God like that?"

Mrs Wallace stopped and took Belle's hand. "You hold the small amount of trust God has already planted in your spirit – it might be as small as a mustard seed... and you plant it and allow God to grow it. See? I am an incorrigible gardener. We water this trust by learning about Him – by reading the Bible and talking with God... and spending time with other followers... then our trust grows into friendship. That is what trust is about. Friendship with God." When Belle nodded, she gently asked, "Would you like to start this trust journey with God? We can talk with Him if you like."

So quietly, she tenderly started a conversation with God. When Belle looked into Mrs Wallace's damp eyes as she quietly said "Amen", she kind of expected the blue sky to be cloudless and the dry grass to turn green. Nothing had changed on the outside. She didn't even feel that different on the inside – except for the knowledge that a tiny seed of trust had been planted in her heart and the moist soil of her circumstances that been patted firmly around it… and it was starting to grow.

13.

Belle waited until Toby left and stood before the machine. She stared at the ungainly thing, remembering the first time her father had levered it over to start. He had made such a ceremony about that first mix. Funny that Toby had been hovering about that day also. She had forgotten that. Is that why he felt such a connection to it now? This evening, in the silence of the shop closed to her customers, she hesitated again about starting the machine. Toby was so confident it was fixed, but then – how would he know? She wished she had asked him to stay while she started it up. But, if he didn't want any part of her offer for the partnership, it hardly seemed reasonable to ask more of him.

She had filled up the bowl with the plain white baker's flour, and hovered over it uncertainly. If she could use the machine for the majority of her orders, handling the smaller whole-grain and brown batches by hand would be so much easier. She swallowed and closed her eyes. "Oh God. Help me trust you..." She pulled the lever. It hissed and clunked and ground slowly as the large unwieldy mixers started to turn, around and around.

The familiar sounds of the machine hummed so normally, she turned, almost expecting to see her father in his little calico baker's cap and apron leaning over the machine, levering the dry flour mix to the centre of the stirrers. She grabbed the large wooden spatula and went to work. She knew that re-establishing the routines with the machine would take a bit of extra work to fine tune, but in the long run the solutions to her dilemma were materialising. Slowly, slowly, with time, it would be okay. The turning of the stirrers seemed to gently, rhythmically, make the affirmation that things would work out. They had to.

Belle wearily allowed Bronza to trudge back to the shop. Her success in getting the machine to mix up the evening batches had drained her. She had worked very late, but she was aware her exhaustion had more to do with the emotional resources she had to call on to work the machine without her dad. It felt wrong. She had never worked it by herself before... and cleaning it seemed to take forever. Toby's reaction to seeing the machine in use was a little understated. She had expected him to glow with pride, jumping up and down, excited over her resolution to start it up. After all, he had been on and on about it for ages, and he was the one who had fixed it. He had only smiled, and she was surprised that all he said was, "You did the right thing Belle. Your dad would be pleased to see it back in service for his girl."

Bronza seemed to sense her fatigue and his rocking slowly nudged Belle to the verge of sleep. He headed to the stable for a fork load of hay and a nose-bag of oats that Toby had started bringing in from their farm. There was something quite comforting in the reliable regularity of Bronza's trust in the sameness of life. Belle roused herself and unhitched the cart. She went through to the shop and put on the kettle for a cup of tea and toast. This was her regular breakfast fare that she had eaten since she could remember. Even when she was little, the morning mug and toast was part of the special Dad and girl moments she cherished. For now, she just sat, tired and bone-weary, sipping her morning cuppa, her mind numb.

The bell on the counter tinkled. Toby must not be at his post, serving customers and she was annoyed that he hadn't told her that he would not stay this morning. Tommy Wilson was also as regular as her morning cup of tea and Belle automatically got up to get the order. But as she came out to the shop front it wasn't young Tommy who stood at the counter. It was Mrs Craddick looking quite flustered. "Well? How can you bear it?"

Belle paled. "Have you news from the hospital?"

"About your father? Well I'm glad he's not here to see this. There is nothing that would break his heart quite so thoroughly, and if this was your idea of what a stroke could do, then it is eminently clear that you have never seen a broken heart in action."

Her indignant prattle clogged the airways around the tired thumping in Belle's head. Had Mrs Craddick heard she had used her father's mixing machine last night? Did he have another stoke? All she could register was that something had changed… and that something was sending panic signals shooting through her.

"Stop! Stop! Is Dad okay?" she shrieked.

Mrs Craddick raised her eyebrows while collecting her thoughts in an offended rejoinder. She lifted her chin just a little. "My goodness – no need to get so stroppy young lady. This is all your own selfish doing! In my day, family hung onto their heritage and was not afraid to work for it. You should be ashamed of yourself Mabel Kane – after all your father has done for you…" She quietly cluck-clucked and tut-tutted in moral horror of the vile state that had befallen the baker's daughter.

Belle shook her head. She felt quite incapable of comprehending whatever she was going on about. The door opened again. Mrs Hollis and Miss Francine Redding came into the shop supporting each other as comrades at arms. They stood, staring wide eyed – one through her cataracts and the other, over small round glasses. Mrs Craddick had beaten them to it. Nancy Hollis quickly gathered her faculties. "Now don't you go minding what she says to you Belle. You have as much right as the next person to be wanting an easy life. We all knew it was just a matter of time."

"Did you now?" said Mrs Craddick shaking her head in disgust at this pair. What right did they have to come here and put in their tuppence of shallow and moralising insights uninvited? However, she was quite overwhelmed with the need to articulate her personal ethical observations. She turned back to Belle. "It is devastating to think that everything your father strove so hard for is now suffering this flagrantly public display of corrupt mercenary gain… with him still lying in that hospital bed and…"

Suddenly it clicked. "No!" screamed Belle as she pushed passed the three grey-haired Job-comforters and ran to the front of the shop. Under the bull-nosed awning… hammered to the weatherboards near the front door, was a garish red "For Sale" sign. It boldly declared that the historical and community value of the Bakery was as significant as its business generating capacity. Jameson unapologetically had splashed his name on the bottom.

"He can't!" she shrieked again. Belle pulled at the sign, tearing the thin wooden sheet away from the heavy nails. It had all the hallmarks of a crucifixion. What she loved was being slaughtered and hammered by the destructive intent of evil.

"Jameson will go to hell for this!" She stomped and tore at the thing like a mother grizzly attacking to protect her newborn cubs. "His greasy, lined pockets are not getting Dad's shop! If its blood he's after, he's going to have to find someone else to sacrifice!"

Belle flew around the corner of the building – unable to stand still in one place. What would she do? God! God! This was the most complete of all wrongs.

"God, please help me…" It was a plea: to fix it; make it go away; to wave a magic wand. She buried her face in her arms; unable to stand the sunlight glaring brightly when everything should be cringing in horror at this indescribable injustice. She so desperately wanted someone to tell her what to do. She was willing to put up a fight, but how?

In the aloneness of the moment, she felt her remaining reserves of fight being actively sucked out of her and all that was left was the knowledge that her Dad would have waged war for his bakery. But like so many things… what her Dad would do, and what she *could* do were very different. How does one fight with your hands tied behind your back, thrown headlong into financial quicksand? She was no longer sinking, she was being sucked down at a rapid rate, and she felt her breath being squeezed out of her. Surely it was too late now. The writing was on the wall... in the form of Jameson's For Sale sign.

Someone touched her shoulder and she jumped. "Belle – it's me..." Toby stood in his town shirt and tie. "Come inside. I've got something..." He paused and cleared his throat. "I'd like to talk," he finished simply.

"Toby – no offence, but I'm done talking. I just want to be alone. I wish they would all go away."

"I'll get rid of them if you come inside. Really. I need to talk with you."

Belle shrugged. Life suddenly seemed very hollow. The substance had been knocked out of it. What did it matter? She didn't want to be bothered with whatever story Toby might have. Other things were more important. She had hoped that her discussions with Mr Jameson would have forestalled this. But if he was hell bent on getting his grubby, corrupt paws on the business, it probably would not matter what she did or said.

True to his word, the unwelcomed visitors had gone by the time she detoured around the back and into the shop. Toby put the kettle on and got her to sit down at the table. She put her head in her hands; it seemed too heavy to hold up by itself. She picked up the cup he offered and took no notice that he remembered how she liked her tea.

"This morning I went by Doc Wallace's... and got him to witness the partnership agreement. Both copies are here – you've already signed them, so this one is yours."

Belle shook her head in bewilderment. Why would he trot this out now? "Too late I'm afraid Toby. But thanks," she added, as she reminded herself, he didn't know any better.

"I went and saw Jameson. He doesn't want the bakery. All he is interested in is recovering the money from the mortgage." He stopped. Belle's eyes were glazed with tears.

He repeated himself. "He just wants the mortgage paid out. Once that's done, then it's off the market, you have the bakery back."

Belle sighed. He was trying hard but this was obviously out of his league.

"Toby you want to help so much, but this is exactly what I was trying to anticipate. The partnership would have helped, but now time has run out. I have nothing to pay out Jameson with… and I have a lot of medical bills," she added. He could have no idea at the depth of the hole she was in.

He took a deep breath. "Wattle Creek needs its bakery. It is an excellent little business. Your father's name adds significant value. And since Jameson doesn't want the bakery per say – that works for us."

"Us? Toby – there is no 'us'. There is no point in a partnership when the shop is going to sell."

"The thing is Belle, there are a number of ways Jameson can get his money back. He could sell up the premises, but it would be better to sell it as a going concern – as the bakery. Any number of businesses in neighbouring areas would be interested in this bakery: it has reputation. The possibility of an outside buyer is excellent. Jameson said so himself."

Belle looked up at him and smeared the tears in her eyes with the back of her hand. "What I am saying," he continued, "is that any time that you thought we might have, in reality – doesn't exist. You need action - now."

"Yes Toby… very insightful."

He continued, trying to gauge how much she was absorbing.

"Well, I have a plan… and I wanted to run it by you." Belle put down her cup of tea and pushed it away. It was ridiculous to think that any sort of plan could possibly have potential from this quarter. She looked at him with a dismissive quip on her lips, but his gaze held her. She was stunned by the clarity she saw there. For the first time since they had been working together, their eyes drilled into each other. Their gaze held for a long time, neither one willing to be the first to look away. Finally, Toby spoke quietly… his eyes steadily looking deep into Belle's blue eyes that fluctuated from curious, to intrigued, to confused, to outrage, to intense determination. "Do you want to hear my plan?" he asked.

"I think there is a lot about your plan that I would like to understand," she flashed back scathingly. The control needed to sustain their gazes gave a measure of restraint in their dialogue that was unfamiliar in their history of feuding. Both dug into their trenches waiting for the other to falter.

"I spoke with Nat and Mal, to see if they would buy out my portion of the farm… and what that would come to. I also checked with the solicitors to see how it would all hang together, and if I was able to use that to take over the mortgage." They continued in their death stare headlock. "As you can tell, this doesn't happen overnight. I have been working through this for a while."

"And you didn't think for one small moment that I might be interested in knowing some of this?"

"I wasn't going to raise your hopes on a solution that may not pan out. Sure, they're my brothers, but Nat is very protective of the farm. Even Mal wouldn't buy into the plan if it wasn't a fair bet. I have to respect that, even if it's not my way."

"What is your way Tobias Lawson?"

"Whatever it takes… usually – although lately, my track record has been marred somewhat."

"Meaning?"

"Meaning that… lately, winning has not been so important."

"And why would that be?"

"The plan for the shop is what is important at the moment."

"Really? Why would my father's shop be important to you?"

"Because it is important to you…" There, he said it.

"Your loyalty is quite touching…"

"You doubt it?"

"Well, what do you think Toby? You seem to be quite miraculously back to your old self."

He had nothing to say. He sat opposite, looking into her fiery eyes. She was so hurt and disappointed because of what she saw in *his* eyes. It didn't make sense to her. Again, the desire to win dissipated and left him wanting her to trust him, to collaborate, to be friends. What hope did he have? His record was self-condemning. He stood up and willed himself to drag his eyes away.

14.

Toby stood leaning on the wooden cooling rack beside the ovens. He watched intently as the totality of the revelation continued to dawn on Belle's face.

"But the accident," she stammered.

"There was no accident," he said matter-of-factly.

"But you said..." She looked at his face – open, an eyebrow raised in challenge. "I'm sure you said..." Belle scanned the recesses of her clouded memory. Surely he had said there was an accident. How else would she have known? "But you went to the city for investigations... you had tests... the results were to tell..." she stopped as she realised that she had never asked their outcome. "I take it they found nothing wrong?" she asked with her lips pursed.

"The medical tests were pre-med entry exams. I passed."

"Pre-med? University exams?" she spat out the words. "You deceitful... you told Mal to be intentionally ambiguous!" Her eyes narrowed with distrust.

"I never said there had been an accident," he stated unequivocally.

"But your mother?"

"We talked about it – she agreed not to correct any assumptions you made."

"This has been full blown conspiracy! Why would you do that?" Then before he could respond she gasped at another thought. "The Doctor! Doctor Wallace – he did exactly the same! How could he? He asked if you had been aggressive!"

"He did?" He turned away so Belle did not have to look at the smile playing on his lips. "Oh, that is too much," he murmured quietly in spite of the horror on Belle's face.

She was not fooled. "This is not funny Tobias. Not funny at all. It was all directed in exactly the same direction – to get me to believe that there was a problem with you."

"Belle – you wanted to believe it. Maybe not to start with … but lately - nothing would convince you otherwise."

"You can't say that! How could I possibly know that all this time there's been nothing wrong? You spoke like a simpleton to…" She turned on him, her whole body livid with anger.

Toby's face turned pale. "No, Belle. No. It wasn't like that at all."

"No? Then tell me Tobias – how was it?"

"I…" He shrugged helplessly. Doctor Wallace was very clear. Doc's offer would not stand if Tobias told anyone - that principle of the "left hand". But where was the line? As he stood there, not sure how to answer Belle, Tobias became aware of a change in his approach. Before he just wanted to protect his own investment in the agreement; now he wanted to honour the man's wishes. He was amazed at the regeneration of his thinking. He made a mental note to go back and explore this more totally. Just now, what he had to do was to keep Dr Wallace's name completely out of this conversation. Eventually he just said, "You needed help. I needed work away from the farm. I guessed pretty accurately that you wouldn't give me the job – if it was just me."

"You are right about that Tobias Lawson! Because with you there is always another motive."

"Is that so?" Now he had to make himself look at her – how well she knew him. There *had* been another motive… a very strong one.

"Yes – it's so." Her voice was ice-cold and quiet. "You play to win. You smug, arrogant impostor! Tobias Lawson: You think you've won again!"

"You forget I wanted out – no, I *tried* to decline your offer. You were determined to have your way."

"That is what you would have me believe – that you *tried* to refuse. But *you* forget I did not have all the facts. I'll contest it."

"Contest what?"

"The partnership. The whole thing is null and void."

"Why? Two adults of age signed a legally drawn contract. You made it pretty water-tight."

Belle's hand gripped a loaf of bread and flung it at his head. He caught it smoothly and put it on the rack behind him. "Belle – there's an easier way."

Belle sank to the floor – her back against the stone-wall. Her hands swept her hair back off her face and she held it there, her elbows resting on her knees. This betrayal, this deception was more than all the others Tobias Lawson had ever committed. She had been duped… and it made her feel more retarded than any of the pretences Tobias had pulled off. "God, I don't trust him," she whispered in her heart.

"Trust Me. Toby is the same as any man. He will make mistakes."

"Really?" she responded almost audibly. If this was about God and not about Toby - it sure didn't feel like it.

Toby stood still studying her sitting on the floor. Again, he felt the curiosity that there was none of the past vestiges of victory in seeing her beaten. There was no delight in seeing her like this. He wanted to protect her and at the same time recognised he had probably destroyed any hope of being able to do so. "Yes really. There *is* an easier way. I won't fight you Belle. If you want me out – I'll go. You know if you can handle it or not. Consider my offer to buy out the mortgage. But I will need to act on it immediately. Jameson is not a man known for his patience."

Belle said nothing. What had changed for her? She was still alone – she still needed help – partner or not…

Toby came over and sat down – his back against the cold stone wall beside her. He said nothing for a while. "Belle you are a fighter. You always take things head on. You have more spirit and grit than any girl I know. This is what I like about you. Just be sure you know who the enemy is."

He stood up and left.

Belle sat for a long time. She thought about her only stand up fight with Tobias. She couldn't even remember what it was about. A circle of grubby school faces chanted, "Fight – fight – fight", as they flew at each other like two young sparring cockerels, down by the back fence. Mr Hewitt's firm hand pulled them apart and his grim mouth ordered them to his office. When he proceeded to stand Tobias up for the cane, he dismissed Belle with extra copybook lines for homework, but she refused to go. "I was in the fight," she said with a ten-year-old flick of her pigtails. "Whatever you dish out on Tobias, I will take the same." She didn't want him winning by being able to flaunt his physical punishment as a sign of strength.

Mr Hewitt shook his head in frustration as to why his best two students were so bent on destroying each other. So instead of giving Tobias six of the best, he gave them three each. He was not like some of his colleagues. He took no delight in corporal punishment, and was loathe in dealing it to girls. They both left subdued, but out on the verandah Tobias stopped and said, "That was a good fight Belle. I'll stand up with you any day." He spat on his palm and held it out to her.

In return, she spat on her own stinging, red fingers and they shook. "'Till next time," she said.

He smiled and said, "'Til next time…"

Their fighting became more sophisticated and intellectual after that. There never was another hand-to-hand brawl. Thinking back, Belle thought that was strange. She had been vowing enmity, but perhaps he was shaking on equality. Was it possible she had been fighting for a respect that had been there all along… and she never recognised it? This was the first time she imagined that Tobias Lawson was not just after blood.

15.

Belle came in to sit by her father's bed and hold his hand. Where his palms were once work hardened and calloused, now they were white and clammy and soft. It seemed his wasting body belonged to another person. Yet every day she came, usually for just a short while. On a good day, she could see his eyes show response. On other days he slept or stared vacantly into a world unreachable by her. She walked quickly into the ward; her eyes automatically went to his bed scanning for clues as to what sort of day this morning might herald.

This time her heart stopped. His bed was flat: the covers creased in tight cardboard folds. The emptiness of the bed rose up and wailed her grief. She stood paralysed. Even her tears were frozen in the ghastly knowledge that it was over. Her heart screamed in her chest and she felt the ward tipping dangerously to and fro. "Oh Daddy, Daddy..." she whispered.

"Miss Kane?" said a gentle voice beside her.

"Ohh..." Her voice was barely audible as Belle responded to the pain in her throat. She was glad that the Ward-Hun was not on duty today.

The nurse looked compassionately to the direction of Belle's drawn expression and gasped. "Oh Miss Kane, we moved your father today. He is down in Bed Seven - at the end of the ward with the other long-term patients. You will find that he slept quite well."

Belle blinked, confusion clouding the moment. "What? I thought..." her voice trailed off. Why didn't they notify her that they were moving him today? Then she felt another flood of emotions equally confusing. With a bizarre stab of disappointment, she realised she would have to journey through these emotions again, perhaps next time for real. She let out a slow breath of relief as she stared down the long ward trying to locate his new bed. At least for now he was okay, yet the move acknowledged most convincingly that a discharge was slipping further and further away. Perhaps this was all she could hope for her father, for the rest of his life.

Although she didn't keep a tally, it seemed to her that there were more, far more, poor days than good. It became harder and harder to make the trip to the long-term patient beds where bed number seven was sitting under the window. Each time she went, she vowed to make her visit the highlight of his day - so she always put on a brave face for her father and his bed-neighbours, who became like family in their support. She had a particularly soft spot for old Wallaby Joe in the next bed, who always had a smile and a sweet-treat for her. But no matter how smoothly her visit went, she always went home drained. It was a marathon she ran every day. She just could not get used to seeing her father there.

Toby was sitting on the doorstep when she walked up the path to the back door. She stepped around him and opened the unlocked door. He grimaced as she ignored him, and continued to avoid the decision. True – they had worked every night and morning since the exposure of his ploy. But even if the cool August weather was warming, it was still very chilly in each other's company. The wattle-trees along the roads were starting to bloom in clusters, annually re-creating its renown golden tracks through the district.

"Belle, we need to talk!" She said nothing but indicated with an impatient sweep of her hand that he could pull up a chair. She automatically put the kettle on, for if she had to listen to him they might as well have a cup of tea. Toby was blunt. "I must know what you want to do. I have people hanging on until I give them the go ahead. What's it going to be?"

She paced; like a lioness trapped in a corner with nowhere to go. She felt her hackles rise and the fight in her starting to activate. Then she remembered something. Trust. "God how do I know who to trust. What is the best way to go?" It was not like there were a hundred options open. It was, in reality, pretty binary: yes or no. And still she could not be sure. Her entire father's heritage was hanging on this one response. It seemed there was too much at stake to choose, even though it appeared to be gone either way. Was a slow death, better than a quick one?

Trust. Okay. She stopped and took a deep breath. "God, I've read in the Bible that you give wisdom, that you are with me in every situation... and Mrs Wallace says you can make everything work out for my good. I don't understand any of this, and it doesn't feel safe, or wise, or good... but you have also said you want me to trust you. So that is what I am going to do." Turning to face Toby, it seemed to her that the most realistic thing was to leave him out of the equation. Before she could formulate these words into a sentence, she heard herself say, "I'll take your offer Toby." She stared at him in disbelief.

He stared back equally stunned. He was so sure that she was going to tell him "Thanks, but no thanks".

"Really?"

"No, not really. I had no intention of saying that!"

"Well, what is it? Yes or no?"

"Well, I don't know. I was going to say no... but I said yes... so maybe... Yes?"

"Are you sure?"

"No, I am not sure! How can I be sure? I don't have the luxury of a crystal ball like some gypsy! Since I don't have one... I'll..." she hesitated again. Trust. This was weird. "Okay, I'll go with the yes. Yes."

"Yes?"

She nodded, biting her bottom lip. "God – if this is trust, I'm none too keen."

Trust Me - I am trustworthy. It was a whisper in her heart, unspoken.

"Well then. Partners." He stood up and came and shook her hand. For a moment it seemed like they were ten again, standing on the school verandah... enemies calling a truce.

"No need to bring out the matches to burn the documents after all... since the agreement stands." He smiled in spite of her overwhelming lack of enthusiasm.

"I'll go and get it rolling. As soon as I know the time frames we are looking at, I'll let you know. From what Jameson has told me, there'll be no hold ups from his end."

There was nothing else for Belle to say, so she nodded.

"I did have the tin of matches handy you know," he said as he went to the door. "Thanks Belle. We work well together." And she frowned as she heard him whistling as he went around the back to the stable where his horse was tethered.

16.

They laughed as they walked across the street. "We should have made a reservation – that way it could feel like a real date," said Ali as she fiddled with the buckle on her bag that matched the buckle on her boots.

"At the splendid Creek Hotel?" scoffed Belle. "Be reassured that this establishment requires nothing more than showing up and paying up."

Ali looked offended. "I've made reservations before. It gives an occasion an aura of... formality."

"Without Jimmy? I didn't think any outing would be complete without the man behind the rock," said Belle with a twinkle.

"Oh you. I have Jimmy for the rest of my life. One night is not going to kill us. He was very apologetic! I kind of sprung this on him. He said he had other things organised already. Shame really – then you could have brought Toby along as well."

She ignored the Toby comment. They were business partners, not best friends. "Spontaneity is not a big thing with Jimmy then?" observed Belle. "You'll have to create a running engagement calendar so that he can keep up with your social life Ali!" Belle knew she was pushing it a little, but she felt entitled to get in some overdue mileage. Her confidence in this relationship was growing. Ali was determined.

Ali smiled, completely reassured by her friendly banter. She enjoyed seeing Belle so relaxed. It had been a long time since she had seen that in her friend. "They say opposites attract," she said uncharacteristically philosophical.

"Then that explains it – my most spontaneous of friends!" said Belle. "Here's to a night for celebrating friendships and partnerships!" Belle couldn't help but laugh. The papers had come through. Jameson was out of the picture and with that knowledge she realised a huge weight had lifted from her shoulders. Sure, the debt remained – in the Lawson name, but that was not so terrifying. She knew whom she was dealing with, and the partnership meant that it would be dealt with. In time, with good planning, it would be no more. Nothing had felt so light for a long time. She had jumped at Ali's offer to treat her to a dinner to celebrate.

She pushed open the door and made their way to the dining room. Finding a spare table, they sat down listening to the music and banter coming from the bar. It seemed that everyone was in high spirits tonight. They sat for a while making small talk, waiting for service. Belle got up. "I'll go and see if I can get someone's attention so we can place an order." She went to the swinging doors that separated the bar area, and stared dumbfounded at what she saw. Jimmy sat at the bar with Betsy swinging her legs and large bosom in front of him. She tossed her long red hair over her shoulder and was teasing him for a kiss, obviously enjoying the conquest. The tragic thing was that Jimmy wasn't disinterested. His mouth could barely contain the drool seeping from every crevice.

Belle turned on her heel. She had to get Ali out of there! She caught her coming across the room. "What's got into you," she said brightly as she saw the look on Belle's face.

131

"Sorry Ali – I suddenly don't feel well. We need to go. Now." And she grabbed her by the elbow to guide her back to the table to get their things.

"Whoa there. Not so fast. This is my treat. You can't get sick that quickly."

"Oh yes I can," Belle insisted. "I just did!"

"At least have a drink and then we'll go."

"We need to go now Ali. I mean it."

Ali shook her free. "I mean it too. This is the first time we have been out in 400 years. You can't renege just like that."

"I just did," Belle insisted again.

"Well, sit down and I'll get you some water…" and she spun around before Belle could stop her and she pushed through the doors and was half way to the counter before she saw Betsy Jameson hanging all over her beloved Jimmy. She stood frozen in horror, the music and the talk at the bar gradually turning silent as her look of complete revulsion seeped through to those egging on the wanton display. As the last whispers faded only Betsy's winsome voice could be heard saying, "You're the man for me Jimmy Golders and you know I'm more girl than any others in this town!"

In the silence, the pair turned to find what had muzzled the crowd. As his eyes landed on Ali, Jimmy jumped to his feet, knocking his drink. "Ali – it's not how it looks. I thought you were going to Belle's for dinner."

"Obviously. I'm guessing you wouldn't be here like this if you thought we would be too. 'Other plans?' You bastard! How could you?" She stormed over to where he stood, tugging at the ring on her hand. It slipped off and rattled to the ground.

She made no attempt to retrieve it. Her most treasured possession was trashed in a moment of brutal exposure. She stared in total disbelief at his guilt-stricken face – angry tears spilling from under her make-up coated eyelashes. "Never, ever talk to me again Jimmy Golders!" she threatened in quiet undertones and before she could stop herself, she slapped him in the face and stormed out.

Belle moved the bucket to the next section of window. She had a cleaning rag slung over her shoulder that she used to wipe the glass panel dry. "Morning Miss," said Tommy Wilson as he came out of the shop and tucked the loaf up under his arm out of reach of his exuberant young puppy.

"Hey Tommy!" She glanced back inside. "How'd he go? Did he give you the right change?"

"Toby? Yeah he's smart."

"So everyone keeps telling me. Oh look at this dog! He is all grown up. Is he the same pup you had?"

"Yeah – this is Bandit," Tommy said proudly tugging on the twine that was attached to his collar.

"Goodness – he's growing up quickly. You must be looking after him well. Bandit seems to like my bread!"

"Mum'll kill me if he gets it."

"Better not risk it then. Take care on the way home!" He trotted off, the dog bouncing excitedly beside him. He had barely turned the corner when another voice behind Belle startled her.

"Mabes…" Jimmy stood hanging onto the shop-awning post, a fixed, determined look giving him a fierce expression. He took a step towards her.

"Jimmy – you've been drinking." Belle turned away as his breath blasted her with a gust that threatened to knock her unconscious.

"Gee Mabes, what'ya reckon? Me girl dumped me." She picked up the dripping cloth from the bucket and attacked the next panel of glass. Like that was Ali's fault. "Mabes – I want ya to talk to her. Make her see sense." His words were slurring slightly, and his eyes stared in glazed concentration.

"Jimmy, I don't think you understand that I'm not exactly your greatest ally here."

"But it ain't my fault. I never asked Betsy to come."

"I was there Jimmy. I saw you. You have legs… you could have walked away."

"But it's not like she caught us in bed or anything. I was just having a drink with my mates…"

"Some mates you have. Real value."

"Mabes – can't you just talk to her? Tell her to come back…"

Belle paused and dropped the cloth back into the bucket with a splash. "I can't Jimmy – it's her life."

"But she'll listen to you…"

"Well, doesn't that say something? You're the one she was engaged to." Belle looked over at him. There was a dreadful moment of raw remorse that dropped Belle's guard. "I am going to see her tonight…" she conceded.

"Just make her see it was a mistake. I never knew she'd be there."

"Pardon?"

"Well, Betsy might have more… of her Dad's money, but I wouldn't want to marry a girl like that. If I'd known…"

"So, what you're saying is that… you're sorry."

"Yeah Mabes, it's killing me. I'm busted. I know it."

Belle stared at him. "You fraud! You're so cut up because you got caught! Not one word about how you've broken Ali's heart. Not one single thought about how she is doing! I have a news flash for you Jimmy Golders: It's not all about Jimmy Golders! If you really loved Ali – if you wanted to be with her for the rest of your life, that would be *all* you'd be thinking of!"

"Mabes…"

She cringed at the familiarity of using Ali's pet name for her. "Jimmy – my name is Belle: Ma-bel. Excuse me, I have work to do." She picked up the bucket. Jimmy stepped forward to block her way into the shop.

"You stuck up..."

In a flash Toby was between them. "Jimmy go home and sleep it off. You'll think more clearly when you're sober." His voice was ice calm… his body strung tight like a leopard on the hunt.

"I'm think'n fine already. You and your snobbish girl-friend here, think you're too bleedin' good…" He staggered forward swinging and clobbered Toby on the chin. Toby recoiled quickly and returned a punch that knocked him flying off balance. Jimmy picked himself up and barrelled Toby in the middle with his head. In an instant there was an all out brawl in the street.

Belle stared in shock as the two stumbled and lurched around in the dust. How could this happen? It was only half past eight in the morning! It was a ridiculous display of testosterone and liquor. The proprietors of the other shops came to the doors to see what was going on. Morning shoppers stopped and stared in amused astonishment. Jimmy crawled to his feet, staggering to reposition himself to wrestle Toby to the ground, his face bloodied from a split lip and a bleeding nose. Toby smeared the blood and dust from his face as he stepped up and punched him, slowly and deliberately, on the jaw – and he toppled like a tumble-weed.

Belle looked intently as he did not move. She ran to the crumpled form of Jimmy lying flat on his back. "Go and get Doctor Wallace! Now!" she demanded of Toby. He stared at her in disbelief. "Now Toby – this is not the time. Go and get him." Then he moved: the weight of tragic possibilities dawning on him as he ran.

Doc Wallace stood up from the bed and snapped his black bag shut. His mouth was grim and his eyes drawn thoughtfully. Belle and Toby watched him approach the two hard seats in the corridor where they sat.

"Can you explain what happened?" he asked quietly. The hospital echoed with the firm tread of nurses' shoes and squeaking trolley wheels. Toby said nothing. Belle looked away. She didn't want to expose Toby's foolhardy behaviour.

They were summoned yet again to the school-teacher's desk. "Well?" he repeated.

Belle took a breath. "Jimmy wanted me to talk to Ali. When I refused, he started getting in my face…" She paused as if something quite significant had just occurred to her. She looked passed the doctor to some undefined blotch on the hallway wall.

"I see. Well, tomorrow we will know more. He needs sleep."

"His breath smelt. He'd been drinking," she added as if this information would add weight to what happened.

"There's nothing you can do here now." The Doctor dismissed them.

They walked mute along the road back towards the shop. Toby had felt the wind had been knocked out of him… and that wasn't Jimmy's doing. Belle had slaughtered him with a vicious and disparaging look as she knelt over Jimmy in the street. He had no intention of letting it go so far. It happened so quickly. God. What if it wasn't just a harmless fight in the street? What if he was permanently… He couldn't even fill in the gaps. How does one fail so quickly?

Belle's thoughts were on somewhat of a different vein. What Jimmy had said echoed around in her brain like a bat in a cave: *"You and your snobbish girl-friend…"* Girlfriend? Is that what people thought? Another bat winged past: It was the look on Tobias' face as he intervened when Jimmy stepped up, agitated and drunk. Toby had been furious… mad… protective. She had recognised it instantly. He had been defending his ownership of the bakery. Or so she thought. In fact – she was kind of pleased it had meant so much to him. It had given her a sense of kinship with him. But now, as she turned down towards the shop with Toby striding silently at her side, his hands deep in his pockets, she didn't think that was the case at all. He had stated his case so quietly – so formidably. Belle realised that even if Jimmy had been sober, the result would have been the same. Jimmy's destiny that morning was to be pulverised into the dust... for he had threatened what Tobias Lawson considered his own: Belle.

Her mind then flitted back over the last months: previously unrecognised glances, unheralded comments, unprompted acts of redemption – like a mortgage and a partnership. Belle groaned. "Now what do I do?" she thought hopelessly. She would have to buy him out. She would not stay in business with a man who thought he owned her. Then another groan escaped her: the reality was... he did: he owned her – lock, stock and barrel.

She wished with all her might that she could return to her state of blissful ignorance. Just fifteen minutes ago, it had never occurred to her that Tobias Lawson had taken emotional ownership of her. He might call it love. She doubted his love would ever tempt her. She was not one for infatuations and doe eyed sentimentalism. Ali was testimony enough to the dangers of that. Yes, reality is not hard to bypass if one is unaware. But now she was going to be living in a state of perpetual awkwardness – until she could escape her chains.

17.

Belle stood by the window near her father's bed. She watched the sun dip low in the sky and stood quietly, hoping that the Ward-Hun would be distracted and allow her to linger a moment longer by her father's side. The nurse had never been accommodating before so Belle wondered why she hoped for it. The regimented control of the hospital reeked of marshal law. Right on time, Belle heard her come, stomping past the beds, the keys rattling on her belt like a warden. She stopped at Bed Four and addressed the patient's son; her voice clear in the silence of the ward. "It's coming from the city hospital. We don't have stores here." There was no apology, no sense of frustration – just a statement of facts.

"But how long is this going to take? Doesn't he need it... now?" The son's voice was not loud, but aggravation rang in every syllable.

"Doctor wouldn't prescribe the linctus if it is not needed."

"But…"

"Visiting hours are over now." He stared in disbelief at her frozen, iron expression; no response forming on his lips. He gathered his coat and hat wordlessly, and stormed out of the ward. A couple of patients weakly clapped his defiant exit. Belle failed to see how his impotence measured up as a heroic stand. Her desire to stay a few more moments abruptly left. She bent down and kissed her father. "Goodnight Dad. I'll see you tomorrow."

Belle watched the morning sun melt the darkness into a grey-pink light through the bakery window. She had tossed under her bedcovers until she could reasonably start the day. Now, as the sky faded into morning, she worked to get the loaves ready for the ovens. It didn't seem long before the risen round loaves in dark, heavy tins were slid into position in the brick oven. It was a couple of days since Toby had decked Jimmy in the street. He had slept it off and was discharged with no ill effects. It was a matter of pride that neither spoke of the incident again. Belle felt no closer to resolving her dilemma.

Toby paused by the door, watching Belle scrub the benches in an automated frenzy. He swallowed awkwardly. How could he proceed when she so obviously despised him? Nothing had changed from grade school after all, when she had stood on the other side of the room, tossing her pigtails and proceeded to talk her way through some argument with articulate poise. Nothing had changed indeed: except for one thing. By some strange biological phenomenon, his tongue now held no fluent rejoinder, but morphed into a dugong that wallowed incoherently around under his pallet. He was supposed to be her clever counterpart, so why should he be suddenly tongue-tied when it came to this dark haired, blue-eyed master of the verbal retort?

Suddenly Belle jumped, jittery like a cricket. "Toby? How long have you been standing there?"

"Hardly at all." Well, time is a relative dimension after all. He cleared his throat. "I wanted to tell you that…" She stood up tall, an angry flash to her eyes and a grim line to her full lips. He paused awkwardly. "Belle – I had no intention of knocking Jimmy down. It happened so fast."

"Yeah right," said Belle scathingly. "You had no intention of letting him go until you made a point."

"Excuse me – he started it. He was behaving far from decent."

"Decent? Oh Toby – give me a break! You weren't exactly debonair yourself."

"You told the Doc what was going on. He was drunk and getting in your face – you said so yourself."

"And? How does that give you licence to knock his lights out? I never asked you to Toby!"

He stared at her in frustration. He paced the floor in front of the ovens. What was he doing wrong? He didn't get it. What did she want? "Why should you have to ask? I don't like seeing people treat you badly Belle – it's not right."

"I can handle it Toby – I'm a big girl you know. All grown up ..."

"Don't I know it, Belle! Well, it beats me! Tell me! What is it you want?"

"You want to know? Do you *really* want to know what I want?" She stared at him defiantly – daring him to ask her what that was.

It never failed. Without exception, that look and a challenge never failed to push him to the edge. "Yeah. That'd be fresh – not having to try and work this out in the dark!"

All the frustration, all the disappointment, all the hassle, all the feelings of not getting it right, and not matching up, all the claustrophobia from being confined by what everyone else wanted and not knowing what it was that she wanted... it all welled up and threatened to overwhelm her. She felt emotionally cramped and desperately needed to stretch her legs. She just wanted to get up and run... and yet she felt crippled. She stood, picking at her fingernails, scraping away dried dough at the edges... where the soap had not penetrated the crusted exterior. She turned around abruptly and cried out. "I want to be left alone! That is all. I just want to be left alone!"

He stared at her. It was that simple. He felt again the wind being knocked out of him. Nothing would ever make it feel right. He spoke with difficulty. "You live a charmed life Belle Kane. You have your wish. I have been offered a position at University. So... in two months I'm gone." He had wanted to talk to her about his dream. He had wanted to know how she felt about that. But she had pre-empted it, and made everything so very clear.

Belle paused, immobile, as if someone had doused her with icy cold well-water. She turned around to look at him to see if what he said was real, or some tortuous scheme to get back at her. "Really? You're leaving Wattle Creek? Just like that?"

"Well, that's what you want." She really did. She had made it plain.

"I... yes... I... just didn't expect it – that's all." Just like that. Problem solved. He was going anyway. She felt that it should have been a relief. Yet it shocked her that it wasn't relief she was feeling. A mild sort of panic was hovering around the fringes of her emotions instead.

"I saw Terry down the street yesterday. His arm's pretty good now."

Belle turned away, her voice as cold as the morning air. "Well, I'll drop in and see Mrs Levin on the way home. I'm sure she'd be happy to organise Terry to come back to work…"

Belle pulled up outside Levin's yard, and grabbed the bread-basket as she jumped down from the step. She felt a stab of conviction that she had not managed to come back and 'visit' with Doris. She had not actually promised to do it, but she was suddenly aware she only ever came here out of necessity. Even Doris Levin deserved someone to be her friend. "God, I'm sorry. Help me to be a friend to Doris…" she said as she pushed the gate and it swung crookedly on a broken hinge, screeching loudly in the morning quiet.

The Levin household normally had at least one little tot buzzing around the yard… no matter how early. Belle eyed the empty yard warily for the teeth-snarling dog. When he didn't appear, she knocked tentatively at the door. Something felt very wrong. The Levin's never went away. "Mrs Levin? Doris? I've brought your bread delivery… Is anyone home?"

Silence.

She put down the basket. "Hello? Its Belle, Doris…" The door was ajar slightly. "Hello?" She knocked again and it scraped open a little further. She saw the small face of Fanny peek from behind a torn curtain. Belle let out her breath in relief. "Hi Fanny – it's Belle… from the Bakery. Is your Mum at home? I came to see her…"

She said nothing. Quiet and peaked, she came out a little further. It reminded Belle of a possum being coaxed from the rafters with an apple core. "Fanny, what's wrong? Where is everyone?" Belle compared the mite in front of her, to the capable, organised young supervisor of the bread distribution on her last visit. It seemed a lifetime ago.

A tear tracked down Fanny's grubby face. "Mumma's hurtin'. I don't know what to do," she said helplessly.

"Hurt? Oh Fanny..." Belle's heart melted in the face of such powerlessness. "Where is she?" She reached out to take Fanny's hand, but the girl turned abruptly on her heel and went back inside. Belle followed in silence.

The chaos that greeted her was shocking. Flimsy, old furniture lay shattered in fragments. Miss-matched chairs were upturned and broken. She couldn't distinguish anything in the mess. "Doris?" Then, she heard a moan and her eyes locked on a crumpled figure by the back door – its splintered remains were sprawled on the small porch by the stairs. "Doris? Oh no! Doris?" She ran forward, shoving stuff out of the way. "Doris – It's Belle. Please! What happened? Can you talk to me?"

Another moan escaped her and she turned her head. Hot feverish eyes were fixed in a vacant forgetfulness. "Me, babies..." she whispered through dry lips. Belle turned around. Where was everyone?

"Fanny – where are the kids?"

"Terry took them..."

"He took them? Where? Why?"

"Dunno – away. Mum told him to. Pa went berserk."

Suddenly, a wild moan - guttural and intense, came from Doris and she reached out and clutched Belle's arm in panic, her whole body stiffened in spasm. Belle stared at the hand gripping the life out of her forearm as if she couldn't quite understand the pain it caused. Belle moved her eyes away and registered Doris's tight, swollen abdomen. "Oh my... Doris? You're in labour? Oh no. Yes?" Belle's eyes took on a terror of her own. Slowly the grip on her arm relaxed. "Doris how long? How long have you been hurting?" She shook her head, unaware. Belle's mind twirled... "God what do I do?"

Before Belle could move, another spasm wracked Doris' body and she arched her back, unable to hold in the moan any longer, she let out a slow, deep, agonising scream.

Belle felt the blood drain from her face. "Oh God, help her! Help me help her." Suddenly she remembered Fanny. She pulled loose from Doris' vice-grip.

"Fanny. I need you to go and get help!"

She was only little, but a look of determination framed her face. "Terry made me promise I wouldn't go away... I have to stay with Mamma."

Belle looked into the girl's serious grey eyes. "Oh, Fanny I'll stay with your Mum... but we need some help. Okay?" She took the girl to the front door, and knelt down beside her, and turned her frail body towards her. "Fanny – I want you to take Bronza back to the Bakery. He knows the way – he will take you there. You must tell Toby that I need him. Okay? Tell him to come to your place straight away. Then leave Bronza at the Bakery, because he won't want to go anywhere once he is home..." She gently held the girl's face in

145

her hands. "Then… this is important: Fanny - I need you to run over to Doc Wallace's house and tell him that your Mum's baby is coming."

She paused and took the time to gently smile at her. "Will you do that?" Belle thought the wisp of a girl could faint at any moment. Who knows when she ate last. She grabbed a cob loaf from the basket still sitting beside the front door. "Fanny – I know your Mum is so proud of you. Here, take this bread, and eat it on the way into town. Bronza will take care of you." She nodded mutely and Belle helped her up into cart. Bronza turned with a flick of the reigns and trudged stoically into town.

Belle rushed back to Doris. At least she was here. If she hadn't come… She shuddered at the reality that Doris was alone… with no one but a terrified child. She knelt beside her, holding her hot hand and Doris let out a bellow when the next contraction came. The sound sent shivers of horror through Belle's veins. Belle looked around. Nothing in all her experience had ever felt this desperate. She had no idea of what she could do… so she prayed. Helpless, hopeless, frantic prayers for this woman she hardly knew, to a God she was only just getting to know. Even in her inexperience there was no question of *how* she should pray. She didn't consider prayer etiquette. She just banged on the door of the Creator's throne room and barged right in. Only his grace could work this out and save her life.

She understood nothing about mothers and babies… but she believed that Doris was in very grave danger. She prayed that Fanny would faithfully deliver the messages; she prayed that Toby would still be at the bakery; she prayed that Bronza would do the same thing he had done every day of his life… without deviation; she prayed for the Doctor to interpret the urgency of the girl's mission; she prayed for Doris – for her life – the life of the baby – for the life of her kids – for Terry. She felt in her spirit that even in her desperation and powerlessness, she was moving and working with One who was powerful. That gave her courage enough to stay and hold Doris' hand and whisper unheard words of comfort.

Time stood agonisingly still. Minute after minute… relentless wave, after overwhelming wave of agony, persistently wracked Doris' body. Tears streamed down Belle's face as she tried to infuse some reassurance through the sheer force of her will. Oh God, make them hurry!

18.

"Belle?" Toby had come! She knew he would.

"In here! Toby – she's is hurting so badly."

He stood in the doorway – gapping at what was before him. Belle was still kneeling, tear-drenched and compassionate beside Mrs Levin. Even he, with limited exposure to life and death, could see this woman was exhausted and dying, and his heart stopped at the cruelness of life.

"Toby please... What do we do?"

He came and knelt beside her. He looked at this woman and gasped. He swore under his breath. "Look at her... bruises..."

Belle stared with new insight. What she had thought as the dirt of low living, was actually dark purple bruising across her face, arms and legs. Welts she hadn't even seen appeared clearly on her skin.

Toby shook himself aware. What was it that Dr Wallace had said? *Tobias, medicine still is about cure more than any other one thing.* What would he need when he gets here? He looked around. Clean area. Dr Lister's work was controversial to be sure, but Dr Wallace was convinced. It suddenly gave him something to focus his energy on.

"Belle – you are doing the best thing. I know little Fanny has gone for the Doc and he'll be here real soon. We've got to get things ready for him." He ploughed into the rubble and started shovelling things out of the centre of the small room. He tossed the legs of chairs and the remains of home-made stools made from wooden packing cases to one side. The rest he piled on an old springless sofa. He disappeared into the other room and tipped rubble off the mattress, dragging it back into the room. He laid it beside Doris and in between the screams they levered her heavy body across. He dragged it to the centre of the room. Normally the Doc would use the kitchen table… but it had splinted into rubble also.

"Pretty sure that Doc won't be able to move her… that means that what's got to be done, has got to be done here."

He went to the stove – cold and damp and miraculously found a flint. He made his own tinder out of some rubbish, the remnant of an old tea towel and used splinters to fan a small flame into life, fuelling it with sticks of furniture and the left over door. The stove smoked heavily and he jammed opened the windows with a chair leg to let in some fresh air.

"Can we just burn someone's house?" asked Belle uncertainly.

"Pretty sure that she won't be using this stuff as it is," he said as he shortened another board by cracking it over his knee. "We might be doing her a favour..." He went looking for some pots and cleaned them the best he could. He went out to the tank and filled them. He put the largest on the stove to boil. He searched for clean linen and towels, but couldn't find any. He found a used sheet and folded it in quarters and slid it under her legs. "Keep talking to her Belle – she can hear your voice…"

"It hardly seems enough."

Toby stopped. He knew it wasn't enough but now he could protect Belle from the harshness of this cold reality. "It mightn't seem like much, but you are saving her life. She needs to know she can fight. In the end – that will tip the scales."

With renewed compassion Belle spoke soothing words of comfort and reassurance… none of which she felt were very convincing. But in a strange way, hearing the words, even spoken by her mouth, built up her belief in the fact that all would be well.

Toby found a bucket and some soap. He proceeded to scrub the floor around the mattress, and wipe it dry with an old shirt he found. He emptied the dirty water and filled it with clean water.

The gate squeaked and Toby bounded to the door. Never had one face seemed so welcomed. Doc Wallace stood, intensely taking in data from the scene. He took her pulse, and checked her skin by pinching it up… hot and dry. From his bag he took a pair a scissors and cut her dress straight up the middle. He placed a small metal cone on her abdomen… listening for her baby's heart-beat. Around and around he searched shaking his head, then he stopped and smiled. A beat: frail but present.

"I've asked Sister Tyler, the nursing sister, to come. She will be here soon - we will start." He looked at Belle as he drew up an injection in a glass syringe and administered it in Doris' thigh. "How are you doing my girl? If you can stay to grab things we need, an extra pair of hands would be welcome. We won't be able to help if you feel queasy – so you will have to go outside yourself. Okay? Don't leave it too late. Tobias – you need to help here." He handed him a cloth mask framed in metal. Toby poured ether into it and held it gently to Doris' face. Her body relaxed and her breathing evened out. He quickly examined her, then palping for the position of the baby. Again, his face was sombre.

"The baby is presenting by the shoulder: impacted. Any labour is dangerous in these circumstances… this has been going on too long. We will have to do a caesarean section. By some miracle there's a heartbeat. Mrs Levin is in an unrivalled position of danger. We have to act now. I won't be able to move her." As he spoke, he was scrubbing His hands in the bucket.

Belle squeezed her eyes shut when the nursing sister arrived. The Ward-Hun. With brief and military efficiency, she also washed and scrubbed in the primitive conditions. A tray and linen materialized from her suitcase. Clean areas appeared; instruments and other portable medical paraphernalia emerged. In what appeared to be seconds, the doctor had started: a cut, and a retractor and a baby boy. It happened so fast… but there was no cry.

Doctor Wallace paused. "He's small," he observed. "Too small." The shocks had not stopped. "Twins. This one is a girl," he said as he lifted another bottom to the surface of the cruel world. Some feverish work, constant talking and monitoring… and she was born. The Sister snugly wrapped the tiny mite and it weakly gave a cry. She sat Belle on the floor by the warm stove and handed her the tiny bundle with instructions what to watch for.

The sister immediately went back to assist Doctor Wallace. What they did and how they did it, Belle had no idea. She was completely absorbed by the tiny life she held in her arms. This was the first time she had held a baby – and this baby was just minutes old. She seemed so small, tinier than the little doll she had as a child. She snuffled and wheezed, and sneezed twice… and although Belle thought she did not possibly have any tears left, she cried and cried. This new life, so unspoilt and full of promise, filled her with amazement. If this little baby girl could emerge from all the pain and evil and destruction that lay on this side of the railway tracks, there really was hope. That one thought moved her profoundly.

Belle went out along the ridge and picked a huge bunch of wattle. She took it with a little teddy bear to visit Doris and her new daughter at the hospital. The resilience of Doris amazed every one. She was quickly recovering the trauma of her delivery, and no other injuries were evident - bar a cracked rib. For weeks, the life of little baby May Levin teetered precariously on the edge of death. She was early – a month premature… and small. Yet she showed all the spirit of her mother… and refused to give in. The nurses shook their heads with pride, as if their nursing milk had made all the difference. They acknowledged that each day was a milestone. Belle went with Doris to the small funeral of May's little twin brother. "Belle, I've called him Wally," she said soberly. "Toby and you and Doctor Wallace saved my little May… so all my other kids still have a mum."

Terry had reappeared with his six siblings. They had camped out under the stars… down by the creek. The adventure was still fresh and exciting. Fanny's younger twin brothers had caught a few fish and a rabbit or two; Terry cooked them on an open fire. Their big brother now had the status of a hero. Hermie was seen permanently attached to Terry's leg, and – for now… it didn't seem to bother him none.

Belle took extra fresh loaves of bread to them every morning. She conspired with the kids about how to fix the house up for when their mother came home. They finished burning the busted up furniture. They got rid of the rubbish. Fanny helped get the baby bassinette ready – a converted fruit crate that had been sanded smooth. It had another crate underneath, turned upside down as the base stand. A whole generation of Levin's had spent their early days in this crib.

The constable took George Levin into custody and Doctor Wallace was called to the witness stand. Doc had seen too much to turn the other way. He was criticised freely for the stance he was making. Domestic matters were a family affair – whatever happened behind the veil of matrimony was private. It was feared that he was opening the latch on an assault against personal privacy that would turn the tide on traditional freedoms. But they also saw the kids around town, and the story of May's birth was sensational enough to make diehard prejudices cringe in disgust at the treatment of the fairer sex, even if it was a Levin.

Early mornings again became a refuge for Belle as the machine rattled and stirred the next quantity of mixture, and she punched out the dough. The routine with Toby almost resumed a place of comfortable normality again… yet there hovered in the distance the reality that he was going away. One morning as she was setting up and listening to Toby firing up the ovens with Terry, it hit her forcefully that he was going. She needed to prepare. There was urgency as never before.

Life would be forever changed... again. She longed for some stability. The changing landscape felt like she was trying to build her life on a wave... and nothing was staying up. What would it be like without Toby? She started listing all the things that she had inadvertently come to depend on. He was like clockwork - she could set her watch by him. He knew what needed to be done... and did extra jobs, like taking out the rubbish the day the garbage-cart came around. He was also the bread machine expert. He knew it inside out and was quickly able to locate any kinks in the way it ran. He always had Bronza ready in the morning for the deliveries and brought in extra oats for his nosebag after she completed the rounds. Toby stayed to help with the shop during the day. He'd brought study books over to read in between counter sale customers. He made a good cuppa... and the list seem to continue to scroll, as she remembered the times when they had sat, close to the warm ovens in the early morning, chatting about Wattle Creek and the bakery shop.

"You look pleased with yourself," said a voice, quickly jolting Belle to attention.

"Just like the cat that stole the cream. What are you thinking about?"

"Toby! Ahh... caught napping." She cleared her throat in embarrassment and looked around to orientate where she was with her tasks. She felt unreasonably flustered.

He looked at her queerly... curiosity burning a hole in his vision. Some deep desire wished that he could be the cause of such a gentle expression. What an impossibility! He knew what she thought about him. There was no evidence anything so tender was ever cast towards his shadow.

"So," said Belle very business like, "How is Terry going? Is his arm strong?"

"Well, it seems pretty good. Doc's happy with it. Belle – he's just a kid. A good kid mind you... I'm sure he'll get there. The thing with his Mum really shook him up. He's changed."

Once she would have said 'that's a relief', but the truth was... it had changed them all.

Toby continued. "Taking the kids away like that... fair nearly wrecked him. He said he was a yellow-belly running from his Pa. He only did it because his Mum pleaded with him so hard. He told me that she is the only one ever been proud of him and he couldn't let her down."

"What did you say to that?"

"Just that there are times to fight... and a drunk on a rampage isn't one of them." He paused at the irony of his words. Would that he had heeded his own good advice! He still felt the sting of Belle's rebuke over the Jimmy incident. But that was different... but maybe not. Perhaps Terry had the same need to defend his Mum as he had Belle. "You know Terry probably saved those kids' lives by getting out of there. It takes guts to do that, especially when it doesn't feel that clever. His Mum knew what was going on."

"Toby – how did you do it? You were so focused. Doc Wallace said the way you had everything ready, probably saved them..."

"Nice thought, but I am absolutely sure that God saved that baby… and her mother. Not Tobias Lawson, or Doc Wallace or Sister Tyler, or Belle Kane. We all did our bit."

Belle stared at him in amazement. He said that? Tobias Lawson just attributed to God a miracle and took no personal credit, even when it was handed to him on a platter? But he did take personal delight in seeing the astounded look on her face, and he knew exactly where it was coming from. "Wow." She blinked her eyes as she went back to her dough.

"You're shocked by the God thing, aren't you?"

"I'm… well – I've never heard you speak like that before. I'm impressed."

"No harm in impressing you I guess." He smiled again. "The God perspective…He has been a rather recent modification to the way I look at life. More than that… Doc Wallace would say 'I met with Him'. It's changed a lot for me."

"Don't I know it," said Belle quietly. Again, he looked at her intrigued – his eyes drilling through to the core of her being. She nodded to his unspoken question. "Jesus got me too."

He laughed. "Now it's my turn to be impressed!" He turned away thoughtfully. "Someone's been praying hard on our account. I wonder who was on His case?" he mused quietly to himself.

"Is that why you decided to go to doctoring?"

"Well, kinda cemented it, I guess. It has been a dream since I was a kid – since my Dad was killed. I thought that if there had been more doctors in small places like The Creek, perhaps my Dad did not have to die. I just got to the point where I gave up believing it could happen. But Doc showed me that God is a dream thrower. I'm learning His plans are not thrown out to torment us... but to be fulfilled... even if they present the biggest of challenges."

Belle turned away and suddenly threw herself into the dough trough, cutting out risen lumps to punch down. Why didn't she have something that she could call her own? Why was she always caught in someone else's passion? She just wanted to have one thing that was her own... originally hers... not inherited, not caught like a contagious disease. Something – like baby May... a unique, precious, specifically created miracle just for her. That was the dream she was looking for. You wouldn't fail to match up to a custom-made dream, because it would be tailor-made to fit.

19.

Belle sat down at her Dad's desk and started sifting through the accounts and books on the shelf. This writing bureau was such a contrast to the desk her dad had made one year for Christmas. He had polished back an old door, and cleverly changed the door-knob into the inkwell. Her desk was orderly and tidy, so it wasn't a big stretch to know why bookkeeping and the accounts had been her job since grade school. Her father was not a stickler for records – he had left that to her. It used to be a mystery to Belle, that her father was so successful when he lacked anything that resembled a system. But she also knew that he had the most incredibly detailed memory – nothing ever escaped him. Perhaps that was his one failing: in relying so heavily on his natural ability he made no provision for those that would follow in his steps when things needed to change.

She half-heartedly rummaged through the papers and found a number of unpaid bills that had never made it to her desk. She put them aside and made a separate pile of unfiled flour orders. Her mind was not really on the task; she was thinking about the mixing machine. How would she trouble-shoot problems when Toby left? This bothered her. She didn't have the confidence in Terry that Toby had. She couldn't afford the chances of it lying dormant again if something went wrong.

Then Belle remembered something. Her father had a book that he recorded all his brainstorming notes and ideas in… a lot like a technical notepad, or a visionary journal. She had only seen it a couple of times, just after he had started on his mixing machine. She had come in from school and asked what he was building, and he had shown her a picture of the machine he had drawn in this book. The page was crammed with technical diagrams and jots of information… right down to the installation of the steam boiler working off the oven fires that would generate the power for it. Looking at that page had not interested her then, and her father quickly put it back into the large pocket in his overalls.

She went through the drawers. She found another wad of invoices with nothing to indicate whether they had been paid. She put them to one side. He wasn't deliberate in his untidiness, but the muddle frustrated her. "Come on Daddy. Talk to me. There must be something here that will tell me what I need to know. I know you are stuck in bed number seven… but there is more than one way of dialogue!" Belle stopped. She was talking to her father who could not possibly hear or answer her! She closed her eyes and changed her tack. There was someone who could hear. "Lord God, I know You can hear me no matter where I am and what I am doing. You are the One who knows everything… You show me where I will find what I need."

She continued to sift through layers, sorting as she went. In a very short time, she was absorbed in putting a semblance of order to her father's desk that had always been off limits to her. It had been left dormant for a long time, but now that she started, it almost took care of itself. She felt embarrassed that she had let it go so long, but she realised it was a type of denial.

If his desk stayed untouched, Dad could sort it out when he came home.

Mr Hewitt had taught very practical principles of bookkeeping. He had a rather unconventional approach to teaching... lessons that were life-useful. Belle was amazed how applying these lessons made the translation of the day-to-day business of the bakery onto paper quite painless. It was repetitive, unimaginative bookkeeping, but many times she would have happily hugged that man with the small rimless glasses – even in front of a class full of peers. She was also amazed how much of this information – facts and figures, were in her head and retrievable at a moment's notice. Perhaps she was Sam Kane's daughter after all - more than she ever imagined.

She smiled and lifted out the last sheets of paper from the bottom of the drawer. Her eye caught the bottom of the drawer. There was a piece of timber covering the base of the drawer. It was a little tight and Belle prized it out carefully. Underneath was a low-sided box that held a collection of envelopes tied with a ribbon, a couple of documents and the notebook. She had found it.

Her Dad's notebook was leather bound and it had his initials embossed on the cover. She held it in her hand for a long time, wondering if she was breaking some sort of code in wanting to see what was inside. He certainly had no intention of showing her. It felt like she was about to read the last will and testament of a live person.

"I'm just after the plans of the mixing machine," she told herself. She opened the cover.

"To my dearest Samuel,
For every dream and great idea,
for all the processing of every good thing God gives –
'write down the vision so that it won't be lost –
though it linger, it will certainly come…' (Habakkuk 2:2,3)."

~ Nell.

Belle snapped the book shut. Her mother gave this to him? Her mother quoted the bible? The familiarity with which she wrote, spoke of affection and love. Not only devotion for her father, but God? How could that be? Her father refused to talk about God: absolutely, resolutely refused to go to church… they never discussed God or spiritual things. The only religious thing he had allowed Belle was her mother's Bible. But she had never thought that her mother understood God… in the same way as she had discovered him: as a God who cares, and who actively invests in his children. A tear rolled down Belle's cheek. She felt an unexplained closeness to the mother she had struggled to remember through the tears she cried at night. Even though her face had faded in her memory, a knowledge grew in her spirit, that her mother had actively prayed for her… her mother had committed her into God's hands before she left… and God had faithfully answered the plea of her mother's heart. She *would* get to see her mother and she could enjoy her for eternity. Even as she thought these things, it didn't strike her as morbid. Just comforting… all those lonely, motherless years: they would not last forever.

Belle was finishing serving a customer when Ali came in. The agonised look on her face cut short any chit-chat. Without hesitation Belle went to the front glass window and flipped over the "Back in 10 minutes" sign and locked the door. Ali needed her friend. Belle followed her out the back and sat her down in a chair. Ali's shoulders slumped in defeat. Her clear complexion had a tired, blotchy tone and her eyes were flat and dull. Belle knelt on the floor in front of the chair and gave her a hug. They didn't say anything for a long time.

Belle looked up at her friend. Ali's red eyes spilt tears and there was resignation written all over her sagging limbs. "Why Mabes? He was so perfect. What did I do wrong? I was so sure. We were in love…"

Belle closed her eyes. God! I have no idea! "I don't know Ali. I know you… and I know where you stood. Jimmy? I'm not so sure. He was pretty cut up afterwards."

Ali voice rasped, uncharacteristically cynical. "In one way – I don't care… and another part of me screams – I sure hope it hurts as much for him! And another part of me just wants to kiss and make up. I can't do all of that at once!"

"Oh Ali – you need to give yourself time. Nothing is going to make sense just now. Just take it easy… then perhaps things will get clearer."

She blinked her eyes and squeezed away tears blurring her vision. "Did I do the wrong thing? Should I say I'm sorry?"

"Sorry? For standing up for yourself? Believe me, it is *not* wrong to expect your fiancé to be unquestionably loyal – regardless of who throws herself at him! I would seriously doubt your sanity if you expected anything else. I cannot see how that deserves an apology... not at all Ali. You said yourself that Jimmy has never apologised for what happened. No – I didn't think so. He doesn't think anything was wrong. That is hardly the way of a man who is in love."

"It was so perfect. I just want the dream to go on..."

"I know." They were quiet for a long time. "At least you had the dream for a little while. I haven't had the pleasure..."

Ali smiled through her tears. "Mabes – one day you're going to wake up and realise your dream was walking around with you all the time..."

"What is that supposed to mean?"

"We all want a dream Mabes. You just haven't admitted it yet."

"Well, I think that the dream thing is over-rated! It would be nice if I could tell you that the dream will come back and you will 'live happily ever after'. But after you wake up from a dream Ali, you can never recapture the moment. The fantasy isn't going to come back... no matter how desperately you try to force it. It's been corrupted by reality."

"That's it – isn't it? You never liked him!"

"No – that's not it. I saw you Ali. I have never seen you like that before. What you felt for Jimmy was intense... and I don't understand how that can be so mistaken."

"What if I'm wrong and I'm supposed to go grovelling back to him? What if I am walking away from the only chance for my dream?"

"Ali… what if this happened *after* you married? What if Jimmy is not the best for you? What if there is something better that you can't see yet?"

"I can't see anything at the moment. I just want to wake up and find it never happened."

"Come on Ali – finding a red headed brazen tart draped all over your fiancé, is not a dream – that's a nightmare! Who needs it?" The look on Ali's face – pulled Belle up short. "Yeah I know… apart from that… it seemed good." She got up and made a cup of coffee for them both. They sat musing in their own thoughts for a long time while they sipped their brew. "So, what are you going to do now?" Belle eventually asked when the dregs in her cup had gone cold.

"Me?"

"No – your grandmother's cat. Of course, you."

"I can't stand the scrutiny any longer. It seems that everyone is on Betsy's side and somehow it must be my fault."

Belle scoffed in disgust. "How is it that money buys morality in everyone's eyes? They even know the truth!"

"Truth? The truth is that I can't stand it. I've given notice to Mrs Craddick."

"Ali don't! Ali, don't let them bully you out. You have every right to stay on. You did nothing wrong!"

"I was going when I got married anyway. It is just a little sooner, that's all."

"Ali – what are you talking about? Where are you going? You can't keep board without your job. You can stay here - you know that."

Ali just closed her eyes and sighed. "I'm going back home. Mum and Dad suggested it. I need some space away from everything. I won't get that here Mabes... the bakery is too close. I'm sorry."

"Ali - you always wanted to own your own shop. Working at Mrs Craddick's was helping you understand business. Are you sure you're doing the right thing in going back to the dairy?"

Ali stood and quietly gathered her bag. "No Mabes... I'm not going back to the dairy. I'm going home... to Mum and Dad. And besides, it was you who always wanted to own a shop. You were always so excited when you talked about it. Your goals seemed incredibly clear compared to mine. I guess I just wanted to feel part of that. Well Mabes, you've got your dream... and I've lost mine."

20.

Belle threw herself into the shop. She did an audit on the books, tidying up loose ends, and cleaned out the flour store. She looked over the documents she found in the secret drawer. Two of them were of particular interest... one a pending patent on the dough machine, the other was correspondence to an engineering firm. So that was why the mortgage had been taken: to finance a dream of marketing this brain-child to the baking world. She wrote a letter making enquiries of the status of the project. She showed Doc Wallace the letter before she sent it. It seemed logical to at least follow the lead. She may be able to recoup some of that money.

Ali's assertion fluttered around her ears: *you always wanted to own a shop.* Owning a shop was her dream? She had forgotten all those child conversations. Ali was so sure, but it didn't seem so clear to Belle now. How could that be? If it was supposed to be the thing that she always wanted why did it feel so second hand? And Toby... Ali was wrong. He wasn't her dream. Toby was... well, just there... always around... there to listen, and challenge and counter as she spoke her mind. At least, he had been. The prospect of his absence suddenly made the world take on a colourless and cold aspect. It was wrong the way she had frozen him out. The inevitable would come soon enough. How different things would be.

The next morning when Toby came in, Belle had the kettle boiled. Toby quietly looked at her and nodded when she offered a cup of tea. He was trying to work out what was going on in her head. There was more than just tea and toast on the menu. As he sat down, Belle blurted out, "I owe you an apology. I have been very inhospitable lately. I want to say I'm sorry."

He took a mouth full of tea and swallowed. That was unexpected. "Apology accepted," he murmured.

Belle squirmed. That was not the response she expected from her humble outburst. She wanted him to demand an explanation, or give a dismissive shrug, or make a comment that she could return until there was a trivial circle of dismissals and reciprocated apologies. Tobias sat drinking his tea. He didn't even look at her.

"Oh. Well…" Belle hesitated. Fancy finding it hard to say something… especially to Toby. "I know that you are going… but, you hold the mortgage on the Bakery and I wanted to know how you would like me to handle that when you go."

"The same as now. Just deposit the money when it is due. It will help pay my way through school."

"But Toby – what if something happens and I don't have the money one month?"

"Then it will go towards a balance in the partnership. Just like now."

"But you don't want the partnership."

"I never said that."

"You're going to be a doctor! Why would you want part share in a Bakery?"

"Sound business. Good manager. Can't lose."

"But…"

"But what? It's an investment."

"Sure… I…" She stopped and sighed. She didn't know why she needed a better explanation. It just seemed too simple. Not restrictive enough… not worthy enough. A bakery was not medical science. Her Dad always said, "*it ain't Medical Science Belle: good bread and hard work — virtually fool proof.*" Besides, how could he just up and leave… it changed so much, so quickly. "I don't know how it is going to be without you. You have…"

"I don't know how it is going to be without me here either. To be honest - I hope it doesn't work."

"What do you mean by that? That's ridiculous! You just told me it was an investment that couldn't lose! You want me to fail… as always."

He sighed, tired of the circles they tracked around each other… staring… waiting… like a wrestling ring. "Belle, I don't want you to fail… no listen…" He held up his hand as she went to interject again. "There are two different things happening here. The business – no problems… that is a done deal. What I am talking about… is how life will work for *you* without me here… that is different. That is personal. That is what I don't want to work without me. Belle, your life and mine… we are meant to be in life together."

"We are?"

"If it works well without me being here… if your life is complete without me… Belle, oh boy - I don't want that to happen."

Belle shook her head. "You… mean…" She must have heard incorrectly. Tobias Lawson was acknowledging her autonomy. So where the emotional bondage that she feared so fiercely?

He raised his gaze from the bottom of his mug and looked directly into her eyes. "Belle – I know that we have always hammered each other tooth and nail... but we are a match. I know it. You are a part of me. I can't do anything without wondering what you would say... how you would counter it... what you would think."

Her mind went into a spin. Tobias? He was saying... How could he echo her very own thoughts that she had just such a short time before? It boggled her mind: Toby enjoyed that too? Is that what he wanted... a mental equal, as well as an emotional partnership? She stared back at him, seeing something she had never noticed before. It was a desperate tenderness. It scared her to death. It took all her will and self control not to run for the hills.

She stopped. No. She was not going to run! Anger again started to rise from her belly. She was not going to be chained through a desperate business deal. "Toby! I want to make it perfectly clear that you don't own me. You have no..."

"Whoa... stop right there. I have never claimed to *own* you. You are Miss Independence. I guess that's my point. I have never *presumed* ownership over you Belle, just because of a financial partnering in the Bakery. I want you to choose to be my friend... all by yourself... just because you can."

Belle sighed in relief. Just friends. That she could do. "Friends? Sure."

"Belle, the friendship I'm after here is more than being ex-school buddies. I'm talking life."

"Life? What do you mean?"

"I want to go courting with you Belle."

169

"Courting? How can you be serious?" She turned away and steadied herself. "Well, don't you think that is a little ill-timed, considering you are going to be leaving town in a couple of months?" Why couldn't he leave things the way they were?

"With you Belle – I will take any time I can get. I just want to start. These last months – they have been the most infuriating in my life. You drive me nuts… but when it comes down to it, I'm done for. I know it. And I think if you let yourself, you know it too."

"The flattery is killing me. And all of this helps… how?"

"Just say yes."

"So, what happens at the end of the year?"

"Nothing perhaps…"

"Nothing?" For some reason it gave her hope. There was no foregone conclusion.

He shrugged, his heart beating loudly in his ears. "There might not be anything to work with. If it comes to nothing… that will be that. It might be just a romantic, fanciful notion of mine that has no substance."

"And if it's not?"

"Guess it would be best to find out first, don't you think?"

"So, you're not expecting fire-works?"

"Belle – my heart is exploding right now. It's not me who has to find out if there's anything to discover here."

"Oh." She studied her cup of tea with uncharacteristic fascination. When she looked up at him and said, "Okay then…", it was the most calculated, unromantic instant in her life. Best get this over with, so he could get this out of his system and they could go back to talking again. She missed that.

He closed his eyes and whispered, "Thank you Lord." It was the only time he could remember when the stakes on winning were so desperately high.

21.

Belle stepped inside as Fanny pushed opened the squeaking door. She could hear baby May crying. Immediately Belle knew that all was not well in the Levin household. Her breadbasket was swooped upon by little Levin's like a swarm of hungry seagulls; their round, wide eyes eating up the crumbs like desperate scavengers.

She forced lightness she did not feel into her voice. "Hi. I came to see how you were all settling in at home…" Fanny swept aside the littlest kids to allow her access to the table.

Belle sat down and looked around bewildered. The sink once again looked like a mass murder had been conducted in its depths. Dirty clothes were strewn from one end of the house to the other. The baby was crying so hard that Belle went over and picked her up and realised that her nappy had not been changed in a very long time. "Fanny? Would it … I have never changed little May's nappy … Would it be okay if I had a go? I'd like to try."

Fanny nodded, but looked as if it was impossible to believe that a person of her age was so completely unexposed to the very basic realities of life. It was a bit like admitting that you had never learnt to tie your shoe-laces. Belle found very quickly that it was not as simple as it seemed. May kicked and cried. The nappy unfolded itself a dozen times and she had to put in considerable effort, juggling legs and bottom and nappy and pins. It left Belle feeling quite exhausted. Finally, she lifted May to her shoulder and held her tiny body as she shuddered through more sobs. "Where's your Mum Fanny? I had wanted to…"

"Wanted…? What?" Doris stood in the doorway to the bedroom. She looked like death. Her eyes were ringed in dark circles and her dress hung in crumpled creases. Belle turned around and took in the tragic sight.

"Well…" She took a deep breath. She recognised that Doris was just as fragile this morning as the day May was born. The amazing thing was that Belle never questioned the truth of this insight, but she wasn't sure what she should do with such intuitive knowledge. "Would you like to sit here and feed little May and I'll make you a cup of tea. I would like to… well, ask you something."

Belle knew she was stalling for time. Doris's face was expressionless. She nodded and sat down heavily. Fanny helped her put little May to the breast. It seemed so back to front that a child would have it together. Her mother seemed lost. Belle had never seen her like this. It would have been a relief to hear her scream at the kids again.

Belle stoked the fire and put the kettle on to boil. She could only half fill it because of little rust holes that were developing in the side. At least they weren't towards the bottom of the kettle. It still held some water. She spent time stacking dishes and pots, then washed up some cups. *Help me Lord!! Why did I have to say I was going to ask her something? Like what? I can't ask why she's such a mess and isn't looking after her family? I don't think so!* Finally, she made the tea and sat down opposite Doris. Belle watched her pick up the cup. Her chipped and grimy nails clutching the handle as if it was a life buoy. After the third sip, she stared at Belle expectantly.

What a shame. She hadn't forgotten.

"I... ahh... well, this is rather awkward. My friend Ali... Alice Dampier – Did you know that her engagement to Jimmy Golders recently broke up? Ali does really lovely manicures and I... noticed your nails. I was wondering if you would let Ali give you a manicure – it would really help her to think about something else rather than just feeling sad all the time." Belle looked away. She didn't think she would buy that.

Doris put down the cup and looked at her hands as if seeing them for the first time. "I used to have nice nails... before George and I got hitched."

"I think it would really help Ali... would you mind?"

She shrugged nonchalantly. But Belle had the impression that it did appeal to her sense of dignity. She nodded in consent. Belle let out a slow breath.

Belle kicked herself all the way out to the Dampier dairy-farm. What could she be thinking to draw Ali into this? How would she ever get Ali to give Doris a manicure? Hello! To say that Ali was devastated was a complete understatement. Belle had been to visit just once since Ali had moved back to her parent's farm. She had spent the entire visit looking at the walls, ceilings, furniture... anywhere but at Ali. She couldn't handle the scrutiny and would burst into tears with just the wrong lilt to someone's voice, or the most innocent comment would send her into floods of grief. Belle considered the likelihood of getting Ali to do anything other than cry was as remote as the possibility of setting up house on the moon.

"Hi Mrs Dampier. Ali up for a visit?" she asked lightly meeting her mother at the house yard gate. Her heart felt anything but 'light'.

"Of course, dear. She'll appreciate the distraction."

"How is she, Mrs Dampier?"

"Oh… not so good really. She's had a hard knock… it's going to take a while. We just want our little girl to smile again… but all in good time."

"How long does this go on for?" The whole thing was very disturbing.

"Maybe it never goes away. I don't really know. I've lost family… but never this."

Belle took a deep breath and went to join Ali on the back verandah. She was looking silently out over the yard. Even standard greetings seemed superficial and inappropriate. Belle gave her a hug from behind; until Belle could feel Ali's tears roll off her cheeks, and fall onto her sleeve. Her heart ached for her friend. Part of her wanted to wrap Ali in cotton wool and never let her out again; another part of her wanted to slap her across the face and yell at her to pull herself together. She suspected that neither was going to be very useful. "Dear Lord… I need to find the middle road… help me to love her. And the mess with Doris… I'm really sorry about that. Please help me to explain to Doris why it can't happen." Distraction – Ali needed distraction.

"Ali - I have some news. I'm not sure how you're going to take it, but I don't want you to hear this from someone else."

175

Ali stood up and turned around. She raised her eyebrows expectantly, interest wavering through her green, red stained eyes. That was a start. Belle took a deep breath and let it out slowly. "I have agreed to go courting with Tobias." There. She said it. She braced herself for the flood that would come.

Silence. Belle stared at her. Oh boy! Why did she ever say yes to Toby? She should have known it would back fire. It wasn't worth it. "Are you serious?" Ali said quietly.

Belle nodded, embarrassed. "I am so sorry Ali... I didn't think about how you would feel..."

For the first time in a long time a half smile played on her lips. "I just can't believe you are saying this as if you were asked to amputate your leg."

"You're not mad at me? I kind of expected you would hate me and run away."

"Mabes - you should be happy. You were destined to be with Tobias since 4th grade. You two are the only ones who couldn't see it."

"I've only agreed to go courting. I'm not going to marry him!"

"Why not? That's why you go courting..." Her eyes shimmered suspiciously of tears.

"Well, because... I'm not sure. Well, for one, I don't want to marry someone I fight with all the time. When people love each other, they don't disagree."

"That's stupid. Who says that?"

"No one has to say it – it's just general knowledge."

Ali went very quiet, and large tears gathered undisputed. "I don't ever remember having a fight with Jimmy. We never disagreed." Belle held her breath. "But I don't think that is evidence that he was madly in love with me." Belle could not help but notice that Ali's eyes didn't spill the large reservoir of water gathered there when she said it. "Okay – maybe fighting all the time might not be a good plan... but certainly you don't have to agree. I've thought about this a lot... I think it is more about respect. If you respect the other person and their feelings – then it is okay to disagree with their ideas. It doesn't mean you don't love them."

"Whew..." Belle let her breath out slowly. She never gave Ali much credit for deep thinking. She had kind of thought that the most painful aspect of the Jimmy mess, might be that she was not able to wear a veil or change her name to Mrs Jimmy Golders. "You've got me there," Belle conceded.

Ali's face seemed to relax some. Belle registered that her eyes remained a flat green... lifeless almost. She didn't say anything for a long time, so Belle got up to leave. "I need to go Ali..." Ali roused herself and walked back through the house with her. As they got to the door, Belle suddenly remembered the other reason for her visit. "Oh! I went to see Doris today... she isn't coping with the kids, and the house is in chaos. But I noticed her hands. They are in a state Ali... I wondered if... you might give her a manicure...." Belle's voice trailed off. Ali stared at her, almost vacantly. "It is only something small, but I thought it might give her something else to think about... her having a new baby and all..."

Ali hesitated, and then said, "Sure Mabes... I'll do that for you..."

Then, as if the last slice of energy was being sucked from her system, she went into the living room and sat down on the window seat, stony faced. Belle finally gave her a hug before she left. "Ali Dampier – you are my best friend. We're going to get through this... I know it."

Ali watched Bronza trudge down the driveway out onto the road. Then she turned her face to the wall and cried, and cried.

22.

Belle looked at her wardrobe in despair. She had never worried about what Tobias saw her in before. Why should it matter what she wore now? It was totally ridiculous. Suddenly she felt complete envy for Ali's fashion sense. She was always elegant – no matter what she had on. Belle sighed and struggled into her best outfit. Even she could tell it looked tired. She fussed with her long straight hair, and felt miffed that it never bounced into it's own perfect style like Ali's blonde tresses.

She stared at her reflection in the mirror. What on earth possessed Tobias to want to go courting? Was he desperate? Was he sorry for her? That did it - she wasn't going! She would *not* put herself through this. When a knock on the door came moments later she flew down the stairs and flung open the door. "I'm not going. I'm sorry – I've tried and I can't."

"Oh. Well then, " said Ali as she pushed passed Belle, "You will have to store these for some other occasion." She dumped a whole collection of outfits on the table.

"Ali! What are you doing?"

"I've cleaned out my wardrobe – won't be needing these."

"Oh Ali, I am so glad to see you! I thought you were Toby."

"Well, I'm glad I'm not Toby! I would hate him to see you looking like this when you are supposed to be going on an afternoon date. Come on Mabes… you need to do this properly."

"Ali? Oh Ali – you're back! Oh, thank God!" She ran and engulfed her friend in a hug, tears brimming in her eyes.

"Mabes." She pushed her back and turned away quickly. "Hate to be a stick in the mud, but Toby is due to come calling any moment and I know I am good… but you have to help."

"What do you mean? I'm not going!"

"Yes you are. You have given him your word… and one thing I know about you, Belle Kane, is that you are not a coward."

"Oh Ali – I can't.

"We all have our challenges," she said significantly, "and this is yours. Let him see you dressed like a lady instead of a baker's apron." She went over the table and picked up two outfits and walked upstairs. Belle rolled her eyes and followed her objecting. Ali dumped the dresses unceremoniously on the bed. "Choose one."

"Choose? Why?"

"Because you can't go out stark naked, and I am not letting you out in public with that on."

"It's not that bad…" Ali raised her fine eyebrows. One thing Ali knew was clothes. "Okay… it might be. Which one?"

Ali picked up one of her cast-offs, quite amazed. "You really have no idea. Try this. The blue will bring out the colour in your eyes. Or, this… the cut is flattering. Either is okay. You choose."

"Alright. The blue." She put it on… watching Ali out of the corner of her eye. She was suspicious. Her friend a week ago was an emotional wreck – today she is solving her problems? Maybe she was having a breakdown. "We could stay in and chat…" she suggested.

"No! Mabes you are not going to use me like that. It is just one date. You can do it." She piled Belle's hair on her head and twisted it into a knot. Suddenly Belle went to her dressing table and she drew out a small velvet bag. She poured its contents into Ali's hand. It was a small gold locket that had belonged to her mother. Ali fastened it at the nape of her neck, and then rummaged in her bag and applied some lip colour. "There…" She turned Belle towards the mirror, and tilted her chin. "You look amazing!"

"Oh Ali – this isn't who I am. Why should I try to kid him… or myself?"

"What do you mean? It certainly isn't me in that dress. This is all you."

"It doesn't feel right."

"All you mean is that it doesn't feel familiar. You have made an effort and that shows you respect him – nothing more."

Belle stared. Where did the blonde ditsy thing go? She was still gaping at Ali when there was the dreaded knock at the door. "Now Mabes, allow him to compliment you without saying anything stupid… or at least, just say thankyou, okay?"

"What makes you think that?"

"Because I know you Mabes – just let him say something nice without having to justify it." Belle shook her head in bewilderment. When did the rules change? Why couldn't it be simple?

She braced herself and walked towards the door. It seemed to shrink further and further away. She stopped dead. Ali nudged her towards the door. There was a pause and then he knocked again. Belle put her hand to the knob. Tobias turned around as the door opened and stood there, holding a bunch of white dog-roses and gardenias. She stared at his hands and recognised the flowers from Mrs Wallace's garden. Tobias had momentarily paralysed, his mouth gaping in dumbfounded astonishment.

Finally, Ali coughed slightly. "Well, I have to go now... have fun," she said and gathered her things. As she brushed passed, she gently lifted Tobias' chin with her finger, closing his mouth.

Tobias stood on the doormat, awkwardness filled the space between them. Eventually he handed her the flowers, blinked and cleared his throat. "Do you need a wrap? There is a bit of a breeze."

Belle was grateful for a place to focus her attention. Tobias' eyes had not left her face. She went back and filled a vase for the flowers. She grabbed a shawl that hardly matched the rest of her outfit, but she wasn't about to fuss now. It would cover her embarrassment anyway. She just wanted it over. For that to happen, she had to start. She pulled the door shut. She felt foolish. "Where are we going?" she asked impatiently, and stopped when Toby did not immediately reply.

"Somewhere," he answered cryptically and he offered her his arm.

"Shouldn't we have a chaperone?"

"Yes."

"What exactly are you planning?"

"Not telling." A smile played on his lips, and he struggled to regain his composure.

She ignored it and stepped out. If he wanted to be smart, he could do it alone. He quickened his step to keep up. For a long while they said nothing.

"You know, I was serious about the chaperone... we should..."

"Belle, I agree. Trust me."

She was struck into silence. Did he know that, of all the things she doubted, it was her confidence in whether he could be trusted that troubled her. They walked for a while and then turned into the entrance of the Hospital. "You're taking me to the Hospital?"

"We're going to visit your Dad."

"Why?"

"He is your family and should be the first to know my intentions."

"What intentions?"

"To go courting, Belle."

"Oh." She had forgotten that bit... even in the frenzy of dressing for a date.

Tobias pulled forward a chair and Belle sat down at bed seven. She took hold of her Dad's hand and sat helplessly quiet... becoming once again the little girl who couldn't help her dad enough. She wanted to be perfect for him. Yet she knew that he loved her and she adored him. Her father was her hero... but he had never been a talkative man. The communication stalemate that shrouded his body in silence now, in some ways, was not that different to the quiet silence she had grown up with. So why did it hurt so much? She mused over the thought and decided it was probably more about intention than actualities. Back then... if they wanted to say something to each other, they could just out and say it. That option was now gone.

She completely forgot Toby was standing behind her until he spoke. "Mr Kane, it is Tobias Lawson. I have brought Belle to visit you. How are you feeling today? Can you squeeze her hand?"

Surprisingly Belle felt his hand flex in hers. She quickly glanced up at Toby. "Toby! He squeezed my hand! He can hear you... he can understand!" she whispered. He seemed completely self-assured – as if this was the most usual thing.

"Mr Kane, I wanted to ask your permission to go courting your daughter. I would like to get to know her better, Sir."

A large tear gathered under his lid and pooled there until it could be contained no longer. Again his hand moved. Belle stared at it absolutely amazed. "Toby – he did it again! He did – he heard you. I know he did!"

Toby stood very still. "Belle, did he squeeze once or twice?"

"I don't know – he moved it, he's okay... he's going to be okay!"

"Belle – once or twice?"

"I don't know. What does it matter! He moved it – in response!"

"It matters because it is the difference between yes and no."

"Yes or no? You mean you *asked* him? Really asked him?"

"Yes, I asked him. He is your father Belle. It is right that he knows who is looking at his daughter."

"Oh... once or twice? I don't know Toby – I wasn't listening! Oh dear... once or twice?" Just then his grip flexed intentionally, deliberately again: once.

"Toby – he did it again...just once. What does that mean?"

Toby's shoulders slumped momentarily. And then he straightened with a smile. "Once is okay... Yes! He has given his consent. Thank you, Sir! Thank you very much! I promise you Sir I will look after her. Absolutely!"

Toby left Belle to have a few moments with her father. She sat there quietly talking to him. "I love you Dad. Do you know that?" *Once.* Tears of relief streamed down her cheeks. "Oh Daddy! This is wonderful. You are going to be okay! I know it." *Once, twice.*

Belle blinked through her tears. He squeezed twice? Didn't he mean once? Why would he think that he was not going to get better? "Dad – you have to believe it. You have to hang on!" Twice.

Belle's head was swimming. He should fight! This was wrong… totally unfair.

Old Wallaby Joe in the next bed softly spoke. "Excuse me Miss. I just wanted to say me congratulations. I reckon your young bloke is a fine fellow… a man of his word. He'll look after ya mighty fine."

"Thanks Wallaby Joe…" She smiled at him neutrally. Old Wallaby was taken in by a youthful, handsome smile and an impressive two-minute speech - hardly enough to see what a person is made of.

He raised his eyebrows a little – almost indignantly. With the radar of age and experience, he detected her scepticism as loud as if she had yelled at him. He quietly said his bit. "Now Miss – I know your father… we're here beside each other all day and all night. Your visits, and Toby's visits, they make this bearable. If Toby says he'll look after you, your Pa knows that he will. It will be a comfort to him to know that you and Toby are okay."

"Oh Wallaby, I never meant…"

"It's okay Miss. You're Pa hangs on for you… and only you. You are his whole world, you know. He needs to know you're okay. If he says he's had enough… it's not because he's ain't a fighter… it's because he sees that his job is done."

23.

As Belle walked out onto the lawn of the hospital grounds, Belle turned to Tobias and asked, "Exactly how long have you known my father can hear you?"

"Oh. A while," he answered noncommittally.

"And you never told me?"

He paused, as if he was uncertain how to explain. "Look Belle, I visit your Father. I have since he was moved into the long-term bed. We worked out this yes/no thing a while ago... so we could communicate. Old Wallaby Joe talks to him too... I'm a kind of interpreter."

"And you thought I would not approve."

"Maybe."

"You have a way of communicating with my father that I never knew existed and you didn't know whether I would approve?"

"Okay – it wasn't only that... it was also the Principle of the Left hand.

"Principle of the Left Hand? What on earth is that?"

"It's something that Doc Wallace taught me. It comes from Jesus. It's about doing good things, kindnesses – and you don't let your right hand know what your left hand is doing. Don't broadcast. It's just between you and God."

Belle stared ahead. It hardly seemed like Tobias. He was changing. "Why would you want to do this?"

"Well, I found out some stuff Doc Wallace has done. Without broadcasting; he just does it. Belle, you said to me once that I only do stuff if it had a double motive. That really challenged me. I had to ask: what did I ever do that didn't have an ulterior motive? I didn't like what I found, so, I decided I would find something I could do... just for the sake of that. Nothing else."

"And you went to visit my father?"

"It was important that I didn't tell you. I had to know I wasn't trying to win points with you Belle. I was doing it for him... and Old Wallaby Joe... and me. Nothing else."

It surprised Belle that they stopped at Doc Wallace's house. Tobias knocked at the door and Mrs Wallace greeted them with a basket and sun hat. "I am ready dear," she said with a glowing smile as Tobias took the picnic basket and pulled the gate behind the ladies. "I was flattered when Tobias asked me to chaperone you both. This is your first outing together?"

Belle nodded. "Yes, this is officially the first." How could it feel so foreign when they had worked together for so long? Yet it was definitely different. Something altered in the atmosphere when an outing had the soul purpose of getting to know the other person. What was she learning about Tobias? Did he like what he was learning about her? It seemed so contrived. Why couldn't the exercise be spontaneous and natural? It lacked the storybook element...

They walked down towards the creek and stopped where the grass was thick in the shade. The water was still and glassy; vivid blue dragonflies hovering over the reeds on the edge of the bank. The full flush of the wattle blooms had finished, but the air was still heavy with their distinctive sweet honey fragrance. Bees hummed on the gentle breeze that blew browning wattle-dust onto the blanket as they spread it out in the shade. They nibbled on petite sandwiches, which explained the extra order of bread this morning. There were some slices of fruit and Toby made a small fire to boil the billy. A cup of tea was just the thing to compliment the little jam tarts Mrs Wallace had made to complete their picnic. As they packed up the plates, Mrs Wallace pulled a book from the basket. "I hope you young people don't mind, but I like to relax with a book after lunch. I'm sure there is no need to break an age-old habit today. I like to read in quiet so I will just go over there and sit on that rock in the shade."

Tobias smiled as she strolled away and opened her book. Belle thought it was hardly necessary. It was less embarrassing when someone was nearby. There was no chance of getting into awkward areas of conversation.

"Thanks for coming Belle."

She looked at him sheepishly. "You know I nearly pulled out. Ali would not let me. How she knew, I don't know."

"I saw her yesterday in town. I am very grateful to her," he said with a smile. "The Left Hand does not extend to every part of life."

"You asked her to supervise me?"

"No. You'd be as mad as a hornet if I went that far."

"Hmmm. You're right about that. It was odd really. She was so like her normal self."

"Maybe she just pushed aside everything else for a moment," he said. "She has been your best friend for a long time."

Belle took a deep breath. "You haven't made one comment on how I look. Ali told me to let you compliment me, but that hardly seems necessary advice. Don't you like this outfit? I wasn't…"

He reached over and touched her hand. She pulled back instinctively. "Belle. You look stunning. I have noticed… very much. I thought you would have felt I've been staring at you too much. I've tried not to."

"I was thinking that you thought it was unnecessary – or silly."

"I'm pleased you took our outing seriously. I wasn't sure that you would. That colour looks beautiful on you – it's the same blue of your eyes…"

Belle looked away and flushed. "That's what Ali said." Belle had never heard Toby say anything like that. She had always thought that he was impervious to such shallow matters as clothes and hairstyles. "It seems a bit over the top for a picnic… but I wasn't sure what you had planned. I'm surprised you noticed, that's all."

"It would be hard not to notice you coming to the door looking like that. Not over the top at all."

She needed to change the subject.

"Toby? When I sat with Dad at the hospital… Old Wallaby Joe gave his congratulations. He said that Dad was pleased you had asked me to go courting…"

"I think he's right. Your Dad wouldn't give his consent to anything he was not happy about."

"Dad also said he would not get better…"

"He has been sick for a long time…"

"I told him he needed to fight… that he would get better. He squeezed twice. He said no. He's given up. He repeated it…"

"Belle, I…"

She rushed on, not waiting for him to continue.

"Old Wallaby said it was because you are courting me. Dad has no purpose left."

"Belle that's cods-twaddle!"

It was automatic, defending a position, even when she did not have a clear idea of where that position was going. She lunged ahead. "No – it makes perfect sense. If he has given up, and his fight has gone because I am courting… then the only thing left is for me to stop."

Toby stared at her. He didn't like where this seemed to be headed. "Stop what?"

"Dad can't give up. He mustn't. The responsibility lies with me. I have been misled. This will not work. We must not see each other Toby."

"Belle! Your father gave his consent! That means he approves – not that he wants to relinquish his role in your life. He could live for a long time yet. But he may not either. I don't think we have the kind of power you are projecting on us."

Now that she had started she was not about to back down. "I'm sorry… I can tell you are disappointed… but my father's life hangs on my choice. It is true. I would never forgive myself knowing that I had willingly taken his life..."

"Belle! Listen to yourself! This is completely irrational! Your father has had a stroke! *Two* strokes. This is not your fault."

"Perhaps the strokes are not my fault Toby... but the outcome is. If he needs a reason to go on... and I am that reason, then I will give it to him." She stood to her feet. "I am sorry Toby. Goodbye." She turned and walked away, a touch of the dramatic tragedy filled her senses. She would not look back.

Tobias scrambled to his feet and raced after her. "Belle! This is right out of nowhere. You need to think about this."

She did not alter her pace. "Toby. I cannot afford the luxury of contemplation when the right course of action stares me in the face. I am determined to follow through."

"Belle at least let me walk you back to the Bakery."

"No Tobias."

"Oh Belle. Please..."

"Honestly, you have no obligation now. I am choosing to walk alone. Quite literally, thank you."

"Belle!" A catch in his voice caused her to pause. She stopped and looked at him. She expected disappointment, she even expected him to be distressed, but she didn't expect to witness the raw anger that filled his eyes. When he spoke his tone was very low and he strained to retain control. "Okay – you work this out. Whatever you have to do. When it is done... I will still be here. I promise you!"

24.

Belle was in the process of mixing dough in the trough to bake up some Christmas hams. Every year, town's people brought in their hams: she'd encase them in dough, and bake them in her large stone oven. It had the smell of Christmas about it, and the festive season preparations could not truly begin until the bakery fired up its Christmas bake. Doris stood by the cooling racks… and looked in amazement at her hands. "I used to have nice hands…" she murmured to herself again.

"I think they look really lovely. Your nails have such a nice shape now. And your hair… I never thought a trim would make long hair sit so well when it is tied up all the time." Ali had done a beautiful job… hands and hair. How could such simple things make such a difference? She didn't think too much about how her own hands looked. She went along the trough mixing in more flour into the water. This work didn't make for soft, genteel hands, but she always made an effort to ensure her nails were trimmed and clean.

Doris watched her with interest as Belle worked solidly, and finally finished the mixing. She washed and wiped her hands on her long calico baker's apron, and rolled out the doughs to wrap up the hams… little pigs in a blanket, she smothered each little porker and pinched up the join. Then each dough-covered ham was slid into the oven and Belle checked the time. "There, that does it. This is a treat! We should be able to have our afternoon tea now. Toby said he was going to show Terry the delivery run in the morning. It will be good to see how he goes."

She brought over the coffee pot and sat it on a metal trivet. She brought in a cake she had baked in the stone oven after the last of the bread had been removed that morning. She poured generous lashings of fresh milk in each mug. "How's little May?" she asked as she settled in to her chair. She was in very unfamiliar territory when it came to discussing parenting, but little May… she was different. Belle couldn't hear enough about this little miracle that was her name-sake.

"She don't smile much… mostly she cries like a stuck pig... poos and pukes."

Belle cringed as she thought of the tidy row of hams baking in her oven, that were sending wafts of Christmas flavours through the bakery. She was continually shocked by Mrs Levin's bluntness, but today she decided to translate Doris' roughness with wording she might have used, something like: "Guess what? May gave me her first real smile yesterday! Otherwise she does what every healthy baby does... she cries, drinks, sleeps, toilets, grows. She is getting so big…" As Belle did that, she could hear the mother's heart of Doris beating and did not begrudge her apparent, awful callous indifference. They sat and nibbled cake and then she made another pot of coffee. Belle was surprised how her own attitude had undergone an enormous metamorphosis. Doris had not really changed… but then, in some ways, to Belle she was a completely new person.

"You know Belle, I feel so ungrateful…"

Belle looked up at her startled. Candid confessions. "What ever do you mean? Don't you like the cake? Would you prefer a fresh sandwich?"

"I mean that… my little May is such a darlin' baby… perfect she is… and I know she is a miracle from God… but…" she paused and tears welled up in her eyes. "Belle, I miss my baby boy. Oh, I miss my little Wally so. When I met George, he was so handsome and clever. My little Wally had that look about him. I know people think I should hate George for what he done… but I can't bring myself to. I just can't help thinking, hopin'… that maybe, maybe… maybe tomorrow will be more like it used to be."

Belle stared at her across the table. What was it with women this week? She had always prided herself on being one of the few people in this town who reflected about things deeply. Now she had begun to think that instead, she was the only person who had not had a profound and sensible thought to her credit at all in recent times. The only thing she had done was say she would go courting with Tobias Lawson, and then had intentionally created an excuse to end it. She had always considered herself to be a woman of her word.

"Belle?" Doris stared back at Belle. "It is bad… I know…"

"Doris – No! No, I don't think so at least. I am just shocked at myself. I guess I thought that since you were not expecting twins… and since May was alive, losing little Wally would not matter so much. I'm so sorry. It was very insensitive. Please forgive me." Doris' eyes filled with tears. Belle handed her a freshly ironed handkerchief as the sobs came to the surface and her heart spilt out onto the tablecloth. "Oh Doris, I'm sorry – truly," she said quietly as she dapped her own tears on her sleeve.

As the storm calmed over, Doris looked up at Belle. "Do you know you are the only person who has called my Wally by his name, since we buried him. Everybody just says... well, at least you have May... and they think... well, at least George is locked up in the slammer. They don't understand that everything has been turned upside down. Things won't ever go back to normal... they won't. I have to pick up and get on... and I'm not so sure I want to. I just want... I... just want things to be like I thought they'd be right at the start. But I know... I know it won't be. I know it never will be..." Belle stared in compassion at her new friend. She reached out and held her hand across the table. She didn't know what to say... so she said nothing, and waited for the fresh tears to pass.

Eventually it was time to slide the hams out from the ovens. Sam Kane had always said, "The baker is the chef... a taste test is as good a quality check you will ever get." Belle stood up. "Doris you are here at the most perfect time. It is a rule in this bakery that if you are present when the first hams come out of the oven you have to give your professional opinion and taste-test the ham crust." She carved off a small section from the leg bone and poured a fresh cup of coffee and set it before her guest. "Now tell me what you think..."

The baked bacon-flavoured crust sent waves of warm memories through her being. New tears glistened in Doris' eyes as she nibbled on the corner of the salty sample. "This is the first thing that has tasted like Christmas since... forever."

Belle was working the evening dough when there was a knock at the door. The windows were shut against the warm summer sky, to stop the insects flying in around the lamp. Terry had completely taken over from Toby now, but he had left after he had poured out the flour into the trough for the mixes and chopped more wood. Belle had not seen Toby all week. It shocked her that he had been so restrained. She would catch herself talking to him, telling him things… all in her mind. How she would phrase a thought or pose a question without even realising that she was doing so. Then she would check herself… and try to imagine doing the same with her other friends… but it never worked. They didn't have Toby's spark. She defended her position over and over, and still it seemed she had carved a hole in her chest with a butcher's knife without anaesthetic.

She paused in the mixing. The knock came again. She could hardly pretend she was not at home. The whole town knew the bakery routine. She wiped the flour off her hands onto her calico apron and went to the door. Mrs Wallace stood there with a small basket of salad vegetables. "I came to visit while you do your evening chores." Belle opened the door for her to come in. She was disappointed and relieved at the same time. She felt so ashamed. Mrs Wallace had been the solitary witness to their one and only attempt at a date. "I brought some veges from the garden. Sometimes it's hard to eat properly when you don't have another person to prepare for... I'll just put them on this bench?"

"Yes, thank you Mrs Wallace. Did you want to boil some water for tea? I've still quite a bit to do." She went back to the trough mixing the water, yeast, and improver, working in more flour.

"Please just go ahead. I'll get the kettle."

Mrs Wallace comfortably made her way around the benches, stoked the small stove and put the kettle on. She pulled up a stool and sat on it as if it was a drawing room chair. How could this lady seem so at home in such diverse settings? It didn't matter if she was sitting on a rock down by the creek, or a stool in the bakery surrounded by flour dust and dough, or in her own parlour with tapestries and vases. Her contentment – that's what it was, rattled Belle and she plunged her arms into the flour again and worked the moisture through the dry flour furiously. It was not the way her father showed her. *Rhythm, pace your-self, let the water do the work… it will take up the flour… it has to, it's the science of nature*, he would say. Sometimes it just felt better to break the rules. She knew in the morning she would wake stiff, but just now it seemed to channel the tension in her limbs.

"You are very good at what you do Belle. You have every right to be proud of your work here. It is the mark of a community – a quality bakery. I think it sets the tone for the whole area."

In spite of herself Belle smiled. It was not exactly what she expected her to say. "Do you think so? I would give credence to many other things first…"

"You mean, like Doctors?"

"Perhaps."

"It is interesting that people tend to think highly of certain professions over others... but ask any doctor if his morning toast, or lunch bread is stodgy and he may not be so dismissive of the basics. What ever we do… if it is done poorly, people notice… and it adds up to the whole picture. A community can build on quality essentials."

"Thanks Mrs Wallace. I appreciated the sentiment," said Belle. "It was the way Dad thought. He was a very clever man and yet he never felt under-utilized because of his chosen profession." Then why did she feel so restless? Did she presume to be better than her father? Why did she feel like she needed more? She moved around the trough not taking her eyes off her work. Not that she couldn't – she knew the job blindfolded.

"Belle…" Mrs Wallace looked compassionately at her frenzied movements, agitation stealing Belle's normally poised pace. "How are things going… really?"

Belle shuddered. She knew it was coming. Mrs Wallace could read her like a page in large type. They had not been together to talk about things like this for a while. "I don't feel settled… or satisfied. I just mustn't be a good enough Christian. Something seems to be missing still. I thought that a relationship with God would fix everything."

"Depends what you're trying to fix, I guess. The eternal question – that's settled. Relationships with those around us – that's an ongoing journey… with abundant times and dry times… a bit like the seasons. God gives us principles, Jesus demonstrated them and the Holy Spirit helps us apply them. One thing about God, He never claimed to be a magician… or the master of the quick-fix. He could change our circumstances instantly … but often He doesn't so it forces our characters to grow. No quick-fixes, but principles, strategies… and strength."

Belle absorbed her words, like the flour and water and prover in the trough. Belle reflected out loud, "The Bible says that the Kingdom of God is like yeast that is blended in and permeates the whole dough. I think of that every time I mix up the nightly doughs. Do you think Jesus meant his values were to become so much a part of us that we cannot separate them out from our lives?"

Mrs Wallace smiled. "What an excellent interpretation! Jesus' stories apply on so many levels. I've generally thought of it as the Church, growing and improving the quality of our world. But we are certainly part of the Kingdom of God. I imagine that a poorly mixed dough would result in a loaf of poor texture and quality… am I right?"

"Of course! So, if we segregate our lives into compartments, like work, friends, hobbies, Christianity … it is like not mixing the dough thoroughly. It might leave areas of our lives lacking texture and quality."

The kettle started to whistle and Mrs Wallace got up to put tea-leaves in the pot. "For someone so young in the faith you have a great insight into spiritual truths. To allow God's Spirit to teach you so well is noteworthy Belle."

"Then why? Why do I feel like I never match up? That everything is a test… that I need to find my place or I will be swallowed up by any person that knows what they're doing more clearly than me?"

"Is that what happened with Toby down by the creek? It wasn't about your father was it?"

"I guess not. It sort of sounded right... but really, everything Toby said was true. Dad wouldn't have given his consent if he wasn't happy about it. I will always be his daughter... always. I just felt I was walking out on him."

"That's interesting... because I was so proud of the way you two young people made such an effort to take account of him in your decision. That's inclusion, not exclusion."

"I didn't think of it like that."

"Have you told Toby this?"

"No, I haven't seen him. I thought it might be him when you knocked."

"Disappointed?"

"A bit."

"Dear, why don't you talk to him?"

"Oh Mrs Wallace, I can't. I want to... but I can't. I know I will get swallowed up. He is so focused, and I have nothing but a bakery shop."

"A very good shop though..."

Belle washed and wiped her hands on a towel, and covered the doughs with flour bags. "Yes, but that is not what I mean. This is Dad's shop. It's not mine. I don't own this dream. I can do it, and do it well... but it has never captured my heart like it did his! I just wonder if I'm looking for something that just doesn't exist. If I knew... if I understood exactly what it is I am looking for... to be honest, I'd marry Toby tomorrow." She stopped dead. Did she say that? She leant her hands on the wooden bench and leant forward as if she felt faint.

"Belle? Are you okay dear?"

"I… I don't know…" She laughed. "I've never said that before. I must really like… love… him. I didn't think it was possible."

Mrs Wallace smiled. "Your secret is safe with me. That is something you need to tell him yourself. He will be delighted."

The laughter died on her lips as Belle looked over at her visitor. "Oh Mrs Wallace. What if I never find it in time?"

"My dear, God is never late. Jesus made a promise that if we look… we will find what we are looking for, and if we knock… He'll answer the door, or if we ask the question… He'll give the answer. God is generous. He didn't qualify that and say it was just about our salvation. After He gave that promise he went on to say that God gives good gifts to his children… just like a loving parent. He wants us to have whole lives. Walking around feeling like we are missing a limb isn't abundant living. Why don't we ask Him for the answer and keep looking in the mean time?"

25.

For weeks, after every evening dough-mixing Belle flopped on the bed, tiredness seeping through her bones. She closed her eyes and tried to drift off into oblivion, but images of Toby's fiery eyes kept burning through her soul. But she was determined; she wasn't going to talk to Toby until she knew the answer. Was that so unfair? She got up and went downstairs and poured a glass of water. She paced for a while, trying to put her brain into neutral.

She went back upstairs and sat on the bed and flipped open her Bible. She looked at it listlessly. Nothing. The words sat stuck on the page where normally she would have felt energy feeding her spirit. She shut it and tried to lie down again. She sat up. Everything felt wrong. She didn't want to face any problems. She just wanted to go to sleep but her eyes refused to close.

She walked around her small bedroom. Her Dad had tried to decorate it for a little girl, but apart from the roses painted on the dressing table drawers, the effect was very tomboy. Why did everything feminine scare her to death? Her mind floated around memories of her dad. Most of them were of the bakery, elbows deep in dough and flour. The smell of proving dough or baking bread even now evoked a sense of belonging.

She spotted her Dad's journal and picked it up. She traced the monogram on the cover. The Bible said to honour your mother and father. She turned the pages of the journal, looking with interest at the things that her father had sketched. She found a page that had the same roses painted on her dressing table. The same roses Toby held in his hands. Spread over the page was a number of phrases. *"A rose by any another name…"; "the fragrance of a bridal bouquet"; "the softness of my Baby Belle's cheek".* A romantic. Her dad was an incurable romantic. She looked over some other technical drafts, but for now she wanted to learn more of this gentle side of her father.

Then she stopped at a page as the opening line caught her eye. *"The widow came to visit again today."* Belle paused. The widow? Was this Josephine Lawson – Toby's mother? She read on curiously. It had to be.

"I know her intention, but I cannot, nay - I will not, walk in the shadow of another man. If she ever comes out of mourning, perhaps it might work. I yearn still for the softness of a woman's touch. Perhaps the only truth in the Bible is the observation that it is not good for a man to be alone. But Matthew Lawson is not a man who is easily forgotten. She is still his bride… and while it remains so, she cannot… will not, be mine. It is that simple. Yet she does not, will not, understand."

Well, thought Belle ironically… that makes two of us! *"I cannot, nay - I will not, walk in the shadow of another man…"* If it was not for the tiredness that pinned her muscles down, Belle would have laughed at the irony of the reflection of her own search. Her father refused to engage Mrs Lawson's advances because he didn't want to walk in another man's shadow. The observation rang true in Belle's heart and resonated with genuineness. Every individual ought to nourish and grow - become their own shape, full of their own potential: living out their own wild and fantastic dreams. "Ahh Daddy," thought Belle through tears of tiredness, "You have such perception…"

The answer seemed no closer than when she had talked with Mrs Wallace. Sometimes it seemed that there were whole segments to life that were locked away out of reach – beyond understanding. If only she could find the key. It was an elusive belief that one small element of truth might be all that was needed to decode these mysteries and reveal a dimension of a whole new world… But where would she find it? She had no idea.

"Every visit the widow grows more resentful. She will not forgive me. One day, in the not so distant future, we will be mortal enemies. It is a shame. In a way it would be a good thing for Belle to have a feminine influence in her life. But the widow lives in the shadow of man who now stands larger than life. I fear that the only outcome will be that I will be diminished in my daughter's eyes because this shadow will be constantly thrown up on the wall for comparison. That I will not allow."

Kanes and Lawsons: was there some cosmic connection that destined these two families to align. If she didn't already understand that connection was God she was convinced she could start a credible sort of cult.

Yes, her premise was sound: no one should be overshadowed by another. Each person should be allowed to grow and flourish. Every time she considered stepping up beside Toby something deep inside her spirit responded to that, but the reality was that the hollowness of her shell felt so fragile that she rejected the idea. If only she could reject the emptiness without rejecting the man.

"The widow's boys are fine lads. I particularly like Tobias. The twerp is an inquiring thinker. He doesn't fear to speak his mind - which is unquestionably his own. His mother has done well with him. I see the sparks that fly between him and Belle. There is another reason to let the potential relationship starve and die a natural death. They could never be brother and sister."

Belle read and reread that paragraph. Her father liked Tobias – because he had attitude? How like her Dad to call him a twerp. Why would he think they could never be brother and sister, yet he was willing for Tobias to go courting? Well, he never said they could not be husband and wife. She returned to that thought again and again, until it seemed less shocking and more familiar. Husband and wife…

Ahh, the relief she felt in coming to an honest conclusion. Yes, honouring her father was not dependant on her state of matrimony, but a position of respect. Her Dad valued her respect so much he had refused to marry another woman because he saw it could jeopardise her high opinion of him. Indeed, marrying Toby would not make her responsible for giving her father hope or plummeting him into despair. He had made his own choices regarding his family. Now Belle had the same choice to make for herself.

Another tired tear tracked slowly down her cheek, too exhausted to fall quickly. She again realised that to find her own self was the desperate plea of her heart, more desperate than finding a husband. When it was all measured and weighed, she had done the right thing. Perhaps her reasoning had been flawed, but in the end, it was far better that she live in the sun and put down her own roots and explore the shape of her own branches, than go to that place prematurely and be smothered and stunted in the shadow of another. Even if this meant she was alone for the rest of her life; being alone was better than not being able to be herself. She had to be true to herself first, before she could be true to another.

26.

Belle paced around the garden as Mrs Wallace worked potting up some of her plants. Suddenly she blurted out a question. "Mrs Wallace – didn't you ever want to make a mark of your own – rather than just tending your husband's garden?"

Mrs Wallace paused and blinked. She almost laughed out loud as she looked into Belle's finely chiselled face – that was just a little too gaunt to be really pretty. She realised she was still knocking, still looking, still asking. It was a struggle that was much deeper than the question itself.

"Well actually dear, this is something I have desired all my life. But only once did I feel I wasn't quite getting there." She paused and carried the pot over to a patch of wandering-dew.

Belle waited for her to go on… but she didn't. "Do you mind if I ask when that was?"

She didn't pause, as she levered out some plants from the garden bed and placed them in the pot. She answered quietly, almost as if she was sharing a very precious secret. "It was after we had been married about two years, and I had little Lois in the crib…. and it seemed that all I ever did was wash nappies and bibs… and I watched my husband who was needed by so many… and I was at my wits' end with one small baby. It seemed ridiculous… and wasteful… and not to mention incompetent. When I spoke to him about it, he said something that changed my life." Again, she paused completely content in her garden around her.

Belle blinked. She would never have believed that someone could be satisfied in telling only part of a story. "What did he say?" she prompted.

"He sat down on the step over there and said to me, "Louise, I have been given a gift to help people's bodies that are hurting and need healing. I am good at this, and I will always strive to be better… but you my dear, you have a gift that is just as valuable… maybe even more eternally significant. You have our precious daughter… you are the one who will have memories of her growing up – more than I will because of the demands on my time. I am not complaining… but I do, at times, envy your closeness to our beautiful baby girl." Mrs Wallace laughed then. "I could have strangled the man. Fancy saying that! I would have happily swapped places with him. Being a parent didn't seem at all as glamorous as he was trying to make it sound.

Belle stared. She had no idea that Mrs Wallace could have ever entertained asphyxiation by brute force, much less confess to it – out loud! It sounded so normal… so un-saintlike. It was a relief in a way.

Mrs Wallace just smiled at her budding gardenia bush, and continued her musings. She had more gardenias than anything else. It was obviously her favourite. Belle was not sure Mrs Wallace even knew she was there anymore. "He must have got the idea that I was none too impressed because then he said, "I work with bodies… but you have an intuition that detects pain that I can't operate on. You have a way about you to soothe people's spirits. You *know* when someone has a need that cannot be heard with a stethoscope. That is not a gift to be sighed at. That is to be grasped and honed just as my skill with a scalpel. You, my dear Louise, compliment everything I hope to achieve in this community... and without you I don't think it would be very noteworthy at all."

Belle stared mesmerised at the water showering from the rose end of the spout over the newly potted plant. It amazed her that Doc Wallace would consider his wife's non-intrusive, background life so essential. Belle always knew that *his* work was important... he was the town's only doctor after all. But two roles... equally important... equally challenging... just different? She blinked. No one had ever said that to her before. Mrs Hollis had recently bailed her up in the bakery and given her the "help-mate" speech. Belle was evidently letting down the side by not attaching herself to some male like a leach, as was her feminine duty. Okay... maybe that was not word for word, but Belle felt sorry for Nancy Hollis' best friend Miss Francine Redding... since she was guilty as any, of the crime of failing the feminine God-given cause in matrimonial obligations. Who could live with Hollis imposed guilt?

In time Mrs Wallace spoke again – a little conspiring whisper that had Belle straining not to miss a word. "I have never spoken of this to anyone since. (Well, except Harold of course!) But since you asked... I did take up the challenge: to grow, and develop and train my gift.... not just to let it happen by default. Let me show you my garden..."

She pointed to a vine twisting itself over the wooden arch at the gate. "I planted this climber when the Blake family moved in, up on the top ridge out of town. When I water it in the morning – I pray for Bill and Melba, for their kids and their cattle – if they prosper, their family will prosper too." She moved further along the path. "This rose I planted for old Mrs Gleeson – she loved the colour red. Her favourite rug was a red one. She always had it on her bed when I went to visit. She's with the Lord now, but I pray for her daughter who lives in the city. I like to have a rose for her to put on her Mother's headstone when she comes back to Wattle Creek to visit. This row of little nasturtiums - so bright and colourful… just like the little faces at the school house… I pray protection over that school yard every morning…" One by one she went around every street and need in the community all represented in her garden. "And look – these corn flowers… they are for your dad. I had to choose a blue flower because of his eyes. You have your father's eyes too… they have a real depth about them, Belle. I pray peace for your dad and also for you."

Mrs Wallace went to the well and hand pumped more water for her garden. When she came back she continued. "You know… it drove me nutty to start with... to have everything laid out so randomly… out of line… but I really felt I needed to plant things this way. I asked the Spirit of God why it was so important… and if I couldn't just have one straight line. And immediately I got an impression… just a very strong feeling that people's lives are not regimented and patterned in the way I would like. They grow at different rates and have different seasons side by side. It was important that I am reminded that I cannot make people conform to my sense of

211

order. They are who they are, with their own special beauty and gifts and they can be appreciated in the most unexpected places.

"So now I get to see many answers to my prayers. And the blessing is, I know I have always had a direct hand in seeing what comes to pass... and sometimes I even get to offer something besides prayer. I might cook a meal, or knit a baby jacket. You see, I don't walk in my husbands shadow... but he has said many times that he walks in mine because I walk closer to the Son as we journey side-by-side. I don't have to do what he does, to be valuable in the lives of people in Wattle Creek. Not at all."

Belle walked home after visiting her father, taking deep breaths of the warm evening air, the smell of summer coming in on the twilight breezes. Christmas day didn't seem to hold the same magic anymore, even though the carols were the same, the story was the same, and the advent-traditions were the same... essentially. Today she had gone to church just a little late, so she could slide silently into the back pew and quickly leave without seeing anyone. She especially didn't want Toby questioning her about her plans for Christmas dinner. He didn't need to know that she felt hopelessly isolated and alone. If they spoke for just seconds, he would know. Then she spent the rest of the day at the Hospital. She couldn't even take her father out for the day. What a dreadful place to celebrate the birth of Jesus. She had brought her father a new razor set as a gift. His old favourite was worn down from years of running up and down the leather razor-strap that had always hung behind his bedroom door. It was a practical gift, but very necessary.

Old Wallaby Joe was discharged to spend Christmas day with his family, so Belle left a jar of special boiled lollies on his bedside cabinet for him when he returned. She stared at them all afternoon, their bright Christmas colours doing less and less to cheer her spirits. They provoked and tormented her into thinking of Toby. It depressed her to think that he would spend so much time in such a place as this: sick beds, aggressive controlling nurses, blood, scalpels, urinals. She wondered what it would feel like to be inspired to be a doctor, or a nurse. With such an ambition there would be no reason why her nature would not grow into its own shape – right along side Tobias. They could talk about carbolic acid and body fluids, at night over coffee.

She smiled. It was funny in a perverse sort of way. Her insides felt heavy when she thought of not having Toby around to wrangle with. His voice echoed, *"Belle – I know that we have always hammered each other tooth and nail… but I can't do anything without wondering what you would say… how you would counter it… what you would think."* He was in her head. She wondered how he would like the idea… of her working beside him.

She remembered the birth of little May. She closed her eyes against the gruesome images of pain and injury. It only left the imprint of horror. There was no point even contemplating the fantasy. There was nothing at all that would induce her to go near such professions. It was not that she did not have compassion. It was simply her lack of a cast-iron constitution. If she could heal in a bread-tin then the problem would be solved. She sighed. Healing didn't come in kitchens or bakeries, it involved coping with blood and hideous treatments... and that - she just couldn't do. It was almost a relief to realise it was not that she didn't want to... she was physically unable.

Tobias settled in the lounge to savour his Christmas supper. His mother's coffee and her irresistible home-baked Christmas fruitcake were unrivalled. He felt rather disappointed that he soon would not be able to help himself to one of her oatmeal biscuits out of the barrel on the bench whenever the whim took him. Could you get homesick over your mother's cooking? He lingered in the lounge-chair, overcome with a sense of nostalgia; his mother was equally quiet. It was a season of celebration, remembering all that God had accomplished through his son, yet Toby could only think of those things that he hadn't finished. Suddenly he knew what it meant to be a mortal man with limited time available to him. His greatest disappointment was embodied in the little box that he fingered in his pocket. It was the only gift this Christmas he had not been able to give. A sigh escaped his heart – one that came from deep within.

His mother sipped her tea and wondered if there was anything to be said. Her own heart was heavy with the realisation that for the first time, one of her fledgling sons was soon to leave home. This had been postponed more years than one would have expected; even so, she was shocked by the way it was affecting her. She thought there was no more grief to be had... yet it seemed that life was just a series of goodbyes. Even if it was not final, there was still the pain of separation that could not be denied. Josephine was not one for tears. She had long done with crying. But she was concerned for her son. A broken and heavy heart was a tragic way to leave. Perhaps it was for the best: to get away and start a new life, to be immersed in new challenges, and explore new passions.

Tobias had always been her enigma. Lately she had seen changes, and identified the sound of a familiar chord. She recognised the softness that came into his eyes when he talked about the bakery, and she knew full well it was not the whimsical smell of baking bread that had won his devotion. It was far more than that. She had also seen the anger and frustration that could only have one source: a Kane. In each of these observations she saw more of herself reflected in Tobias' personality than she had ever previously imagined. The way he spoke of the Kane girl – the baker's daughter – that was the most amazing of all. As a mother, she noticed he was listless, marking time... waiting. Even though she recognised it, they had never talked about it. But now it didn't seem right just to let it wordlessly remain there, to fester. It was a splinter that needed to be pulled. "Was it for Belle?"

Tobias looked up at his mother, his dream flattened and stretched like a peeled fox pelt pegged out on a tree. He nodded, resigned that it no longer mattered who knew and who didn't. While there was an active hope, he had wanted to keep it private. He had believed, really believed, that he would be leaving Wattle Creek with a promise of her love returned. Was he so egotistical to think that nothing he desired would be out of reach? "God – forgive my arrogance. You work this out. It is beyond me..." He had closed his eyes, apparently absorbing the aroma of his drink. The fingers of his left hand restlessly traced the shape of the box in his pocket. "Mum – please don't tell me that I am better off without her. It doesn't feel like that at all."

"Now try for one moment not to put words in my mouth Son. I know what it is to have a grieving heart. You do not travel in uncharted waters."

Tobias looked with interest at his mother and considered her familiar care-worn face. He had never specifically noticed the creases around her eyes and lips from years of hard work and worry. Perhaps she was right... "Ma... you don't talk much of how you managed in those years after Pa died..."

Josie sighed heavily. "Death is probably easier to explain. I'm not sure it hurts less... it's just simpler to understand perhaps. One thing I remember is that I got up one day and I was finished crying. Even if the sadness had not gone away, it was time to start walking through the valley. That was mainly because you boys needed me. It was what needed to be done."

"Mum... I, we were so young. Where did you start with that?" Was the ache in his chest something that would never go away? Where was God's promise to bind up the broken hearted?

"Well, the farm was the most urgent. I knew diddly-squat about farming... but that is what I had to do. I decided that if I didn't have Matt close by, I needed to surround myself with people who knew what needed to be done. I went and talked to each of our neighbours. Not one of them was happy about a woman musclin' in on their territory. They all tried to convince me to sell out and give up - at one time or another. To start with even Alf Dampier was as stubborn as the others. So, I went to him and shed a tear and told him it was out of respect for Matt's memory and because his young boys needed help. That part was true... he just didn't expect me to say it. From then on Alf has been the most faithful of friends. Word got around that I was going to stick it out and they were all too gentlemanly like, to tell me I had no business farming after that. They'd show me what I needed to know. Your Dad had a dream of a farm for his boys. It was something we had talked about together. He wanted this opportunity for you all so badly; this is the legacy he had worked so hard for... it was even the thing that killed him... so, as much as it hurt, it is the dream I was goin' to give you."

"Does it bother you Ma – that I'm not staying on the farm?"

Josie looked at him thoughtfully. "I saw a long time ago that you were made of different dreams. Yes, it upset me. I even went to your schoolteacher – Evan Hewitt, and told him to stop encouraging you like he was. And the Doctor – I saw him too... but he told me that I didn't draw up the architectural-plans for you; God Almighty did that... and I should work with what the Lord's given you. I was mad with him for saying that. It was so hard... to give in and let Matt's dream fade for you when it was so right for the other two. But it reminded me that Matt had a faith in God. He would have said something like – 'Josie, our dreams cannot compare with what God dreams for our boys... just let the lad be.'"

Tobias chuckled softly. "Did he really say that?"

"No. But he could have. When you know someone... you get to know the way they think. Until then I was so consumed with surviving each day that I had forgotten how personal his Faith had been. Sure, I always took you boys to Church until you were old enough to choose for yourself, but you know... your Pa had an edge with God that I never really understood."

She stared at the portrait over the mantle and shook her head in a profound bewilderment. It was something she could not understand even now. "Tobias, losing your Pa was not part of our plan. I didn't want you growing up without a daddy. I cried until I thought my heart would give out. The truth is: my heart gave out with losing him... and cryin' was just lettin' myself be honest about it. I still get so lonesome for him. It was so hard to admit, you boys were never going to have your daddy again. That was the real tragedy. But your life had to go on. So, all that to say... it is difficult to lose someone you love. You will survive and you will be able to do what needs to be done... but just now, let your heart grieve, dear. That is the place to start. You can't stop crying until you've begun."

Josie paused then and helped herself to another piece of Christmas cake, a treat she rarely allowed herself. She carefully poured a cup of tea from the cosy covered pot. She stirred in some milk and sugar, and seemed to disappear as she leant back in her chair and pensively sipped its steamy flavour. Toby expected her to continue once she had refuelled, but she didn't.

There was an extended silence. He stood and excused himself – but before he left, he came over and pressed his lips against his mother's forehead. "I love you Mum. You're the best. Happy Christmas."

Josie smiled gently. "'Thanks Toby. Your Daddy would be proud." She didn't seem to hear him leave to go to his bed, staring vacantly into her cup long after the room was empty and silent. Finally, she got up and went over to the mantle clock. She turned the key, winding it slowly. She looked up at the photo that hung over the mantle. A lone tear escaped down her cheek. "Maybe I was wrong Matt," she whispered, "Maybe I have not done with crying yet…"

27.

Belle had become familiar with lack of sleep. She couldn't remember the last time she had fallen into a swift, deep, healthy sleep after finishing the night dough mix. Tonight, she couldn't even lie on her bed and pretend to sleep. The realisation that a change was blowing in on the evening draught that blew around the window shutters sent her mind fluttering like a flag in the breeze: restless, unsettled, unable to stay still. Tomorrow Tobias would leave.

How she wished it were different! "Oh God, I want so much to be true to you... to have something to offer. But I have no picture of who I am. I don't even understand what it is I'm missing." She turned from the star-studded night window and opened her Bible to the next chapter of Proverbs. The book of wisdom seemed too full to ever understand, but she dutifully read a chapter a day and reported to Mrs Wallace at the end of the week. Then they would talk about what she read and what she had learnt. Mrs Wallace said that because Proverbs had 31 chapters, it would take just one month to read it through. Today she read chapter twenty-nine. She didn't get past verse eighteen: *"Where there is no vision, the people perish."* She read it again. That was it! No vision... this feeling of perishing. "Oh Lord God! You wouldn't save my spirit for eternity, but allow my soul to perish from a lack of vision? Show me a direction, a place to start. I need to grow into who I'm meant to be - not my father's, not Toby's, not Mrs Wallace's! I need to find the shape that you made for me." It was a desperate plea. Tonight's batch was an eight-hour-dough. That was the time she had before she needed to knock the dough. She would wait all night to hear the answer to the question of her heart.

Belle struggled to pull her mind back into line. Her thoughts kept wandering to the hospital: the hard, cold steps and jingling sound of the Ward-Hun's keys echoing around the ice-cold beds. "I should concentrate… not just keep thinking about Dad." Eventually her tired eyes refused to focus any longer and she surrendered her mind to wander where it would. Almost immediately she dosed off, and she watched the Ward-Hun marching down between the rows of beds, stopping at the foot of each bed and checking notes made by junior nurses. She glanced at her Dad's chart and answered Wallaby Joes' question dismissively. "No, his medicine has not come… it won't come… he will have to go without! There is nothing a good dose of castor oil won't cure." She pulled from her uniform pocket a bottle the size of a beer keg. "What a shame I don't have any of that either… this will have to do," and she proceeded to measure out a black tarry goop by the ladle. Out of nowhere, Toby charged in and tackled the Ward-Hun to the floor. "No!" he screamed at her, "No! Don't give him that!' Belle tried to pull him away… "Please, please – just give him his medicine… just give him his medicine!" The Ward-Hun stared through her, "There is none," she said. The phrase rang around her head; "There is none, there is none…"

Belle started awake, her hands sweating, her breathing heavy. Belle stared out the window. She massaged her eyelids with her fingertips and continued down the sides of her temples in a circular motion. How pathetic, how bizarre: to doze off into a weird dream, instead of searching out her purpose. Almost immediately she had a thought. What if there wasn't one... what if her only destiny was her father's dough trough and brick oven. Her father enjoyed his business. She had always wanted a business too... but one of her own.

"There is none, there is none..." The Ward-Hun's words echoed again. No dream of her own? No – it appeared not...only the distorted nonsensical jumblings of an over-tired mind. *"There is none, there is none..."* The Ward-Hun was not talking about a shortage of dreams. There was always a dream to be found. How did Toby put it? God was a Dream-thrower. How do you learn to be a Dream-catcher? "God throw me my dream. I'm ready to catch."

It was still dark when Toby's brother, Nat, drew the sulky up outside the house gate. Josie had made a big breakfast as if it was the last decent meal Toby would ever have. He ate it dutifully and tried to keep the jokes coming. Today his new life began. It should have been filled with the excitement and anticipation of a new season. Mal came to wish him well, "Hey, big guy, you have my sympathy.... all that unfortunate aggravation you have to suffer... living in the city and all. Still, keep your shirt on and don't get too big for your britches." Eventually Nat cleared his throat and headed for the door. "Come on Toby. You might be headed for a life of luxury... some of us still have a full days work ahead of us." With that Toby gave his mother a hug and swung up beside his brother. He smiled at the picture the warm glow of the lantern made through the shuttered windows. Home was always home, and already his changed perspective added value on it being there to come home to.

Progressively – like the fanning of tinder, encouraging an ember to burst into flame, an idea glowed in the back of her mind. At first it was barely noticeable... hardly perceivable. But it persisted; it swelled and ebbed with promise, until a flame flickered forward. It was so intriguing that Belle stopped and pulled away from the window. She stood, completely absorbed in the ideas that were growing brighter and more intense with every passing second. She ran to her desk and grabbed a sheet of paper and scrawled down the framework of what was starting to burn in her belly... and in the end she could not keep up and surrendered to the flames.

When the urgent blaze had gradually tamed, she walked over to the window and looked out over the eastern sky that was fading the darkness of night. She knew it would soon be iridescent with shades of pink and gold and purple. Tears rolled down her face. It made perfect sense. Her own darkness was receding in front of the brilliance of the vision before her... filling her mind and soul with life. Belle sunk to her knees by the windowsill, "Oh Lord Jesus, thank you! Thank you for the privilege of being your daughter!" and then she added with a smile, "Toby will be *so* amazed by this!"

A morning mist hung over the railway track and lay in the hollows along the street. The sun had not yet risen, but above the horizon a glow held the promise of a warm day. Nat helped Tobias unload his trunk from the back of the sulky, and tossed his bag and coat down beside it. His older brother shook his hand firmly. "I won't stay to see you off if that's okay. I need to get back to help Mal."

Tobias genuinely felt relieved. They were very early. It suited Nat to start his day with plenty of daylight in credit. "Yeah. Don't need soppy scenes out here," agreed Toby. He put on his coat and settled on the station bench. He didn't mind the wait really. He pushed his hands deep into his pocket and traced the shape of the little box he carried there, with his fourth finger.

Belle bounced up and down on Bronza's bare back. He was so slow, but she knew what time the train was leaving and she was sure that she would meet them going to the station. But the road was silent. She went past the Dampier dairy-farm and the cows were trailing out past the bails. She spurred Bronza on, heeling him in the ribs. "Gidup!" she cried frustrated. It would be quicker if she got off and crawled! Bronza wasn't built for speed. She needed to see Toby before he left. He had to know!

When she turned the corner towards the Lawson farm she sighed with relief to see Nat was just hitching the cart. "Nat!" she called out. "Good morning! I came to see Toby off! Are you ready to go?"

"Gee sorry Belle. Just got back from town. Toby's already at the station."

"You're UN-hitching? I thought the train didn't go until after half past six."

"Yeah. Sorry. Went in early. Big day."

Belle stared. She had to see him! She had to! Frustration stung her eyes as she yanked Bronza's head around and headed back towards the road. She would never make it.

"You're saddle horse is looking a bit beat," said Nat with a grin. "Why don't I get Toby's horse? He's a little fresher."

She hardly wanted to wait. She hopped and fidgeted like a four-year-old with a bladder problem, and as soon as the girth was tight and the stirrups shortened, she hitched herself up. One thing about Wattle Creek, there were no fancy pretences made about girls riding side-saddle.

She let the horse have his head and headed for town. The rhythm of his gallop under her thigh pumped through her being. It was imperative that Tobias knew about this. He had echoed her thoughts and said, *"Belle – I can't do anything without wondering what you would say... how you would counter it... what you would think."* Oh, she understood what he meant. She needed to find out what he felt about this. It was as essential as breathing... and she spurred his horse on faster.

Toby looked at the station clock and sighed... the hands relentlessly moved forward. Sparrows were hopping around under the benches, pecking at crumbs and breaking the stillness

225

of the morning with their busy chirping. He stood up and unwrapped a red and white boiled lolly from his pocket. The sweetness stung his throat and he started to pace. Every road led to Belle's Bakery. Now he just wanted to get going. He tipped his hat as other passengers starting to arrive for the early train. He turned and bumped into another, he mumbled an apology by tilting the brim of his hat, and bent down to collect the things that spilt from her bag all over the platform. "Ma'am, I am so sorry…"

"Sir," she smiled up at him and for a moment Tobias caught his breath… her eyes were blue. But they were not the right blue. A pain shot through his head like a bolt of lightening. He quickly returned her belongings and went back to his bench. He looked at the clock again. Right now she will be done knocking the dough and pushing Terry through the morning rush hour. Any hope that he carried close to his heart, to say a farewell, died as he watched the clock tick over. It chimed.

28.

The train whistle sounded and the churning wheels slowed as the train snaked its way through the town. She stopped by the rail crossing and her heart sank, the warning bell clanging a death knoll. The train wasn't late this morning. The whistle blew again, carriages passing, clanging and squealing as it pulled into the station. She bounded off the horse and ran to the platform hunting through the few passengers for Toby's familiar tall frame. He wasn't there. She quickly paced along the platform, sweeping back her dishevelled hair that had tangled loose on her ride. She stared through the small windows into the dark carriages searching for his face. Then she worked her way back again, looking over each carriage carefully. She spun around in despair. She never imagined that in getting to the station, he wouldn't be here to spark and spar with her. Perhaps he had decided not to leave...

Her gaze swept over the platform again. Toby was coming out of the men's room and making his way back to his hand luggage. His chin clenched in, there was a despondent perse to his mouth, and his hands were plunged deep in his pockets. "Toby!" She ran towards him. He stopped - frozen for a moment, thawing the instant she went to throw her arms around him. He caught her, holding her at arms length. If she got hold of him properly he would never get on that train.

"Belle?"

"I need to tell you something!"

He said nothing. He couldn't... his throat constricted. He looked at the energy burning in her eyes. Something enormous had happened.

She plunged in. "Toby you said once that you *can't do anything without wondering what I would say... what I would think.* I want you to listen to this. I need to know what you think."

His heart stabbed with disappointment. Perhaps this was just a frantic, last minute business meeting. Yet he nodded, led her to the platform seat and sat down beside her. Passengers were milling around their luggage saying farewells. Porters hustled around organising things to be stowed.

Belle wouldn't let herself pause. She had to say it all before they called for passengers. It had to be said. She mustn't think about how he might respond. "When you asked me to courting I wasn't too excited..."

Nothing like making a man feel grand, thought Toby wryly. Suddenly he didn't know whether he would prefer if this speech was about the bakery-partnership. What if she came to close the door forever? At least the Bakery left that door prised open and the thought eased the pain somewhat.

Belle hardly drew a breath. "It wasn't that I don't like being with you... it just seems that you and I are always competitors... not partners... well, I know we are partners in the Bakery, but that was not what..."

"Belle – the point."

"Oh yes, okay. Competitors. Competitors don't get married. Partners get married. I realised I was competing because I didn't want to get swallowed up by your dream. It is incredible what you want to do... but I could never do what you do or even something like nursing. I just don't have the constitution. And I couldn't just be your shadow and hang around while you lived your dream. I need to have a dream of my own and I never knew what that was. I just did the next thing... and the next thing was always the Bakery."

"But Belle..."

"No Toby. Just listen. I asked Mrs Wallace how she did it... how she could just live in her husband's shadow... but she said it is not like that at all! She told me all about her own dream and how she's living it! Two different dreams, living side by side... not competing, but important to each other. And then, I remembered what you said about God being a Dream Thrower. I asked Him to throw me a dream of my own. And He did! All of a sudden... the most stunning thing... and it makes perfect sense!"

He couldn't take his eyes off the blue depths that sparkled and reflected her excitement. He thought he would drown. "Are you going to tell me... or is this a secret?"

The steam train snorted its impatient call to get rolling. Passengers started to board.

"Making... pharmaceuticals! The medicines that you need to help your patients. So many little towns don't have a druggist who can prepare these... and people wait so long to get what they need. Like my Dad... like your Dad. It would really help people. And I know it's not what most women do, but I like business. This would make us partners... we would be supporting each other, not competing for sunlight because we are growing in each other's shadow."

"Are you sure?"

"Oh yes! But the weirdest thing is... once I got the vision of this... it was like I understood more completely that it is not about what I do... but who I am. Oh Toby! I know Dad is no less valuable just because he has had to close the door on his life work. This is not the sum total of who I am... but it is a direction, a place to walk towards. Toby this is so exciting! I feel that..."

"What about your father?"

"Dad? What do you mean?"

"Your father. His reason to go on living..." The guard blew the whistle... and then blew it again. Tobias made no effort to move. Out of the corner of his eye he could see more activity at the stock carriage designated for passengers' luggage. Goods were being unloaded.

Belle swallowed. "I, I... it was an excuse to buy time. I'm so sorry." Suddenly she felt her heart beating like a run away train. What if this was not as perfect as she thought? What would she do if he didn't think so, if he had changed his mind? "But Dad did give his approval. I will stay with him until next year. That is when I would come down to the city and start... when you go back next year. If he is willing, perhaps he can come with us..."

"You have this all worked out. Is this a proposal?"

"Oh. I'm sorry Toby. I never meant to presume. If you have changed your..."

"Is this a proposal?"

"I want to be your partner... in life. Not just medicine."

"What about love?"

"Love? Ah. You said you didn't expect fireworks..."

"No. I said I was not the one who needed to discover if there was anything more…"

"I'm not a great fan of the giggly romance thing. I saw what it did to Ali. If you want me to blush at your name, you've got the wrong girl. You know what I'm like. This is it. This is what you get."

He smiled at her defiance. "I love what I get. And just so you know… it wasn't the romance that did that to Ali… it was the wrong suitor." He paused. "Am I the right one?"

"Of course. That's why I'm here."

"Do you have a ring?"

"No…"

"Well then,"

"So, you think that makes my proposal null and void?"

"Yes." He smiled again. He loved this unconventional girl. Oh, so much!

"Oh." She looked away. She was kind of enjoying having all the answers. As always Toby found a hole. He got up to go. It felt incomplete. She sighed… disappointed. She had wanted his words to seal what they had, so she could take that with her as he went away.

He stood before her. "However…" he said quietly. Then knelt on the platform in front of the bench and gently took her hand. Belle held her breath. She dare not move in case the moment would collapse under the force of her breathing. He took out the little box that had been his constant companion for what had seemed a hopeless forever. "My-Belle, May-belle Kane… will you be my life partner? Will you marry me?"

Belle stared mesmerised by the circle of gold he held in his hand. It was studded with the most brilliant blue sapphires – that distinctive Kane cornflower blue. This circle of gold would bind them together… life-partners. An overwhelming softness filled her being and she could contain it no longer. Tears filled her eyes and she made no effort to stop them from falling. She knew such a ring took preparation and sacrifice. He had been bold enough to invest in both – planning this, because he knew what he knew… and was not deterred by the fact she had taken so long to see what he already saw.

"Tobias Lawson… yes!"

The stationmaster cleared his throat and suggested his workers start reloading the carriage. The two or three that stood around rolling cigarettes, nodded amiably. The engineer came storming across the platform. "What's going on? We were exactly on schedule and now we're behind!" He coloured his complaint with adjectives that brought a smirk to the workers' faces as they continued to carry packages unhurriedly across the platform.

"Well Mate," said the stationmaster calmly disregarding his ranting. "It's like this. We're doin' our darnedest. There's been a muck-up in the transport notices…' The engine driver blustered and fumed in disgust, describing colourfully every threat to their job security he could devise on short notice. The guard shrugged unconcerned and turned back to take charge over the luggage-cabin. As he sauntered past Tobias, he gave him a nod. "Sir, we'll be ready to leave in about seven minutes…"

Oblivious to the tempers on the platform, Belle's eyes blurred as she felt Tobias slide the cool band over her finger. He lent forward and whispered. "You said so yourself: twelve months. I will come back for my bride."

Belle reached out and encircled her arms around his neck. "I will be ready. I promise you that." Just then, like a warm morning blanket, the first smell of hot, stone-oven baked bread covered the town in its morning greeting. She tightened her embrace in amazement. "Terry's started the baking!"

"I'd say he's just about finished. It's going to be okay Belle. It'll work out fine." Toby grinned reassured.

The guard blew his whistle again, and Tobias forced himself to stand. He swung onto the rear metal balcony, watching the station recede into the distance, coal smoke and steam churning over the tracks behind him. Belle carefully engraved the look on his face into her memory until the train disappeared around the curve of the creek where the bridge runs over the gully. The green of the wattles shone silver in the morning sunlight.

She stayed there long after the platform was deserted. The stationmaster quietly came and stood beside her. "The thing I notice about trains Miss, is that they are never on time and they always come back."

"Yes, I believe you are right." Belle turned and looked at his portly smile. "Sir, exactly how delayed was the train in leaving this morning?"

"Well Miss, it's the railway," he said with a wink. "I reckon we lost a good half an hour over that luggage debacle."

In spite of her normal reserve, Belle reached up and gave him a hug. "You old romantic! Sir, may I have the honour of issuing the first invitation to our wedding!"

"And I accept with pleasure. There are some facts about the railway that no amount of ranting by officialdom can change. It is the way things are…" He stood there comfortably beside her for a while, looking down the rail line, each absorbed in their own thoughts. "You're Sam Kane's girl aren't you… the Baker's daughter?"

Belle did not shift her gaze from the railway line… tracking its destination into the future. Next year she will be on that train. She held out her hand and traced the circle of gold on her hand. "Yes, that's me… my name is Mabel, my friends call me Belle; a Kane to the core. I'm engaged! I'm a business woman – going to be a druggist in fact. I'm a daughter, a friend and a partner.

He smiled and extended his hand. "Pleased to meet you Mabel Kane. Pleased to meet you indeed."

Part 2

Citygirl

"Dear Nathaniel,

What astounding contentment engulfs me as I sit here, quietly watching you sleep on your mother's arm... oblivious to the street sounds that traffic relentlessly up and down outside our window. How gracious is our Heavenly Father to allow me the privilege to experience this glimpse into his heart. Was this how he felt when he reached down and breathed life into Adam? Was His parent heart protective, and deliriously joyous just to have him there, resting so confidently on his hand? Did He anticipate as much as I, the years ahead when He would guide and teach him things as they worked the Garden together?

The sound of the pot and saucepan hawker is clanging his way around the block. Suddenly this city, with all its people and commerce and industry is too small for us. I want a larger horizon for you, my son. I want us to learn and grow and be familiar with the smell of the soil ... to know the taste of a hard day's toil, forged from the work of our hands. I am captivated by this idea of creating our personal Eden... a place of refuge where our family can work together... walk together.

It sounds like I am smitten with an idealistic, rose-coloured vision... but in reality I see dust, and flies, and blisters. I'm sure I don't even know the half of it yet! Still, I am confident that, just like Adam, who started from the dust... that out of these things God will form quality character. Adam went walking in the evenings with his Creator, because God breathed life into his being.

Nat, never forget to walk in the dusk... and the dust, with your God. He is the source of life ~ the breath of love that defines success, regardless of what things look like on the outside. Only God can measure the heart of a man, and nothing compares with that.

~ your devoted father, always"

29.

It was impossible for Belle to stand on the station platform and not to think of the day Tobias left to go to university. She had written letter after letter; read and re-read every reply. She hadn't expected this urgency, the compelling need to communicate her heart with him. She wondered whether sharing her thoughts would have mattered so much if they'd had a normal face-to-face courtship. Perhaps this remoteness was a net – catching all the wasted time; allowing her to sweep up and capture on paper her ideas and emotions that were swimming around in her head and her heart. It was a way she could share things she would not ordinarily have the courage to reveal about herself. Sometimes she felt she would write Tobias Lawson letters for the rest of her life…even after they were married… and post them on his pillow!

Alma Dampier quietly touched Belle's shoulder. "Belle dear, I am so grateful you came to meet the train. I have no way of knowing how Ali will react."

"You said yourself, Mrs Dampier… it is all going to take time… wagon-loads of time. Things will get back to normal for her."

"But that is just it, Belle… I cannot presume we have so much time. That is why I really appreciate you coming out to the farm with us. At least until the wedding…"

"Oh Mrs Dampier... you are my second family. You know that. When Ali told me Emmaline was the sister that she never had, I was so jealous! I thought that was my place! It took me ages to forgive Em for that!" She laughed. Emotions run high when you are nine-years-old. Belle stopped and looked at her best friend's mother. Ali had her mother's handsome features, but now Belle suddenly noticed that the woman before her had aged. Her hair had greyed and the lines around her eyes were much deeper. She reached out and took her hand reassuringly. "It won't be so bad... you'll see. I know it's been a while, but having Emmaline here again will be like old times."

Belle was never sure how Ali would be the next time she saw her. She wavered between being very much her normal self, to being distant and untouchable. Now Ali was remote again – Belle hardly saw her. Between her Dad having yet another stroke, and the bakery – it took time... a lot of time. But perhaps that is no excuse to neglect friendships.

Doris Levin had taken up the bakehouse baton, and with her help Terry's apprenticeship had accelerated. It was Doris who gave the bakery the dependability the community expected. The process had taken Belle every second of the past year to help them be ready for when she left Wattle Creek after the wedding. What a couple they would be: Dr and Mrs Lawson. There is a lot of study to finish before they will be able to work together as their dream team.

Mrs Dampier looked at the station clock. Her anxiety was putting Belle on edge. It was nearly time. Alma sighed and restlessly moved on the railway bench. "Belle, there is something you must know..." The graveness of her tone pulled Belle's thoughts back from the millions of pre-wedding things that she had started to think about. "Fred and Janie have announced their wedding date. We were hoping that they would have a longer engagement and let things settle with Ali a bit. But we can't. Not now…" She paused. It was difficult for her to continue. Her voice was barely a whisper. "Fred said it wasn't fair that they were expected to put their lives on hold because of Ali. Him and Janie, well… they are determined, and now I think Janie is in the family way… and the wedding – just a small one you know… it will be in March… that's why it has to be."

A tear glistened in Mrs Dampier's eye. She looked frayed around the edges, like a thread had been pulled and her life was unravelling. "I know Fred loves his sister… but I also know that Janie is not happy at home. It almost seems as if this is deliberate." She didn't say "tart", but the sour taste in her mouth tainted her words. It was a trap, and she was angry at the danger it was putting their family in. Weddings were supposed to be happy celebrations – not an escape ticket for discontented girls who couldn't wait to be brides.

Belle looked straight ahead. It had seemed kind of fast… but then romance was like that sometimes. Her and Toby for example… it seemed like they were mortal enemies one day and… She never finished the thought. Mrs Dampier sat stoically on the bench clutching her handbag. This burden was one she could never share with her peers. Belle felt very much exposed. She treasured her friendship with Ali, but she really didn't want to know about their family skeletons. Not a few of days before her wedding. She felt tainted by what Mrs Dampier whispered.

"I told you that because of Ali…" Mrs Dampier cleared her throat, and dabbed a handkerchief around her eyes. "Oh Belle, I know you and Toby… your wedding will be so special, but she's still hurting. Time is not healing her heart as we thought it would. Oh, she seemed better, much more like her old self… like she was running a clean broom through her life and starting again. She gave back all the engagement gifts, and was giving other things away too…"

Belle smoothed the fabric of her dress. "I did try to give some of her dresses back. It seemed too much."

Her mother nodded, her eyes wrapped in worry. "That is what I am talking about. No one could talk her out of it. So we just let her be. Then…" Mrs Dampier's shoulders shuddered a little, and her breath rasped. "Her father found her down by the creek. She had taken knives from the meat-house… she had three of them… she was getting set to…" With a tremble her voice went silent. "Alf found her in time… but only just." Fear and shame covered her like a shawl, and she retreated under it.

Belle couldn't breath. The beautiful dress she had on was one of Ali's. It seemed to get tighter and tighter, strangling the breath out of her. Never would she have imagined anything so … grave. She shuddered. How close that thought really was.

A little girl danced along the platform waiting with her mother for the train. She had a wand and a jar of bubble soap, blowing bubbles and catching each one as they floated on the breeze. Belle stared at them. Her life, her dreams, her friendships… they all seemed illustriously hollow – like bubbles – beautifully floating in the sunshine, sheer and transparent,

241

rainbows marbling the fragile surface, ready to pop and disappear into nothing at any moment. Oh God. Was nothing sure?

"Of course, we've told no-one outside the family... well, except Doctor Wallace. This is why I asked if we could invite Emmaline to the wedding. I thought if she came... it might be a support to Ali... it might help her get through, after you go. Oh Belle, I know that sounds like an awful thing to say to the bride... but I know you'll understand. Ali might regret this later if she is not there. Em knows nothing about Ali being ill, or about her and Jimmy. I just couldn't tell her something like that in a letter. What if her Grandmother found it? The scandal she'd create would be unbearable. Belle dear," tears welled in Mrs Dampier's eyes, "I didn't know what else to do."

Belle reached out and held her hand, pain fusing them together as they heard the train whistle blow, signalling it was passing the crossing on the edge of town. Oh, she sincerely wanted to believe they were all over reacting, but how do you measure such a thing? She felt helpless. In the few minutes before the train grated and hissed into the station, they quietly sat, surrounded by others waiting for the train. It felt very much like watching fish in a bowl – creatures that belonged to a whole different ecosystem. The bubble girl had abandoned her wand and was excitedly jumping and dancing around the skirts of her mother. They both wanted to believe that it was just the happy occasion of her wedding that welcomed Emmaline back to Wattle Creek.

Belle remembered Emmaline as a shy, quiet kid. Ali always protectively defended her timid ways. Emmaline's parents drowned in a tragic accident when she was five. Afterwards she was ushered into the stuffy halls of ELLIOT HOUSE and lived with her crusty grandmother. As a child, Emmaline looked forward to her holidays in the country like fresh air. Her cousins at Dampier farm were the people she loved most in the entire world. There was even talk of them adopting full custody at one stage.

That was before Grandmother Edith came to collect her from the farm one day and found her helping Fred rescue some calves from a flooded yard after a water tank burst. They were up to their knees, sloshing around in muck, manure and hay – having the time of their lives. Visits were promptly confined to short summer stays with the rural relatives. There was a certain prestige in having relatives on a country estate, as long as the details were not too specific, or realistic. Emmaline's visits to the farm dwindled under Grandmother Edith's discouragement. It had been ten long years since she had been back.

The train snorted to a standstill. Crumpled passengers alighted, carrying hatboxes, leather overnight bags and hand luggage. Mrs Dampier nervously scanned the milling gathering. "Aunt Alma?" She was there before they even realised. The cut of her dress was simple and elegant. Belle hardly recognised the plain city-kid that had usurped her sister-status in Ali's eyes. Ali was tall and had thick fair hair that fell in flaxen waves. Emmaline was the exact contrast to Ali. She was petite and her straight auburn hair had been described by Ali in romantic terms as "flyaway fine – like fairy tale spun gold". But in spite of her slight figure, Emmaline was well and truly grown up.

"Em – darling! I am so glad you've come. Welcome back to Wattle Creek dear." She enveloped her in a hug. Belle watched with relief. It was bizarre, Mrs Dampier was so insecure about this visit. Mrs Dampier chatted nervously on the way back to the buggy. "You remember Belle don't you? The blushing bride she is too. We've offered to help with some things for the wedding... cooking and flowers mainly. The roses have done quite well this summer considering. She's coming out to the farm for a couple of days just before the wedding. I've cooked a special roast dinner for tonight my dear... I remember how you used to be partial to it. My, you grow more like my sister every time I see you. You have the same gentle way as Edith about you dear. Here, let me get some help with your trunk. You're quite the young lady now. Your Uncle Alf will be quite surprised. I think he may not have his best cow-maid in the bails anymore. Fred's still at home... him and Janie will be living in the old house, just off the kitchen, until we get to build the new one when they get married. Did I tell you that they have announced their engagement? We lived there ourselves before the kids came along. They've started to clean out all the storage and doing it up nice. Its kind of cosy for newly weds... well at least I thought so when I married your Uncle Alf. It is most unusual to think that Fred will soon be married... or Belle for that matter. I can hardly get used to it. You are all growing up so fast."

By the time they climbed into the seat and were on their way, Em was well and truly up to speed about the entire family

244

and neighbourhood: except Ali. Belle silently wondered when Mrs Dampier would talk to her about Ali. But with the skill of a conversational gymnast she avoided the topic with adept agility.

When they pulled up at the house gate, Mrs Dampier secured the reins. "Ali will be resting until dinner." Belle sighed. Once Ali would have been the first to want to know Emmaline was here. She watched Em's face and tried to interpret what was behind her placid features, but it was like reading a plaster wall… perfectly smooth, powdered and fine. She nodded and smiled as if such weird neglect by her cousin was completely normal. Well, it had been a long time.

Dinner was served in the dining room just like every other Sunday and special occasion. The yellow lamps gave the room a muted ambiance and Em could well have been forgiven for thinking that she had stepped into a time warp. Her farm holidays had many happy memories for her, but she had been a child then. Now, with her socialised, cultured awareness Emmaline looked around the farmhouse dining room through a lens that made everything plain and dull. Uncle Alf, Aunt Alma, Alice… Ali, Alfred… Fred: Emmaline smiled cynically. Why had she never noticed the corny names her country cousins had? How time changes things.

Ali pushed baked potato around her plate with a fork and nibbled on her carrots as if they were woodchips. Em looked across the table at Fred. She had always considered her cousin was as handsome as Ali was pretty. Fred responded to

Emmaline's gaze with an amiable smile and started reminiscing, almost too eagerly, about their childhood escapades. She nodded occasionally, spurring Fred on to add even more fantastic details to his accounts. Uncle Alf added his perspective with a laugh. Emmaline didn't need any placards to tell her this was a longed-for diversion from undercurrents running deep in the Dampier family. Living with Grandmother Edith had taught her how to ignore the obvious. She smiled and tried not to cringe at his stories or the chips she noticed in the china.

Belle sat across the table and poured another cup of tea. Had it been too unreasonable to insist Ali be involved in her wedding just like they always planned? Mrs Dampier desperately endorsed the idea of Ali taking part, but now Belle worried she had put an unwarranted amount of strain on her friend. The wedding was on Wednesday, and the ceremony would be held at Mrs and Dr Wallace's home in town. It was the logical choice in the absence of Belle's parents as they supported Toby in his studies and Mrs Wallace had mothered them both through their courtship. It had taken Belle a long time to realise her father would never recover from his strokes sufficiently to live at home independently. She had talked with Dr Wallace about this many times. As much as everyone supported Ali attending as Belle's bride's-maid, their childhood vows seemed so long ago. Belle wondered if they hadn't both outgrown such childish promises, but she wasn't sure how to change things now the countdown was set in motion.

30.

The next day started early. There were lots of preparations to be finalised. Belle had been up for hours when Em finally made her way to the kitchen for breakfast. Belle offered a light good-morning on her way to the laundry. "Good morning Em… did you sleep well?" she chirruped cheerfully. Emmaline's sober silence did nothing to douse Belle's buoyancy. "Country air tends to help me relax. Early mornings come pretty easy for me… growing up in a Bakehouse and all… much like dairy farming really."

Em grimaced and helped herself to a cup of tea. "How delightful," she thought cynically, "I'm keeping company with essential services: milk from Uncle Alf's dairy farm; bread from Belle's bakery. All we need now is dinner with a butcher and supper with the ice-man, delivering blocks of ice with his tongs and ice-pick to pack up the ice-chest." She remembered Belle as a strong willed competitive nine-year-old who was always vying for Ali's attention. The whole country thing, well, her Grandmother had been right. It was just a little too base.

The house was in an uproar. Fred and his mates were carrying out chairs and forms to take over to the Wallace's place. Ali, Em and Belle had the job of collecting flowers. Mrs Wallace's garden could amply supply bouquets for the bride and maids. But there was a bridal arch that was to be woven with ivy and roses, and draped with damp tea-towels so that it didn't wilt beyond recognition before the bride got to stand under it. It was one of those whimsical wedding-dreams that the practical

Belle was not quite sure she should pursue. But as she thought of the roses her father had painted in her childhood bedroom, it got the better of her. She was compelled to add this symbol to their special day.

The job for today was to collect the floral donations that were going to come in from every rose garden in the area, and cut as many roses as they could from the Dampier garden. Then they had to bring in enough long strands of ivy that trailed over the old part of the house to cover the arch as well. They had the laundry tubs filled with water to keep the cuttings fresh overnight. So, with an old Hessian bag to pile on the plunder from the vines and bushes, and a pair of scissors each in hand, they started the pillage. Ali listlessly gathered the strands passed down to her by Em and Belle as they balanced on a wooden ladder to retrieve the long strands of ivy. Slowly they worked their way around the ivy-covered shed.

They stared at the arch, as it stood naked under the tank-stand next to the laundry. Some things are easier said than done, and it definitely seemed an ambitious undertaking to make this stark chicken wire frame become the voluptuous dreamed-of bower. It looked very unstable and ungainly in its exposed state. "We're going to need masses of ivy to cover this," said Belle grimly. A skimpy bridal arch, with wire showing through sparse strands of ivy would look pitiful. Em sighed. If she had to do this task because there was no real domestic Help available, there was no way it was going to look meagre. It absolutely would be the most plentiful, full, stand-under-it-arch in the history of Wattle Creek weddings.

Ali stood listlessly by as they continued their harvest. They piled the bag high with ivy and were dragging it back to the laundry to immerse their harvest in the cool tubs, when the impatient, shrill tones of Janie Pearce – Fred's fiancée, carried across the yard. It was evident she would not let her frustrations go unvented. "I absolutely don't care what she said. Ali is ungrateful and spoilt. She is sabotaging the celebration of my engagement just because she wasn't able to hold onto a man of her own!"

Belle stared at the retreating full figure of Janie in shock. "Ali – bear her no mind. She's got no idea!" But before Ali had time to react another voice interrupted.

"Ali! There you are. Got some things for you…" Their neighbour Nat Lawson stood with his rabbit-felt hat planted firmly on his head. He smiled hopefully at Ali, but if he was waiting for some recognition he waited in vain.

He paused, and then cleared his throat. Suddenly he became so businesslike Em almost expected him to pull a delivery docket from his pocket. "Mum told me to bring these buckets of flowers over. Plus there are chairs and benches to take into town. Where do you want them?"

Ali looked stunned that he would ask her. She had no idea. Nor did she care. All she could hear was the voice of Janie Pearce ringing in her ears. Tears welled in her eyes as she turned and deserted them in overwhelming distress. Nat stared after her in bewilderment. He had no idea chairs could be so emotive.

Belle shrugged helplessly. "Nat, thanks for your help. How's it going over yonder?" Toby's older brother was abrupt, but she was not put off by his manner. She knew him well enough to realise he was a time-line guy. Nat liked to have his day thoroughly planned.

He grinned. "I left Toby pacing like a lion. He's thinking he should have eloped. He'll be fine... by Wednesday," he added quickly as he saw Belle's brow pucker. "Pre-wedding jitters. Ma's absolutely set that he won't break any traditions and see you before the ceremony, and he's pretty ticked off about that. Feeling all left out." Nat's obvious opinion was that he wished he could trade places and have an enforced exclusion zone around the preparations himself. "Still, you picked a good man there Belle... I can't deny it. Mal's busy doing Lord knows what... being best man and all. I've been given a list of things to do. I couldn't find anyone," he said indicating towards the house. "Don't s'pose you know where the flowers and chairs have gotta go? Ma told me not to bother you..." he added apologetically.

"The flowers can go around to the laundry – we've tubs and buckets there. Chairs... no idea... there's a lot going on. I'll go and find Mrs Dampier and see what she has organised with Fred. Oh, by the way – you remember Em... Emmaline Farrington... Ali's cousin? Emmaline – I'm sure you remember Toby's older brother. I'll be back in a tick."

Ali's cousin? Nathaniel hadn't remembered. But he nodded anyway and stuck out his hand. "Emmaline... Hmm? Family get togethers are such fun."

Emmaline stared at his hard, calloused hand. It was dusty and unwashed. His hat remained on his head. The boys from next door had left an impression from those innocent farm holidays... especially the youngest who had spent a lot of time with Fred. Back then, she hadn't been immune to his good-looking oldest brother and one summer she even privately harboured a crush. Oh, that was a long time ago! She looked at the man before her and couldn't believe she had ever thought that way! She shuddered in disgust at his social ineptness, and juggled ivy and scissors in a ploy to avoid his offered hand.

In the end he held his bucket of flowers in one hand and picked up the bag layered with ivy strands with the other. "Where have these got to go? Laundry hey." He had asked a question... and then answered it. She nodded with a raise of her eyebrows and followed him around the back. The bucket clanged noisily as he dumped it unceremoniously on the hardened, compressed floor besides the tubs. The ivy from the Hessian bag sloshed into the water and he dragged the bag back through the water, spilling it everywhere. Emmaline cringed. He was like a gorilla lumbering around a florist shop. "I'll go and get the other buckets for you." He almost ran away, but was back before she could take a breath. He deposited them clumsily beside the others, tipping the stems out. He shoved them back in and straightened up – mission accomplished.

There was silence. Belle had not returned with any information about the chairs and trestles. "Hmm. How long are you here for then? Just until after the wedding." He did it again... answered his own question. There was nothing for Em to say. She dearly wanted to get rid of his hat since he was insisting on talking to her. It was very basic etiquette.

Nat cleared his throat again. He wasn't used to having to mark time, especially in the presence of a lady. It was disconcerting. How could he not remember Ali's cousin? She was stunning – elegant. Her hair shone like gold in the afternoon sun. The effect was quite anaesthetising. She seemed very much out of place in the farmhouse back yard, cutting ivy strands with her gloved hand.

Em looked around for an escape. "I'd better keep going or we'll run out of light. There are still a few more collections we need to make... and then the ivy... Nice to meet you, Mr....."

He got that. He shook his head as if someone had jabbed him back to consciousness. "Lawson. Nathaniel Lawson. Call me Nat. Live next door. S'pose I can help you with that while I wait."

The last thing she wanted was more of his inept company, especially when he conversed in dot-points. "No need. Belle will be back in a moment."

Nat was not a guy used to being told 'no' when he offered a hand. He followed her out to the yard and picked up the scissors Belle had left and preceded to hack away at the ivy. He was cutting the lengths way too short, stripping the stems of the leaves. Now Em was agitated. There was not an endless supply of ivy, especially when so much was required. "If you're determined to assist, please cut them longer. We need them at least a yard in length, longer if possible. We are finding it hard to get the height."

Well! Was that possible? Absolutely. Height was definitely something he could help with. His tall frame and long arms reached up over the eaves when he stood on the ladder. So now, in an uncharacteristic attempt to please, the ivy cuttings were trailing all the way across the yard. She closed her eyes and groaned. Surely, he hadn't thought she meant a "back-yard" in length?

31.

The day dawned softly. Emmaline took her morning cup of tea down to the laundry and sat on a chair, watching Belle thread layers of ivy through the wire. "Not a morning person hey?" commented Belle through teeth that held a thread in place as she placed another tendril of vine over the frame. "Me... come evening I collapse... a bit like the fall of Jericho at sunset. It happens every night. I have no social stamina for long evenings at all!" She paused and stepped back. "So, what do you think? Has this arch got the potential to bless our bridal vows in marital bliss?"

In spite of herself, Emmaline smiled. "I'm sure you will be blessed anyway... with or without a bridal bough." It was quite unexpected Belle would be so down to earth... when it was her wedding. There were plenty of others who seemed to suffering the fluster and panic that was normally attributed to the bride. Belle was just doing what needed to be done. "Belle, it was nice of you to invite me. I was quite surprised."

"Glad you're enjoying the experience. It can be quite disconcerting... wedding preparations."

"I will confess I'm not used to the all-in approach of country weddings. It seems a bit intense for me... too many cooks. You seem very calm, considering."

It was quite intentional that she was doing this arch: one thing to focus on. This was Mrs Wallace's idea: one task to give her attention to. Belle really wanted to be relaxed for her wedding day, but she was not the kind of person who could sit and buff her nails watching other people do the work.

Belle looked at Em through bundles of ivy. She knew Emmaline was not comfortable with the country wedding setting, but felt a little perspective could help. "You know your aunt wasn't sure that Ali would want to be involved in my wedding... " She stopped. No. She wouldn't say anything. It was not her place.

"Why? I know time changes things, but I thought Ali would be a natural choice given your friendship."

Belle focused very intently on the wire, and used a little string to tie up some strands to stop them from sagging. "And I guess that's why Ali is going along with it. She hasn't said anything – but I know it is hard for her. Ali was engaged earlier last year. This *could* have been her wedding..."

"She was engaged?" Emmaline blinked. How could she not have known that? Why wouldn't she be told? Why wouldn't anybody say anything? Suddenly the whole dynamic at Dampier's farm made sense. It was as if big slabs of puzzle pieces suddenly joined together simultaneously.

"Oh. So, is she... well, you know? I wondered if... her needing extra rest and all... and Aunt Alma has said she has been sick, I wondered if she... might be... well you know... " Could the beautiful Ali have fallen so far? The boys were always chasing her.

Belle laughed, but there was no humour in it. "I can assure you that if Ali was in the family way, it would be well and truly passed the time when she could hide such a thing. Ali hasn't looked at a man since her engagement was broken..." In her mind she saw Jimmy standing by her bakery shop, guilt stricken and drunk after being caught red handed with the town-mayor's daughter. "In truth, she is heart-sick, and it is mostly from broken faith in humanity... well, one human specifically. I've tried... but it seems I am just another person who is locked out of her life. Oh Em... she needs you."

Em was quiet for a long while. Her unsavoury presumption felt humiliating. Yet it was the realisation that she wasn't invited to the wedding because Belle considered a friend that struck her. She was asked here because of Ali. Why was she not surprised? Ali always outshone her. Em bit her lip thoughtfully. Funny how such a revelation hurt even when she wasn't nine years old and life had moved on. It would be nice just once to be liked for herself... and not because of Ali.

Belle continued to thread the wire frame. It was tedious work and jagged bits of wire stabbed her fingers, even through her gloves. She stopped and stretched her arms behind her back. She wriggled the arch around to face Emmaline. "I'm not sure we have enough roses to cover the whole thing, so I'm thinking we should place them across the top edge... just here?" Em didn't even notice that Belle continued to give the project a joint status, even though she hadn't lifted a finger towards it.

Abruptly Em got up and left. She went into the bedroom and shut the door. Ali was sitting on the floor beside her bed. Her eyes were dry, her mouth grim. Em latched the door and sat on the floor beside her. She looked around the room. She had forgotten the hours they had spent here as children, just like this... on the floor. But instead of silence – they would chatter and giggle late into the night, until Uncle Alf would grump past with a switch and threaten a tortuous death by flogging if they didn't settle down: there was milking to do in the morning!

Remembering made Em realise she had got out of the habit of being a friend. The people in her Grandmother's world didn't confess to friendships… they majored on contacts and influence. These people had engulfed her world, and the loneliness of it suddenly hit her as Belle's words scalded like a strong carbolic soap, washing off layers of dust that covered that part of her memory… *"Oh Em, she needs you…"* Here was someone who did need her. Just as she was.

She saw the grim, acid profile of Janie storm past the window, and Em got up and drew the blind. In spite of Janie's attractive features, there was something about that girl that reminded her of Grandmother Edith's parlour acquaintances. Em determined she would try… at least where Ali was concerned… she would try and remember how to be a friend. Sure, there is a lot of history in ten years, but she could attempt to spin new threads of connection. They were still cousins after all.

"The arch is nearly done. Belle's got it well in hand…" she said conversationally. Ali hardly seemed to register. "It's going to be interesting to see how they get it into town on the wagon. Do they really think it would be easier than transporting the buckets of flowers and finding somewhere to construct it in town?" Emmaline paused and didn't say anything for a while. "Ali, do you want to go to the wedding?" she asked quietly.

Ali blinked. "Why would you ask?" Lots of people were happy to tell her what to do; even how to feel. Few had asked. She couldn't actually remember even one... perhaps they had. She couldn't be sure.

Em slowly leant over and lifted up Ali's hand. "Ali – because you may not want to..."

Like a frozen pot cracking from contact with a warm surface, Ali responded to her cousin's touch. Oh, how she had missed her. When Grandmother Edith refused her cousin to visit, it wasn't just one little girl's heart she was breaking: it was two. Just then, on the floor of the bedroom with the havoc of wedding preparations flurrying outside their little bedroom, two lost little girls found each other again.

Ali leant on Em's shoulder as she cried the tears that had refused to come. She cried for the neglected years of their sister-hood, the destroyed opportunity to enjoy her best friend's wedding, or her brother's engagement... the lost ability to retain any joy, because the plug had been pulled from her life and everything worthwhile seemed to swirl out of reach of her fingers.

Em turned Ali to her. "I have missed you... missed us. I'm sorry I didn't write... or something. I could have..."

"Why didn't you? I waited for your letters... I wrote... for a whole year... I couldn't understand that you didn't want to be my pen-cousin..." It was a challenge to her faithfulness, just as Jimmy Golders had failed in his sincerity towards her.

Em felt the cold hand of control slide down her back. "You wrote to me? Oh Ali!" Now it was her turn to sit winded from reality. It felt like a cliché, like some badly written novel, with her name on the cover. There was no proof; only the snatched correspondence and strained looks from

Grandmother Edith when the house-staff brought in the mail. It became some sort of forbidden privilege. "But Ali… I didn't get any letters. I can't explain it, but I would have written back. I know I would have found a way. I was never brave enough to send the first letter. I thought you would hate me for not being able to come. I'm sorry… so sorry..."

Em pushed down the tears that prickled the back of her eyes. She had to help Ali through this. Now it became her commitment. Bridal boughs fell off her priority list. So, what if people could see wire? There was something far more exposed that needed protection from prying eyes and caustic asides. She was very unsure how to do this. She stood up and walked the room. Suddenly she stopped and repeated her question. "Ali… do you want to go to the wedding?"

Ali sighed. When Belle approached her about being bridesmaid her heart faded in fear. She wanted so much to pretend this, or any other relationship, was not really successful when her own engagement was botched so thoroughly. The day loomed closer. Toby's return from university was much anticipated; Belle could hardly speak of anything else. Ali breathed deeply again. The air was warm and still, and dust swirled in hazy patterns as the morning sun streamed in around the blinds at the window. "I already said I would, but Emmy, I'm just not sure I can. It's so hard…"

Emmaline took a deep breath. She tried to sound non-committal. "What do you think Belle would want?"

"I don't know… someone organised… efficient… to keep things on track for her… not having her mother and all..." Ali sighed. The expectations were so hard to keep up with.

"Belle said this is what she wants you to do?"

"Well, no. But she hasn't got her mother to help her."

"Ali… in all honesty… if Belle needed those things… it's well past the time. Aunt Alma and Mrs Wallace have helped her with most details. I think she just wants her friend to be with her."

"Well, it is easy for you to say that. You've never…" Her voice trailed off.

Em looked at her. "Never what?"

"Never mind… it was nothing."

"Never been engaged?"

Ali swallowed and took a deep breath. How harsh it sounded when it was said like that. "I said I would, so I have to go."

"Why?"

"Well, because… everyone expects it now."

"I don't."

"I would have thought that you would be the first to do what is expected."

Em cringed. That was borne from years of being told that she couldn't visit because her social responsibilities came above all else. "I confess… it would be mannerly: Belle is your best friend, and Toby is your neighbour, after all. But you decide. Are you up to it?"

"I don't know."

Em believed her. She probably didn't know how shallow or deep her resilience ran. How could she know how many layers of defences had been eroded away, or how many were left? "Would you like to be there for Belle… if you thought you could manage it?"

"But I can. It's just here at Wattle Creek."

"That's not what I mean…"

Ali's head was niggling with a headache. It was stretching her ability to follow what Em was getting at. "I'm not sure. It already seems so hard."

"Okay… let me put it this way. This is Belle and Toby's wedding day. They are the people we should be considering. Now, I don't know Toby, so let's just focus on Belle… just Belle."

Put like that… for Belle – her best friend… that was different. Yes, she would like to be there for Belle. She nodded. She would.

Em came over and gave Ali a hug. "Do you want to know something? You're tougher than anyone gives you credit for. You will do fine! Where is your dress? We need to get it out to take with us." She again saw Nat in his heavy overalls and grubby rabbit felt hat, hacking away at ivy tendrils. He had blended in so well with every other person who had swarmed over the house in the last few days and she mentally pictured the wedding party in denim and drill, bridesmaids in heavy cotton skirts and mud-crusted boots. She had no confidence in country residents to be suitably attired. When Ali went to the wardrobe and brought out her dress, she was genuinely surprised. "Ali – this is beautiful!" Even though the fabrics were not expensive, the simplicity and cut made the outfit look stunning. She sighed from relief.

32.

Belle's friend, Doris Levin, had a tribe of kids. Her twin boys were given the duty of standing at the front gate of the Wallace's residence to welcome guests. They stood with their ears scrubbed, hair slicked down, and their long socks sliding uncooperatively to their ankles. Within minutes their shirt-tails were swinging in the breeze and from their pockets little pea-shooters materialized. They loaded them expertly with spit-balls – little chewed up wads of paper, and in between the flow of visitors, they competed their pocket money for the highest tally of dead flies hit off the oil light that hung at the front door. In one glorious, unfortunate moment they miscalculated and decorated Mrs Hollis' hat with a particularly juicy specimen – fly corpse and all. Instantly every hat became fair game. Reverend Bernard wore a chewed up projectile on the back of his ministerial robes. As Doctor Wallace ushered his wife to a chair, he copped one on the seat of his pants, from one of the boys hiding strategically in the shrubbery beside the house.

Nat Lawson arrived with his mother Josie, escorting her on his arm. Nat offered her a seat before he gave the tails of his jacket a perfunctory adjustment, and excused himself to stand with Toby at the altar. His younger brother Malachi stood beside the arched bower of ivy and roses scanning the congregation of guests. Three brothers. Ali's brother Fred was the fourth musketeer... and today, they stood inseparable in solidarity - sober and solemn, befitting the close of an era. They had spent a great deal of time cooking up tomfoolery together.

Nat was none too surprised to see mischief brewing in Mal's eyes… some practical joke cooking for the newly-wed couple later on. No doubt there would be plenty of likely opportunities to talk with young ladies later on as well; an apt privilege for the best man. He spotted some young girls giggling sillily as they ducked out of sight and skirted the house, positioning themselves for the bridal entry.

Little Fanny Levin stood serious and responsible by a pedestal planter near the French doors that opened out onto the back courtyard. The duties that befell her as head flower girl weighed heavily on her little shoulders. She soberly waited in her pretty dress with her two little sisters, who were dancing around with their baskets of flower petals. It was nearly time to walk through the garden before the bride. The petals left a glorious fresh, tangy, crushed smell.

Nat noted Ali's petite cousin Emmaline slip in behind the little portable organ and take charge of the ivory keys. He wasn't expecting that. He just assumed that they would use the regular Church organist. The minister nodded, and Emmaline played a quiet fugue. He found it an interesting piece of irrelevant trivia that she could play music, and quite well it seemed: pretty *and* clever.

Uncle Alf and Aunt Alma sat with Josie Lawson. The Doctor and Mrs Wallace were on the benches under the shade of the spreading camphor laurel trees that lined the lane that ran down the back fence of their yard. The railroad Stationmaster sat beside them with his buttons polished with pride. He was, after all, the very first to receive a wedding invitation from Belle, straight after Toby proposed. A few friends of Toby's lounged casually about. Nat couldn't see Ali anywhere at all, but breathed easier when he saw her set Fanny and her sisters on the carpet and gently nudge them towards the altar, baskets of petals in hand. Em struck the rousing chords of the Bridal Entry.

Toby stood with his brothers staring at his bride as she emerged from the house in white. The lawn was smooth and green. The long carpet-runner went down to the marriage altar set out under the shade. Belle walked down Mrs Wallace's path, out into her garden.

By her side, a nurse wheeled Belle's father in a wooden, large-wheeled chair. He tilted precariously to one side, the weakness down his side unable to support his body. He was propped up oddly with lumpy cushions. Mrs Wallace reached out and touched Josie's gloved hand. A tremor of emotion that Josie rarely allowed herself, fluttered in her throat. Oh that Toby's father could witness this moment. How proud Matt would be. Perhaps from eternity he looked on with pride anyway. It was a small consolation.

Belle's father was to be taken back to the hospital ward immediately after he had given his daughter away. The matron had dogmatically decreed he could only cope with a short outing. A large, uncontrolled tear slid down Sam Kane's drooping cheek. There are things that only a father should complete. This was one of them: a concluding moment for him… and a starting point for the young couple as they stepped out into a new chapter of their lives. "Who gives this woman to be this man's bride?" Reverend Bernard gently lent forward placed his hand in the invalid's limp hold. He paused and waited… a limp flutter of a squeeze. Yes… consent; a formal release… a blessing. Belle thrust her bouquet of white roses, sweet smelling gardenias and blue corn-flowers into Ali's hands and threw her arms around her Dad's neck, tilting the chair on its wheels unsteadily. "Oh, Daddy I love you. Thank you... thank you for being here," she murmured.

That was just about the end of every dry eye in the garden. Handkerchiefs were pulled from clutch-bags and pockets. The nurse unashamedly groped up her sleeve and pulled out a man sized kerchief and snorted quite inelegantly. "Don't worry Mr Kane… I don't care if you sleep for the rest of the year. We're going to stay and see your little baby girl get hitched right and proper."

Reverend Bernard blinked and cleared his throat. "Dearly beloved, we are gathered here today to join in holy matrimony Tobias Herbert Lawson and Mabel Joyce Kane." The words of the ceremony, unchanged and conventional, rolled off Reverend Bernard's tongue in a comforting liturgy. Belle reached out and held Toby's hand under their bower-framed altar as Reverend Bernard led the couple through their vows, sealed with rings and a kiss. Ali and Mal witnessed the formal register. With a nod and a breathless, wheezy "Amen!" from the Reverend, Em quickly returned to the keys and played the favourite by Charles Wesley "Love Divine, all loves excelling". The hymn concluded, the group clapped and every one smiled. A new family was born in Wattle Creek. Then Mr and Mrs Tobias Lawson were announced. They led their guests into Mrs Wallace's drawing room for refreshments, and then retired for their photograph portrait.

Nat stared at his kid brothers with a certain amount of fraternal pride. Toby was now a husband and Mal was talking with Ali with animated energy. It occurred to him at that moment that Mal was no longer a kid. He was moving and thinking as a man. He felt a familiar tug at his gut as he watched them. Ali had been in his life forever.

One of his earliest memories of Wattle Creek was when his mother had visited Mrs Dampier next door to welcome her new little baby girl. He had been so taken with the lace and white frills that splattered her nursery. Her tiny face seemed to smile even when asleep. She had seemed so fragile and from that moment he had helplessly taken on the role of protector. He was like an older brother - defender against the pranks of those pesky brothers. It was Nat who taught her to shoot spit-balls to defend herself against Fred and Mal, and their plots of sabotage. Under his tutorage, she became proficient at using a shanghai... and came out victor from one notable battle when she discovered an old nest of deserted chicken eggs to use as arsenal. The smell from that battle was still a note-worthy affair. Nat was the neighbour that stood up for her in the school-yard. He couldn't actually remember when this possessiveness started – it had just always been. It was strange that he had not felt jealous when he was told that Ali was dating Jimmy Golders. It was not even unexpected when they got engaged. He assumed that Ali had found her worthy someone who could now take over his role. Yet he had been furious when he found out about Jimmy's scandalous behaviour. At first it was the disgrace it reflected on his gender. Then it was rage at the pain inflicted on one so innocent. He knew Ali's heart gave devotion without reserve.

He stared at Mal talking with Ali. His little brother had better show her proper respect, or he once more would be readying his fist to defend her. Nat sat down with a drink in his hand as he watched on, protectively, guardedly, lest any should suspect him of improper surveillance. It was then, quite unexpectedly, that he realised that Ali would always be Ali to him. Her face was so familiar. Yet he knew what he felt for her was very different to the romance he witnessed between Toby and Belle. He would not have believed that something could change so dramatically as it did between those two. But it had. The neighbourly protection he felt for Ali was akin to that of a very dear friend, the sister he never had, not of a thwarted suitor. His anger with Jimmy Golders was as one who wanted to rectify the mistreatment of family. It came as a revelation to him that it would never be any different. Nat felt relieved. This was far less complicated than romance, and less complicated was good. Very good.

Emmaline carefully put down the lid to the little organ and packed away the music. Guests hung around in clusters waiting to go inside. Nat was among those who lingered at the door, letting the other guests through. "Miss Farrington, you play the organ well…" It was a compliment given easily, with a nod.

Emmaline blinked and looked twice. Was this Mr Lawson who blundered around the laundry full of flowers and buckets like a hulking Neanderthal? It caught her off guard. "Uh ahh. Sir? Oh. Thank you." She looked away self-conscious. That was certainly the most ungainly thing she had ever said.

"Perhaps you don't recognise me," he said apologetically, noticing her embarrassment, he indicated his Sunday best attire. "Nat Lawson. We were introduced a couple of days ago… out at Dampier's place. I think ivy was the focus at the time…"

She smiled tersely. Of course, she knew exactly who he was. How embarrassing! "Mr Lawson? A pleasure..." She made no attempt to be convincing. She turned to look for some escape, but the bottle-necked doorway seemed permanently clogged with chatting guests, not wanting to rush in out of the shaded, pleasant garden atmosphere.

Nat considered her, uncertain. This Emmaline obviously was not in a hurry to be pleasant. Well, he wasn't about to be pushing in where he wasn't wanted. He paused, as an afterthought crossed his mind. "Oh, just be wary if you're around those Levin twins: they have … pea-shooters." He grinned at her shock, and confided, "They have been systematically decorating ladies' hats during the ceremony, and in all honesty, that spit-ball is spoiling the effect of yours." He reached up and picked off a saliva soaked glob of paper from the brim of her hat. He handed it to her before he nodded and excused himself.

She stared at it sitting in her gloved hand in complete amazement. Never had she been given such a token! The barbarian may have chewed up the vile thing himself just to make a mockery of her. She shuddered with disgust and flicked it off into a pot-plant. "Err! How could he?" Country weddings! That's when she remembered her vow to Ali and quickly made her way through the lingering guests, to find how her cousin was fairing.

She found Ali perched on a seat in the courtyard beside Mrs Hollis who was giving studied attention to the guests, who were clumping in groups on the shaded lawn. Mrs Hollis was unwilling to engage in small talk with Alice Dampier. There was scandal – a love triangle with the mayor's daughter. Emmaline could palpate the disapproval. Em lightly fanned her face and mustered years of honed social graces into service. "It is very balmy in the open air. Summer weddings… Ma'am would you like a cool drink?"

Mrs Hollis acknowledged Emmaline and nodded as she handed her a glass. "Warm indeed." She disdainfully shifted her position away from Ali… whom she apparently held personally responsible for scandalous un-bridal like weather.

"Come Cousin, please introduce me to some of your neighbours… it is my one opportunity to experience the warmth of rural hospitality." She glanced around desperately at the sea of strangers. "Look there is Mr Lawson… we should go and pay our neighbourly respects." She gracefully extended her arm to Ali and led her, smiling as they made their way to where he stood, hugging the shade on the other side of the courtyard. Nat looked as comfortable as one might expect a dressed roast lamb to feel, waiting to be served on a platter.

They could sense Mrs Hollis throw daggers at their backs as they took their leave. Ali just nodded to the folk on the lawn and smiled forcefully through gritted teeth. "Thank you for rescuing me. I only wanted to sit for a while... without having to explain myself."

Em smiled. "No need to explain to me either! Ali, you're doing great... by far the handsomest lady here. Bride excepted of course..." Em had no intention of going to speak with Nat and quickly diverted their destination. "Ali, please introduce me to the Doctor and his wife..."

"Doctor and Mrs Wallace... my cousin, Emmaline Farrington," said Ali obligingly.

Em bobbed a greeting, as someone handed both her and Ali a glass of cool juice. "It is lovely that you opened your home for the wedding. Your garden... it is a beautiful setting." The sweeping sculptured lawns out the back, were quite a contrast to the cluttered cottage garden that greeted the guests at the front gate.

The Doctor smiled. "This is Louise's palate. I can take no credit for her passion. This is just the place for the photographer to immortalise this occasion in sepia. Am I the only one who finds it suitably ironic that extracted cuttlefish ink, that creature's natural camouflage, becomes the medium for photographic exposure," he asked with a grin.

"Their portrait should be lovely; they do make a handsome couple," offered Emmaline politely, a little bemused by his trivia.

"Oh yes, every Bride and Groom has the enormous privilege of looking youthful, gloriously groomed... and morbidly dismal."

His wife nudged him affectionately. "Harold has a particular distaste for grim wedding portraits. He declares

270

memories should be able to depict celebration and delight, not made look like a funeral moment. Even though it has been explained that the event has a certain element of sobriety and photography requires sustained postures that could never capture frivolity. I feel it cannot be considered inappropriate. Yet, he absolutely refuses to admit it. For us – it meant we never had a wedding portrait taken."

Emmaline warmed to this lady's unaffected manner; fancy making such a transparent confession to a complete stranger. It should have reeked of impropriety, but it didn't feel that way at all. "I must also confess that I have never seen a glowing bride and contented groom in a portrait. They all do seem to be suffering under the severe punishment of being sentenced to the vilest of institutions."

"Would you suggest the institution of marriage is a vile state?" spoke a voice at her elbow.

Emmaline jolted, her drink tipping in her glass. Nat Lawson? Where did he come from? She quickly gathered her wits that seemed to have scattered themselves all over the lawn. She glanced at Ali who seemed completely immune to his presence. Emmaline turned to Nat and said, "Mr Lawson, *marriage* is a state that has less bearing on the nature of the institution and more on those who would inhabit it. So vile it can be… however my optimistic belief remains that marriage can also be quite satisfactory."

Mrs Wallace smiled, "Ah, I would go one step further and suggest that given the proper attention by both parties, the institution of marriage has every potential to be a very contented state. Why settle for anything less than complete happiness?"

Emmaline raised her eyebrows and blinked twice. "How long have you been married Mrs Wallace that you feel so ardently towards the state of marriage?"

Mrs Wallace's eyes twinkled with a mischievous glint. Em studied that with interest. This lady had her intrigued. "I could say thirty-four years and five months, but I fear that would give too much away. Just to say... that sometimes it feels like a mere moment, and the glowing bride we speak of... is just a heart-beat away!"

Emmaline thought of all the hard-bitten, cynical acquaintances that lined her Grandmother's drawing room. She glanced over to the Doctor. "But is it possible to have a contented groom so long into a marriage as well?"

The Doctor smiled and touched his wife's arm tenderly, "Contented? It is true we have no frowning portrait to deny it! But perhaps 'contented' is a little too comfortable a word... it implies a lackadaisical and careless approach that is not in keeping with my nature. I would prefer to say my devotion is 'ecstatic' or 'crazed with affection'." Emmaline did not quite know how to take his frivolous remarks.

"Harold! You tease these young ones. It does them no harm to see that marriage, as God designed it, is worthy of our attention."

"My dear, you are a fraction of a moment too late for such explorations. The bridal couple have completed their frowning for the photograper, and all good manners now dictate that we must lavish the honoured duo with compliments and politeness." They all turned and clapped the newly weds as they made their way through to the tables that had been loaded with a delicious bounty.

33.

Em linked arms with Ali as they strolled out along the road that wound through waves of tall bleached grass, a light breeze rippling the surface like the ocean. Their sun hats and long skirts billowed like yachts bobbing on this sun-drenched bay. "Ali, what would you think if I asked Uncle Alf and Aunt Alma about staying on for a couple of weeks? I would love to spend a little time here before I go back to ELLIOT HOUSE."

Ali looked at her. "Why, I thought after experiencing a full-blown country wedding, you'd be dying to escape back to the refuge of your Grandmother's parlour." Ali was not being entirely cynical. A cool, quiet, muted Victorian parlour sounded like the perfect sanctuary.

Em blinked. Every one had been pussy-footing around Ali and her broken engagement. The Dampier household skirted the subject as if breathing a word on the topic would somehow cause an outbreak of black plague. Now that Toby and Belle's wedding was over, they avoided talking about that as well. Yet Ali brought up the topic without hesitation. Perhaps it was her way of saying she didn't want protecting… or denial, any longer.

"Hectic describes it pretty well." Em's sensibilities were shocked by the extraordinary efforts gone to practical joking. Someone had unhitched the buggy, but in such a way their horse gave all appearances of being securely harnessed. And Toby had even checked the straps… as well as the bolts and the axles of the sulky. As he flicked the reigns, he and Belle were left sitting in a horseless seat as some generous fellow spooked the horse and sent it careering down the road in its full harness and poles. Neither did they suspect that the room where they were staying was set with flour bombs and booby-traps that were as creative as they were numerous. The couple were doused in showers of flour as Toby carried his bride across the threshold... just the thing for the groom of the town's baker.

Such complex escapades were not part of the weddings Emmaline attended, but it had a kind of genuine warmth behind it. There was nothing malicious in their pranks. Regardless of what people thought about their sudden romance and their rather unconventional plans, everyone really wished the best for them. That was what she appreciated most. Em smiled at the thought. "It's just that I was thinking… Ali, once I would have given one of my eye-teeth to stay here. Now I can! I am of age. I can choose certain things for myself; I don't want to be excluded any longer."

Ali stopped and turned to her, shocked. If Jimmy didn't want to be with her, she had sort of assumed no one would. It was like she had a placard hung around her neck that read: "Jilted and unsavoury woman: poor company – avoid at all cost." Here someone was taking no notice of the sign. It was a rather curious idea. "You want to stay?"

"Of course."

"For me?"

"There is certainly no other reason I can think of." Well, there were some practical benefits of course. As a girl she enjoyed the freedom of riding just like every other kid around

Wattle Creek, but she had lost her confidence. Grandmother Edith's insistence on a side-saddle and nothing above a very slow trot frustrated her. Horse riding was something that she thought she might like to try again... if the occasion arose.

"Well, you were talking with Nat Lawson at the wedding..."

Em laughed out loud. "The chair and bench man? He who only had eyes for yourself because you were unintentionally prettier than the bride? No. I can assure you that I have a beau at home who has more manners and income than Nat Lawson could ever accomplish. I expect Richard and I will be engaged when I return to ELLIOT HOUSE."

She looked across at Ali who paled a little, the lines around her eyes twitching restlessly. Em paused and reached out to hold her hand. Then she said very gently, "Are you shocked that I would say that? You know Ali... Belle told me about your engagement, and I am sorry. I really am. But it won't really protect you if I go around apologising for my life and pretending it doesn't exist."

It took a while, but something inside Ali smiled... just slightly. "You know, it is a relief in a way. You are the first person who doesn't seem scared of me."

"Oh, rot Ali, you have more spunk than that. I'm sure of it."

Ali paused and quietly confessed, "I nearly couldn't do it. It was too hard."

Em swallowed. She had heard the rumours. Perhaps there was more truth in them than she had allowed. Still, there was an element of pride that refused her to back down now that she had made the declaration of confidence in Ali. "There you go. You said so yourself: *nearly*. That means that there is something inside that still wants to fight."

"Mum put you up to this, didn't she? She's asked you to stay on…"

"Oh, Ali. Please don't take away the glory of my one good idea! I thought so much about those letters. I want to see what it will be like to be back here for a while. This is as much for me, as for you. I'm not even sure your parents will be inclined, with another wedding to plan and all."

Ali's lips held a grim thin line. "I'm sure Fred and Janie will be exclusive enough not to notice… at least for a while anyway. You know, it has been nice having you around. I'm sure if there is any doubt about you staying… I can add weight to the argument. Belle and Toby will be leaving Wattle Creek soon…" It seemed Em's proposal was a mercy beyond her wildest hopes, filling the pending vacuum.

"Ahh, there's my girl. Ali! I feel like I'm nine years old and plotting our next great adventure!"

"Perhaps we are."

Nat sat quietly with his Mum in the lounge room sipping coffee. He couldn't believe how long it was taking for Toby and Belle to excuse themselves after their evening coffee. He feigned intense concentration on the calculations he was making on his notepad and barely grunted whenever they tried to engage in polite social chitchat. Even his mother was deep into reading an old novel that had not seen the light of a lamp for at least seven years. Eventually, she got up and walked over to the mantle clock and wound it deliberately. That was the mark of concluding the day. She kissed her sons goodnight and trailed off to her downstairs room. At that Toby shrugged and led his bride off to bed. He couldn't explain his reluctance to retire tonight. Soon they would be leaving. This felt more final than when he had gone away to study the first time.

Finally, Nat stepped quietly out onto the back verandah that overlooked their yard. He peered into the night and nodded. "Have they turned out the lamp yet?" he asked barely above a whisper. Em jumped when he spoke. She had been miles away.

"The light is still on in their window. Do you think they know?"

"Tell them to wait a little longer... just to be sure..."

Em gave the signal, and Ali sat down wearily in a cane chair and waited. This was just as hard as the wedding day. Once she would have been the main conspirator. Finally, she could hear the whispered count-down out on the porch. Four, three, two.... one!

Instantly pandemonium erupted! Cans and saucepans, horns and whistles, jars and tins filled with stones were thumped and rattled, banged and shaken. A hullabaloo of yahoos and piercing whistles filled the night and someone let off a cracker or two. Kids screamed and yelled as they ran sticks up and down the corrugated iron walls of the shed, delighted that tonight, no adult was going to "hush" them. Dogs barked and Henry Hills brought along his famous howling healer that was more dingo than cattle dog, as a special treat. She was howling up a storm! A baby cried and to Ali - that was the only sound that made sense.

The chant started to rise: "Mr and Mrs Lawson, Mr and Mrs Lawson!" They would carry on… escalating the bedlam indefinitely until the newly weds emerged from their bedroom and served the supper everyone brought along. It was a community game: Who could survive a tin-kettling the longest? Yet it wasn't just survival, they had to be able to achieve that diplomatic blend of waiting and hosting, irritation and amusement, being caught off guard and being expectant. Cut it short and the fun is all over too soon; wait excessively long and it is considered a community offence of the highest order. It is an initiation test of social skills, selected and agreed upon by the community. Most brides dread and delight in it all at the same time.

With laudable adeptness in timing, Belle and Toby emerged in their dressing gowns, hair tousled and coy grins on their dials. Three cheers roared as the home brew was set out. Phil Pollock pulled out his banjo… and the din miraculously turned to a carnival. Some brought their hand-made instruments… the rhythm makers of the bush and the kids started dancing. Mrs Lawson – junior, and Mrs Lawson – senior… opened up the doors to the verandah and lamps were set out as party food emerged out of picnic hampers and hidden baskets. So let the party begin.

Wattle Creek was changing… life was moving on at a bullet's speed. It was essential that little moments of celebration were captured before they passed and were lost forever. Farewell Toby, goodbye Belle. More than one person from The

Creek looked back on that night and felt it ushered in a new season.

34.

Ali snipped around her father's hair with a deft hand. He was calculating something on a slate while she razored his neck and trimmed his side burns. He blew the clipped hair out of the way, and continued his computations undisturbed. Alma was sitting in a chair near the open window allowing the morning light to fall onto her darning, her needle swiftly weaving a grid across the heel of an already patched sock. It was her constant challenge to keep this dairy farmer's wardrobe complete with hole-less socks, and waterproof boots. Alma's father had been Wattle Creek's cobbler – the town's master boot-maker. She grew up with stockings and boots being her family's pride and priority, much like good cream and butter were for her husband. It wasn't right to compromise some things regardless of the inconvenience of sustaining the standard.

Fred came in and started sifting through papers on the china hutch. "Has anyone seen the catalogue that came the other day? Janie asked me to take it over to her house today."

Alma looked up from her darning work. "I gave it to Em, Dear. Ali will be done here soon, and then she will be ready for you."

Fred mumbled something and abruptly left to find Em and the missing catalogue. Later, as he passed the door, his mother hailed him. "She's ready Fred… don't keep Ali waiting dear."

He stopped and looked awkwardly at his sister. He shrugged uncomfortably. "No need to wait for me. I won't be getting you to cut my hair anymore Sis…"

Janie had already openly confessed that hair-cutting was not in her repertoire of domestic skills. It was a duty Ali felt safe to continue, without treading on his insecure fiancé's toes. But it seemed that in her possessiveness, even this was not beyond her touch. "Doesn't she want me touching your head? Come on Fred. I'm your sister."

"Janie thinks I should get it done professionally in town… at Hendricks' Barber Shop." Just then Em arrived at the door with the mail catalogue in her hand. She was immediately confronted by the awful silence that occurs when someone makes a very improper noise in a public place. All eyes stared at Fred in disbelief except his father, who carefully continued to work his calculations on the slate.

Finally, Alf, not lifting his gaze said matter-of-factly, "Now why would you be paying old Hendricks to butcher your head Son, when Ali can do it tidy, and much, much cheaper?"

"Dad – you don't get cheaper than 'free'," said Ali emphatically.

He did not shift his gaze from his slate. "Guess that's my point."

"Hendricks is not that bad really. Janie feels that a professional barber is more… proper." He didn't look either convinced or thrilled about the idea.

Alma was shocked. Her eyes darted worriedly from Ali to Em and back to her husband. "But Fred dear, Ali has done your hair since she could hold a pair of scissors and a blade. Don't you think that this is a little unfair?"

Alf returned to his calculations with renewed vigour. "Goodness boy, if you're compelled to part with your hard earned pennies, why not pay your sister and be done with it."

"Pa," Fred sound exasperated. Trampling on loyalties distressed him, but he had a new loyalty now that he was obliged to accommodate.

Ali blinked her eyes. She remembered what Em had said: *"You're tougher than I ever gave you credit for. You will do fine!"* Suddenly Ali burst out laughing, and sat down shaking her head. She felt stronger. She was not the one being pushed about by the whims of another. It gave her a feeling of freedom that had eluded her for a long time. "Don't fret yourself Fred. If that is what you want, then give it a try." Fred's eyes widened, in relief.

Em was suddenly assaulted by the idea that his farmer-boy good looks were wasted on dairy cows and the impetuous Janie. How good he would look in a society jacket and smartly polished boots. Ali folded up the throw apron, and smiled a little. "I'll even fix up the mess when you get back. Still for free."

Malachi Lawson sat in the kitchen chatting to Mrs Dampier with a mug of hot tea. He casually dunked the biscuit in his hand and ate slowly, savouring its nutty flavour. The hours spent here as a kid after coming in from rabbiting with Fred, gave him status higher than mere guest. "Mum was very definite Mrs Dampier.... just come. She knows how busy you have been… and thought it would give you a break to have a meal at our place."

Mal smiled. He knew her well enough to know that it didn't matter what he said. She would come piled with things to contribute. He couldn't resist giving her some guidance. "Do you know Nat has never tasted one of your apricot pies? I told him exactly what he has missed all these years but he doesn't believe me!"

"All those times he's been over here? Really! I can't imagine how that has happened."

Mal laughed. "Yeah, I tell him. His loss. Remember – Ma said. Absolutely: just come." He could not be accused of not delivering the message accurately.

"Of course, dear. Tell your mother we will be delighted to accept. I do have some of my sweet preserves here in the pantry…", and when Mal left she had already pulled down a couple of jars, so that the pastry could be baked first thing tomorrow - in the cool of the morning before church.

Ali sat on the back step wrapped in her dressing gown with a coffee mug in her hand as Fred pulled on his boots to go to the cow-bails in the crisp cool morning air. "Fred! Are you seriously going to Church like that?"

"Actually, I'm heading to the cow-bales. If you don't think my hair is suitable for public scrutiny… well, I'll stay home from Church. Janie wouldn't mind… I could go over there and have some time to ourselves."

"You can't go like that. Your head looks like it got stuck in the chaff-cutter…" And it wasn't just his hair that suffered. "Fred, he cut you! Besides, we're having lunch with Lawson's remember?"

Fred paused. He looked like a boy grounded from playing with his mates. "Don't suppose being a hermit until it grows some is really necessary. Janie mi…"

"Don't be silly. Janie has some weird ideas, but even I can't possibly imagine that she can be delighted that you look like a walking eagles' nest."

Fred bristled in her defence. "She doesn't know. Hasn't seen it yet…"

"It's your head Fred! You can't avoid her forever. At some point you are going to have to go and see her…"

It was true. Nor could he go around wearing his hat forever. "Well, the cows don't care none!"

"Cows don't go to church! And even if you miss this week… it isn't going to fix itself. Look. Sit here on the step. I'll tidy it up in five. I won't hold you up." Ali already had her scissors and comb in her pinafore pocket and whipped them out. She gently pushed him seated to the step. He didn't even seriously resist. She stared in horror at the mutilated mess as she combed through the uneven chunks. "Hendricks's getting worse. Only the mentally deranged would do this to themselves! It's criminal."

"Thanks." Fred went very quiet. "He was under the weather a bit… but it seemed like a waste to go all the way back into town again later. There'd be no telling if he'd be any better next time anyhow."

"Does the Doctor know …about Hendriks?" Ali snipped and evened, combed and razored. In the end it was very short.

"The whole world knows."

"It's a dying shame. He has such a great little shop. Look, tell Janie that you wanted to get value for your money and you asked for it to be short!"

"I thought you'd be mad… and do the whole 'told you so' thing… since you and Janie don't get on…"

Ali's grip stalled and she almost cut too close. She loved her brother. It never occurred to her he would be hurt by her feud with Janie. "We think differently that's all…"

The dark morning air, and the quiet smell of morning coffee settled over them. "Oh Ali… Sis - the fun we used to have… well, it changes, that's all. Janie loves me… she makes me laugh."

"So, this is my fault?"

"No… I ain't saying that. I'm just saying things are different. Janie ain't perfect… but she ain't the devil either. And I love her."

Ali paused. In fairness she had to admit that her brother deserved his shot at love. What if everyone only got one shot? Had she missed hers? "I'll remember that Fred…" she whispered. She flicked off the cut hair from his shirt with a cloth, plonked his hat back on his head and gave him a shove. "Your dairy awaits Sir Alfred. Be gone with you!"

35.

The congregation shuffled to their feet to sing the final doxology. Alf looked at his pocket watch. Reverend Bernard had gone on a little longer today. He should mention that to the session clerk. The minister cleared his throat and instead of leading the strong starting note, he spoke firmly. "Brothers and Sisters in Christ..." The organist stalled as he tentatively pulled an envelope from his pastoral robes and a heavy silence thickened the air as the fidgeting quietened. They sensed the gravity of the moment – Reverend Bernard rarely did things spontaneously, and this was way off script. "I have here a letter. It is my incumbent duty to inform you that the content of this communication is to tender my resignation from this parish, effective immediately. I assure you that it is due to the gravest of personal reasons that I retire from this position."

A wave of gasps and whispers rippled through the congregation in shock. Reverend Laurie Bernard had been here since... well, fifteen... eighteen years... maybe more. The organist seemed uncertain what to do and so proceeded to start the doxology again, but only murmurings and anxious whispers accompanied the music. The final cadence and three-fold amen did little to close the meeting with its usual tidy conclusion. With the last wavering chord, the church erupted with every demand of confirmation, explanation, and clarification. Can people just resign from the call of God? Can a minister just leave a church like you might leave a restaurant after a meal? All those years of unwavering service, didn't that count for anything? No one exactly said it, but why would he leave when he wasn't dead?

Reverend Bernard had little to say that extended the explanation given in the letter. He had just this week received a communication that his beloved sister was seriously ill and was rapidly declining. He desired to spend her final hours attending to her care. He could not delay. Someone suggested special leave, compassionate leave... any sort of leave... but the Reverend shook his head. "One knows in his heart when it is time to move aside. God has blessed us, but it is time to usher in a new season..." That sounded quite spiritually profound... although no one knew exactly what it meant. Except to say he was determined to resign and stay resigned.

The congregation continued their anxious speculations well after the church would normally be locked up and deserted. An urgent meeting was instantly called. As Reverend Bernard walked out the door, there was decisiveness about his step. He was not coming back. Someone hovered around to give the news that the manse was indeed all packed up. Only the furniture and household items remained... even the cat was gone. Everyone knew that it wouldn't be easy to get an itinerant preacher to come to Wattle Creek. The announcement brought with it the wind of change, and that inevitably had an omen of restlessness about it. Life was not as it should be... if for no other reason than it was not as it always had been.

Alma and Alf drove home slowly, each absorbed in their thoughts. It seemed inconceivable that Reverend Bernard would not be there next week to welcome them at the door and then to put them to sleep during his sermon. Suddenly their comfortable and predictable world, even if at times it seemed a little dry, had at least been safe in its dependability.

Alma finally spoke. The shock of it unsettled her. "I had absolutely no idea. I mean… did anyone even know he had a sister? How incredible that he would want to leave Wattle Creek!"

Alf nodded. It was not often he was thrown by something. "Well, I guess he wants to be there for her. That's what family does."

"All I'm saying is that it is all very sudden… and it makes you wonder." She paused. "Fancy thinking that Belle and Toby's wedding will be the last ceremony that Reverend Bernard ever performs at Wattle Creek. What if they can't get another minister? It throws a whole new light on Fred and Janie's plans. I don't want them married in the Catholic Church Alf. We might even have to go over to Mallee Hill." She lingered to let the significance of her observations penetrate the silence.

"Now Alma – don't be getting yourself all het-up about problems that don't exist yet. We'll just have to take it as it comes. Who knows… the man might get half way down the road and decide to come back."

Ali also kept turning the news over in her mind. It would not have been honest to think that she wasn't troubled by his resignation. It was another example of the lack of stability in an unreliable world. But she was rather encouraged to realise she wasn't devastated by it. She had never found the Reverend warm… but she hardly remembered anyone else. She wondered who among the congregation counted the old bachelor as their friend... not just some remote, austere father-figure. She couldn't identify even one.

Fred leant back, his Sunday hat hard down on his unseemly short-cropped hair. It was all a lot of hoo-hah. Someone else will turn up, appointed by the pope or whoever organises these things, in time to marry them. It was better to let the man go in peace.

Emmaline sat in the back of the buggy, musing over her personal observations. She had watched the trauma of change dawn upon each face, but it was the older ones who were most rocked by the news. She couldn't help wondering what would have given the announcement the appropriate amount of decorum. Urgency always left the unfortunate taste of shock in people's mouths. Preamble and the subtle hints that lessen the shock are not very viable in "effective immediately" decisions. If the man felt he had few choices, what had to be done, was best done quickly. Surely.

Em thought it was a relief that they were going out to lunch – even if it was next door. It would provide relief from talking about the minister's resignation given she did not immediately belong to the parish. However, from the moment that they set foot on their driveway, right up to serving coffee after the meal, nothing else even hovered on the horizon of conversation.

"No one begrudges the man his family duties - it is admirable in a way... but *is* this the way it should be done... springing it on us like this?"

"Alma, I couldn't agree more," said Mrs Lawson seriously. "It is not so much us... we can cope well enough.

Goodness knows we've had worse shocks than this and survived, but some of the others... I'm not sure that it was handled in the most appropriate manner."

Ali suspected that some were probably more disturbed by the fact they had not been privy to the "inside news". Gossip of this magnitude generates power. What is more, there was now no prospect of manipulating such privileged knowledge to any influential advantage.

Em listened to the circle of conversation go around and around and said little. She felt detached. The whole thing had been terminated too fast – like the amputation of someone else's limb: over and done with. She could see that people were disappointed, perhaps sad... even angry, that the ceremony around saying goodbye to the shepherd who had guided them for so many years, was abruptly cut short. Mal and Fred had given up and left the table, urgent business in the stable used to make their escape. Even Nat, who generally relished the politics of life – whatever arena, was struggling with the need to rehash it over and over. It was done, irreversible, so the best thing was to get on your horse and move on. He wasn't one for massive amounts of verbal processing. Em looked over at him. She could tell he was unsympathetic to the conversation, and thinking about other things. In a way it gave her a sense of common ground. "So Nat, this man has always been your minister. This news must affect you also. Do you feel forsaken by The Cloth because of this sudden announcement?"

He looked up with interest. This was the first real exchange that Emmaline had initiated voluntarily. He smiled at her efforts to make something out of nothing. "Whether I feel forsaken or not, is not up to the Reverend. It was not his job to mollycoddle me."

Em raised her eyebrows. The direct, no-fuss answer was not what she expected. It made her feel uncomfortable and curious at the same time. Richard would have shrouded his response in smooth platitudes, an odd blending of irrelevant ideas that usually made no sense. She could imagine how Richard might have responded; *"Take it from me, sheep without a shepherd wander aimlessly through the wilderness, vulnerable to any wolf in sheep's clothing. It absolutely is his responsibility…"* She wondered why she was so sure Richard would consider he had licence to speak at all, especially since he didn't like churches and attended just often enough to retain his "club membership". At least, that was how he put it. Richard always had an opinion. That confident self-assurance was one of the safe things about Richard. He and his flunky gentlemen friends never had any doubt about what angle to take.

Funny that Nat was equally self-assured, but head on. At ELLIOT HOUSE Emmaline would have offered more cake and engaged in her own evasive action by steering the conversation to safer ground. Here on the Lawson's verandah, she felt an expectation that even as a visitor, she was to submit a tuppence worth of reflections. Mrs Dampier cut another serve of her apricot pie, and put the saucer in front of Nat. Emmaline watched him tackle it like restraining a stray calf for branding. She thought it the most undignified approach to pie she could imagine. Nat grunted his appreciation. It met every acclaimed expectation. "Aunt Alma, this pie is as good as Mal

292

has been sprouting all these years. You've been holding out on me."

Alma beamed. "You go ahead and make up for lost time. I hardly know how you missed out like you did."

Emmaline felt put out. Alma wasn't his aunt. How dare he be so familiar? All this fuss over a pie! She pointedly went back to her observations about the minister, steering the conversation back to the topic she had wanted to avoid. "But Nat, surely the shepherd of the flock should think about the care of his charges after he moves on to greener pastures. This is his trust; regardless how urgent his exit may be."

Nat raised his brow and looked a little puzzled. Why couldn't she just speak plain, without making everything sound so high and mighty? It was kinda draining, trying to carry on conversation when so much effort had to go into translating everything she said into normal words. He shrugged and had another spoonful of pie. "Whatta ya mean? I know Wattle Creek is not exactly paradise, but going to nurse a dying relative is hardly greener pastures," he said finally through the crumbs.

Emmaline cringed as she watched a shower of crumbs fall to the cloth. She was shocked that her observations weren't considered articulate and clever. Richard would have thought it a very revealing question. "Yes, well. I guess not. It is just that a minister of religion is responsible for the care of his congregation. So – regardless of whether he needs to leave quickly or not, surely that role cannot be abandoned…"

"Why not?"

Emmaline shook her ears, as if water was stopping her from hearing correctly. "Over the years he is the person the community has looked to for support and care. There is history in that trust."

"But he's resigned. It's not his problem anymore."

"It's not just a job... it's a sacred calling. People feel quite deserted in times like this."

"I don't."

"Why ever not? He is the shepherd of the flock!"

"So, you are disappointed I am not reliant on an old man to gauge how I feel? You would have it that I feel abandoned and desperate?"

"No – not at all. Put like that I would expect a degree of independence from you. But there are others to consider here. Not all have your sense of self-reliance. What of those individuals... should they be cast alone into the sea, ship-wrecked by lack of care?"

Nat looked at her warily. His lips were pursed in an amused sort of line. He couldn't seriously believe that she was one hundred percent in earnest concerning her assertions. It was just a little too dramatic. "I believe your question was directed to my personal reaction to Bernard's resignation. I can't speak for anyone else."

"I find it hard to believe that you don't you have an opinion..."

"Opinions I have in plenty. Airing them isn't always entirely constructive. What's done is done. Those who are worried about the lack, will no doubt work to sort it out."

"Is that you... are you worried about the lack of pastoral guidance for the people in your congregation during this crisis?"

Nat considered his challenger. If he said he wasn't worried, she would consider him heartless. Heartless is not his style, but he wasn't going to enter the circle of gossip-mongers who were out fishing for a scandal by getting over-involved in what was none of their business. "If the choice is between being seen as heartless or meddling… then I would have to lean towards heartless. You are right: I have no great concern about the souls of our congregation being 'shipwrecked'. There are sufficient good people about to see to it that they will be cared for. Like most things around here… people rally when people need to rally. We don't need a public memorandum to look out for each other. You just do it." It was obvious to him, but then a city girl wouldn't have a clue.

"You seem confident of that. Are you one of those good people who rally?" persisted Em.

Nat almost laughed. She wasn't going to give up easily. Did she need to have him nailed down as some weak, washy, religious type? He could guarantee he wouldn't be doing any super-sensitive morning teas for anyone who wanted to cry over this. Prying wasn't his thing. There were others more equipped for the touchy-feely soppy stuff. He didn't know who exactly, and that didn't bother him. He was responsible for looking after his own back-yard first and foremost. He had never baulked at giving a hand when a hand was needed. That would have to suffice for now.

36.

The committee sat around the table. Doc Wallace had finally asked for a vote. Nat gnawed the end of his pencil looking at the others as they considered the options. Alf Dampier wanted to wait until more prospective candidates put their hat in the ring. Henry Hills was of the opinion that waiting would cause an untimely death to their congregation. He'd seen a lot of churches go down the gurgler because they weren't able to place someone, anyone, in the top job quickly. At least – that is what he said. And then there was lanky Phil Pollock. He wanted to pray, and Nat was pretty sure he was talking about a week's sabbatical of serious, down-on-your-knees pleading-by-your-bed intercession.

Nat chewed violently on the wood and snapped the pencil between his teeth. He sat bolt upright and tried to cover the boredom that prompted the energetic munching. As far as he was concerned, there was not much of an upside to this sort of deliberation. Nat could think of a million other places he'd rather be on a Thursday night. But Dr Wallace had asked him to be involved, and well, he could hardly say no.

Okay, Nat had to admit there were a few advantages that swayed his willingness to be here. There was a lot of talk about "God's man for the job", that the Lord would call his chosen to the fold. Religious mumbo-jumbo. Why didn't people just call a spade a spade? When it came to being spiritual, Nat did not get it at all. Here was just a practical opportunity to inject some young blood into the position.

Besides, he could hardly resist the chance to show that Farrington girl he was a man of action. That was far more important than just being one of those "caring-feely" types.

Phil Pollock cleared his throat. "Now Doc, I know this is your show, but I reckon we gunna be pray'n before we start throwing our vote in the hat. This is too important to go stuffin' around like old hens in a chook-yard. We need the Lord's guidance," he said matter-of-factly.

The Doc just smiled in an accepting, agreeable way. "Phil – you know better than to think this is my show. That is why we have brought everyone here together… to find God's mind on the matter. I couldn't agree with you more."

Nat frowned to himself. He had always considered praying to be an open admission that they were joining ranks with the greying female contingent. Surely real men could make a decision without emasculating themselves on the need to consult the Almighty on every little thing. It was pathologically co-dependent.

Nat nodded sagely and mentally filed the need to ask the Doctor for a more specific meeting agenda next time. They could save hours of their time with a little bit of trimming. Phil bowed his head. "Almighty Father God. You know everything about everything; and we're simple folk. But I reckon You've got real solutions; and we're wanting to be in step with 'em. Your Book says that if we lack wisdom, we just need to ask. Lord we know You give mighty generously, and we take You at Your Word. We're askin' You to bring the right man along. In Jesus name, Amen."

It was over before Nat could settle himself in for the long haul. He blinked and sat straight up when it finished. Phil sounded like he was chatting about the weather with the Guy who could turn it on or off. It wasn't at all how Reverend Bernard prayed.

Nat remembered the Reverend once said that prayer was where God and man met in the supernatural realm of humility. Bernard said that humility was not a trait of people naturally gravitate towards, because we generally only look out for ourselves. He said that humility was something we have to consciously put on – like a coat, and that's where we got the phrase, "being clothed in humility". Nat couldn't really understand why it was a sermon he remembered. It was probably because he found it quite confusing and had gone home and made some very practical interpretations on what "being clothed in humility" might actually mean.

Experience told Nat that humility more realistically means, "humiliating". It wasn't too hard to work out any number of recognised and acceptable religious ways that were humiliating, and in doing so he defined his own theology of prayer. He was sure praying in long sentences was a fail-safe approach to being a humble prayer. That also made it exhausting and not something one would want to do very often. He was confident that remembering to use a lot of "thee's" and "thou's" and other antiquated King's English words, was also helpful when praying. One of his favourite things was doing that Catholic cross thing across his chest. He had no idea what that was about, but it looked very sincere – more than the protestant's routine of bowed head and clutched hands. That just looked desperate.

When he thought about it, there was only one thing about the mechanics of praying that was useful, and that was the art of eye-squinting. This was his favourite aspect of the hallowed rite – it meant he could pray and keep an eye on things at the same time. Nat became a proficient squinter at an early age. He had to, so that he could keep tabs on Tobias and Mal, since his mother was often on the organ roster. Back then, his young brothers had been terrors at pulling pranks while Bernard launched into his marathon-long prayers. Once the boys conducted a full rodent dissection with their pocket-knives under the pews and then attached bits of it to Mitsey Timms' new patent leather shoes. Even for boys – that was kinda gross.

So, Nat figured he had the prayer thing pretty much nailed, and now Phil Pollock just pulled the bottom log from the pile of neatly stacked ideas, and it was in serious danger of crashing. "Was that enough prayer Phil? I mean… it seemed a bit short. Anyone else want a go?" Nat asked tentatively. The Doc seemed unconcerned but looked around expectantly.

Phil shrugged. "I ain't got Reverend Bernard's book learning, and it ain't any good pretendin' I'm a master at fancy words. If Jesus can take simple fishermen and use them to build the church from scratch… I reckon he ain't above taking the heart of a simple farmer too. He knows what I mean without me having to sound all superior about it… by being something I ain't." Something within Nat's heart applauded. That made sense to him.

No one had anything to add, so Doctor Wallace smiled. "Well then. On to business..." They had put forward the three names; their references were brief and unembellished.

One had a similar profile to Bernard... educated. However, he'd been an assistant-minister for a millennium, and was now looking for his own church. He sounded old, frustrated, and wishy-washy.

The second candidate was coming on middle aged, married with six kids, a dog, a budgie and two cats. The whole affair sounded like a zoo. There was a smear of something unidentifiable across the page of his letter.

Nat tried to stay serious as the last applicant's letter was read. "Dear Brethren at Wattle Creek, My name was Lloyd C. W. H. Jacobson. I am born and bred in the city and yet mysteriously feel a burden to minister in the country..." Yeah right! Was one of the criteria to having the call of God that you also had to be a little dim-witted? Mr Lloyd C. W. H. Jacobson obviously had no idea how to win points in the country. Announcing roots in the suburban world and alluding to a missionary call, similar to one to darkest Africa was not a good way to start.

Nat's brother Tobias had told this young man about the position and given him a reference. Nat hoped Tobias wasn't losing his edge by going up to the city too. There might be truth in the idea that if you run with turkeys long enough, you start to gobble. Still, Toby's friend didn't come with a portable menagerie, and he wasn't old and frustrated. Even if he had no idea about the real world, Lloyd C. W. H. Jacobson fulfilled Nat's priority of injecting young blood into the role. He also didn't sound like he was going to upset the apple-cart too much. By the sensible process of logical elimination Jacobson had his vote. Besides, his kid brother had endorsed him. Doc handed out ballot. When they were collected and counted, one went for the Menagerie family, one preferred the Bernard-look-a-like, and three went with Lloyd C. W. H. Jacobson. They had a recommendation to take to the congregation.

Generally speaking, the wheels of protocol turn slowly in Wattle Creek country. It was hard to explain how the recommendation to call Reverend Lloyd C. W. H. Jacobson, was voted on and passed in such a short time of the resignation of Reverend Bernard. It was also inexplicable why no one complained on how inappropriate the brief period of deliberation was, or how inexperienced this new candidate obviously was. He didn't even have grey hair. Normally, such warning flags would grind everything to a halt. Instead, little proverbs were whispered among the pews in support of the move. Mrs Hollis had it on her mind that "a stitch in time saves nine", although the extent of their decision resembled nothing at all to do with mending. Nat was relieved Mrs Hollis had decided to make her stand for positive action. That alone compelled people to bow to weight of her influence because they knew how it would be, had she decided to drag her heels in this process.

The congregation filed passed, each giving him a critique on the service and his first sermon. "Reverend," gushed Mrs Hollis as Reverend Jacobson took her gloved hand and bowed over it graciously at the Church door. "It was delightful to hear teaching on the Love chapter," she said with raised eyebrows and her uncharacteristically red lipstick smiling all over her face. It gave her a quizzical appearance that could be best described as a startled possum caught red-handed stealing apples. "It has been years since we have heard such a sermon."

The Reverend brushed his unruly fair hair back out of his eyes. It gave him a charming schoolboy look that had Mrs Hollis irresistibly wanting to mother and flirt with him at the same time, regardless of her seventy-three years. "I believe it is a topic close to the heart of God. It is wonderful that you share His passions, Mrs Hollis," he said slightly embarrassed.

"Passions…" she said softly. "Oh, and please, call me Nancy." Everyone then knew that Mrs Hollis was in crisis. No one, in the known history of Wattle Creek had ever been given the golden invitation to address Mrs Hollis by her Christian name on a first meeting.

It bemused the young man that the topic of most interest regarding the new minister was his marital status. Mrs Hemming was first off the rank. "You'll be coming out to visit my bed-ridden father, Reverend. Why don't you come in the afternoon and stay for one of my special roast dinners? Phyllis will be pleased for company her own age… and young Tommy has a horse he has been working with… he'd love to show it off." Many more invitations were extended to the handsome new minister. Before he knew it, he had a string of engagements. He saw it as a blessing from God that he wouldn't need to eat at the hotel for the foreseeable future.

Phil Pollock shook his hand warmly and said, "We're mighty glad the Lord ain't blind and deaf. He's seen our plight and heard our prayers. Welcome to The Creek, Reverend." Lloyd looked the tall fellow in the eye and smiled at the warmth and sincerity he saw there. Phil felt like family. That was definitely agreeable. Most of his invitations made him feel like a new novelty show-pony... one they wanted to preen and show off and parade around for a while. He wondered how long he would be endured before they would get bored and discard him in the back paddock when the showing off part was over. He was not sure how long it would take to establish real credibility so they would take him seriously as a minister of the Gospel of Christ.

Lloyd Jacobson took a deep breath as he ushered the last of the congregation from the church. Finally, he was here at Wattle Creek and meeting the people that were to be in his safekeeping. His emotions wavered between the elation he felt on the train-ride into town, and sheer terror. Was this the enormous responsibility that Moses felt, when God told him to go back to Egypt? Is that why Moses pulled out every excuse he could think of, as to why God should not send him?

For a moment Lloyd thought he had made the biggest mistake of his life. Whatever arrogance inspired him to write his application at the urging of Toby was well and truly snuffed out now. How could he possibly think he could do this? It was about then that a small voice reminded him that God provided his appointment. There is no job-security in a resume, yet to establish the credibility he sought would require a lot of consistent hard work. The thought occurred to Lloyd that the only time the credibility of a prophet had been handed to someone on a platter was in the case of John the Baptist. Pretty graphic but not too far removed from the truth given that he felt like his head was on the chopping block. Well, there was nothing to do but to go for it. He was committed.

Nat locked the back door and closed up the windows of the church. "Ready Reverend? Ma's dinner should be past cooking if we don't make a move."

"You know Nat, if it's no different to you, I would prefer to be called Pastor... instead of Reverend."

"Not Reverend?" Nat paused. He hadn't counted on something so unconventional. "I don't get it Rev. Remember what it says in the Bible: "A rose by any other name would smell as sweet..." You can call something a name - any name, but it is still that same thing regardless of what you call it."

"That was William Shakespeare: straight from one of his tragic love-stories... and I admit – Billy had a point: we sometimes get hung up on names and our prejudices. But the Bible says God gives the Church those who have the gift to teach and pastor... that makes me a 'Pastor' – not a Reverend or a Monk or a Padre or a Vicar or a Minister." He shrugged, trying to appear reasonably non-committed to the idea. "So, since I'm here to pastor, I wouldn't mind being known as that... if it's all the same to you," he added apologetically.

Nat stared at him as if he had just grown antennae from his forehead and was trying to communicate with blips and whistles. It was about as sensible as walking on coals with bare feet. "What's wrong with Reverend? We've always had a Reverend."

"Nothing I guess… like you say… it's just a name. But I always thought I'd like to keep it close to the source. The fire is hotter there."

Nat looked back at him. This was obviously a thought he had been stewing over; most people don't respond like that on the spur of the moment. It opened the window to air something that had been disturbing Nat too. "Ya know, I actually agree with you there, Rev. Names are important. You paint a picture with the handle a man goes by. But…"

"But what?"

"Well, I dunno if you can take it. You mightn't be too keen to hear the truth."

Lloyd stared at his friend's brother. No two people could be so dissimilar. The challenge was thrown out – roughly, like a test. Lloyd felt he was being set up. *Jesus – I'd appreciate your help here. Don't let me put your Name to shame.* Lloyd considered his words carefully. "Until you tell me what is on your mind, I won't have the chance to respond to it. If you feel it is important, I would like you to proceed."

"See. That's what I don't get. Why do you city creatures have to beat around the bush like a scared rabbit looking for a log to crawl into? Ali's cousin, Miss Farrington is exactly the same! Why can't you just say it straight– "Yes!" or "No!"?"

Now it was Lloyd's turn to wonder if he was talking to the same species. *God – am I really in the right place here? I don't even speak their language!* "Okay. Tell me." He prayed he would have the courage to live through the consequences.

"Hmm. That's interesting. I wasn't too sure you would."

"Either was I. Get it over with."

"That's the style. Well see… it's your name. Goodness man – in this district you might as well call yourself Daisy. There's not a full-blooded Wattle-Creekian who would give their boy a name like Lloyd. Keep that handle and you'll be need'n to prove your manhood to your death-bed."

Lloyd starred at the tall man before him, broad-shouldered and strong. Tobias had said that Nat could be as subtle as a rampaging bull once he had something in his sights. Yes, he said, his big brother was blunt, tough… but as solid as gold. Why would he quote Shakespeare over the irrelevance of a ministerial title and then slam his birth-name? Lloyd prickled and felt his knuckles itching to preserve his name-sakes' honour. But how can you defend the parental wisdom in such a choice, if you had always doubted it yourself? Lloyd Charles William Herbert Jacobson. As a kid such a name was almost too big to carry. It contained the entire weight of their family's legacy in these names. It was more than just names they were playing with: it was a God-filled acknowledgment of his hand through the generations. Lloyd's one encouraging thought was that Abram, Jacob, Simon and Saul all had name changes when God called them out from the past for a mission. "Nat, what do you suggest?"

"Shorten it… take the city out of it. Jacobson is enough of mouthful to make a grown man choke! Besides its tradition you have a handle to go by… so I reckon just Jake. I don't really get the "Pastor" thing… but fair enough, I guess we can live with it – Pastor Jake…" His tone rang with conclusion. He had finalized the change: non-negotiable, sealed, confirmed.

Well, at least it was clean. He was bemused that Nat even bothered to talk to him about it. Very few arrivals to The Creek ever got to discuss what abbreviations their names would go by. Nicknames usually evolved or were voted on by majority rule. Perhaps this was Nat's way of respecting his position, or helping him integrate.

Lloyd shook his head in bewilderment when Nat strode out the door, his duty complete, ready to get the sulky to drive home for lunch. *God – I have no idea what happened just now... if that was You or him. But either way, it looks like people around here will know me as Pastor Jake from now on. Perhaps it is your way of showing me that here I cannot rely on my heritage to get me through. God – it's you and me: no past, just present and future. "Pastor Jake," He* stopped as the sound of it rang foreign in his ears. *"...Oh, my Lord, may they only know it as the name of a servant of the living God."*

37.

Ali looked out the window in eagerness. "The mail is here! Everyone – the mail has arrived!" An air of excitement rippled through the hallway as the mail was brought inside. Letters were distributed to each recipient who gathered their treasures and left to find their own private place to settle down to enjoy their correspondence. Emmaline always had a respectable number of letters to keep her occupied writing replies. She had found a secret little nook in behind the water tank stand where the garden had grown over. In there she had rolled a cut log from the wood heap, which served as a common bush seat. This was her space whenever she needed solitude.

She escaped there to read her letters. The sun was dipping low on the horizon and mosquitoes started buzzing in the evening dampness when Ali tapped on the tank stand. "Hi… do you mind if I interrupt your visit back to the social set?" Em looked up and shrugged. She shuffled across, making room for Ali to sit beside her on the log. "Everything okay?" Ali whispered, sensing her soberness. "A letter from Richard?"

Emmaline didn't say anything, but shrugged again. It took a while for her to gather her words. "No, nothing from him. But I have a letter from Grandmother…"

Ali cringed at the lack of familiarity of that word. It didn't describe a relationship, just a genetic placement. Ali closed her eyes. She had known it was coming, but she had wanted to believe that it would be later, rather than sooner. "I thought you asked to stay a while longer."

"I did."

"Oh." She didn't know what else to say. Obviously, Emmaline was being summoned home.

"She says that I must go back... immediately." There was a catch in her voice. She was upset. Again, her plans had been thwarted.

Ali sighed. "Oh well... it was good while it lasted. But hey – we will write this time. Okay? We'll keep in touch."

Emmaline looked down at her hands. She held the crumpled piece of paper. "This is her second letter. She writes that if I don't come home without delay... she is going to cut out my allowance and give it to Maxwell.

"Cousin Max?"

"He's her only grandson."

"Can she do that? What about your parents' will and legacy... all that stuff?"

"Grandmother does whatever she wants."

Ali leaned over and put her arm around her shoulders. "Don't sweat it. You've got to do what you've got to do. We all know your family." Ali was sounding more understanding than how she was feeling. She was family too! Why did they always have to bow to the wishes of the rich and small-minded?

Emmaline smoothed out the wrinkles in the fabric of her skirt. She had been sitting far too long. "After her first letter I wrote back and told her I wanted to stay... just as I had planned... for a few weeks. But I guess I knew nothing would change her mind."

Emmaline's voice started to rise as she continued. "I don't even feel like her granddaughter. I am more like a piece of furniture that she positions in a room. In fact, I think one of her Chippendales would be given more consideration."

Ali extended her hand. "Oh Emmy... I'm so sorry!"

"Yeah, so am I!"

"I wish that there was something we could do to change her mind. But one thing about your Grandmother... she's kinda set in her ways."

"If I go back, I will have named my price. I go now, and she will always own me. There will be nothing that she will not hold me to ransom for."

"They are your family Em..."

"Your understanding of family is very different. Very different."

"What about Richard?" Ali held her breath. She wanted to believe one man would hold his ground and stick up for her cousin-friend.

Emmaline shrugged. "Richard is kinda flexible. He bends with the wind... and Grandmother is a rather blustery airstream."

"But if you explained..."

"Ali." It was a full-stop, as if she had finally come to the end of the sentence. Ali halted half way through inhaling and turned towards her golden-haired cousin. Her chin was lifted just a little. "No Ali, I am not going back. I will stay until I can find a measure of dignity to go and visit my grandmother as the daughter of her only son – not some chattel to be shuffled according to the seasons."

"Emmaline! You can't!" Aunt Alma stared at the little slip of a girl. Her sister's daughter was showing more will and determination than Edith ever had. It seemed impossible.

"Aunt Alma, I can. I am of age. I should start to do what is good for me... not just what she wants."

"But – you said so yourself... she will cut your allowance... all your inheritance. Don't you know what that means?"

"Do you really think I haven't thought this through? This is not some fly-brain reflex decision. I have gone over and over this. Most likely it will mean Richard will just never get around to finalising our intended engagement. He won't marry if Grandmother disowns me. I will become the leper of ELLIOT HOUSE. But the alternative is no longer a choice. I need to able to hold my head up and be confident that the person I am on the inside is reflected on the outside."

Uncle Alf smiled around his pipe as he leaned over the rail on the verandah. "That's my girl..."

"Oh Emmaline... I know you mean well... but it's not that easy."

"Well, you are wrong Aunt Alma. It is that easy. I don't get on the train."

"But what are you going to do? I don't want to seem like a wet blanket... but life on the other side... goes on indefinitely."

"I... you think that I won't make it?" It was a thought that had not occurred to her.

"No! Of course not. It's just that... well, you will have to do your bit."

"I don't want charity. I will work – just like anyone else. I will. I must."

"Oh, Emmaline darling – you're not going to find this easy, you know. You haven't had to work before. Any time you did, it was because you wanted to... it was fun. When you have to... it is not so amusing."

"Ali has had a job. And I will too. Don't be so surprised. It's a matter of *do or die*. I'm now penniless and unskilled, but I will always be able to say it was my choice. Many of the world's poor have not had that luxury. Besides, survival is a great motivator." She stood and stretched – as if trying to lengthen the shortness in her legs. "Do you know what the ridiculous thing is? If Grandmother had just let things be... and allowed me a few more weeks... she would have had me for the rest of my natural life. She was just too near-sighted to realise it... and I suspect... she's done me a favour in the process."

Ali gave her a huge hug. "You've been telling me I have strength. It must run in the family. Who would've thought you would ever come out and stand up like this?"

Em smiled and swatted a mosquito that landed on the back of her hand. "Yes, who? You know, this just might be the adventure we were after!"

Em woke with a jolt as Aunt Alma gently lit the lamp by her bed. "Mornin' Honey – I've put the kettle on the stove and will make some pancakes before you go down to the dairy-bails." Em sat up. Her stomach turned. Food at this hour was abnormal. She was pretty certain she would never get used to this. Was it silly of her to assume that anything they can do – she could do just as well? There was one thing that she would never get used to… getting up before the rooster crows. It was not biologically benevolent.

She shivered as she struggled into her overalls and tied back her hair. She peeled off the cotton gloves that covered the grim looking salve that she put on every night, and looked at her hands in the lamplight. The cracks along her knuckles did not seem any better. As the weather got cooler, they seemed to get worse. The cold frosty mornings and having her hands immersed in cold water at the dairy, was not allowing them to heal. Em sighed and determinedly pulled on her socks. She was not going to give in. She said she would work and she would never put Uncle Alf in the position to have to tell her she was not pulling her weight.

Aunt Alma would freak if she saw the way her hands were, so she pulled her gloves back on over her hands. Em sighed as she put on her coat and boots on at the door. "I'm a little late Aunt Alma – I'll have the pancakes later." She trudged down the track to the bails.

She could see the hurricane lantern swinging as Fred was calling up the cows. In the clear crisp night under the setting moon, the shadows of the cows lining up for milking trailed like a march of giant ants. Calves bleated and their mothers moaned from over-full udders. Scoops of chaff puffed into the troughs at the head of the bails and the warm smell of the cows hung in the still morning air as they waited patiently chewing their cud. The first cows filed into the bails and Uncle

Alf pulled up a stool, washing the udder with clean water. Holding the milk-bucket between his knees, the first twang of the milk-stream hit the bottom of the bucket. Within moments the rhythmic squirt of milk frothed into a warm, clean swirl. Bucket after bucket was emptied into the milk cans ready for delivery.

Em pulled up her stool in the next bail and secured the rope behind the cow. She tied the leg rope and lent into the cow's warm side and positioned the bucket between her knees. Her cold hands took a while to find a regular tempo. It never occurred to Em that her efficiency in the morning and afternoon milking was a measure of success. To her, the physical fatigue and her soft tender skin breaking under the demands of this type of work was a sign of failure as a working-class girl. The other shock was the internal dissatisfaction that plagued her.

The reality of drudgery that Aunt Alma alluded to was shocking beyond her wildest imagination. Her vision was tunnelling into a greyness that was not at all how she imagined independence and self-sufficiency to be. She felt it should bring a type of equilibrium that would give her a personal satisfaction or at the very least, a vague sense of contented peace. But it didn't.

She was not a stranger to this feeling, but she had always privately attributed this hollowness to her Grandmother's domination. Now, morning after morning... in the quiet routine of cow flanks, leg ropes and milk buckets, she had no distraction that could deny that same vacant sensation still existed. It had nothing to do with forced social expectations or shallow, meaningless daily agendas. Here, at the Dampier farm, there were no social expectations other than being true to your family, and her daily agenda was now packed full of meaning... the purpose of survival.

38.

Ali was flapping around the kitchen like a caged bird trying to fly. "I'm sorry Mum, it's just that the house will not be big enough once Janie is here. And when the baby comes it will be worse. I need to go before I end up hating Fred for marrying her."

"Alice Eloise! I cannot allow you to say such a thing. He is your brother and his bride will be accepted in this house!"

"Oh Mum, I know you want everyone to be happy... but it won't work. It can't. I've tried to accommodate her like you want... but I feel pushed out... and they are not even married yet. I hate it!"

"Oh, my dear... this is your home – first and foremost. But it will be Janie's home too. You know I want you both to be happy. Surely there is a way..."

"Well, I don't know what it is... except a bit of space. Quite a big bit of space. There are just too many females in one small space."

Her father looked up from his paper with a mouth full of toast. "Honey... just imagine how I feel..." Ali shot her mother a victorious glance until her father continued. "But you can't just go off like a half-cocked rifle. When you have a plan, I'll give my blessing. 'Til then – you and Janie will have to work it out."

"Pa. Come on. I'm not staying until she moves in here lock, stock and barrel. I've given it a fair shot. I don't..."

"Ali..." Her mother pursed her lip. That look reminded Ali of when she was twelve and was reprimanded for spending far too much reflective time in front of the mirror modelling dresses rather than doing her chores.

Em sat on the pianola stool swinging her legs contemplatively. "Uncle Alf. We might have a plan..."

Ali shook her head silently and mouthed a very cautious, "No. Not yet..." in Em's direction.

Uncle Alf looked from one face to the other. "Things don't have to be watertight before you explore 'em, ya know. That's what plan'n is: checking out the possibilities."

Em raised her eyebrows in question. Ali shrugged and then conceded. "Okay then. But it's just an idea. We're not really sure how to..."

Em stood. "Uncle Alf, you know I appreciate the opportunities you've given me here. But I can't stay at the dairy indefinitely. I need to get another job. It hasn't been easy for me working through this, and I guess I am shocked that being willing is not enough. Everything I have thought of so far hasn't been very successful. Ali had a job... but it seems the only draper in town has already replaced Ali and is not likely to hire any more personnel." Em took a breath trying not to look at Ali's blushing face. Her last days at Mrs Craddick's Store had been a crushing nightmare for Ali. "Well... we had a look at the things we can do. Ali can cook... I can serve tea. Ali can sew. There's book-keeping... I've only done a little committee work for our charities, and I'm sure I could brush up. That sort of thing. Not a very impressive skill-set to say the least."

317

Uncle Alf nodded and folded his newspaper and picked up his cup of tea. His attention was fastened on his niece's intense face. She was obviously not finished. "As far as I can gather almost everything we *could* do, relies heavily on Ali... and my limited ability to contribute. I pretty much will have to learn everything from the beginning. So, with that in mind, we thought a good place to start would be what Ali really loves doing. And what we came up with was..." Uncle Alf raised his eyebrows just a little. He had never thought of his darling Alice as a girl in possession of a passion. "... starting with raw potential and helping people look their best! ... making it come together. There is no business in The Creek that offers this but we could and we want to try. We want to start our own business that does just that. We could really do this!"

Alma stared from one face to another. "Doing what exactly? This might work in the city where people worry about this sort of thing... but in Wattle Creek? This is all sounding quite concerning! I don't see how you..."

"Mum!"

"Stay with us Aunt Alma. Just because it is the country it doesn't mean that people don't want to look good... or be fashionable. It just needs to be done on a budget. On this I can really assist. But that would be a long way out. To start with it would be something much simpler. In fact, the only business that comes close to this in Wattle Creek is the barber."

Even Uncle Alf could not resist being amused. That Hendricks' service statement might be helping people look their best was hideously unexpected. Em eyed the twist of his mouth and quickly followed on. "Sure, he has let it run down, but we're thinking – these ideas are all very rudimentary… of course, but… well, we're thinking - we could work at Hendricks' Barber shop… and put it back on its feet…" There. It was said.

"The man's a drunk! I won't allow it. I positively won't!" said Aunt Alma mortified.

"But Ali can cut hair. She's a natural. The shop is closed up a lot. We'd like to *manage* it for him. I think the town would appreciate a reliable and responsible service again."

Ali looked at her Dad. "I've never heard of him being violent."

Em glanced over at her Aunt, her face ashen as she clutched a hot cup of tea. "Alf – you cannot allow this! They are just girls. They can't possibly manage a shop full of male clientele! Their reputation would be gone like a morning fog."

"Your mother has a point." Uncle Alf quietly picked up his slate and scribbled some computations.

Ali sighed and gave Em an "I-told-you-they'd-never-go-for-it" look. She had walked this road many times before. There was no point fighting her mother when she was like this. Ali was so disappointed. This plan had stirred her like nothing ever had before. Now it was over before it had started. She felt flattened by a steamroller… her chance to be more than two-dimensional, squashed out of her.

But Em was not so easily put off. "Uncle Alf, we've thought about this. I won't be a burden to you! I need to support myself. I *want* to learn. I really do. It doesn't have to be *this* hare-brain idea… even though it is our favourite! Another would do just as well. I need to change things for me.

Out here... people consider work differently. It is an honourable thing – supporting yourself. That's not what Grandmother thinks... to her it is humiliating. It wouldn't matter what type of work it is; nothing is ever going to seem respectable to her. Even a successful business, at least in my Grandmother's eyes, is symptomatic of failure... just because it is business."

Alf stared at his niece, and then glanced over at his wife. "This idea is not as silly as you may think... it has potential... a little raw at the moment..."

"Alf! You can't be serious. That drunk would take advantage of them!"

He scribbled some more. "I could offer to buy the shop..." But before their hopes could rise, he added, "but everyone knows Hendricks would drink himself into hell within the week. I'm not prepared to watch a man die in front of me because I helped fund his boozin'. Besides... your mother is perfectly right. If he thought he had a regular income without havin' to lift a finger, he'd wring every ounce of money out of that till for his thirsty lady in a bottle. You'd never see your pay. If you go for the Barber shop idea, it's gotta be without Hendricks."

Em shook her head. "You won't buy it off him – because he will drink the price. We can't rent it for the same reason!"

"Well, I'll ask around. We'll show your Grandmother a thing or two about country work-ethics. And Em – you know... a valuable partner is not about having the same abilities... its more about being able to work together. What you said about book-keeping – things need to be taken care of; customers, property, supplies, time, money – it's all got to be managed. Partnerships work when you can chip in and help each other. Take Alma and me. I do the outside stuff… she looks after keeping me on track. If I had to do both, we couldn't work the farm so effectively. That's what a business is… partnership - but not many people see it that way."

So, they considered it more… fleshing out the idea - putting meat on the skeleton. Ali picked up her flattened dream off its steam-rolled pavement and carefully watched it start to become three-dimensional again. They looked at alternative premises… but somehow the little shop on the corner with the flaking paint, bay window and the faded red and white pole at the front was home to their dream. Ali's private hope was that some-how her dream would not have to be relocated.

Alma poured a rather stiff mug of coffee the way Alf liked it and set it down beside the newspaper. "Alf, I want to suggest something," she said positioning some of his favourite melting moment creams on a plate just out of range. He reached with a grunt of approval, but she whisked them skilfully out of his reach. He stared at the plate irritated. "Alf – you need to listen…" His vision was firmly channelled in on the plate. His coffee was begging to be accompanied by one of those sweet biscuits. It had been a while since Alma had made a batch.

"Alf…" she hesitated as she picked up the small jug of thin cream and set it beside his mug, holding onto the plate of biscuits thoughtfully. "Please… allow me." She figured he would have got the idea after twenty-seven years of marriage. Only when there was something important at stake did she ever break out his mother's famous Melting Moments recipe. Obviously, the connection was never made... not that he would admit anyway.

"Well, spit it out Alma. My coffee's getting cold."

Alma blinked. Perhaps he chose not to acknowledge her Melting Moments strategy because it would concede that the woman of the house was misusing power. Old habits were hard to break, especially when they were effective. Didn't Queen Esther use good food to soften the King of the Medes and Persians?

"Alf, I have arranged for Em to go through book-keeping with Josie Lawson."

"Fair enough." He nodded as he stretched unconcerned for a biscuit that again swayed just out of reach. "Oh, come on woman – my coffee's dying a slow cold death here. What is the problem?"

"That is okay?"

"Of course, it's okay. Why wouldn't it be okay?"

"Because you were determined to show her the books. It is not like you to relinquish this so meekly. Why is that?"

Alf Dampier sighed. His wife would beat this to death until she was satisfied. His coffee would not survive it if he didn't cut to the chase. "Honestly Alma, I just got to admit...I'm doubting she'll really make a go of it. Josie's welcome to try her darnedest."

"Alf!" Alma hissed. "Don't say that about my Edith's daughter! You can't blame the pupil for the teacher's lack of skill."

"Now hang on a minute. This here is a scheme you have fought tooth and nail over… so you are blaming me for it not flying? It's not my fault the girl's got no head for figures. Ali is exactly the same. There is nothing wrong with my book-keepin'. It was exactly as my Pa showed me… with extra stuff I've picked up along the way. I'm thinking I was naive to assume a woman could enter a man's world. Just because I want it, doesn't mean it will… that's all."

Alma thumped the plate on the bench and raised her hands to her hips. This had gone on long enough. "Alfonzo Dampier, I don't believe I just heard what came out of your mouth! Those girls are full of get-up-and-go to drive this thing forward; the likes of which I never thought we would see. I don't *ever* want to hear such things… that is going to squish the life out of their dream, when we have worked so hard to fan something like this into poor Ali's life since…" Her vigorous defence faded as she stood helpless, her face quivering in fear. "Alf… this has to work. It must. She couldn't take another blow… not after last… time… please…"

Alf stood up and put his arm around his wife's shoulders. He honestly didn't want to argue over this. He was just surprised as any that Em was not showing the adeptness to book-keeping he thought she would have. That wasn't his fault. He didn't want it to fail either. He had invested too much already. He had resigned himself to managing the books himself. "Come Alma, really… I'm not squishing the life out of their dream because I get some sort of morbid pleasure out of it. If it ain't gunna work, we gotta get our heads out of the clouds and start being realistic. Now there are other ways around this. Em doesn't have to be responsible for the ledgers."

"But that's just it, Alf. They do have to be responsible. This is their project. They want to do this on their own... to be independent - not put extra strain on us. They don't want us to take the control out of it for them. They need to be able to do this... all of it. Can't you see that?"

"There are things a father is entitled to do for his daughter. She doesn't stop being my baby girl just because she all grown up and wants to step up into something she may not be cut out for. Come Alma... she's still my girl."

"There! You said it yourself. She's more her father's daughter than both of you realise. She's stubborn and proud... and she's determined... her and Em. Both of them are."

"Then they get it from their mothers! Sisters tarred with the same brush."

"Alf, they want to do this."

"Well, I don't see much alternative. They both have no idea when it comes down to it. It's awkward."

"For you or for them?" she said pointedly. "Like I said. Josie will show Em the ropes of book-keeping. Woman to woman... she's survived in a man's world and knows how a girl thinks."

"Numbers are numbers. You can't mess with absolutes."

"No one's trying to dear. It's just a matter of understanding where they sit on the page. Josie can do that. You'd better drink your coffee… it is getting cold." She pushed the plate beside his mug and picked up some mending and returned to her corner chair.

Alf sipped his coffee. It had already reached the tepid side of a first-rate cuppa. He got up and tipped it into a pot plant, poured another cup from the stove and added cream. He scooped up some biscuits and grabbed the paper before he went out onto the verandah to read under the lantern before retiring. He would only persist so long. The insects were thick tonight. They might get some rain.

39.

Em walked over to Lawsons' farm after the morning milking was finished. She wanted to be sure that Nat and Mal would have left the house. She didn't need them observing her struggle to get a handle on the books. It completely floored her that the charity work she had done could not compare with the requirements of a business. But she was determined. She had to be in a position to contribute to this venture. Now was not a time for self-preserving pride.

As she walked, she felt her throat smart with indignation. She wanted to prosecute her childhood tutor for gross and criminal negligence. Did he do anything to earn his fees all those hours she sat with him in the ELLIOT HOUSE nursery? But even as she thought about it, she remembered a time when he had gone to her Grandmother with allegations of her lack of enthusiasm for lessons. Grandmother Edith was very unsympathetic to his complaint. "Why should the girl be immersed in Latin? There are far more practical lessons that will hold a girl of her position in good stead. Geometry and Latin roots will not." So even though Emmaline's basic mathematics was sound, she forewent solving advanced arithmetic calculations and majored in music and art instead… and social etiquette lessons that made her Grandmother nod with approval. Her smug adolescent victory hardly seemed like a battle worth winning just now.

Em hardly knew what to expect from Josephine Lawson. It was all she could do to keep an open mind. She threaded her ledger-books under the fence and climbed through the railings, brushing from her full skirt the seeds that had glued to the fabric from swaying strands of paspalum. She picked off some of the seeds, but she didn't want to take too long and keep Mrs Lawson waiting. She bent down and picked up her books, and then orientating herself towards the homestead, she made her way across the yard. Suddenly she froze.

Emmaline felt it before she saw anything. She spun around, not sure what was staring her down. A large bull, heavy and strong from years of pampered breeding was glowering at her from the corner of the holding yard. His thick woolly head lowered, its dark coat shining in the high morning sun. Heavy hooves slowly started pawing the ground, dusting his underbelly. Em dropped her books and ran. In panic she steered towards the house, but she tripped on her skirt and sprawled into the dirt. In panic she scrambled to her feet. She knew she would never make it.

She whirled around to go back to the fence where she climbed through, but suddenly it was three hundred miles away and receding. She started back in horror and instinctively scrambled for the single shade tree in the yard. It was a rather substantial Pepperina tree; its long leaves swaying madly as she flew into its arms. The beast thundered towards her. She clambered up into its branches, its bark feeling safe as it scratched along her forearms. Clinging in panic she waited for the pounding against the trunk to start. He rumbled passed in a fuming rage, infuriated that his target had disappeared from the ground before him. He pawed the earth crazed in frustration, scratching up the dirt in wild bursts as it snorted and fumed, pounding around, blaring fierce guttural moans that came from the very depths of his belly.

Em clung in terror as the ground swirled with dust below. It seemed to sway, ebb and flow. She squeezed her eyes tightly shut. She could not fall; she must not fall. Somewhere a voice was calling. "Some of Dampier's strays must be near that bull again, he's going mad over there!"

Then she heard Nat. His deep voice irritated by the inconvenience of interruption, as he pulled his stock horse up along the rails. He swore. "Fair go Dampier, can't you keep your stock under control?" It had happened before. As if he had nothing better to do than to sort out their bull from the neighbour's heifers at this hour in the morning. He whistled - sharp and loud. A blue-healer scurried under the fence; fearless as it rushed in to nip his hind-heels. The bull spun around, glaring at its new, tangible target. Nat called the dog off, and threw a tussock of hay over the fence, the fragrance rising like calming incense. Slowly the madness subsided… and the dust settled.

Nat looked past the yard railings for the offending heifers… and spat on the ground when he realised they had probably spooked and high-tailed it back across the flats. Now he'd have to ride the fence and check the prodigals had really returned home. He didn't need strays in his crops. He checked the yard again. "Striker" was pawing up the hay and tossing it about. There is nothing quite as fearsome as a bull in the full heat of rage, aggressively stomping his stuff. It commanded respect. He turned his horse to go.

"Nat…"

It took a moment to register he was not alone. Striker raised his head, his flanks quivering in a bad-tempered mania, staring at the dog who came back and barked at the tree.

"Nat!"

Her skirt, torn and dirty slipped into view from its leafy hide. "Ali?"

She could not believe that she had to admit it. "It's Emmaline..." She wished she could vaporise into the dusty air.

Nat stared at her. "I'll be... the Dampier stray," he swore in disbelief. This could not be happening! He flew into action, certain the girl from the city was going to fall to a trampled death at any moment. He bounded over the fence and lowered the rails. In one deft movement he stripped off his shirt and spun it around his head, impersonating a Spanish toreador, tormenting the beast through the gate. He whistled and Pike spun in and nipped his heels, driving him into the neighbouring yard in a tornado of dust and fury. Nat deftly raised the rails in swift, exacting movements. He scooped up more hay and dumped it unceremoniously over the fence. There was a solid railing between them now. He went and stood under the pepperina-tree... and looked up at the pale, horror struck, humiliated face of Emmaline. Instinctively he reached out to soothe away her fear.

"He's in the next yard now... you can get down."

She raised her eyes from her arms, stiff from her claw-hold on the wood, and closed her lids in dismay as she realised Nat stood bare-chested in the heat, his shirt slung over his shoulder waiting to assist her to level terra firma. She couldn't move... not forwards or backwards. Would she ever live down the disgrace? It was likely she would die of old age glued to the branches of this sappy tree. It was an undeserved demise!

"Miss Farrington ... you can come down now... the coast is clear."

She grunted in despair. Of course, she would come down... if she could! It was not like she was enjoying making a spectacle of herself in this elevated possie! "I... I can't..."

"You can't? You want me to come up there?" She had to be kidding.

"No! I'm fine. Really. I just need a moment."

He raised his eyebrows and waited. He saw her gloved hands clawing the branches of the tree. It was a genuine possibility she'd graft herself into that tree, if she stayed immobilized much longer.

He reached down, and played with the ears of his dog. "Pike... my mate – what do you reckon about this?" he asked his canine off-sider quietly with a smile. The dog panted and sat down in the shade. Nat leaned against the tree; a presiding governor's smile lingered around his jaw. He was secure in his own province. Her pride demanded that he should only assist if she asked for help. His pride demanded she ask. She remained frozen, and continued to insist she was fine. It was very apparent that she wasn't. Nat wondered how long she would persist. It didn't matter much anymore. His day was wrecked anyway, and this was providing a whole new dimension to the word entertainment.

He took his shirt from his shoulder and wiped the grime from his chest before he put it back on, and sunk on his hunches, and said just loud enough for her to hear, "So the question is Pike… 'How long?' What do you think - what's the gentlemanly thing to do? 'Cause I'm reckoning with this one, the proper thing is kinda important. Don't want to be interfering by jumping in unwanted… or don't want to be uncouth and uncaring by being tardy." In all honesty – it was amusing, and he was happy to get mileage out of it. He could hear her huffing in disgust above him and he didn't care. This game she played did not inspire his wits. Moving targets and guessing games were unfair. He preferred to know the rules, then you could decide which ones to break, how often.

Finally, he could stand it no longer. He swore under his breath. He was not keen that it came to this. He swung up into the tree and put a firm hand on her calf. She jumped nervously at his touch, and he resisted the temptation to linger there. "Miss Farrington, you will have to move back into the main trunk of the tree… plant your weight here… now lift yourself to sit up… don't look down…" He coached her the whole way… and finally she dropped a short distance to the ground into the support of his arms. Emmaline swayed uneasily and leaned heavily on him for a moment before she realised where she was. Self-consciously she pulled away and sunk against the trunk of the pepperina-tree. It was the only time she could remember when she wanted to hug a tree… and kiss the ground it grew from.

Nat pulled a canteen off his saddle, and offered her a drink. "So, do you want to tell me what that was about?"

"No."

Nat couldn't help noticing that she had not thanked him for his efforts. "Then you usually go courting bad-tempered bulls, in the middle of the morning?"

"I didn't mean to walk into the bull yard. I was coming to visit your mother."

"You don't *walk* into a bull-yard. You climb. It's not like he's invisible."

"Well, I don't know… I was thinking about other things."

"Okay. Next time – let me suggest you walk around…"

"I'll remember that," she said ungratefully. She picked up the books that sat stacked beside the tree where Nat had gathered them and stood with a resolute set of her jaw. There would be no way she could focus on numbers now. "Could you please give your mother my apologies? I'd best come back another time." She self-consciously tried to dust the dirt off her skirt and… wobbled ungainly.

Nat reached out and steadied her. She wouldn't be walking home. "Look, I have to check the fences along the creek anyway, so why don't you hitch a lift back to your Uncle's place?" He looked significantly at his horse and saw the fear return to her eyes… until her face smoothed and was unreadable. She was not at all like Ali. He knew Ali. "I could go and get the cart – but that would require a great deal of explanation," said Nat helpfully. "I know Mum would insist you stay and rest. If you want to avoid detection… making-do might be the plan."

Her tense expression relaxed. It surprised her that he'd understand she would want that. "I can improvise if I need to. Please don't go fast."

"Comet here is a snail…" he good-naturedly insisted, as he stroked his lean dun-coloured stockhorse. It flicked its dark tail over his fly-covered flanks. "He's tired… been working this morning… wouldn't raise a trot."

Emmaline nodded and acknowledged the lie for what it was: a tease, a way to allow her to retain a shred of dignity. It seemed to be the first thing that she had ever seen worthy of appreciation in Nat Lawson.

Josie opened the door and smiled as Emmaline made her way up the path. "So, how's the kitten?"

"Kitten? As in a cat?"

"It's alright…" Josie added with a conspiring whisper, "Nat passed on your apologies from the other day. He told me you were detained rescuing a stray kitten from a tree. He said it was a bit feral, spitting and carrying on…"

"A stray feral!" That was unbelievable. The image of the pepperina tree loomed large in her mind.

Josie quickly added, "But he did say he actually thought it was cute in its own way."

"He thought it was cute?" She wasn't sure which was worse. She blushed. Oh, that was too much!

Josie heard the irritation in her voice and looked at her curiously. She shrugged. "That's what he said."

Then Em paused. This was intriguing. "Oh. Well, I guess... I was worried about... ahh... its safety."

"Well, I'd like to meet the little mite some time. Nat was quite taken with it."

"Perhaps he should have kept it..." Emmaline said glibly. Yet he really had chosen to protect her from embarrassment, even when it was a situation going begging for humiliation. That was a little unexpected, impressive in a way.

Josie led the way into the kitchen table. "I see you brought your books, but I hadn't wanted to get into them today very much. Let's just talk about what needs to be done. Alma said that you had worked on some charity committees. Do you want milk in your tea?"

"Yes thanks, just a dash." Emmaline pulled out a chair and sat down. "My charity work apparently doesn't help me any. Women's League is a long way from the reality of business it seems."

Josie carefully poured the milk. "Well, let's have a look... you might be surprised." She sat down opposite Emmaline and looked at her slender face, and she suspected she was not quite as delicate as her fine features may suggest. In a good way... there was resilience there... and an intelligent shine to her brown eyes. Josie always read people's eyes. She believed quite sincerely in the adage they were the 'windows to the soul'. She was sure this girl was not stupid. Alma was probably right. It might just take another approach. She knew the difference that could make.

Matthew had a very precise way of recording the books. His system was pristine, and his coaching had guided Josie through the maze of accounts and ledgers, when they were starting out. But when he was gone, she had to substitute his immaculate columns with an interpretation that was her own. It was hard, struggling to follow a man's world with a man's mentality, when she was striving just to breathe... coping with grief and farm-work and boys. She had adapted... but she had felt she had betrayed the purity of his system in the process. "What did you do at the Woman's League?" Josie asked as she placed the cups beside them when she sat down.

"Well, I looked after the money tins, and just kept track of donations... nothing more. Took them to the bank sometimes if Mrs Zeller was not able to."

"Did you record it?

"In the minutes… and there was a book. I only assisted really."

"It seems everyone has their own system, but the principles are basically the same. This probably won't seem like business record keeping, as your Uncle Alf describes it, but just humour me…" She pulled out some leather boot-laces and made three circles on the table. "With the Woman's League, how did you raise your money?"

"Dues, street stalls… collections… donations…"

"Okay…" Josie opened her button-box and added half a dozen buttons into the first circle. "Money in the money-tin." Emmaline smiled, and tried not to think this was being far too simplistic. Josie continued. "This is what you were responsible for… right?"

Emmaline nodded. Josie smiled encouragingly as she continued. "Well, there is more to it than that. You raised the money for a purpose. What were your charitable causes?"

"It varied. The League was for the hospital, so it depended on what was the agreed project. One year we made improvements to the boiler house. Another time we financed a new anaesthetic table. The Nurses' Quarters were a regular recipient."

"Well... all worthy projects, that is for sure. One operating table will cost four buttons, a couple of chairs for the nurses. We'll put outgoing money, all your costs, into this circle..." She moved three more buttons into the other circle.

"Here – you place the buttons. This is a donation from Mr and Mrs Jones. This is a bill of two buttons for fire-wood. This is the income from the annual show. Mr Smith doesn't have money to donate, but he will give four buttons when the shearing is done..."

Emmaline hesitated... "Pledges... the third circle."

"Exactly..." She placed the buttons as a reminder of the amount. They followed the buttons around the leather-lace circles for a while longer, becoming more complex with the scenarios of ins and outs. Like the dawn lighting up the mysterious shadows of night, Emmaline quickly started to see the correlation to all those numbers that previously sat meaningless on her uncle's ledger.

Josie got up and refilled the kettle and stoked the stove. "That's all there is to it... book-keeping is just shuffling buttons. Obviously, we can't keep buttons, and boot-lace circles are clumsy... so we record the state of these circles in the books. Columns make it easier to compare the status of each circle. When you get down to it… it's still buttons and boot-laces, and making sure there's enough in one circle to cover the other." She laughed a little self-consciously. "Even now – if I'm not sure of where something should be recorded… I think in buttons 'n boot-laces."

She placed the fresh cups of tea on the table. "Extending credit to your customers is allowing them to make a pledge that they will pay… usually after the service has been rendered. You can't let that circle get too weighty, because recovering it into your expendable income can sometimes be a challenge. The health of your business depends on your ability to have your expenses covered. That's what you are responsible for." She pulled out Uncle Alf's ledger book he had bought for her. "May I?"

"Yes – of course…" Josie went through the columns and asked Em to explain which circles they belonged to. "You will have to decide if these columns accurately describe the boot-lace circles you need to record. Simple is best. You may find you need to add others – little circles within the main pools, just to keep your thoughts organised… like donations, fund-raisers and dues may need to be tracked separately. I colour code which circle they belong to, so I can see at a glance what I am looking at. I bought artist pastels so I could do that… blues and greens are my colour-codes for credits, warm colours (orange and red) are debits. I don't think that's the usual way most people would do it. On the farm, we keep the income from the grain, separate from the cattle… and the costs for each that relate to that part of the business… that way we can see if one area is doing better than another."

Em shook her head in amazement. "Just buttons 'n boot-laces."

"That's it… buttons 'n boot-laces. If you ask me… the simpler it is, the less likely you will double up or make mistakes." She paused and smiled. "So, The Creek is getting a new barber after all…"

Em nodded, her eyes serious. "Would you mind if I brought over the books until I get the hang of it… it may take a while… I'd like you to check the state of my buttons 'n boot-laces."

Josie smiled. "It would be my pleasure Emmaline Farrington. We business women need to support each other: it has been a long time coming."

40.

Ali hopped and buzzed. The morning sun burst over the rows of buildings along the street. A horse lazily rocked his rider home after an all-night stint. Dust puffed under his tread, swirling through the streams of morning-light in hazy country waltzes. The Barber's pole was freshly painted, red and white spiralling its way to the white knob at the top. The daybreak smell of baking bread burst over the town like a canopy. It was as predictable as the dairy cows lining up at the bails for their morning milking. Always that earliest morning aroma felt like it was happening for the first time.

Ali swept the step... just one more time. Em repositioned the placard for the eighth time. It announced to Wattle Creek what everyone already knew: "Under New Management". The straggling grass along the easement was trimmed and Uncle Alf's gift of two wooden planters, made from hollowed logs, were filled with Mrs Wallace's reddest geranium plants, freshly potted.

As if on cue, Belle's Bakery horse and cart plodded steadily around the corner with Terry on the tailgate ready to run in the morning deliveries. Wattle Creek was stirring for their morning bread. The cooking smells of breakfast started to stir along the streets. Bronza stopped in front of the shop. Terry jumped off and handed them some fresh bread. "Compliments of the boss..." he said simply.

Ali smiled as she watched the cart disappear around the street. There were new adventures on every corner. Belle was off now to her new life as a wife. And they… finally… were open for business. The months had dragged in one sense… and there hardly seemed enough time in another. "Come inside and let's have breakfast. It'll be awhile before our opening rush," said Emmaline as she ushered Ali through the swinging doors. The makeover inside the little shop was equally as dramatic as its external transformation. Scrubbed and polished, the worn leather chair was oiled and patched so that now there was a subtle saddlery smell of linseed. They could not afford to paint the walls, but they cleaned off the years of smoke and grime, and revived the dark panel of shellacked timber to regain the room's distinguished gentleman feel. The sparkling mirror, the orderly array of combs and razors, a picture on each wall, made it barely recognisable. It felt like a place of industry.

Emmaline and Ali bubbled with pride as they shifted the stools up to the bench and positioned their teacups next to the fresh breakfast buns from Belle's breadbasket. It was a treat to celebrate success with a friend. Even if she wasn't there in person, she had not forgotten them. They could imagine the waiting patrons sitting along the bench just inside the door. The newspapers that sat there would be read with interest as they passed the time before they filed into the leather chair for their cut.

All that was needed was that first patron.

They waited.

After church Ali busied herself tidying hymn books and washing up vases. She offered to swept the floor and insisted Mrs Hollis go home. Then she attacked a small storage cupboard in a cleaning frenzy. Ali jumped as she suddenly became conscious of Pastor Jake watching her. She looked up to see a rather grim look on his face. He had loosened his tie and taken off his jacket. She dived deep into the back of the cupboard, her forehead flushing red. This was not going to be easy. "You know…" Pastor Jake said seriously, "the Sabbath was intended as a day of rest. Perhaps you could leave these cupboards for another day."

Ali shrugged without looking up, her voice echoing around the inside of the shelves. "Guess they have been left for another day too long."

Pastor Jake leaned against the window and folded his arms. He just wished that he could get rid of the perpetual match-making. It was a huge barrier to just about everything he was working towards. Every mother wanted to know if her daughter had a chance. Every father wanted to know if he'd be able to provide a suitable living. *They should know*, he thought wryly, *after all, they pay my stipend.* He cleared his throat. "If you could finish up, your father has asked me to take you home."

She nodded and bumped her head. She wanted to stay inside the cupboard to gather more courage. Perhaps this was not such a good idea. He could end up despising her. "I know. I asked Dad to suggest it because I wanted to ask you something."

He knew it. Pastor Jake braced himself. He actually didn't mind Ali. Of the single young ladies in his congregation, there was something about this lady, a melancholy sigh that seemed to surround her in a halo that made him want to bring back the laughter that he suspected lay buried. He was surprised that Ali would be throwing herself at his feet. Even Ruth in the Old Testament was a little subtler. And it perplexed him that her family was willing to support her overt pursuit of him. "Oh Lord Jesus, give me the grace to be kind."

She sighed and extracted her shoulders from the cupboard. She removed the apron and hung it on a nail behind the door. "The kettle is still warm, would you like a cup of tea?" She had deliberately overlooked that in washing up the crockery.

He shook his head. "Miss Dampier…"

"I know, I know. I'll just come straight to the point."

"Miss Dampier please… I don't want things to be awkward between us. You are a valuable part of this Church family."

This was not going well. He called her Miss Dampier. Ali flinched. He hated her already. "I promised Em I would at least talk to you. I understand the way you feel to respond… that is entirely up to you."

A hint of interest played around his eyes. Pressure to match people's expectations was constantly around him. It was disarming that she would at least acknowledge he had a measure of control, however symbolic, especially since her family were so confident as to invite him over for Sunday lunch. He would excuse himself from the Dampier's invitation once he dropped her off. "No pressure. Well, that is encouraging at least. If you must… say your piece."

"Really? Okay. Are you sure you don't want a cup of tea?" He shook his head.

She inhaled deeply. "You know Em and I are working the Barber shop while Mr Hendricks is in hospital. Doc Wallace fixed it so we could take over the lease. It is not a permanent arrangement… only on trial really, but it is not going well. It seems that people don't trust women to cut hair. I wanted to ask if you would come as our customer because, well, you are a preacher and all. We thought that if you were a regular patron it would help others to have confidence in us. Give us a kind of credibility… like a reference – but in person."

Pastor Jake turned away and looked out the window at the tall gum trees that lined the neighbouring block. He tried to gather his composure without staring at her suspiciously. She wasn't making a pass at him? How bizarre that she felt he could offer the very thing he struggled for: credibility.

But Ali was not looking at him. She studied the wall, the window, the floor; anywhere but where he stood. "But of course we wouldn't expect you to pay. No, no… I could just do it as a service… to the church, or as a favour because you're a friend of Toby's and Belle's… and she's been my best friend forever. Em just thought it might make a difference. Please consider this Sir." Tears welled on her lashes. She had not realised that the success of this project meant so much to her.

Pastor Jake turned and stared at her. He felt crushed that he could so clearly misread the situation. That he had assumed Ali was throwing herself at him like a tart made his hands burn with shame. Was there no end to his vanity? He was kind of intrigued that nothing was further from her mind.

He unfolded his arms and ran his fingers through his hair. It was getting long. He had not even thought about a barber. He was in front of the public eye and even though he was a great proponent of the maxim that 'appearances are not an indication of the man within', he did need to be neat and respectable. Oh boy. He wanted that cup of tea now. He went over to the kettle and poured two cups. They were tepid from sitting out. He handed one to Ali. "I'm a little surprised... and grateful, that you think my position would hold so much influence." He paused. "Is my hair that bad?"

"Oh no. No, no. That is not what I meant. I just... Yes. It is really. Sorry."

"Can you cut hair? I mean, are you good at it?"

Ali bristled. "Well of course! I wouldn't offer to cut people's hair for money if I couldn't do it. That would hardly be honest... and certainly not a good way to make our venture work."

From what I hear, it hadn't stopped Hendricks, he thought. He pulled out a bench and sat down. He shook his head again. It was not often that he was taken by surprise.

Ali pursed her lips and sighed. "You don't want to get involved, do you? Em said preachers don't like mixing business with their spiritual duties."

He blinked at that and smiled. "People are my business – so if that means becoming familiar with their livelihoods, I've no problem with that. You're not asking me to do anything unethical. You're offering to cut my hair – regularly. Apparently even pastors require haircuts... unless their name is

344

Samson." He laughed at his own joke. "I would be quite prepared to pay."

"Oh, that would be wonderful! Not about offering to pay, of course," she clarified quickly, "It is great that you will consider our service. If you don't like what we do, you don't have to keep coming. But I know you won't be disappointed with us."

"You're quite a persuasive business woman Miss Dampier."

"Miss Dampier?"

"Would you prefer I call you Miss Alice?"

"Just Ali. Dampier is so official, I thought I had done something to offend you."

"Oh no. I think I have been the offensive one. I'm sorry."

"What do you mean? You said yes."

"I… yes." He nearly let it go. She need never know, but something in his heart urged him to be straight down the line with this lady. "I was worried when you said you needed to ask me a question. I thought you were going to ask me to consider to go courting with you. I'm sorry I did not give you credit for higher motives when you asked your father to suggest I offer you a lift."

Ali stared at him. Did he really think that? She looked around and remembered his stern expressions. She softly laughed – a cold heartless chuckle. She couldn't help it. "Oh, Pastor Jake – you must not have heard. I'm not going out with anybody; nor am I likely to. I was engaged last year. I will never marry now."

"Oh, I'm sorry. It was inappropriate for me to surmise."

"Don't be sorry. My fiancé did not die... although I did want to kill him. No, Jimmy is alive and well. For someone who had declared undivided and undying devotion, he recovered quite quickly it seems. He is married to someone else now..."

"Oh. Jimmy and Betsy." He saw her flinch. "In time you may have reason to change your mind."

Why was it that when people learned of her intentions never to pursue another relationship, they were all so very determined to unlock the cover she had placed over her heart. "No, I don't think so. A few have asked me out... but I don't want to go courting, or get married. But I do want to be independent. That is why this business is important to me."

He sat still for a while. He was shocked again. There was so much that he didn't know about the lives of the people around him. How could he ever minister to people who refused to uncover their lives to him because he was an outsider? It seemed that everything was on hold until he chose a local girl... that *this* would be his mark of credibility. Only then he could move on and be accepted. He understood a little more of the journey that Reverend Bernard would have walked, as a man who had resolutely chosen to stay untangled from romantic enticements in the district. What happened to the time honoured values of hard work, consistency, compassion and truth in building trust? But perhaps when Jesus gave the Great Commission - he had not considered what it meant not to be born a local in Wattle Creek.

Yet here was Ali - one slit in the solid impenetrable façade of Wattle Creek's community. She had been honest – transparent about her business and her position. He had found a friend. "You know Ali... I know exactly what you mean. I don't intend to marry either. I want to be able to commit to this work whole heartedly."

"Really? I thought that you were courting Phyllis Hemming."

"And where did you hear that?"

"I work in a Barber shop. Where do you think I heard that?"

"Well your sources are not reliable. I have never asked her father for the privilege."

"Tommy Hemming was in the other day. If her brother would not deny it..."

"Of course, he wouldn't deny it. There is nothing to deny!"

"Phyllis is also very convinced of your attentions."

"Phyllis? Oh, dear no... sure I've had limited contact with her family, and apparently that is all that is required." It was the last thing he needed, and it was the very thing he had not encouraged; yet somehow it had quickly got around town that he and Phyllis were an item. "I can't see where she would get such an idea. I have never encouraged her attentions or ..." Jake stopped, frozen as he suddenly remembered his Wednesday night bible study group. He replayed the evening in his mind. The first week Phyllis turned up unexpectedly, she was sporting the biggest bible he had ever seen – straight off the family mantelpiece. Her being there had genuinely surprised him and consequently he had wanted her to feel very welcomed.

Phyllis had smiled disarmingly and sat down beside him… just a little too close he had thought at the time. She had seemed very attentive to the lesson, and had asked many questions. Her interest had encouraged him to devote a fair amount of the study time to promoting her grasp of the topic, especially when some of her questions had not a lot of sound theological understanding behind them. No – perhaps that was a little too generous. She was asking a load of dumb questions – mainly about the classical coloured illustration plates in the middle of the bible. Still, she had seemed anxious to know more. He had been relieved when the group finally dispersed. The evening had been quite exhausting. He was surprised when she came back the next week, and the scene had acted out almost identically. He had no idea she was preening herself to become the pastor's wife! It was a shame she was not clever enough to think of new questions. Somehow, he had acquired a potential fiancé he had no intention of courting.

Pastor Jake sighed. "I went to visit her grandfather, since he's bed-ridden. Phyllis' father offered to sell me a horse… but I can't ride, so that was pointless."

"You can't ride? Why not?"

"The parish provides a sulky. Besides I grew up with trains and bikes. Nothing that ate straw was really needed."

"Oh dear… you are seriously disadvantaged."

"I fear to ask what you mean…"

"An eligible bachelor, in a district of desperate singles… no saddle-horse, and in need of a hair cut. Life, for you Pastor, is looking seriously grim!"

He laughed, glad that she could make light of it. "Perhaps you might be able to help… a kind of exchange for gracing your barber's chair."

"Pastor Jake - I would be only too happy to assist you in your wretched situation, in any way I can. I know a hair-cut could tip the balance in your favour."

"I'm thinking… you don't want to be bothered by potential suitors. I don't wish to give young ladies the impression I am available when my heart is not. I tell them this, but it does not seem to mean anything."

Ali looked at him queerly. "What do you mean?"

"By convention the Pastor gets invited to all the local functions. I suspect it is a courtesy thing… and I understand that most of these invitations were declined in the past. Reverend Bernard – although people respected his ministry, there is a residual feeling that he was exclusive, almost a recluse. I want to meet and get to know people at the coal-face… where they work, where they do the hard yards, and where they relax and wind-down as well."

"Why don't you accept the invitations then? You don't have to follow what Reverend Bernard did. People expect you to be different."

"But Ali, to accept these invitations there is also an expectation I will not go alone. If I could have someone to accompany me to upcoming functions… the locals would think I'm off the suitor smorgasbord. They would leave me alone to do my work. If you were that other person, they would leave you alone too – to concentrate on your business. It could be a solution for both of us."

"You want *me* to be the one who'll go to these functions with you?" When he nodded, she swallowed hard. "You have not heard me… I don't want to go courting."

"Oh, I heard you perfectly well. In this situation, we're not dating… just turning up together. I will collect you, be the attentive gentleman while I get the opportunity to rub shoulders with the locals. Then I'll drop you home on time… until the next function. If you don't want to go I could put in an apology for both of us… or just for yourself. It would not hurt to miss some events. You see, this is a very proper solution, because it would not be decent for me to be flitting from one date to another. I would be branded a womaniser, and be treated with deserved scorn."

"So, everyone will *think* we are courting."

"You and I will know what we have privately agreed to… it would seem appropriate to keep this between ourselves."

"But people will eventually ask when we are getting engaged…"

"In time we could discuss it further… but we don't have to tell anyone anything if we don't want to. If it seems inordinately long and inappropriate, we can officially break off the arrangement. Everyone would leave us alone for a while. We would have officially broken our hearts. It's not an uncommon plight."

Ali grimaced and turned away. It seemed flippant for a religious man to say that. She did not suspect for a moment that her plight was common! "It doesn't seem very honest. What happens if you change your mind... and you meet someone you really want to marry? How will that work?"

"Not honest? I think we are being up front with our expectations. That's truthful, don't you think? I trust you Miss Ali. I'm not sure why, because half an hour ago I thought you were throwing yourself at my feet in desperation. Now I feel like I'm the frantic one. If the agreement is not working, or we change our minds, we stop."

"How often do you think it would be needed – to go out like that?"

"I'm not sure. There is a theatre-night next week. Mrs Hollis wanted me to buy tickets, so I bought a couple. I gave those away, but I can buy more. I'm pretty sure it will not be a sell out performance. Oh Ali... if you think you could stand it, having this understanding would really help. I will need a haircut before then," he added as if that would make the weight of the argument conclusive.

"I think I can... it would suit me as well."

He smiled and lifted his hat from the peg near the door. "Miss Dampier, it would be my pleasure to drive you home. I will need a moment to ask your father's permission to take you as my guest to the theatre-night."

Ali took his arm. "Be careful. Dad might kiss you. He will be so delighted."

41.

Emmaline was surprised and a little bit honoured when Mrs Wallace offered an invitation to afternoon tea. She remembered her unusual comments about marriage at Belle's wedding and she was very much interesting in getting to know the woman behind them. They sat outside under the trees, lace napkins gracing the white furniture, Sarah – their housemaid hovered attentively to their needs. Emmaline sighed. This felt so comfortable... so like home. How she missed the ordinary comforts of her ELLIOT life.

Small talk wafted around the edges of life in Wattle Creek. Mrs Wallace had a private rule to avoid entering into specifics... and the fascinating allure of gossip. Em found that rather different. Her Grandmother was the first to dive into specifics... the more specific the better. Mrs Wallace enquired about the shop and how she found the changes to her life in Wattle Creek. In any other setting it might have been suspiciously like gathering gossip-fuel, but Em had no reason to doubt Mrs Wallace was true to the pattern she saw as they shared tea.

"I enjoy the shop... because it is my independence. But it is so different to the usual things women do in Wattle Creek. It seems that there is a general principle around here that there should be no other expectation out of life other than that of getting a husband and having a house full of kids."

Mrs Wallace smiled and nodded. She had a far away glint in her eye when she responded. "I remember making those same observations at your age. I screamed about the world being full of possibilities… yet it always seemed to be swallowed up by this predictable, ordinary doorway that everyone I knew was being sucked through. I didn't know whether I wanted to be on that run-of-the-mill train. I wanted to know if there was something more exceptional that I could be part of..."

"Yes! That is exactly what I mean! Yet…"

Mrs Wallace smiled. "Perhaps you think I succumbed in the end and boarded that matrimonial train?"

"Well… I think there are points in life where we get to make choices. It is so hard to know which is the best way." Emmaline sipped her tea. Choices… like not going back to ELLIOT HOUSE.

"You know… some of these choices are not necessarily good or bad… they just change the route of the journey we travel – we turn right or we turn left. If we commit our choices to God, where we end up… that is set by Him. Our destination stays the same… but the scenery changes a bit… that's all. I don't have my daughter Lois with me now… I didn't have a choice about that. If I could have held her... Still…" A wistful sigh escaped her lips and she sipped her tea.

"Oh, Mrs Wallace I'm so sorry. That was very uncaring of me. I did not know…" Emmaline felt the jolt of her *faux pas*. Why did no one tell her she had a daughter?

"Oh, Emmaline, don't distress yourself dear. How could you know? Lois has been gone for years. She was just sixteen when she left us to be with Jesus. It has not been something that we have hidden… but it is generally not something that comes up in everyday conversation either."

Emmaline shifted uneasily in her chair. Certainly not the typical type of afternoon tea conversation. Mrs Wallace had a daughter who died. Yet she sat here, looking serene and accepting. It was abnormal. Surely the woman was maladjusted or mentally unwell. It just didn't seem like she was. That's all.

Mrs Wallace looked at her quickly and smiled. "But you know – even though that was something that we had no choice about, it does not mean that we have not had the opportunity of a fulfilling journey. God chose this road to take us to the fullness of His plan. I cannot judge His wisdom. He has His reasons. God will not issue shoes that are too big to fit."

Emmaline sat twirling the lace napkin in a preoccupied, charmless way. Her Grandmother had scolded her many times for such distracted ill-manners. Em quickly put down the napkin and looked at Mrs Wallace, but she hadn't noticed. Mrs Wallace poured another cup of tea. "I used to think that when the unconventional ambitions of youth faded, it was a sign that a person's character had become flabby. By compromising the vigour of our young days, it seemed to indicate a downward spiral to mundane insignificance."

"I always feel there should be more…"

"Oh Emmaline. What you seek won't be achieved outside of walking in step with God who has made you. Take your money for example. I know many girls who would think that if they could have your dresses, your parties, your amusements and your education… that all their problems would be solved… or at least a good part of them. Yet you had those things and still are looking…"

Emmaline pulled at her serviette again. "Those things are just a distraction that filled up the days. But when I stop I realise… I am essentially still at the same place. Don't misunderstand me, I don't despise my lessons… but there are many in *this* community who would consider my education very deficient. Understanding the masters in classical art does not hold a lot of weight around here."

"Ah – that is clever… 'just a distraction'. Emmaline, how very insightful."

Em raised her eyebrows. How could she say she was insightful? She felt like her head was being pushed under water and she couldn't breathe properly. Her nameless struggles loomed large in her mind as she listened. It was a struggle to keep going. "I guess we run our own races…" She wasn't even sure why she said that.

"The thing is Emmaline, I never understood until much later who would take on the next leg of the race." Mrs Wallace smiled gently. "What made it clearer for me was that I noticed God made His world to operate in a special way. The Bible speaks of when our world will be fully re-established in time. It says that every man will sit under his own vine and fig tree… times of security, family, peace, and contentment. These are the ambitions that God has for His people – when everything is in order. The reign of King Solomon was considered the pinnacle in history for the nation of Israel, and the most notable thing about this time was recorded as *'each man dwelt under his own vine and fig-tree'.*

"Gradually I saw that being part of a family, and raising the next generation to be active and healthy – not to add to the worlds problems… but to be part of the solutions; living securely in our relationships and being content in our circumstances… this is its own reward - just like Paul said, *"…godliness with contentment is great gain."*

"That is when I truly started to enjoy the miracle of those family years with Lois. Even though they were short… they were a blessing beyond measure. I'm so – ever so, grateful that I understood that then… oh what I could have missed out on. Being part of a family is a huge honour – something that God gives to his people to show his favour and grace, and I very nearly despised and rejected it.

"How could I face my Lord and say that His greatest gift was seen as a burden, or worse - a curse? How could I tell Him I rejected His gift because I thought my family would tie me down and stop me from reaching my potential? Oh – did it ever stop me from growing into who I am intended to be? Believe me, I grew in those family years, more than I ever imagined possible."

Em stirred another spoon of sugar in her tea. She felt encouraged to keep going, to find her own race to run, and to run it with all her might.

Em lifted her basket of books onto her lap as the sulky pulled up at the gate of the Lawson's farm. Uncle Alf looked at her one more time. "Sure you'll be okay to walk home?"

"Yes thanks, Uncle Alf. I appreciate the lift." He flicked the reigns and clicked his tongue. Sometimes it seemed he worried more over his girls than was natural.

Oh yes, Alf was so grateful he had been blessed with his Alma... childhood sweethearts... and now, comfortable companions. Why couldn't history just repeat itself? He knew his daughter's heart had been scarred from her broken engagement. He wanted to give her every opportunity to be a woman who could find her own way. Alf hadn't liked the idea that Ali had apparently chosen spinsterhood over being a wife and mother. He knew his darling Alice had so much to offer. Not that he blamed her really. Still, it was a relief that the Pastor had taken a shine to his Ali; and he was kinda surprised that Ali had been so amiable towards his invitation. Perhaps it just took the right man at the right time. There had been many suitors, willing to pick up what that mongrel Golders had tossed aside, and he prayed this preacher was a man of his word. He would hate to go and do something desperate to a man of the cloth because he failed in his duty.

He thanked God that Emmaline had come along. His niece was totally entrenched in Alf's fathering-heart. It wasn't just her friendship that was the saving of their precious Ali. No, Em belonged with them. She had been away too long. In hindsight he should have held his ground back then. But, at the time, it seemed Edith Farrington held many more cards that would benefit the girl.

Things weren't going so swell at the shop. It was beyond his understanding how disgruntled patrons who never had a good thing to say about old Hendricks couldn't cope with the unconventional initiative of having a woman cut hair. In so many other things this town prided itself on bucking the system, but apparently not when it came to the tradition of barbering. The very idea that women would have the audacity to take on barbering generated quite passionate criticism. It was 'immoral', 'unnatural', 'perverted'... among other things! Yet at home every wife did this at sometime or other. It seemed that if they *really* were ladies of ill-repute there would be more respect in *that* profession than trying to earn an honest living doing something other than teaching children, nursing old women, or being a nun. It made absolutely no sense – even to Alf, who didn't consider himself a revolutionary by any means.

He shook his head. If only they could break through the hard headed prejudices of Wattle Creek's small town traditions. It was only hair after all. Hair grew back, or fell out... which ever came first. It hardly seemed worthwhile establishing a revolt over. Alf wasn't really a praying man, but at that moment he had to admit that the Divine needed to intervene. He glanced up at the sky as he turned the horse homeward and made his appeal. "Father in Heaven... have mercy... help my girls find their way."

Emmaline walked slowly to the Lawson house. She was in no hurry. She had come to pay a debt, and she was not too keen to address it. Still, she understood the proper etiquette, and she had resolved to do what needed to be done. She had agonised over the most fitting token of appreciation, and this is what she came up with. She knocked on the door and waited on the verandah until Josie came. "Oh, Emmaline, what a surprise... come in!"

"Mrs Lawson… I… well, I brought the ledgers over if you have a moment to check them. I…" she hesitated. "I also wondered if Nat was around."

"Nat? Oh. Yes, I think he's working in the stables… I'll call him for you if you like."

"I… ah." Emmaline stopped when she saw Mrs Lawson looking at her strangely. Surely she didn't think she was trying to get Nat's personal attention? Nothing could be further from the truth! She laughed nervously as she realised, that well, actually it was personal…sort of. "I'm sorry. That must sound strange. I brought him the kitten." Em pulled from the basket a gangly turtle-shell kitten – mottled and blotchy – a white patch covered its eye that gave it a perpetually wounded look. "You said he was really taken with the cat we rescued from the pepperina tree the other day… and… well, Uncle Alf's dairy has more cats than cows sometimes." Em had searched through the dairy cats for the perfect substitute for the mythical rescued kitten. It had to be the right age and have the right feel. This was the ugliest kitten she had ever seen. "I thought he might like it… since he helped save its life."

Josie laughed. Her boys never cease to surprise her. "Oh, he neglected to mention *he* helped in the salvage. Probably thought it wasn't manly or something. It's certainly an interesting looking specimen. You've been able to tame it down some. Poor thing was probably scared out of its skin," she said, looking at it curiously.

"Well, you said Nat was taken with it…" Em repeated with a blush. Had he just been talking about a mythical cat or what he really found up that tree?

359

Josie laughed out loud. "Still, one has to be careful. I've noticed people can become very attached to what they have rescued. The boys found a Galah once, just a baby one. It had fallen out of a tree. Something was wrong with it because it was always half bald. That bird went everywhere with Toby. For something that didn't have much covering, I spent years picking up pink and grey feathers."

Emmaline was confident that with Nat she was safe from any such attachment. He was increasingly giving Ali some attentions that indicated he was interested in more than her ability to cut hair. This intriguing observation amused her, because Em knew another card in her strong hand of immunity, was objectivity. There was going to be some interesting developments with Pastor Jake talking to Uncle Alf like he did.

Josie went to the corner of the verandah and picked up a rod and ran it around the metal triangle that called the men in for lunch. It clanged and jangled, and the kitten, lying quietly in Em's arms, bristled instantly and catapulted like a coiled spring from her hold. It skedaddled along the rail of the verandah and straight into a wilga-tree that stood sentry by the stone steps.

"Oh no – not again!" Emmaline exclaimed, forgetting that she had never rescued this cat, or any cat, from a tree. She had taken Nat's convenient story and embedded it into her personal history. Em quickly kicked off her shoes and climbed up onto the verandah rail. It was clinging to a branch within reach. Surely she could get hold of it. This was a token-gift to acknowledge Nat's assistance and close the matter. It was not suppose to create more embarrassment. "Here, Kitty, Kitty…"

She swung out over the rail, determined to retrieve it quickly before Nat answered the smoko call.

Josie barely paused. "I'll be back in a tick," she said and disappeared inside. Em was kinda pleased. She didn't need an audience, she just needed to get the cat down so she could present it to Nat and be gone. The kitten turned around at her coaxing and edged away. With a victorious thrill she could see success within inches of her fingertips. "Kitty, kitty…" It hissed and backed away further, its fur puffing up in agitation. "Oh, come on… we were friends a minute ago!"

"I'm guessing that won't make much difference… I've noticed things stuck in trees don't like to be disturbed."

Emmaline jolted. Stocking footed and swinging out from the verandah rail like a ten-year-old, she recoiled very self-consciously. "Nat! Oh…" She quickly slid down and slipped on her shoes. "I… I'm…" she blushed. How could she explain this? "Your mother said… I…" Oh this was too awkward. "You told her that I rescued a kitten," she said accusingly.

Nat looked bewildered at the bristled, mottled bundle of fur clinging precariously to the swaying branch. It was as ugly as sin. "I also said that cat was feral… and not very cooperative." He smiled, now very amused and looked back at Emmaline fascinated, her face reddening under his scrutiny. "Still, doesn't look like the same one to me…"

She stopped. There was really no come back. They both knew it wasn't. She felt like that cat – cornered in an unstable, insecure and unfamiliar situation… and that made her irritable, wanting to lash out. "I brought it over because there was something about it that reminded me of you." That should be obvious enough!

He couldn't help but be amused. "It wasn't me up the tree."

"Well it wasn't intended as a self portrait that's for sure." Now she regretted the snipe. Why did he so effectively unsettle her composure? "I… oh boy… this has not gone well. Nat, I wanted to thank you… truly."

He continued to study her face, and she refused to look at him. He glanced back at the kitten… fear taking over its tiny frame again, as it clung unsteadily in the swaying branches. "I might be mistaken. It is behaving much the same… trembling all over like that. I could guarantee it's got her claws out again as well…" He was enjoying the lack of composure in Emmaline's citified manners. It was so much easier to handle than that stiff upper-lip thing she seemed to specialise in. "You brought this as a thank you for 'the rescue'? That's kinda thoughtful."

"It was your idea. I appreciated it." There she said it. She wanted to say nothing more about his efforts to retrieve her from her Pepperina tree predicament.

"May I?" he asked, indicating the kitten mewing in a faint tremolo. Emmaline nodded. She could hardly say no. He swung onto the rail, his long arms quickly scooping the kitten from his hold and bringing it back down to earth, just as his mother emerged with a saucer of milk.

"Oh, you were able to get it down. Poor little mite. I've warmed some milk… may help settle it some. It's a nervous little thing… not the wild-cat you painted at all."

"Just different circumstances perhaps. Yep… pretty nervous." Nat said with a grin as he held it up to his face. Em wanted to hit him. So much for the peace offering! He set it down and gently dipped his nose into the milk. The kitten spluttered, flicked its milk-laden nose and sneezed. And then lapped it up with gusto. "I'm going to call it 'Pepper'. It reminds me of the time we extracted it from the pepperina-tree."

Emmaline sighed. He wasn't going to let it go.

42.

Ali swept around the chair, humming softly, and stepping in time with the broad sweeps of the broom. There was lightness in her movements. Emmaline tallied the money from the home made wooden till-box, constructed from recycled packing timber. Things were improving. The satisfied smile on her face faded when she looked up and saw Nat striding towards the shop. That same uneasy, unequalised feeling she felt on his verandah set her quickly stacking papers… an activity that had nothing at all to do with what she had just been doing. "Ali… I think we have another customer before we close up today…" she said as Nat strode through the door into the dimness of the shop.

"Got time for one more?"

"Sure Nat, come in. We don't turn away business… any time of day."

He sat down on the barber's chair, and Ali flicked a cover over his shoulders. Ali was never a slouch at small talk, and her skills were becoming quite honed. She unashamedly used the efficient community grape-vine to stay in touch. Nat partially closed his eyes as he relaxed under Ali's efficient care… curiously watching Emmaline in the mirror that was strategically positioned on the wall. She was interesting – this City-girl.

"So, Nat… tell me what is news at the Lawson spread?"

"Just the same ol' same ol'. A couple of new calves… oh… and a cat. Called it Pepper." This was for Emmaline's benefit. He smiled when he saw her jolt.

"A cat? Well you are full of surprises. Pepper and Pike! How does he like that? Couldn't imagine Pike getting along with anything that would challenge your total devotion."

Em blinked and then stiffened. She had forgotten Nat's loyalty to his dog, and the dog's loyalty to him. How could she have been so stupid? A cat was not appropriate at all. The whole thing was wrong from start to finish.

"It's surprising really. The two most unlikely critters… get along like a house on fire." He watched her busily recounting the till – again… and then she counted it again. The cat and the dog was not the only unlikely couple that had his attention.

"Nat, are you going to the dance next Friday night?" Ali enquired casually. Nat was not a great fan of this particular monthly Wattle Creek tradition.

He blinked and opened his eyes as he focused on her question. He had been completely distracted. "Ah, well… are you?"

"Sure." Ali snipped and combed. "Should be fun. Pretty much everyone is going."

Ali was going to the dance? She hadn't been since… well, since… a long time. "Oh. So, you're going… without a partner?"

"Oh, no. As liberated as I am, I really wouldn't feel comfortable going by myself. I have an escort… all very proper."

He sat up straighter. Ali had a partner? Surely not Pastor Jake again. Hadn't the Pastor told him he didn't want to get involved with anyone? He told Nat quite irritably that to settle down was the last thing on his agenda. So, what was he playing at?

"Wouldn't it be great if we could all go together?" Ali quipped excitedly.

Nat looked at her. Ali almost sounded like her old self. That was good. Or it could be concerning, if Jake was the reason for it. Nat cautiously responded, "Yeah. That's what I was thinking..."

"Great! You could partner Em. It would make such a pleasing group!" Ali said with a rush. Ali mentally substituted the word "pleasing" with "safe". She knew Nat hadn't just turned up at the Barbershop because his mother had suddenly forgotten how to trim beards. She hoped Nat's intention was not to try and woo her, because he must never be allowed to verbalise it if that was his plan. It could never be. Absolutely never.

Partner the Citygirl? Nat was thrown by the simplicity of the suggestion. Emmaline looked up from her refuge at the till. "Me?"

Ali blinked. She discovered she was deriving some strange delight by the shock in Nat's voice. She could never remember him doing anything spontaneous. He was always that way: the grown-up in a kid's body... taking over where his father let off. It would be interesting to get him out of that zone. "Oh, I'm sorry Nat, you already have a partner?"

"No. I hadn't seriously considered it. However,..."

"Well, do you want to go?" Ali insisted.

"Apparently so…"

"Well, there you go Em. Nat has no partner for the dance. This is perfect."

"Perfect? What about you - who are you going with?" Em demanded.

"Me? Oh, Lloyd asked me to go with him." Relief flooded her. She didn't even need to invent an explanation why she wasn't available!

Emmaline stared in total disbelief. "Pastor Jake is 'Lloyd' to you? When did this happen?"

"Well, Pastor Jake sounded a bit formal for a dance partner. He thought it was a good idea."

Nat narrowed his eyes and stared at Ali's reflection in the mirror. "You went to the theatre night with him too…. and now the dance?" It was just as he suspected.

"He says he can dance, so I'm assuming a person in his position would not lie."

"But he's the Reverend." This was not good. Didn't he know how fragile she was? The man was supposed to protect and care, not take advantage of other people's vulnerabilities.

"And… I'm the Barber. People don't always hold onto traditions as tightly as others. We are people Nat, not pre-written scripts." How delightful was their secret. She was doing this so well, and she knew it. Ali went back to cutting his hair with her most innocent dove smile on her lips, snipping just a little too rapidly for Nat's comfort.

"Ministers don't go to dances!"

"But you are planning on going. What makes it sinful for him and okay for you?"

"Well, he's a man of the cloth. They just don't." Shouldn't.

Ali lifted her chin defensively. "Em also assumed he wouldn't get involved in his parishioner's businesses, but he has happily supported our venture from the very beginning."

"What do you mean?"

Emmaline stepped around to get a look at Nat's face. "Pastor Jake comes into the shop every morning for a shave and a trim."

"What? Every morning? Can't the man wield his own razor?" He made it sound like a handicap – akin to having a limb amputated, or at the very least, an unforgivable incompetency in the basic skills of war-craft.

"Of course, he can. He does it as a gesture of support for our enterprise. I think it is very generous of him."

Nat screwed up his face sceptically. "Bet he doesn't pay the full fee!" Would he take advantage of their economic situation as well? How low could this man stoop?

"Our credit or debit arrangements with our customers are strictly confidential! Your mother taught me that," said Em abruptly.

"It's alright Em, Nat's like family. Of course Pastor Jake pays the fee. He's not like that. But actually, you do have a good point. Such loyalty should be rewarded with a discount of sorts."

Nat pursed his lips and frowned. Money and the church: it was always about money. For some reason he thought this guy was different. Evidently not. Perhaps he had been blinded by his contribution to his appointment.

Emmaline looked back down at her ledger. "If we donate every tenth haircut…that would reflect the ten percent tithe."

Ali was enthusiastic. "Yes – that's fantastic! I must remember to tell him."

"And now you're going to the dance with him," Nat scowled.

"Nat – what is the problem here? It was a perfectly legitimate invitation… and I accepted."

Nat looked at Ali poised above his hairline with a razor in her hand. "I wouldn't have thought him so desperate that he needed to buy his date," he said challenging. She should stay away from him. She was not strong enough to be torn apart by some bloke who had declared himself unavailable.

Ali pulled back and stared. She had seen Nat defensive before… but this had taken on a personal intensity. She loved Nat. Why would he spoil all their history by misplacing her regard and wanting to become possessive? It wasn't that way with them. Besides, if Pastor Jake was desperate because he was willing to be in her company that meant Nat was too. "For your information, not everyone around here who wants to keep company with me is desperate."

"That's not what I meant Ali. A Pastor…" She was twisting his words.

"I have had many requests to go out. My father is weary of excusing me from their talons on my behalf. When Lloyd asked, he also said he wouldn't go if he couldn't find a partner

369

without a great deal of fuss. I thought it would help him to get to know some of the people he wouldn't normally meet at Church."

"So, you're not going out." If she needed to be eased back into the public arena, it would be better if he personally did that. She would be safe with him.

"Yes, we *are* going out! We are going to the dance."

"But nothing more… like…"

Ali refused to dignify that with a response. Emmaline considered both of them. For someone whom she could normally read very well, the look on Ali's face was unfathomable. Nat glanced at Em out of the corner of his eye, as Ali was completing the final touches of his grooming. He could see she was as equally confused by Ali's enthusiasm for the outing. Now he definitely needed to go to the dance to keep an eye on things; a bit like squinting through a prayer. He cleared his throat, a rough, raspy sort of sound. "So Citygirl, do you feel like going to this dance?"

Emmaline recoiled inside. The man was irrepressible – if wild boars rampaging through scrub appealed to her, Nat Lawson would be a find. "I have been to plenty of dances. I have no great need to go."

"Well, would you go anyway? Needlessly?"

Emmaline arched her eyebrows at that. In his poorly executed courtesy, he looked flattened. Something softened in her eyes. "Well… why not? If nothing else it should be an interesting exercise in comparing social climates."

Nat went back to studying Ali's face. He had to say he couldn't blame Jake for taking advantage of the opportunity.

But he had better not mess with her. Ali was… well Ali. Gentle and loyal. Her cousin however was something else. Her unconventional gift of scrawny little Pepper had made a very big impression on him. He liked that cat. It might be ugly, but it had personality and was already proving to be a good mouser. As for pulling her out from some foolhardy stupidity that found her stuck in the bull-pen… that was destiny. He was sure. Still, as curious as he was, Nat was pretty certain that this eye-catching young lady was essentially a snob. That bothered him some, and he didn't want to seem too eager. He waited for the cut hair to be brushed from his shoulders and stood up. "I'll pick you up at seven then," he said to Emmaline as he handed over his coins, and abruptly headed for the door. Em looked through the window as he strode across the street. Already she regretted yielding to her instincts of avoiding this man's company at all costs.

Wattle Creek was buzzing with the anticipation of the evening dance. Ali spent a lot of time doing their hairstyles. "If our hair looks ratty, it won't do any favours for our business. We will be walking, dancing advertisements all night… and we won't have to pay for the publicity."

With the skill of a master artisan at her craft Ali created the illusion of abundance and body. When Emmaline finally looked in the mirror she exclaimed in amazement, "Oh Ali, people always comment on the colour of my hair, but I find it so hard to make it sit well. You are incredible!"

"Hey. It's what we do," she said with a very pleased smile, as she gently brushed one remaining loose strand into the elegant auburn scroll at the nape of her neck. Emmaline felt like a baroness. An event had never felt so special even with all her rich escorts and bejewelled outfits. She couldn't imagine how a plain weatherboard hall could have this effect on her, much less a whole district. But it did. She was really looking forward to the outing and trying not to think too hard that keeping company with Nat Lawson was more than half of her anticipation. They had chattered and giggled their way through getting dressed, making their transformations complete.

At exactly seven o'clock two sulkies pulled up outside their small residence. Pastor Jake jumped down with a light step. He greeted Nat with an enthusiastic wave, the muted light of the deepening dusk enhancing his anticipation for the evening. Nat barely nodded, but for Jake his reserved demeanour was nothing unusual. Jake learnt a while back that Nat avoided socialising with vigour. It was good to see him getting out of himself and taking care to balance up his life with a few social outings. The evening bode well.

"We should have organised to bring only one buggy. Seems a waste to have both of us driving when we're going to the same spot." Nat couldn't agree, so he grunted noncommittally. There is no way he'd be sitting in the back seat, watching that man take Ali's arm. Ali's heart gave devotion without reserve. He certainly shouldn't be messing with it flippantly, just for the social convenience of having a date, if he had no intention of following through. He couldn't help reflecting how it would feel to have such a sweet girl respond to him that way. He would be loyal to the death. Nothing would tear such a prize away. And he thought of Emmaline: The girl from the city... up a tree... leaning on him heavily as she found her land-legs.

The whole thing pulled Nat up short. He suddenly realised that marriage was a very desirable state; something he had never bothered thinking about much before. He had assumed it would be something that would take care of itself when the time came. It was rather inconvenient that in his ordered world, it was probably not going to be the simple process he had always supposed it would be. He hadn't factored in emotions or people... or life... or Emmaline.

Pastor Jake knocked at the door, holding a bouquet of flowers, and a small corsage. Nat stared in horror. Oh my! He had been too embarrassed to even tell his mother about the dance. At least she would have reminded him about flowers. How could he have forgotten something so basic? Pastor Jake turned to Nat as he heard the girls fussing inside. "One would think we hadn't given them sufficient warning... like a fortnight's notice is not enough!" His laughter faded suddenly and he started kicking his right foot against the core doormat. "Wouldn't you know it? I've picked up a stone in my boot. Here hold this for me will you?" Without waiting for a reply he thrust the bunch of flowers he was holding into Nat's hands and ripped off his boot, thumping it upside down against the balcony rail. "Had a stone bruise once. Couldn't walk for a week."

Just then the door opened and Em stared into the evening dimness. "Evening gentlemen..." A serious of thumps and bumps echoed around inside. Emmaline smiled apologetically. "Ali is turning the house upside down looking for her purse. I'm sorry. We were so organised, but now we are holding you up."

Pastor Jake laughed. "No worries… I'm not even dressed myself. Stone…" he offered, indicating the boot in his hand as they looked on bemused. He hopped around straightening his sock so he could get his boot back on. Emmaline felt the whole thing was staged and there was no possible explanation why that would be so. Then they could hear Ali calling, "Emmy, I found it! Put it down beside the bed when I went to change my necklace. This one is prettier don't you think?" She came around the door-jam and froze. "Oh. You're here…" She laughed nervously. Was she so out of practice that she hardly knew what to say?

Pastor Jake smiled disarmingly. "You look delightful Ali, I brought you a corsage. I fear the colour may not be right for your dress."

Ali glowed. "Fresh flowers have the delightful benefit of being suitable with any outfit. Thank you – it is lovely."

Nat found it hard not to gag at the display of soppy courtesy. It was way over the top. "Citygirl, can we go?" he muttered gruffly through his scowl. She nodded, clutching her wrap as if waiting for something. He had a strangle hold on the flowers that looked like he intended to commit murder. She could tell he had no plan of releasing them and was at a loss to know how to proceed. He obviously had no idea she was waiting for him to assist her with her shawl. It was all very unfortunate. The comparison with Richard's smooth escorts was stark. Sometimes it seemed his automated courtesies were so predictable it appeared he had undergone coaching with a time-warden. Couldn't she once have a partner who was not so extreme?

Jake quietly stepped up and taking Ali's stole, covered her shoulders, and putting out his arm, they set off towards his buggy. "Let's give them a little space Ali," he said quietly.

"Like we need space!" muttered Nat under his breath as he watched them walk casually away together.

"The flowers are lovely," Emmaline said pointedly after a pause. He had no choice but to hand them over. He didn't know whether to be grateful for the stone-in-the-boot charade or not. The idea of another bloke buying flowers for his date went against the grain. To take hold of the flowers, she handed him her shawl… and adeptly solved her problem. He held it for her and she twisted her shoulders underneath its brushed softness. *Finally,* they could go.

43.

The music was already playing as they arrived at the dance hall. Couples were mingling and standing around in animated clusters, laughing with each other about the amusing trivia that makes being young thrilling and vibrant. Nat jumped out and quickly came around to help Emmaline down. Em could see that he was playing the part - being attentive, anxious to please... but then she caught sight of Ali on Paster Jake's arm, talking casually together at the door. With a cold realisation she understood his haste to get inside. Ali. Always Ali. Ali always shone more brightly than she.

A wave of remembrance washed over her... moments when the dowdy, plain cousin from the city was left out of goings-on, yet again. Why did she keep doing this to herself? She had a good life at ELLIOT HOUSE... among the influential and the mannerly. Why did she subject herself to these humiliations again and again? At home... she was Grandmother's showpiece... a matter of pride... not second best. There, she was never the date you had to take because there was no other date to have. Em covered her eyes. It was a raw insight, revealing and demeaning. No one should have to feel this way... and she was disgusted that Nat had so carelessly tossed aside her anticipation of the evening.

But the curious thing was Em couldn't bring herself to resent Ali. She was the innocent party... the unwitting perpetrator because of her untainted simplicity. How could she blame Ali for that? Em's regret was that she was not more like her. It seemed she was destined to always be the understudy… even when the leading light didn't want to be centre stage. Ali was one of those blessed, cursed creatures who could not escape notice no matter how faded she might feel.

As Nat pushed his way inside, always keeping Ali in sight, Em excused herself and went to sit down. She was glad that Nat was too preoccupied to notice her retreat. She watched as he hooked up with some of his neighbours, and became immersed in conversation. Somehow, no matter where he stood he was able to position himself so that his view of Ali was unimpeded. From where she was sitting Em could hear snatches of the conversation that carried across the room. He was pointing out, with great force, some significant issues… "the seed has stored well", "breaking a new horse to the team", "planting rain is late this year". She became so absorbed in her observations that she almost forgot her pledge to despise and impose sanctions on his company. She was engrossed – vitality ignited his grey eyes. His solid frame was energised, pulsating life through his broad shoulders.

Blushing slightly she remembered his urgent action at the bull yard. Em had considered his strong build slow and cumbersome – right along with his mind. Now she reluctantly allowed a small dose of honesty, and admitted that, in truth, he was not thick and slow and stupid. His style was different to Richard's that's all. His energy for farming was different to Richard's lithe tennis playing. She amused herself by picturing swapped roles. Richard in Wattle Creek would be adaptable for example. He never seemed out of place – wherever he went. Imagine Nat at one of their city lawn parties! She smiled remembering her impressions at the wedding while he stood stiff-legged against the wall, and compared that picture to the vitality of the men negotiating business across the room. Well, she thought, they may be in their element out on their farms, but it irritated her that these clustered men had neglected their partners for so long and still made no attempt to move. It ceased to be poor manners. Now it was just rude – plain and simple.

Again, the frightening realisation crept into her consciousness: she was as restless as ever inside. The work at the barbershop had surfaced an inkling of what might be, but there was no real mission in that either. The dairy routine was different perhaps, but that mundane, grey drudgery was still there. Did such a purpose exist? What pursuit lit her fire? What was she looking for? If it wasn't tennis parties at Grandmother's private courts, or Richard's charity functions, then what? The consolation of partnering with Ali at the shop was that it gave her a measure of independence, and it didn't involve early pre-dawn mornings like the dairy. A strange disappointment agitated the pit of her stomach. Perhaps that was all that it would ever be for her. She felt let-down to think that might be the total sum of it.

"May I have this dance?" Em blinked. Pastor Jake was standing comfortably before her, hand extended.

"I haven't been dancing tonight," she said to excuse herself. It was humiliating to think that her partner had not emerged for at least a courtesy waltz.

"I have noticed. Please do me the honour. I suspect Emmaline Farrington has been to too many dances in the past, not to have pity on me for just one dance. Ali has taken a break and I am enjoying the country atmosphere too much to take one myself just yet."

Emmaline laughed. "How well, Pastor Jake, you know how to appeal to feminine vanity. I don't consider myself a poor dancer." She rose and took his hand as he led her to the floor. Why would Ali's partner care to notice her lack of floor time? It was very flattering that he chose to know more about her than just being Alma Dampier's niece. Around here, that was most people's entire understanding of her situation.

Nat was partway through his next sentence when he was suddenly pulled up short. He stared at Em and the Pastor twirling around the dance floor laughing and tapping in time to the music. It was not enough that Pastor Jake had claimed Ali for the evening, now he was deserting her and muscling in on his rightful partner. It was obscene, unethical, and downright wrong. No decent guy would stoop to that. Pastor or not.

Nat excused himself and strode over the dance floor. He tapped Pastor Jake on the shoulder to cut in. His eyebrows rose slightly, but bowed out to let Nat take up the position. Emmaline's face clouded in a firm frown. "What are you doing?" she said tersely under her breath.

"Cutting in."

"Whatever for?"

"Well, I brought you here… seems the thing to do."

"You're kidding, aren't you?"

"No, quite serious."

"That's ridiculous. You've stood over there the entire evening having no interest in being my partner at all... until another gentleman had the decency to ask me to dance."

Nat looked quickly at her face and stopped dead in the middle of the step as he was confronted with her anger. It absolutely took him by surprise. Whatever was her problem? Emmaline dropped her arms and pushed away. She grabbed her shawl by the door and walked determinedly outside. Nat stared after her until it slowly occurred to him that she was leaving, like really leaving. As in, not coming back.

He shrugged in bewilderment, and when Pastor Jake quietly stood at his shoulder and said, barely above a whisper, "You'd better go after her mate. She looks pretty ticked off..." Nat turned around, and before anyone could come near, he slogged Pastor Jake on the chin catapulting him backwards into the dancing couples, knocking him out. The music ground to a halt. Nat swore and strode out the door in a rage, grabbing his hat as he went. How dare he act all high and mighty!

"Stubborn Citygirl!" he muttered under his breath. This was unbelievable. "Ah, Em... Miss Farrington... wait!"

Emmaline made no effort to recognise his appeal. She had had enough. She was leaving. If she wrote to Grandmother, perhaps she could go back to ELLIOT HOUSE even now... in spite of everything. Richard had more manners than all the landed gentry of Wattle Creek put together!

"Citygirl!" He swore under his breath. "Let me get the horse!"

She did not look back at him or pause. He had to be completely deluded if he thought she would wait for him. What had she been doing all night? There was no way she would ride his horse again. "Citygirl!" His voice was fading. At least he wasn't following. That was something. At that moment she was grateful he didn't understand any courtly principles, much less the one about driving your date home, come hell or high water. She quickly stepped up the pace. It was a disaster… and she had no one but herself to blame. She knew what he was like… and yet for some brainless, moment of insanity, she had put herself in his sphere. Well, never again!

Pastor Jake rubbed his jaw, as the room came back into focus. The man had a solid right hook, he had to give him that. Ali bent over and helped him up. He was not too proud to wobble a little, being rewarded to have her croon caringly over his split lip and by pressing a damp tea towel folded in a wad to his face. At Ali's suggestion they decided to make it a night.

As he drove Ali home, one thought kept going around in his mind, throbbing in time with the pulsating in his swollen lip. He pulled the horse to a stop, and casually secured the reigns. "Well, that was an interesting night all told. I fear my plan has been thwarted completely."

Ali smiled in the dark. Whatever plan he alluded to, he didn't really seem too distressed over its demise. "Don't worry about Nat. He'll forget what that was about in a day or two. He is a good man Pastor Jake… he just sometimes forgets when his temper lets fly."

"That is a very definite and convincing character reference Miss Ali… for someone who just slogged your friend for a totally unidentified offence." Ali blushed at the reference to their friendship, grateful that the gloom covered her complexion modestly. She had a fair idea what was behind the ruptured lip and fractured tempers. He continued. "Whatever it was about – I can honestly say, my conscience is clear. Enough about Nat… I'm sure he's already caught up with Em and they are sorting it out."

Ali smiled, less than certain. "Perhaps. My cousin might look frail, but she is more than capable of looking after herself. I have more fear for Nat in this case."

"Oh? That's an interesting perspective. I must admit I never considered fearing for Nat's wellbeing. Are you sure they will be okay? Should we chaperone them… if his health is at stake?"

Ali laughed. "No, nothing like that. Nat is fine… he's just out of practice when it comes to women. His Mum and his neighbourly connections have perhaps not been so diligent in teaching him the courtesies expected when on an outing. His usual company is working horses and cows… and his dog – Pike."

"So, this episode at the dance… you are taking responsibility for this as his neighbour? That is very generous of you."

"Generous? Not at all. The Lawson's are not just our neighbours – we grew up together…they're like family. And you said so yourself, this is about friendship."

Lloyd felt a twang in his chest. There was that familiarity of being local again: part of the scenery… part of their lives. Would he ever have this privilege? "I am glad you have said so. Perhaps my evening has not been so thwarted after all. Ali, thank you for coming with me this evening. I have met a few more people, made a few more connections. The one with Nat's knuckles noted of course."

Ali laughed. "You will do fine here Pastor. A beating is part of the local initiation of Wattle Creek. The next phase is being dragged through the streets and being pelted with rotting vegetables. Any subsequent torture is easy."

Lloyd smiled. How fortunate he was to have made such a friend. "All in all, I did have a good night. I suspect that my acceptance has much to do with the way that you have opened your heart to me. It means a great deal to me Ali … knowing your disinclination to… well… to be accompanied. I wanted to thank you… and I wasn't sure how. I bought a gift, and I understand that you may not want to wear it… but I thought it might represent our friendship… between us… as we discussed."

Now Ali was intrigued. Her heart quickened when he brought out a small gift box. She opened it carefully, holding it up to the lamp light. It was a novelty ring… three gold bands that interlocked and joined at the top in a cross. "It is a Russian puzzle ring. I like the idea that the three bands join together… it has lots of symbolism for me. I want our friendship to be bound together with God as the third party… always our chaperone, always linking us together."

Ali lifted it carefully out of the box, but the three rings collapsed before she could put it on. "Oh dear – this is not good. I failed puzzles at elementary school! What if I cannot get it back together... does this mean our friendship has fallen apart?"

Lloyd shrugged. "The failure would be all mine. Perhaps it just means it is a little more complex and we need to help each other in getting it to fit together. The analogy is a poor one though. This is just a trinket. If it breaks or gets lost... our friendship will survive those tragedies." He took the ring and linked the separate rings back together. "See – they fit together so well."

He handed it to Ali... hoping that she would not put it back in the box but would be inclined to wear it. She slipped it on her right hand – and it fell straight off her slender finger into her lap. She tried again to link it together, Lloyd helping her. When it was joined she slid it on her middle finger and, although still a little loose, it fitted better. She felt shy. "Thanks for your friendship too... and the gift.

Emmaline was stunned when she heard the horse cantering to her side. Nat slid off her bare back and walked beside Em, holding the mare by her halter rubbing her chestnut ears as they went. He'd taken her out of the harness. He said nothing, the silence pounding in her ears. She glanced his way, trying to distinguish his face in the dark shadows made from the pale light that the houses cast weakly onto the streets. Still he was quiet, tense and terse, and she waited for him to say something, anything... defend his behaviour, apologise or remove himself. He did none of these... but just walked slowly with his horse, adjusting his pace to accommodate her shoes that were built for dancing, not walking.

She wanted to out-walk him, she wanted to out-freeze him, she wanted to out-class him, but as the distance from the hall increased, and his insolent silence remained, she could not contain herself any longer. She stopped and turned on him. "Look – I don't know what you hope to achieve by being here, but I'll be home soon, so take your horse and go Nat. Never, (I repeat - *never*!) ask me out again!"

Never? To suggest Nat Lawson *'never'* to do anything riled him, like a red rag agitated the bull penned in his yards at home. 'Never' was not in his nature. He stopped and looked at her in the dimness. He was kind of grateful he could not see the anger that he heard in her voice. "So, I take it that you and Comet didn't hit it off when we saved you from a long walk home?" He tried not to think about how it felt to hold her steady and close. That had been a tantalisingly slow ride back to Dampier's place, given it was just across the creek. "This mare is much more gentle… she won't mind you riding if your shoes are not up to it."

"I hope to *never* have to endure your company again. Horse or no horse."

He was shocked that he had so offended her. It was not like he intended to behave badly. "You only have to say "no". Can't stop you doing that," he said trying to keep the defensiveness he was feeling out of his tone.

"Well, that's not a problem. I can manage that! No! There, see, I have saved you the trouble. Now, if you don't mind… leave me alone!" She never spoke like this! And she didn't even feel guilty for her brutal behaviour.

"Just so happens I do mind – gotta at least see you home."

"Well, don't. I relieve you of that responsibility. Consider it my treat!"

He could only be patient so long. Her spite was needling his repentance back to the bone. He was irritated, and annoyed, like an angry wasp wanting to lash out and sting. He bucked against the restraint civility demanded. It had been imprinted into him from the father he idolised from his childhood. "Look, I don't know what your problem is, but I *will* see you home. And I *will* ask you out again *if* that is what I want."

"Don't humiliate yourself again, by your ignorant and unmannerly behaviour. I will only have to refuse you."

"Unmannerly? I hardly call you the pin-up poster girl of manners yourself, for all your snooty training."

"Oh, that is rich! There is nothing wrong with *my* manners. Ali would…"

"Ali? Ali has nothing to do with this!"

"Ali has everything to do with this. You know she does! Take it from me; it is not at all flattering to be considered the second rate date because your original plans were thwarted. You have ignored me all evening! Not only that - as soon as Pastor Jake took pity on me for your rudeness, you cut in. I am absolutely sure you did it to spoil the only pleasant moment I had all evening. I've had it with you!"

He shook his head in bewilderment. She couldn't seriously think that he was jealous of a pastor. He was above the likes of him. Certainly, to follow her adamant directive was not an option. She flagged a challenge: to stubbornly refuse another invitation for an outing. He said nothing, but it was obvious he had no choice but to convince her to go out - to make amends. It's just that he didn't go to dances very often… and her expectations seemed a tad unrealistic. She was used to money and city ways.

44.

It seemed a worthy practice for Jesus to get up early in the morning and go out to a lonesome place to pray. Jake took it upon himself to do likewise. There was so much about Wattle Creek that he didn't understand: the people, their struggles, their silent stoic bearing. He could not explain how the images of their faces were burnt into his chest, branded onto his soul like he was being marked one of the herd. His only response was to get outside and walk it out… and pray. During those walks he prayed wordless prayers for the faces in his congregation, knowing that God knew their silent battles and could meet their need. It was during one of these walks that he knew he had to go and see Nat.

"Whoa!" Nat pulled up the horses and wiped the sweat from his eyes. The dust was thick and the dry heat seemed to turn the earth to powder. He adjusted his felt brimmed hat and stared at the cloudless sky, and wondered again if he was doing the right thing. Always be prepared. You never know, the clouds might start to gather on the horizon. What seemed impossible was that this time last year the grain was already in the ground and starting to shoot. They had waited for the showers… and waited. But the time for waiting was over. If the paddocks weren't ready… any rains that came now, would be lost.

His eyes caught a figure tracking across the paddock to meet him. He couldn't make out who would be visiting at this time. He wasn't exactly expecting anyone. He paused for a moment, waiting as they came closer. His brow furrowed like his paddock when he saw it was the Pastor. He didn't have time for a sermon. What did he hope for... a larger offering on Sunday because of a pastoral visit? Not likely mate. Remote courtesy was not Nat's style. He'd rather lay it all out for everyone to see. "I don't have the time for visitin' Pastor. Me and the horses have an overdue schedule to meet. Sorry you had to come this way for nothing."

"I won't take long. Wanted to apologise if I had offended you in some way... since you landed me one across the jaw at the dance."

Nat looked again at the sky. It was getting that bronzy sort of sheen to it. That ain't good. "Why?"

Jake stared at him, Ali's words were sounding quite insightful just now. Could things really be so close to the surface he truly had forgotten all about it? "You decked me – apparently without provocation. Kinda thought that there might have been a reason."

Nat pulled the canvas bag from the side of the plough and took a swig of cool water. "I'll see you on Sunday. Can't it wait 'til then?"

"Well, the Book says to leave your offering at the altar if you have a brother who is offended and go and sort it out. I can't do a whole week without speaking to God."

Nat shrugged. Perhaps he had been wrong. Ali seemed okay when he went to the Barber-shop yesterday. He pulled up the reigns and readied himself to start ploughing again.

Jake didn't quite know what to say. There was no explanation, no visible remorse... and he obviously hadn't been stewing on any of this, like Ali said. Jake guessed he would have to be content with that. "So… you and me: we're okay?"

"Yeah. If you wanna be. Got a question for ya though."

He sighed. That was over. "What?"

"You and Ali… are you – like, seeing each other?"

Jake blinked. Ali? Had this been about Ali? He wished he could say that they were together, like really together, but the terms of their agreement loomed large in his vision: the appearance of attachment, but no real ties. He could not deny that, should Nat want to, he had as much right to see her as he. For the first time the arrangement tasted bitter on his tongue, not quite right. He slowly shook his head. "No. We are not."

Nat relaxed. There. He said it. Ali was okay. That was good enough for him. Funny – that for all his doubts about Jake, he didn't question his word.

Jake looked at him dubiously. "You're still at odds with me, aren't you?"

"Oh, give me a break. Of course not. But I will be if you hold me up much longer. Gotta keep these horses moving Pastor." He flicked the leather reigns, yelling to his team.

Jake kept pace beside him as they pulled forward. "Could you do with a hand then? Surely there is something I could do, help you out a bit."

Nat kept his team moving as they leant their shoulders into their harness. "You want to *what?*" he said kinda shocked, breathing heavily from the exertion of his work. Just because they weren't in the middle of a feud, didn't mean he wanted to become co-joined at the hip.

"Well, what I mean is – your deadline is so tight, I might be able to give you a hand…"

"Now why would ya want to do that? You gotta job already: pastoring the church folk."

"I'm not looking for a job. I figure if I can help out, I might also get a handle on what you do by getting in and having a go."

Nat sighed. A green-skin would slow him down something awful, and he didn't have time to spare. "Tell you what. I'll let you run the team, for a couple of rounds. Then I'll have to take 'em back over to get the paddock done before dark." That should satisfy this altruistic urge to get his hands dirty.

Jake gave him a grin, the kind bursting with boyish eagerness that made Nat shake his head. It was only ploughing after all. Neighbours used to laugh at Nat's serious old-man manner as a kid of eight who helped his Mum run the farm. He would have left school earlier, but his Mum absolutely would not entertain the idea of his schooling being cut short. "Whoa!" He shrugged and moved aside, showing Jake how to hold the plough and where to stand, handling the team. Perfecting this skill takes training; breaking in the driver as much as the horses. Again, Nat called out his commands, and the team moved off, hesitating under the inexperienced hand they sensed through the tension on the leather straps. Jake stiffened as the team pulled forward. Under the guidance of Nat, he tightened his hold on the plough to keep the furrows deep and in line. Slowly their heavy hooves turned up the dust as they tracked slowly around the paddock.

Nat walked beside him, and as he did, a similar scene began to play through his memory. As a young lad, his Dad had walked beside him just like this, his hand on the plough shaft, covering his in a protective hold, calling commands to the team... watching and guiding as he wobbled his way around the paddock. Farming had settled in his bones that year he turned eight... as they had walked the paddock together.

His Dad said that even though he had not grown up on a property, he was choosing farming as his life, and Nat had that same choice should he want to stay farming. When the seed started to sprout in the furrows, Nat could see the crooked lines where the grain had landed in those first grooves he had made. Nat had felt so poorly about his efforts, and in response his Dad had described his own first amateurish attempts at ploughing. "Well son, just three years ago my first furrows were so twisted the seed got lost trying to find where to put down roots!" They laughed about that. Nat never doubted his Dad when he said he was 'a natural'. His Dad knew these things, and straight furrows had been his passion ever since. That year his Dad gave him all the credit for the extra yield they achieved that season, and he was able to buy his first saddle. Oh boy, as a kid he had been ushered into manhood with a plough shaft and a horse. It was not long after that, his Dad died.

He looked at Jake trailing the team. His inexperience was driving Nat's impatience to the surface. Yet somewhere inside him, he restrained the urge to take over and do the job himself. Although he couldn't express the concept well, he felt obliged to contribute to filling in the exposed cog or two in Jake's repertoire of life skills; whether the rains came soon or even if they didn't. "Perhaps," he mused, "Jake is looking for that same sense of passage."

45.

Nat sat in the leather barber's chair and waited for the Citygirl to brush the hair-trimmings from his shoulders. Emmaline Farrington resolutely refused to engage in conversation during the whole process. Nat stood to his feet when she finally flicked off the throw. "It's kinda chilly in here – I'd back a fortune if I could bottle that and sell it in this summer heat," he said, and stepped towards the exit.

Em pursed her lips. This was personal. Her icy manner remained unwilling to thaw.

"Citygirl...?"

She would not even look at him. Nat Lawson – the lout in disarming farmer disguise.

"I don't get this. I only want to make amends. I behaved badly." See – even he could be humble.

"Yes – on that we agree. There is no need to make amends because there is no argument."

"Ah, but on that we *do* disagree. I need to show you I am sincerely sorry."

"Well – it is hardly possible. I am only going to be working here in town one day a week from next Monday."

"Really? Oh, that is too bad... but," he added hopefully, "perhaps you will have more time..."

"No, not at all. I will be helping Uncle Alf. The Shop cannot support two of us with the drought the way it is." As soon as she said it, she regretted the revelation.

"So, we will be neighbours again?"

She turned away and silently kicked herself. She had been so guarded. Why ever did she slip up? "It seems…"

"Then you can come for a ride with me – we'll check the waterholes. That excursion can hardly be a cause for concern. You will see I can behave decently."

"Check water holes?" At that she laughed. He had absolutely no idea… and still he was not fazed. "That is hardly a scheme to make amends for social indiscretions."

"If I cannot do my character justice in a public social setting, I may have more hope on my own territory." Suddenly he felt very optimistic. He liked this much better.

She was getting desperate. "You have forgotten I don't ride."

"Citygirl, can you not be stubborn just one time? If you can't ride, it is time you learnt. You will be much more use to Uncle Alf, if you are competent on horseback."

That threw her. She had not told anyone of her resolution to master the saddle. But perhaps, if Nat Lawson could be of use, then she might be able to endure an afternoon. It would take some pressure off Uncle Alf if she could ride. "Okay… one lesson – to some water holes."

"Next Wednesday, morning… I'll come straight after the milking. Any later and it'll be too hot."

She groaned inwardly. Her life of early mornings was about to resume. "I'll check with Uncle Alf. He may not need me at the dairy and then we could start earlier," she said as Nat strode to the door.

He stopped dead, and turned and looked at her curiously. "You help in the Dairy?"

"Yes of course. What did you think? That I would be serving tea and scones?"

Nat opened his mouth, and then closed it again and muttered under his breath, "*Stubborn* Citygirl", before he turned and left.

The coach came to a stop; dust swirling in clouds around the harnessed horses. Em absently looked through the barbershop window and watched the passengers step down. She really should send Nat a message saying there was urgent business detaining her in town so she could get out of the riding excursion. This whole idea of a riding lesson was a mistake. He would be a terrible teacher. She should find someone patient – and agreeable, so she didn't end up hating riding as much as she hated spinach. She shifted in her seat. Business was quiet these days. Yet travellers provided a contribution to a district in crisis, because people travelling by coach would layover in Wattle Creek. Often, they were not big spenders because coach was the budget option for travel. Still, they had to eat… and sleep… and occasionally get their hair cut.

She watched as one passenger who had been obviously asking locals for directions, was now heading towards the shop. It was apparent that his first mission was a tidy up at the Barber's before he moved on. That was a bonus – to have one more customer before close today. She tried not to study the man too closely. By his dress he was well-to-do. She quickly adjusted her sleeves and put away a few stray items at the counter, and looked down the street for Ali. A client like this should have Ali doing the haircut. Satisfied customers might leave a tip, especially if they had no cash-flow issues. These types were few and far between these days.

He opened the door and made his way to the counter. Em turned away looking busy with some files so that he could have confidence in their thriving little Barbershop business.

"Good afternoon, Emmaline," said a familiar voice.

Em spun around and stared at the man in the long coat, her face going a deeper shade of pink in the warmth of the afternoon. "Oh," she muttered quietly. "Hello Richard."

"Emmaline," he said with the lilt of refinement. "It has been a while."

She swallowed and nodded. It took a moment for her to reply. "Whatever are you doing in Wattle Creek?" she asked eventually.

He smiled confidently looking around the shop in approval. "I have come to get a hair cut."

"A hair cut?" She couldn't help but laugh. It sounded as if he had just walked around the block to the corner store for his favourite bag of toffees. "That's a rather long way to come for a trim. You didn't come in by train?"

"Well no... just a matter of timetabling really. Heard about your new endeavour and I couldn't wait to see how you're going. Haircut it is." He ran his eye over the shop. It surprised her that he did not seem to despise this humble source of revenue.

"So just here for a trim?"

"Oh, you know me well," he said, with a charming caught-off-guard smile. "It's true. I have another motive." Her

397

smile relaxed. How good it was to see him. How refreshing not to have to play cultural city-versus-country games. "I wish to ask you out for dinner – provided this God-forsaken place has somewhere to eat." His eyes sparkled at seeing her and he pulled her in with his smile.

"Dinner?" she blinked. How tantalising to have an outing with a real escort! She pulled at her sleeves. Suddenly the not-so-white cuffs were embarrassing. Richard came all this way for her? She had assumed… well, their correspondence had been brief and terse.

"Come Emmaline, please don't stand on ceremony. We were practically engaged. I like to think we still are. You couldn't possibly think that I would let things stand as they were between us?"

Em was very aware of their couple status. "The Creek Hotel does meals…" she offered, somewhat self-conscious. How dowdy it would appear when compared to the elaborate dining rooms in the city.

Richard looked disappointed. "Oh, a Pub. I was hoping for something a little more… well, suitable. Is there nowhere else?" She shook her head and tidied up the bench to finalise the day. It was hard to know where to look. Richard took a deep breath and measured his words before he continued. "Well, the Wattle Creek hotel it is then," he said brightly. He had surprised her, and Em had felt her usual composure dissolve under his presence. Richard, as always, was completely relaxed.

"Am I too late to have my hair cut?" he said looking at her in a warm evening light. Emmaline blinked. "You *really* want me to cut your hair?" she asked in surprise. She could not believe that Richard would seriously pursue this. Richard was a snob in a number of non-negotiable areas of his ordered life: his barber being a notable one. She was fascinated. This indicated a change in Richard. Perhaps there were other changes as well. Her curiosity burned to find out how deep those changes had gone… and what had etched them so definitely into his brow.

"Absolutely," he said with confidence. Emmaline's training kicked in with professional efficiency as she flicked out the razor ready to give his firm jaw line a trim. She placed aside ceremony like kid-gloves she would put out on the sideboard ready to go somewhere special. Richards' eyes noted it all. This was revealing an unfamiliar side of Emmaline. "Your reputation as a business woman has even reached the halls of ELLIOT HOUSE. Your Grandmother tells her visitors of your entrepreneurial exploits."

"She mentions this?" Em stopped what she was doing and sat down. Grandmother had not forgotten her… or disowned her? Hope burned in her chest. Her breathing quickened.

Richard quickly sat up on the barber chair and reached out to take her fingers in his hand. He noted the fine scars between her fingers where the scissors had nicked her skin, and the calluses that had formed from lifting buckets of water. These were no longer the hands of a lady, and they made him cringe. "Oh Emmaline, you know your Grandmother. She is not always glowing in her reports. Nor has she had a fanciful personality change... as much as we would all like it. But she talks of it... and of you. It is true."

Em smiled, and her eyes misted out of gratitude. If Richard had done nothing else, this kindness was valued. "I would love to have dinner with you Richard, but it will have to be tomorrow. I am going back out to the farm the day after."

"You say that with such finality. Can't you postpone it?"

"No. It is all arranged. Fred and Janie's wedding is next week and then they will be away for a while. I'm needed to help get things ready and to help out. Besides, I would not worry Aunt Alma. She is expecting me."

"We could send a message..."

"Richard... that would involve going out there anyway. This is Wattle Creek."

"Oh. I..." He turned away.

"Richard, I understand..." she said gently, "I want to catch up also. Why don't you come out to the farm with me? Aunt Alma would be perfectly okay with it. Hospitality is her middle name. It would give us more time..."

Richard brightened immediately. "Let's do that then."

"The Creek Hotel closes early... so dinner can't be too late. Uncle Alf is picking me up after a town meeting he has tomorrow."

Richard sighed. It was all rattled out like the reading of a ledger. Not at all what he had in mind. "This will be interesting. I would love to meet your folks." And even as he said it, he realised the inaccuracy in what he said... and the reality of it, at the same time. He was concerned that something here had taken over Emmaline's heart. He stood and then settled himself comfortably down in the barber's chair. "I'll have to be looking my best then," and he closed his eyes to the mirror so that he didn't have to look at Emmaline cutting his hair.

46.

The glaze on the horizon didn't wane. The summer harshness turned the countryside tinder-box dry. District dam levels were dropping daily. Nat shielded his eyes from the sun and stared out over the paddocks, shimmering in the heat. Silver mirages marked out the fence line, creating an illusion of water lying in rivers along the dusty surface. An uneasy restlessness was stirring in his gut. All that remained of the house dam was a thick muddy puddle and the tanks were getting low. Seed was in the ground… but the furrows looked as freshly turned as the day Jake tackled the plough. There was not even enough moisture to sprout the grain.

Jake stood silently. He could feel Nat's apprehension as he surveyed the hazy sky trying to read the signs that were discussed constantly with neighbours. To add insult to injury, an unseasonably hot westerly wind dried out the remaining brittle brown grass. The only clouds they had seen in weeks were rolling pillars of dust, swept up by the unusual winds. Nat sighed heavily. Powerlessly he had to watch his paddock blow over the neighbours' fences.

"So, Preacher – do you have a scripture for this?"

Jake pressed his lips together. What did he want? Was he anxious to prove his God was unfair, heartless, cruel? It would be unfaithful of him to say such a thing. "What would you like to hear Nat – that the Lord sends rain on the just and the unjust? That the Lord gives and the Lord takes away? I hardly think that is the answer. I can only suggest we allow God to be God and plead a case for mercy. He is still God after all."

Nat kicked up the dust in frustration. "Even in this?"

"Even in this."

"But you don't have to stand by and watch your cattle die... all your work and the work of your family go up in dust! How'd you feel if it was your place going down the long-drop through no fault of your own?"

"And if you were at fault – would that make it easier?"

"It might seem a little more right somehow..."

Jake nodded. He could understand this marketplace theology. Where God is good to the good guys. That somehow we deserve the good we are blessed with... and somehow we don't deserve the evil that befalls us. But even if he understood it... it is not what he understood that the Scriptures taught. The consequences of turning away from God were all pervading. Yet the imprint of God on the eternal soul refuses to accept anything less than good as normal. How else could he explain the design of our makeup other than being made in the image of God?

But Jake stayed silent and averted his eyes... and he groaned for the hardship of his friend. Nat was right. This wasn't the fruit of his labour that was swirling across the flats. He could not say any of this... "God, help me to speak your love so that it will be heard through the language of friendship. I don't want to give a bottled theology, pre-packaged like an imported factory product. It feels as if it needs to be grown and lived, for them to experience its reality." And yet... he had been taught... truth is truth, regardless who speaks it... perhaps even regardless how they speak it. He wasn't sure about that. Truth spoken harshly seemed to lose its integrity.

Em sat silently in the barber's shop after Ali had swept and packed up, ready to go home. "I won't be long... just want to finish up a few things here."

"Em – are you sure? I can do it tomorrow..." It wasn't fair that Em had to go back to the farm, yet she had insisted on going... to survive the drought... to keep the shop alive... even in a comatose state until the economic stability of the community was injected with life again... rain... a good season.

"Yeah I know. I would just like to finish it, that's all."

Ali left with a sigh. Em secured the lock behind her and turned down the lamp. She sat in the dim silence of the barbershop, listening to the sounds of the street go past. There was no urgent work... no work at all, actually. She had long completed it. She just needed a quiet space.

It seemed her life was stuck. Em knew she had been right. She couldn't go back to ELLIOT HOUSE on the terms her Grandmother had demanded. She never regretted sticking by her guns on that score. But she realised that Aunt Alma had been right as well. Work was never entertaining when survival was an obligation. Her future seemed to funnel into a black hole of sameness. She tried to imagine what it was she wanted. She was stunned by Richard's sudden appearance. Did she want to be rescued from her Cinderella life of drudgery? Was she disappointed that Richard hadn't come earlier riding into town on his steed? Or had she wanted to prove her worth, demonstrating her independence and deep resourcefulness by creating her own solutions?

The truth was she probably wanted all of those things. No one, even Uncle Alf, had really expected the shop to come through… but they had defied the odds. They had been resourceful. They had worked hard. They had faced all sorts of challenges and surmounted them. But even that success was a shadow. The drought had inflicted a cruel dictator's hand over the district, and they were nearly back to where they had started. At least financially.

Perhaps what she really hoped was Richard's appearance would make a perfect blend of her old life and her new. Deep in her heart… she wanted them to be compatible. What was so terrible about that?

She sat and listened to her heartbeat. Silence pounded in time with her pulse. A quiet tear slid down her cheek. Perhaps another perfect rider might come galloping into her life… one she hadn't met yet who would provide this saturated fulfilment? Perhaps a Nat Lawson look-a-like... with Richard's confident finesse and non-confrontational ways. Where Nat trampled around her in his rough unpolished boots, Richard's attentions in the past had in many ways been *in*attentions. She cringed at her thinking. Her heart was not for sale to the highest bidder! That would make her just like her grandmother.

She sighed. How she wished it were simple. One person… who would show up at the right time. If that were the case, she would be absolved of responsibility. Yet she intuitively grasped that although the keys were within her reach, her own resourcefulness might not be enough. She knew this was something she needed to sort out herself. No one would do it for her.

Finally, she came to admit that these apparent solutions were not really solutions at all. Not really. It wouldn't matter if her dream came true and a steed arrived gallantly carrying her knight. Ultimately her basic problem remained. She had told Mrs Wallace her social lifestyle was a distraction. Now she added industry to that list as well... being busy could cover an unsettled heart just as easily. But when she stopped and listened, she heard what her heart was saying – and it still sounded hollow, echoing around the aching void. With a flash of insight she saw that this heart-condition could not be filled with human hands. Not a man, country-born or city-bred, not her Grandmother, not her friendship with Ali, or even the resourcefulness of herself.

Was it God? Was this what Mrs Wallace meant when she said she must walk in step with God who made her? Was it true she could not successfully live without her Maker? Even though she experienced a type of success at the shop, it just confirmed to her that it did not provide an internal triumph. It didn't *feed* the essential her.

What was this 'essential her' that needed sustenance? She hardly knew. Who talks about such things in parlours over fine china cups and sweet cakes? Who discusses this while milking morning udders and feeding bleating poddy calves? Who carries the answer in an equation or by adding up a business ledger's bottom line?

She had to admit... only a few. A few shared part of that answer in the way they did morning tea... or their daily chores. Like Mrs Wallace... or Phil Pollock; it was a life thing. Two people could not look more different on the outside, but there was something on the inside that had the same essential feel. A wholeness. Pastor Jake had recently quoted someone saying, *"Lead the Christian life and carry the things of the Spirit into all that you do."* That's what she needed. The things of the Spirit. It needed to pervade all of her life. Completely.

"Hmm. I have attended Church dutifully every Sunday... all my life. I have sat with Grandmother Edith, and Aunt Alma through more sermons than I can remember. But it seems that it has never got down into my spirit. God, I want the things of the Spirit..."

She realised her cheeks were wet with silent tears... the silent tears of her heart. Shame welled up inside her. How awful! The slurs she had made against Richard! She was a hypocrite – guilty of the same crimes. She could feel the disgrace. She was unworthy to even attempt this. "I'm sorry... so sorry." Penance. She must pay penance. She must try and undo the disgrace and cover her shame.

Then something quite unexpected happened. It was as if an ugly, cruel dog with its teeth bared had been hunted from the door of her heart. And in its place, a quiet, gentle whisper offered something new. "There is therefore now no condemnation to those who are in Christ Jesus..." No condemnation? Fresh tears... cleansing tears, and without anyone explaining, Em realised that she had been given a gift of great value: not a club membership – but a family.

This family was not like a father or a mother who would not come home one day, destroying the only life she had known as a little girl. It was not like a grandmother who measured value in pounds and shillings, or a fiancé who wanted the appearance of things to be polished first and only if it was convenient. She couldn't describe it, but it went to the core of who she was. She belonged. She felt that belonging welling up inside of her, washing away the voids, the guilt and the shame that had been imposed by that nameless dog-shadow. Everything was awash in this clean, fresh, light feeling, and her new tears were now ones of relief and thanks to the Spirit of God. Some words splashed around in the corners of the room like golden music. She couldn't remember exactly where she had heard these words before, but they sounded so clear, like fine crystal: "Godliness with contentment is great gain…"

47.

Nat strode up the stone step and into the house. His mother sat at the table with books in front of her, lines around her eyes strained as she adjusted her old reading spectacles. Nat grimaced. He had to admit – life was not fair. His mother always had to fight. Just one day, he would love to let her enjoy the fruit of her efforts. But it always seemed that whenever they were making headway, another tragedy stung them from behind. He went to the water jug and poured himself a drink. The water was strained and double filtered… and still it tasted like mud. At least their well wasn't dry.

He sat down beside her. A gentleness washed over him. The pent up anger he felt was not against his mother. She was as much the victim here as he was… perhaps more so. She had invested more; had more history to lose.

"Mum – just… well, thanks. You're always here."

She sat there, tiredness and fear creating a strong bond between them. Nat was the son most like her husband. Loyalty glued them together, stronger it seemed than mother and son. Together they had weathered many storms. Yet the past battles had been active, doing business together – planning their survival. The fight this time was a passive one: a waiting game, hoping for rain. It hardly seemed a worthy war – no highly tuned wits or skills were needed; just a tenacity of hanging-on… to see who would prevail.

Josie nodded. She had no doubt they would get through this. She hoped the cost would not be too high, and at the end of it all, they would still have family. That was the thing she feared. She had seen marriages split apart; young men leave or shoot themselves because the pressure had cooked their will away; young ladies become bitter old women before their time. And the irony was – the land was still there, demanding and challenging its inhabitants to a duel… mocking them as one who had power to wield and nothing to lose.

What irresistible energy had locked them in this struggle for supremacy? Was it really their choice? Matt had always said it was, that they chose to come, and they could choose to leave. But he always added that he hoped as a family they would elect to stay and fight it out. That's what she hung onto now: they would stay and fight. "Son, are you willing to hang on here? There are other options…"

Nat stared at the glass in his hand; the water it contained was symbolic of the life-blood that was being sucked from his property. His land was going into shock and he had no modern miracle to fix the problem. "Willing? Mum, I don't reckon I have an option. The choice I made long ago was that I would do whatever it took. I'm here for the long haul, so that one day – my son will have this same conversation with me at this table. I can't think of it any other way. I get angry at what it is doing, it will set our progress back years. But if I look at this any other way, I may submit… and live to regret it."

Josie quietly let out her breath and breathed easier. The question for her was never really a choice. That was how she felt too. "I'm glad about that, because I want my grandson to also have something to fight for too."

Alf Dampier rode up on his horse, the dust hanging around his face and hat as he dismounted. "I came to let you know… there have been fires over the gully on Pollock's place. They're out now. They just ask that we all be on standby."

Nat looked at the haze that hung on the horizon. It looked like more dust, but now he could identify trails of bush smoke mingled in it. He swore his concern. "Did they lose much? Are they okay?"

"There were just a couple of small pockets. Phil had more pasture than most around here, and a fair bit went. Didn't get into the scrub, which is a wonder. He got onto them quick, and the wind had died. How it didn't get away though, no one can tell. They were lucky."

Nat let out a low whistle. Bush fire season… It sounded as if it was as regular as the coming of autumn or spring. But it was more unpredictable than that. Every summer there was risk; this year it was deadly peril. The menace should be easing at this time of year… but it was just getting dryer and staying as hot as ever. The whole world was crisp, set up like a tinderbox ready for ignition. The smell of heat hung on the air. And the winds: they could blow a cinder into an explosion within minutes. "We haven't seen the last of it yet… it's a bad one Alf. There'll be no relief until it rains proper."

His neighbour nodded. There were some things that defied reason. The hunger of a raging bush-fire was one. "We haven't had bad fires through this side of the creek for over ten years. God willing it won't be this year either, but I'm reckoning we need to be all set for the worst. Everyone's got their fire carts filled, ready to go… bags, shovels and stuff. They're just askin' me to go around and put everyone on high alert…"

"My Furphy cart is filled too. I'm ready…" Nat looked out over the horizon again. "Alf – I'm needin' to check some of the back waterholes and Em was wanting a ride. Are you okay if I took her with me on Wednesday?"

Alf's bushy eyebrows rose in unison. It hardly seemed the kind of thing that Em would be inclined to do. He had heard her reservations about their neighbour. "I'm doubting she'd be disposed to do that Nat… nothing against you taking her along of course… but the girl has a mind."

In these anxious times it seemed like something that could wait, but Nat was impatient. He meant her to see a better side, regardless of the weather. "Alf – I ain't goin' to tie her to the saddle. She said she would come. She wants a riding lesson…"

Alf looked at his neighbour and snorted. Nat could have been talking about the chooks going off the lay. Certainly, didn't sound like Nat had a shine for his niece the way he was talking. Still, if it was a lesson she'd be wanting – she'd have the best tutor and couldn't be safer. "She'll be in good hands. And I can't be denying it would be easy to have another seat in the saddle when Fred goes away. I've got a few more places to visit before this arvo's milking." He nodded towards Lawson's shed. "Trustin' your Furphy won't be needed this time 'round, but I know we'll all pitch in if it comes." The expression on his face as he mounted was not one of hope, but grim inevitability. It would be a miracle if they got through this summer without a major conflagration on their hands.

Josie came and stood by Nat as Alf rode onto the next place. "Pollock's place – spot fires. Dampier's put everyone on alert." Nat's summation of the conversation was all that was needed as Josie turned her gaze north-easterly and identified the tell-tale smudges through the dusty haze. The atmosphere was increasingly tense … as if the tuner of a fiddle was slowly stretching the strings tight. You could feel the strain – that any moment a string might snap back and flick you in the eye.

Nat stood on the verandah stroking Pepper's mottled fur in his arms. The kitten had given him more than one harrowing, claw-scratching encounter, but Nat's persistence was not to be beaten by something as puny as a cat. The result was that they had bonded in a very peculiar blend of contemptible loathing and spectacular devotion. Pepper gave a guttural growl that other cats might have called a purr. Nat leaned on the rail, allowing Pepper to rub against his shirt. The evening brought some relief as the blazing intensity of the sun turned away for the night. He was looking out to the north mesmerized by storm clouds that were flickering with the glow of lightening behind them. Was rain really going to come? He watched the glow rise and fade, outlining their billowy shapes as they moved closer towards Wattle Creek. The wind rose as the lightening forked between the bulging pillows.

Lightening was as feared in these conditions as an untended campfire. "Well, Pepper me mate, this is either the rescue or execution of Wattle Creek. Rain or ruin… and you or me ain't able to say which one it is."

48.

Nat rode up to Dampier's house leading a second stock horse. He had taken time to ride any restlessness out of the mare's gait, even though he was thoroughly confident in this gentle mount. It was one his mother used to ride. He tethered her to the rail.

He grimaced a little as he strode up the path. He realised he presumed this Citygirl would be a push-over, but each encounter proved otherwise. Everything was a challenge, like she needed others to know she had her own mind. She was obstinate to a fault. He broke into a grin and shook his head at that thought. It was different having to deal with an equivalent version of his personal brand of stubbornness. Few were willing to call his bluff on it, and he couldn't help but admire those who did. Ali's cousin was getting under his skin. It was so unexpected. She looked so fragile – like if you squeezed her she might crumble, but there was ample evidence that was an illusion made up of pretty looks, a petite waistline and city-styled clothes. She was not one to crumble at all.

"Morning Mrs Dampier. Am looking over the water holes this morning. I've asked Alf about taking Em on a ride. She's wanting to get easy in the saddle. Reckon Mum's old Shadow would be up for the challenge."

"So, Shadow comes out of retirement for my niece? That is very generous of your Mum, Nat. Come on in..."

"She's more than happy about it..." and the conversation rambled on amiably while they went inside to wait for Em to appear. They were late coming up from the cow-bales. Nat had already volunteered to go down to see if they needed a hand when Richard appeared at the door in his morning smoker's robe.

"Morning sir," Richard said comfortably as he helped himself to toast and coffee.

Nat stared at him like he couldn't quite believe that the Dampier farm incubated exotic animals along with their chickens. The specimen before him was obviously from another land, and cohabitating quite well in Wattle Creek territory it seemed. It defied reason.

"Oh, excuse me Nat – this is Richard Somerville. He is a friend of Em's. Her grandmother is one of his patrons… in the city."

A friend of Em's? Nat turned to the man in the bathrobe and stared at him. What was he doing lounging around in his bed and bath attire half way through the day? That's got to a sign of moral depravity. "So, what does that actually mean – 'patron'?" he said coolly.

"I am often a visitor to ELLIOT HOUSE. Lady Farrington was… well, *is* - a supporter of my projects."

Anyone who relied on an old woman to make their way in the world was worthy of suspicion. Nothing about this specimen was ringing true. "Don't you have a job? What do you mean by projects?" It sounded like a classroom poster assignment.

"Oh, you know: the usual sort of benevolent undertakings."

"No idea actually. Farmer, see? Humour me…"

Richard put down his cup and rolled his shoulders in an exaggerated morning stretch. "Charity, community benefits… and other such like worthy projects."

That sounded about as specific as space travel to far-flung galaxies. Suddenly class work was much more grounded and ten time more purposeful. Nat continued. "And you… you are involved in these *"such-like worthy projects"*… exactly how?" Richard didn't even look up, but studied his toast with intensity. This was not morning small talk. This was a direct, full on interrogation.

Richard took up a stance for a verbal parry. He laughed amiably, but his eyes were cool. "Well, I get to project-manage a number of significant community development and services committees."

"And which project are you working on now?"

Nat noted his furtive glance before he quickly closed his eyes as if savouring the aroma of his coffee. Nat notched it up to despicable acting. No one had coffee these days that didn't have the underlying flavours of a muddy dam or wood ash that was added to the tanks to act as a water purifier. But no one would dare complain: if they had coffee, they had water.

"Well, the hospital actually – development is progressing on a new wing to upgrade the Doctor's rooms. Our services are always improving."

Nat stared at him in contempt. He tried to make it sound like they were feeding starving millions. Stupid city-dwellers. Worried about propping up the established well-to-do, when The Creek didn't even have a proper anaesthetic table. What really got his goat was that the Bathrobe sounded as if he cared about the hospital project just as much as the average person might care for fleas on a dog. What's more, it seemed his greatest concern was the bored inconvenience it served. He should get a life. Nat looked into the man's eyes and developed a deep dislike in the pit of his stomach. No doubt about it. He clenched his fist and suppressed the temptation to put him out of his misery. "Well good morning to you then." He strode outside – the screen door banging wildly as he pushed through.

"Nat?"

"Citygirl! Finally. You're late… we have a date," he said abruptly. "Mum's horse is 'round by the front gate…" The unintentional rhyme: late, date, gate amused her, particularly as he had no idea he was doing it. But with Nat, she knew that he was exactly as you found him. Something had got up his nose, and it was sucking manners out of him like a yabby pump. Em pulled in her chin and took a measured breath. The prospect of Richard being there to share breakfast took the sting out of anything he could say to her today.

Nat strode toward the front of the house and she called after him. "Nat! It's *not* a date and I'm *not* going riding today. I have had a change in plans… a guest from…"

He spun around and glared at her. Guest? Like he was invited? He was welcome? "Yeah, I know. We met. Jolly good reason for a ride I reckon."

Emmaline glared back at him. He paused and looked at her in her dairy-stained clothes. There was something genuinely tough, yet soft, about her standing there in the shadows of the verandah. He stared at her hat-ruffled hair as if it had some sort of command over him. He felt… powerless almost. He wished he could take her in his arms and make a decree that the female of any house, need never put their hand to the plough – if they didn't want to. Citygirl, Emmaline Farrington would be the first to be given that dispensation. But that wasn't the way of it out here. Necessity ruled the land.

Richard came in his bathrobe and stood beside her, breaking the moment. "Good morning Emmaline. I have been getting acquainted with the local... wild-life." He tapped a rolled cigarette and lit it up.

Nat's lip curled involuntarily. Em stared at Nat in shock. She had seen that look. She quickly tried to smooth the tension she sensed between them. "Richard. This is our neighbour – Nathaniel Lawson. I was going for a riding lesson this morning..."

"Emmaline! Good grief! I mean – horse riding... out here... in the wilderness? I'll guarantee he won't be providing a side-saddle. How can he expect a lady to ride in such circumstance?"

Nat was stunned into silence when he saw Richard look at the cow-mess on her sleeves and wince involuntarily. He dragged on his cigarette to cover his distaste. She seemed oblivious to his disgust, and calmly went over to him and touched his arm with her glove. Richard took a step back. She smiled reassuringly. "Richard, this is fine. I asked to ride the stock saddle. I want to learn so I can help Uncle Alf with the musters and such. It is perfectly safe."

Richard inhaled and spluttered as if she just threw a drink in his face. "Emmaline! Come, ladies don't ride musters! Whatever will your Grandmother say? You can't be serious!"

Again, she smiled evenly; her face glowing with a warmth of regard that made Nat stare in recognition. He knew that look. He had seen it dozens of time when maids were being courted. He shook his head. "Oh no, Citygirl... not this weasel!" he whispered to himself as a solid hand squeezed his chest. Out loud he cleared his throat. "That decision might be up to the lady herself. She's quite outgrown being told what to do, I reckon."

Em turned to Nat, her chin tilted thoughtfully. Yes, that was it. She had grown. She could go for a ride, even if her grandmother might disapprove. In fact, she could do it just because, predictably, she would! She might not have this freedom much longer, if this visit continued going the direction she anticipated. "Richard, I expect we will be back mid-morning..."

"I'd offer for you to come, but I don't have an extra horse," said Nat dripping with sarcasm.

He stared at Nat quite indignant. "I'm not pining for a saddle... and certainly not the stock variety. I can ride equestrian events anytime I want. Go ahead then Emmaline. It should be quite diverting for you."

"This is not just diversion. It is a purposeful lesson. Richard, I'm sure Aunt Alma will appreciate some help. There are plenty of things that need doing this morning. This will give Aunt Alma the opportunity she's been looking for – to get to know you better."

Richard grunted and flicked his cigarette out into the garden. Nat eyed it warily. It smouldered like the fuse of a bomb... and just as dangerous. Nat went over and deliberately ground it into the dirt with his boot. "Keep your butts to yourself. You'll burn our district to a cinder if you throw them out like that." He added helpfully, "But I'm sure you'll not be bored if you're after diversion. There is plenty of 'local wild-life' to keep your attention… like the carpet snake in the long-drop."

Richard paled, and then turned and walked unsteadily inside.

Em turned to him and hissed. "Nat! You stop it… he's not used to this like we are."

He did not miss her declaration. She belonged to Wattle Creek now. She was one of them. "He should grow some hair on his chest…" He shook his head in disgust.

"Nat!"

"Fair go, he's…"

"I'm going to change into some fresh clothes. I'll ask Aunt Alma to pack some breakfast so I won't hold you up. I don't want to subject you to this longer than is necessary."

"Not a problem for me Citygirl. Take all the time you need. We're going out into the wilderness!" he said staring at the space where the Bathrobe had stood.

Em quickly gained confidence in the stock saddle and if she was honest, she found it reasonably comfortable. That was a pleasant surprise. The way Richard went on, she fully expected to feel like she was being drawn and quartered. They stopped for breakfast under a few sparse gum trees near a low muddy dam. It was a long time since she had her early-morning cup of tea with Aunt Alma, and she was feeling quite depleted. Em looked in despair at the provisions Nat extracted from the saddle-bag. "I expected Aunt Alma to pack a little more than a couple of slices of bread," she bemoaned. Em wasn't sure what she expected, but it wasn't this.

He grinned. "I whispered in your Aunt's ear. I thought I might treat you to a genuine bush breakfast... flash enough to match any of your city-joints." He paused and his smile faded as he saw her falter a little. "Seriously Citygirl... sit down in the shade... it won't take long."

She looked at him sceptically. "Normal tea and toast would seem gourmet at the moment. I'm so hungry," she said with genuine regret. She sat down on a log, the heat making her feel faint and she took a drink from the canvas bag he passed to her.

"You'll have your breakfast – don't spin out on me."

"I'm not spinning out... I'm just hungry. Is a fire safe in this weather?"

"No – it's never *safe*. You take triple precautions... and then some."

While Nat took the billy over to the dam, Em closed her eyes and listened to the cicadas drone in the hot stillness. It had a hypnotic effect on her senses. Time seemed to stand still. When she opened her eyes Nat had dug a deep trench on the dry edges of dam pan, and set a small fire in its recesses. He knew the dangers. If he could do breakfast over the flame of a candle if would hardly seem safe enough. He put the billy on to boil.

The wood cracked and burned, he mixed up damper dough and twisted it around a green stick and held it over the coals. He rotated it carefully on his makeshift rotisserie. The air was filling with the tasty aroma and… flies. With a perpetual motion, he waved them away and drizzled golden syrup over her damper stick. He brought it to her with casual assurance of a man who was good for his word. "First course – damper twists with syrup. Energy on a stick. It'll give you a spark in no time."

Em looked at him curiously as he handed her the stick. She tentatively tasted it. "Oh! This is very good. Well done Mr Lawson," she said delightedly as she took a bite. He threaded a second damper-stick, and without shame she proceeded to devour that also. He watched her wipe her mouth, and lick her fingers of the sticky syrup. She saw him looking at her, and flushed some, as if she could read his thoughts. He quickly went back to cooking breakfast. He wondered how the Bathrobe might react to seeing this lady sitting in the dirt, eating ash-sprinkled damper with her fingers. "You look afraid that I have lost all sense of decorum. I can still use utensils," she said.

"I was thinkin' it's good to see that the lack of a fork is not bothering you none." Her manner was devoid of the hoity-toity mannerisms she had in public.

Nat went back to the dam and retrieved a small net. Em stared at the crawling contents... a dozen dark blue yabbies. "And completing our bush breakfast – fresh yabbies on toast and billy-tea coming up. Can't beat it." He tossed them into the boiling billy water and watched them turn bright orange as they cooked. He took them out and showed her how to shell them, washing the muddy centre away. "Bushman's prawns... a treat that becomes far more accessible when the dams are low. This one has always been a good yabby hole... they'll all die when it dries up completely."

Em shook her head in amazement. Who would have thought Nat Lawson had culinary skills lurking behind his farmer façade? It surprised her. With no one to criticize her enjoyment of this particularly 'diverting agrarian experience', as Richard would so disparagingly describe it, she relaxed and tucked in.

If Nat had any illusions that he was in part responsible for her relaxed state, she quashed it as she washed her hands in the dam water by saying, "Richard has come to Wattle Creek to ask me to marry him."

He looked away. A pang of jealousy flashed through his chest. Whatever reaction she was fishing for, he was not going to give her the pleasure. "I take it he hasn't yet... and you're just supposing he might?"

"Oh, he will," she said quietly confident.

Nat sighed. *Oh, Citygirl set your sights higher than a bathrobe. Anyone with your spirit, your quality...* He felt a sense of pride that she had tackled a lot of things that were obviously not familiar territory for her. That was the mark of distinction. A dozen fellows around here would not be ashamed to keep her company... himself included. Himself especially. In shame he remembered the Friday Night dance. He would do it differently if he had the chance. He shook his head to clear his thoughts. "You're doing okay in the saddle, you know. We're not far from the last water hole. I'm pleased the other holes still have some life. This one doesn't seem to be dropping as fast as I expected. At least that is one mercy..."

She ignored the summary of the Drought Report, and resumed the conversation that would needle a reaction out of him. "I will be Mrs Richard Somerville of..."

Nat stared at the live coals and busied himself pouring out the billy tea into two cumbersome enamel mugs. He couldn't understand why she was not seriously upset by the idea of that useless, polished up, yellow-bellied snake. He shuddered involuntarily and looked at her square on. "And *that* would be my business... how?"

"Do you always have to be so heartless? You could congratulate me!"

"Whoa there Citygirl. You said yourself you're not engaged yet. There is nothing to congratulate or commiserate you on... either way it goes."

With her appetite satisfied, her sense of weakness faded. "Commiserate? Richard is a perfect gentleman. You have no right to be so judgemental!"

"If you're so darn sure he's the perfect gentleman his behaviour would speak for itself! And there'd be no need to defend him."

"Oh, really Nat.... I'm not defending him. I know what you think of Richard."

He smiled... relaxed and confident. She had opened the gate on this one. "Really? Try me..." There was no shame here.

His confidence surprised her. Where had the uncomfortable, awkward bushman gone? "What do you mean?"

"Well, if you know so well what I'm thinking, tell me."

"Okay, I will. You think Richard is egocentric, incompetent and self-indulged; you despise his customary pampered life... and you think him more a spoilt child waiting for someone to come and take over where his Mother left off, than a man of society and culture."

Nat raised his eyebrows and grinned some more. "Wow. You nailed that. Citygirl, I have to chalk this one up to you. You win."

That was not exactly what she wanted to hear. How could he triumph, even when he was conceding defeat? She smiled weakly. "That is not what I meant."

"Gotta say.... well done."

Em shrugged and sat back on the log and sipped her mug of billy-tea. She wasn't giving in so easily. "Well it is not really such a challenge Nat Lawson – you are as transparent as a jam jar." Nat raised his brow and studied the yabby he was shelling with focused attention. He held his breath. Could she really see what was going on? He let it out slowly, and was grateful that he realised she couldn't. Some things are better left unsaid.

Her drink tasted like silt, but there was something about the warm, hazy morning, the smoke of the small fire curling upward from that dam-pan, the tea-leaves floating in her mug, the sound and smell of horses tethered nearby. It felt comfortable. She thought it was odd she was at ease out here, in the middle of nowhere... in the heat... in spite of Nat's banter. In fact, she was rather enjoying it. He was so totally different to any other man she knew. She never thought of herself as being confrontational by nature... but she could parry with him. She wanted to. For a brief moment she realised it was because she felt safe. Really safe... physically and emotionally...safe enough to be honest. Safe enough to test its resilience... to see how far it would stretch... to see what distance it would take her. He didn't treat her in a condescending, helpless way. They sparred as equals... and that amused her.

Besides, she *would* make him see how Richard suited her situation. "We have the same backgrounds. Richard's very secure. His social savvy is a rare commodity these days," she said significantly.

He deliberately ignored the dig about his lack of social strengths. It was irrelevant here in the back paddock, cooking yabbies for breakfast, looking at shrinking water holes. "Don't have to convince me. You're the one who would have to live with that savvy year in and year out... until death doth save you." Nat stood to his feet and poured the billy over the small fire, and bucketed some more water from the dam. He filled up the hole with loose dirt and piled it over the ashes until they were no longer visible. He stamped on it decisively. How dangerous some things are that seem benign: fire, coals, ash... bathrobes. He was taking no chances.

Em's eyes narrowed. What did he care? She was nothing to him. This outing was just about assuaging his wounded prided and conscience. "This is none of your business – you said so yourself!"

Finally, he stopped. He had been determined to let it pass, but he couldn't contain it any longer. "Citygirl I didn't bring this up – you did. I just reckon you don't have to settle on someone like this Pritchard…"

"Richard."

"It's not like you're driven to it … you've got independent means."

She almost laughed at his idea of her poor and meagre state being self-sufficient, especially since she had to move back to the farm. But it suddenly dawned on her there was truth in what he said. "You know, I'm not just making do. My circumstances are not dictating this at all. I *can* do whatever I want…"

"Then there is really nothing to say! I can't possibly imagine that *this* is what you want." He stared at her large eyes and she held his gaze without embarrassment, a weird mixture of anger, respect, irritation and admiration swirling the dust between them.

"I *want*… to continue my horse-ride." She walked over to Shadow and went to climb up.

Nat quickly pulled her back. Couldn't she even remember how to approach when mounting a horse? Shadow wouldn't do anything, but plenty of horses might. "Don't go jumping up there like you're getting on a train. This here is a living, breathing individual. You can use it like a machine to get you places… but the fact remains that if you treat it nice, it will be a faithful friend. In the end that will be more valuable than something that will just take you where you want to go."

"Faithful friend?" Em stepped back, biting a retort on her tongue. She shook him loose. She heard the rebuke in his voice, and she knew it was not about horse riding… and about him. Them. Em felt her eyes prickle and she squeezed them tight. Them? What happened to the resolution she made when she first came to Wattle Creek – to be a faithful friend? She didn't want to be her grandmother. She didn't see herself as someone who used people to go places to get what she wanted. She was not that kind of person… or was she? No, a friend is not so much about the other person, as the character within yourself. It is about everyone she interacts with – expansively… not selectively. *"Oh God. I didn't realise this is what I am doing… using, taking, discarding… I'm so sorry..."*

Nat saw her close her eyes and he read it as contempt. He didn't want her to have a choice in this. He wanted her to be tidy and controlled and conforming. Choices. He realised that a companion forced to attend to him would not be friendship at all. He squared his shoulders protectively and conceded that he would try to be satisfied to see her safe and skilled. That he could influence. Definitely it would feel even better if they could choose to disagree and not hate each other in the process.

49.

Jake looked forward to the officially-unofficial outings he shared with Ali with possessive anticipation. He felt a connection. It went beyond the smokescreen of their pseudo-courtship. He tried to divine any indication that Ali felt the same sense of destiny. But there was no sign: no smile other than the one she always gave; no attempt at deeper, more intimate conversation; no hint she had any thought different from her initial direct declaration that she had chosen the road of a solitary life.

He stood in Dampier's emptied lounge room as a guest… helping with the last-minute details for Fred and Janie's wedding ceremony. Janie's parents said outright that their little place could not host a wedding… not on the scale that the bride was hoping for. This was a wedding on a shoe-string budget, costing the bride's family virtually nothing. Pastor Jake expected a quick rehearsal… but he soon realised there was little hope of that.

The upright pianola was still being manoeuvred into the corner, next to the mantle piece where Pastor Jake would perform the ceremony. Ali was to play the music. He busied himself arranging chairs while watching her out of the corner of his eye. She sat twiddling the keys distractedly. When he left, Ali turned to Em, "Oh Emmy, I don't know if I can do this…" Her half-hearted practice over the previous weeks did nothing to increase her confidence.

Em had never seen anything so disorganised. "They were talking about a new roll for the Pianola... to use for the entry..." She hoped the observation would take the pressure off to perform. Pianolas were more of a music-machine than an instrument in her eyes.

"I don't even know if the cylinder came." Ali looked as if she was going to cry.

Her anxiety was genuine. Em could see she wasn't handling this at all. She gently took Aunt Alma aside and explained Ali's reluctance. A feeling of panic ran through the conversation until Em quietly offered her abilities as a substitute. It was the least she could do, taking this worry away from her.

The pianola's new scroll of Mendelssohn's wedding processional had been ordered, but it seemed no one could remember if it had ever been delivered. An anxious search found it tossed safely on the top of the kitchen dresser still in its box. Uncle Alf opened up the front of the pianola and expertly slotted it in. Em was sure the gregarious Janie will be the most blissful bride in all of Wattle Creek, if the bridal music was as dependent on her happiness as she had declared.

The back yard had been tidied... but the grass was crunchy and brown. There were large patches of dirt but there was no helping it. Using precious water for something as non-essential as lawn, was not even conceivable. Trestles were set up under the silky oak trees, and their withered leaves dropped onto the borrowed white table-cloths, which had a name-label carefully pinned to each hem. Suddenly someone screeched out the time... and then, as if a horn had been sounded, all parties disappeared to attend to their ablutions and dress in their best Sunday clothes. Then they progressively emerged, scrubbed and dressed, sedate in their manners, ties and ribbons so that no one could have imagined the harried arrangements that prevailed half an hour before. They all sat down in the reshuffled living room.

Emmaline was given a wave; the guests were asked to stand. With expert flare, the pianola pedalled in the flourishing brilliance of Mendelssohn. The ivory and ebony keys bounced and trilled with a life of their own up and down the keyboard. As she arrived at the door, Janie glowed primly at the gathered guests; and then hissed at her younger brother, the bearer of the rings, who was busily picking his nose. She barely acknowledged the bridesmaids and smiled prettily at the flower-girl who twirled all the way to the front, in innocent, self-admiration of her flouncy, lacy skirt. The little girl was totally absorbed in unaffected delight of the occasion.

Janie arrived, blushed and beautiful, at the altar in seconds. Malachi, Nat's brother, and the other awaiting groomsman, were given a famous frosty Janie glare, as if – for some reason, they were responsible for the fact there was not enough aisle for her glory moment. So Em pedalled on, hoping a satisfactory cadence would allow a pause in the dazzling concert… but the pianola keys rolled on with a life-force that seemed beyond her control. In the end the guests effortlessly sat through the entire rendition; Janie – the only one rolling her eyes in impatience.

Pastor Jake led the couple through their vows. The Bride and Groom said, "I do"; they exchanged rings; signed the

Church registrar and they were announced as husband and wife: "Mr and Mrs Fred Dampier."

Janie spun around and wavered behind the hazy veil. Her face went as white as her ivory-cream dress and she crumpled into the arms of her groom. There was an audible gasp all over the room as Fred stared at his bride in horror, and in sheer mortification of the moment, he stepped back and dropped her. Mal jumped forward and grabbed her before she hit the floor. He handed her back to the groom, steadying his rattled nerves with a hand on his shoulder. Mrs Pearce screamed and ran to the front, pushing Doctor Wallace out of the way. Pastor Jake gawked in bewilderment. Her little brother stood balancing the ring cushion on his head and sniggered in admiration, "Way to go Janie!" The little flower girl started crying. Cousins tutted in suspicious tones and scrutinised the fit of her bridal waistline. Aunties whispered that they noticed the dress was not ice-white.

The doctor swept the couple into the bedroom and sent the groomsman to get his bag from his buggy. He quietly spoke to Mrs Pearce who ordered her husband to fetch some water in a basin. It befell to Mal to debonairly calm the bridesmaids. There was an awkward silence as people whispered in worried tones. Em turned back to the pianola and quietly played a soothing Bach prelude while they waited for Doctor Wallace to come out.

He closed the door behind him as necks craned to see what might be going on. "Ladies and Gentlemen, Mrs Dampier is fine. Such a significant day is demanding and stressful, as I am sure you can appreciate. Fred is with his wife, and I'm sure if it pleases the Bride and Groom's parents, you could adjourn for refreshments, and the couple will be able to join you shortly to start the meal proper."

Well, the Doc had spoken. Em quickly changed the pace of the music to something a little more cheerful, and the guests filed out into the backyard clinging to the fringes of shade, fanning their faces vigorously with oriental paper fans and chatting reassurances to each other as they went. It was decided the bride should best sit, rather than stand, for the photography portrait now, so an arm-chair was moved into place. The photographer repositioned his stand and camera. A couple of mates conspired to enlist additional help to ensure appropriate mischief was inflicted on the honeymooning couple. Everything was back on track.

"It seems your patient is fully recovered Doctor," Em observed respectfully. The colour had returned to Janie's cheeks as she flounced her way around the compliments of those gathered. It was so warm.

Nat sat absently watching Ali. It was a public habit he didn't know how to break. Em sought refuge from the sun inside and fanning her face, went looking for Ali. She saw Nat in the corner, with his attention focused intently on her cousin. She boldly walked over to Ali and watched him in her peripheral vision.

Em's presence had a strange effect on him. Suddenly it felt unseemly that he be watching and he looked away. Out of the corner of his eye he saw the Bathrobe suavely slide up, sipping drinks and wordlessly staring around at the guests with that unblinking gaze of a snake. He caught Nat's glance, and he raised his brow. Nat could tell he considered he had the whole story sewn up. And perhaps he did. After all, Em's face glowed.

It could be the heat, or the excitement of the ceremony... but maybe not. She seemed so blind to the Bathrobe's obvious distain for the simplicity of their community celebrations. Couldn't she see what was as plain as the nose on his face? Nat could stand it no longer. He got up and went outside and stood under the silky oak trees trying to catch the slightest breeze to cool off. He would not disgrace himself in public this time.

"Nat – I brought you a cool drink." He visibly jumped.

"Oh Miss Farrington... thoughtful of you. Thanks."

She nodded in acknowledgment. "It's warm today."

"It could be the romance... plenty of that brewing around here."

She raised her eyebrows. "Fred and Janie... they make an interesting couple."

Nat had his own opinion about that. At least she didn't make it sound like a bottomless sweet cup of tea. Nat knew their relationship would be volatile if their past was anything to go on. "Yes. And you and that Pritchard fellow seem to be getting on just fine. Perhaps commiserations will be forthcoming after all."

"Richard... not Pritchard." She didn't even blink. Nat turned and looked up into the broad tangled branches of the tree. Hmm, he thought so.

Well it goes both ways, she thought tartly. She wasn't the only one. "And... you, you as always, only have eyes for

Ali. See my skills of romantic observations are equally honed." When she saw his confusion, she gave him a "caught you out" kind of look and laughed. "I've seen you. You're constantly staring at her. No doubt who the next bride and groom will be..."

It was his turn to be amused. He laughed outright and cut her off. "Ah, no. I don't think so. Me and Ali are neighbours. We will always be neighbours... even if we don't end up living next door..." He looked at her. "That surprises you..."

"All those hair cuts... the dance..." It made no sense. She repeated her infallible argument. "You can't stop looking at her!"

Nat hardly knew what to say. He shrugged. "I've been looking *out* for Ali so long... I suppose it's a kinda habit. Especially after that Golders disaster. But I guess I realised some time ago that certain things aren't meant to be more than what they are. Hair needs to be cut anyway, so it served a dual purpose." He looked up into the branches and avoided her eyes. He didn't want to argue with her today. He resolved to be mannerly. His neighbour's wedding was important to him.

"Oh, I see," she said... but she wasn't really sure that she did. "Neighbours? Does Ali know this is how you feel? Just neighbours... I thought she thought..."

"Well, I've no idea. I've never wanted to give her the wrong impression. I've never been one to chat about such things... nor am I likely to. Figured I just wanted to have someone looking out for her since... well you know..."

This time when Em laughed, it was a clear, relaxed tinkle that sounded as soft as the music she played. He couldn't help but look directly into her smile. "I hear you Mr Lawson. Caring for the vulnerable shipwrecked souls cast out on the sea of life. You told me you didn't have it in you!"

He acknowledged her satisfaction with a half-smile and a shrug. "I believe I said I didn't need to advertise." He didn't think she really understood... but as she slowly nodded and they held each other's gaze for a moment, he wondered if the transplantation to Wattle Creek might have finally been complete.

That sort of put an end to their conversation, but Em didn't want to leave it there. It felt disappointing, unfinished, inadequate. She was not even sure what sort of exchange she had anticipated when she came to escape the stuffiness inside. Perhaps she wanted more of the one-on-one equality. "Okay, well – it's been a nice day, heat aside..." She turned to go.

"Miss Farrington... Em... Ali's got a good friend in you. Thanks." He looked at her again, this time longer.

"Nat, Oh... Thank you. I wouldn't have expected you to think that."

"Why ever not? You're good for her... doing the barber-shop together... being partners." That thought sent a shock through his body. Partners.

She smiled again through the heat. Nat liked the way she looked when she smiled... however pensively. "Partners... yes well, that's on hold for a while. We have been lucky... just a shame that the drought has caused such a strain. We have no debts fortunately... which is something... though not much."

"Well, you're doing better than most in the district then. Comes with the lay of the land I'm afraid. We're all in the same boat."

"It's amazing that you stick it out… it is tough here." For some reason it did not feel difficult to be open… as if the veneer she normally wore had melted in the heat.

Again, he shrugged. "My Dad was brought up in town… like you. He made a choice about farming… said it was something he always thought would be good for a family. Mind you – it killed him. But he was always big on the point that he chose it… and just because we boys were born into it… he never expected that we didn't have that same choice. I always remember that – he said we could take it or leave it. It's in my bones now. I don't want to make any other choice other than to keep with it."

"Ha!" she scoffed. "All those comments about me being City. We are not so unalike, you and me. We have made that same choice."

He smiled at her and nodded slowly. "Citygirl." For once Em didn't feel like it was an insult but an affirmation. She felt warmth rising in her cheeks unexpectedly. It had nothing to do with the weather. She turned and ran inside.

Ali and Em agreed that there were a couple of highlights that should go down in the chronicles of famous Creek Wedding moments: The flower-girl's waltz to the altar that outshone the bride's gallop down the aisle; the extravagant musical recital; Janie's brother's cushion act; the fainting saga; the dropped bride. And finally, Mal and his mates hitched up the couple's cart through the fence, so the horse was on one side and the cart on the other. For a moment they thought Janie was going to pass out again. It was handled rather well considering; but they could still hear Janie screaming, "We're goin' to miss the train! We're goin' to miss the train!" Janie's aunt gave them a gift of train tickets and the use of her house near the beach for their honeymoon. It just added evidence to their belief that the whole world really had stopped revolving just for them.

It was good to have a laugh about families doing their whole whacky family thing without feeling for once that it needed to be perfect to be real, or valuable, or meaningful.

Em pulled on her boots in the warmth of the pre-dawn stillness. Her eyes were smarting from the early start, and she closed them, wishing she could feel the sheets against her hair for just another hour.

"Em, are you going for a walk?" She jolted at the warmth of Richard's deep voice, a little husky from being bathed in sleep. It seemed out of place here... but the familiarity of his tone was strangely comforting. Her heart quickened a little. Their time together had kindled such warm memories, connections that she had thought were tired and old.

She smiled. "Sort of..."

"May I join you? A stroll might wake me up." He smiled at her knowingly. "Couldn't you sleep either?"

At that she shook her head as she rose to her feet. She slept beautifully last night. Bed always seemed like a privilege, when she knew she would have to leave it early. He joined in her steps with a strange smile that lingered under his sculptured moustache. "Country life seems to suit you surprisingly well, Emmaline. You are looking remarkably fine."

"It is not all that surprising it suits me really. Being here has been my choice." She lingered over Nat's congratulatory affirmations in her mind. Yes, he was right.

"That's my Emmaline – bold and daring… always something to prove."

She made her way out the house-yard gate towards the dairy. *My Emmaline?* She didn't want to do this now, not in her ungracious farm clothes, knowing there was work to be attended to. With Fred away she really was needed, even though the herd had dwindled with fewer and fewer cows left to milk. Their milk supply drying as their condition failed. Already the heat of the day was swirling dust along the track where the cows trod.

Richard stared; the dairy loomed closer in the fading grey morning. Heat hazes already smudged themselves across the horizon. "Surely it is an unrealistic expectation that you visit your uncle at the dairy every morning…" She detected an edge to his voice.

"Hmm…every morning," she said with a non-committal nod as she rubbed dust from her eyes.

"Well – it is thoughtful of you…" he said, tersely.

She looked at him quickly. She had expected a rebuke… a tirade about inappropriate chores for a lady from ELLIOT HOUSE. His cool approval made her realize that Richard had absolutely no idea she really *worked* the Dairy…

cows and all... and not just "visited" it. He was blind because he didn't want to see what was obvious.

Nat hadn't expected that she helped at the dairy either. What did he say? *"Stubborn Citygirl,"* Well, she had to be stubborn to keep on going. It was what got her through.

Richard cleared his throat. Already the smell of dairy cows reached him. He didn't want to go closer. "Well, I might mosey back to the house then, while you visit your Uncle. I have some reading I need to do."

She shook her head as she watched him wander amiably back along the house track. Reading. Oh. There was so much reading that needed her indulgence also. But that was a luxury that was pushed aside when encumbered with the responsibility of being a working class girl. As she lowered the wooden rail and went into the bails she wondered if the price of independence was just a little too high.

50.

"Good to see you in church Nat," said Jake as he walked to the front of the church and closed the windows at the conclusion of the service. "It's almost like old times."

Nat didn't even look around. "It ain't nothing like old times," he said. He was distracted watching Citygirl walk along the path towards the gate on the arm of the... well... the Bathrobe-bloke. It was offensive to think he would put himself into Em's class. It wasn't 'city' that bothered him... it was something else: that hungry, not-quite-fed look in his eyes.

Jake stopped, listening to the anger seethe through Nat's whole body. "So, Nat... what did you think about Church this morning... did God speak to you?"

"Maybe not God – but you had plenty to say."

Pastor Jake's right shoulder gave a shrug. He could hardly deny it. Sometimes it felt as if he had a whole stack of revelation bottled up, bursting... hoping it will help someone, anyone, to get a greater handle on the truth that will set them free. It was a compulsion – an obsession. Jake's conviction was that if God said His truth will set us free... then more truth is a good thing... a releasing thing... a powerful activating catalyst. But Jake was the first to admit – freedom came at a price. It reminded him of a favourite history lesson he remembered from his Presbyterian-college school days, about the Scottish freedom fighter William Wallace. Jake wondered if Wallace would agree with his understanding of freedom.

What William Wallace triggered all those years ago in Scotland inspired a nation. His life was more than interesting history: it was a call to liberty. It held a principle that challenged him. Jake did not feel the need to go national; he just wanted his friends to understand that political domination, or circumstances outside their control... like this drought... was not the only form of oppression. They also had to fight their own personal battle for truth and freedom. When Jake understood that, it changed his life. This was what Jake wanted to... needed to... pass on.

Nat stood silent for a while, the heat beading across the back of his Sunday shirt. "I don't think I agree with you. I'm thinking the story of Job is about a real person, not just poetry... or a play."

Jake quickly came back to his Sunday sermon. "I'm interested that you think so, although some theologians disagree with you – they consider the book of Job an ancient, symbolic work. Why do think that?"

"Well, I'm figuring that if someone just wrote it as a good yarn... the average bloke would have cursed God and pulled the trigger. Sure, the things he went through are like a melodrama... but he hung in there even though he lost everything – his kids, his spread, his health. Ain't much to go on... in sticking by God, in my book. Looks like God left Job high and dry."

Jake grinned. "So, it's the blackness of the story that gives it authenticity?"

"Grief! I'm getting real familiar with black... but that isn't it. The way I see it... if it was just some perverse storyteller's way of making him out to be a hero, then they would have written God up as congratulating him at the end for sticking it out. But God didn't do that. Job didn't impress God, even for all his effort. Why didn't God pat him on the back?"

"I guess that's the power of the story: God is still God. That doesn't change even when we don't grasp the extent of His nature or His purposes. God doesn't answer to us – we answer to Him. That is the order of the universe, because He made it. Job didn't understand what was going on, but still he didn't give in. He might have wanted to… his wife certainly did… but something in his spirit demanded to see the whole thing to the end. It's the fact that he chose to talk to God, even in his torment… that encourages me most."

Nat looked past him out into the dry, heat of the paddocks. He felt a fear smother his chest. "You're totally serious about this aren't you? You expect normal people be like this today!"

Jake shrugged. He was less inclined to be dogmatic now. "Well – if it is as you believe… that means Job could have been living down the road and his name could have been Bill or Tom or Jake or Nat. I think it's more about the Spirit of God helping us and keeping us. It gives me hope because it's not about the type of person I am – but about the kind of God He is. So even when I fail… God will not. Without Him, I am a dead fire. The coals have no life."

"Fire isn't our friend at the moment Reverend." He looked again towards the horizon. He had never sweated so much in his spirit. "Damn it, Jake… the whole district is ready to explode… and there's not a thing we can do about it."

443

"We can pray. We have prayed... we can keep on praying..."

"Lot of good that's gunna do us."

Jake shrugged. Once he would have been shocked by the audacity of an infidel who would say such a thing. Now... he appreciated that, like Job, he was desperate enough to be honest. "Oh God. Help me to love with the hands of Jesus." And even as Jake prayed it... the school bell clanged out an urgent toll. "Fire! Fire! It's got into the gully and heading towards Town! Fire!"

They activated, scattering like a fly swat had been smashed into a swarm of insects. Orders were flung around, but no one heard what the yelling was about. Men jumped on horses, or ran towards the battlefront to contend for their town. Women screamed for their children and herded them around like sheep dogs that hadn't been given directions on where to go. Finally someone yelled louder than the others and they headed towards the open horse paddocks near the school. The ground there was bare and barren, eaten down to a dust bowl by the kids' horses that were ridden to school. It was the safest refuge in a world that was set like a fire hearth, ready to burn.

Water carts were being pulled into position, bags dampened. Urgently they worked to widen the wind-break line. The flames roared with ferocious intensity gathering heat and momentum along the trees towards the first line of houses. Jake ripped off his ministerial robes and ran to join the fighting front.

He stared at the smoke that billowed in an ominous pillar of menacing destruction. Oh God. Where would the people go? How could they survive such instant destruction? Didn't God command the prophet Ezekiel to "prophesy to the mountain"? A praying man once told him... *Be an Ezekiel: Don't talk to God about your mountain... talk to the mountain about your God.* "God!" he screamed in urgency. He planted his feet. God would come through or he would be incinerated along with his town, making a stand against this mountain. He stood immobilised as a wind fanned the flames higher, an audible roar rumbling through the streets as the front raced closer. He declared it again... and just as suddenly the wind turned – blowing the fire back across the North paddocks away from town. Thank God.

But it was no victory, just a reprieve – a measure of grace to prepare for the coming onslaught. He picked up a bag and joined the line of people beating out flames. One gang followed the main front, trying to out-chase the fire, to save stock and property in its hungry path. Others took up stands across the wake of the fire, trying to beat it back under control where it flared its nostrils again and again like an angry dragon. Hessian in hand, they beat at spot fires that at any moment could flare into another wall of flame. Fire after fire seemed to appear out of nowhere. They pounded flame after flame as it threatened to reignite.

For days the fire dictated life. The town was on edge. They talked about evacuation, but the roads were blocked further out.

They mobilised gangs and the panic stricken fighting, became systematic warfare. Women worked to support those who fought like soldiers, filling in the vacuum that their subscription created in town. The Bakery cooked around the clock to supply rations. Pantries emptied in volunteer donations.

Slowly there were people coming back with reports... resuming life... picking up the singed remnants of their homes. "Ali... Pastor Jake is coming across the street..." said Em quietly knowing she would soon need to go back to the hospital to help. Ali looked through the shutters of the barbershop as if she couldn't be sure. She saw Jake's tall frame, blackened with char, striding towards the barbershop with determination in his tired step. He softly greeted the town's folk, and stopped a couple of times to quietly offer words of comfort. Ali gave Em an anxious look, agitation swamping her body. "Oh Emmy... I can't do this anymore. Can you stay here for a bit? Are you sure?"

"Sure – it's okay Ali... I understand." Whether she did or not didn't really matter. Her mind was focused elsewhere. They were both exhausted... the strain of the fires stretching all their emotional resources to their limit. The barbershop had become a first aid station... a coffee stop, a refuge. But at the moment, Ali needed to get out of there. She slipped out the back door and ran for her life, escaping down to the creek. She took out her little locket watch that hung in a pendant on her neck, and checked the time. It shouldn't take more than a brisk walk along the creek. He wouldn't stay around for long. He would have many other things to do. How many times had she cut his hair? Ali ran her finger-tips through her fringe under her hat and felt his hair part under the stroke of her hand.

Ali paced up and down the track along the creek. Backwards and forwards, her ankles tiring from walking across the clumping uneven ground, scorched and charred from the fire. The wattle trees along the track to the creek were always a refuge of cool shade from the summer heat, but now they were stark black skeletons arching their arms in a bare framework across the gravel of the dry creek bed.

She checked her watch again… and again. Finally she felt it was safe to walk back towards town. She climbed into the back yard through the missing pickets in the fence. It felt like the time when she had been caught playing truant from school, with Belle and Fred. The belting her father unleashed on her seat deterred her from ever trying that again. She unhooked her skirt as it snagged on the loose splinters in the wood, and stepped free.

As she walked past the boiler stand, near the back laundry, she could hear his voice inside. Abruptly she stopped. Surely not! She leaned weakly on the bricks and caught her breath. Pastor Jake was still inside! Now she was panicking. Quickly she turned and slipped out of the yard again. Was he on some sort of stake out? Would he stay there all day… indefinitely? Did he really want to hold her to their arrangement? Hadn't he said if it didn't work, they could stop and walk away – like a dirty cup left at a teahouse for which there was no further use once the tea leaves had sunk to the bottom? He still needed an accompaniment like a side dish –

she knew that. He thanked her often. Too often. She wished he wouldn't keep bringing it up. It was driving her crazy.

She stumbled back to the creek. A wave of disgust burned in her throat as the sun climbed into the heat of the day, and she found a small remanent of shade in behind the trunk of a larger river-oak that still radiated heat from the smouldering trunk. She sat down on a rock. Well, she could stake-out too. She paced and sat, paced and sat, paced and sat. She felt like merchandise: owned but not valued; kept tidy, but not cherished! Just once she wanted to be special, not a show-piece, not a buddy, not a convenience – but unique, exclusive, prized, captivating. How could she have ever agreed this idea was clever, a solution to the numbness in her heart?

Pastor Jake had made vows. She knew pastors were to stay unfettered so they could focus on the work of God. He loved God so much he would never love a woman. He had said so himself. It was wrong for her to hope that he would be distracted by her friendship. But she had started to be aware of just that specific hope, and a thick guilt clung to her chest because she was not sorry. She had no desire to repent of this very selfish hope.

Tears rolled down her cheeks. She lost one man to a brazen woman of the world, and in spite of her best efforts not to care, she had lost again – to the very opposite spectrum of humanity – a man of God… a good man, one who had become a dear, dear friend. The unfairness of the hurt stung like salt burning unhealed wounds of the past. The pain made her want to scream. The agony was a nameless throbbing in her chest, constricting the life out of her heart. Perhaps it would be better to die than to face the humiliation once more.

Ali sat and looked across at the bare, blackened limbs of the wattle trees. A week ago this area had looked so different. Today all that was left was just the bare bones of the trees... looking like death. Yet she knew that these fires were what kept the wattle alive. New pods needed the heat of the flames to crack open and germinate the hard protected seeds. Fresh life would come from this destruction. It was then she realised something quite revealing.

Like a flash, a thought suddenly ignited like a steady beacon light. It was not something she could ignore. Her heart was hurting... but not because of the increased assault on her sensitive nature. Her heart hurt now, more acutely and truly, because the numbness was passing. Sensation was returning. Didn't wounds throb most, and become the itchiest before the scab was ready to slough off?

"Oh Jesus," Ali whispered in prayer, "has my heart really started to heal? Please... please – it is all I hold in my hand, please take care of it..."

She cried then. Fresh tears. Tears of pure pain... as sensations burst on her emotions with a throbbing newness. She had thought her feelings had calloused over so that they would never hurt again... yet in all the smarting and aching she could not resent what it signalled to her.

She saw then a parade of faces and a new wave of tears flooded her eyes. "Oh God, how could they? I did nothing to deserve what they did..."

A soft voice gently prompted her spirit. "Neither did I. But forgive them, because they do not know what they do…" Tears poured… of effort, of forgiveness, consciously deliberately… for Jimmy… and Betsy – who was now his wife; Mrs Craddick; Fred and Janie; Mrs Hollis; Pastor Jake, all those who hurt – intentionally and unintentionally; all those who judged her, all those who avoided her… all those who threw their stones of disgust at her.

Ali could hardly stand. Spent and weary from the battles she was fighting, but still there was more… more to be said. "Oh God, I confess it… I do admit it! I want to be loved and understood - cherished and special. I don't want to give up the dream. I know I cannot take the vow Lloyd has made as a Pastor. I thought I could… I wanted to… to protect my heart against more pain. I must not be holy enough to stay alone. I want to be known and cared for. Now it feels like I am exposed… and it scares me. I know that with Lloyd this can go nowhere. Yet I still want to be someone's sweet heart; I still want to be somebody's mother. Please forgive me…"

Then came the tears of mourning… for handing over a dream that she hadn't even realised lived on, dormant under the layers of insulated defences. And this time, as her tears were spent, it was like the promise of a clearing overcast sky. Shades of blue seemed to hover just hidden beyond the canopy of grey.

"Oh Jesus… twice now I have failed… please, this time I want to do it your way. I promise… I won't make any more arrangements without you. That is my plan… it is the only arrangement I will make from now on."

And then finally... tears of relief... for having the candour to honestly assess the condition of her heart... and then, exposed and raw, to gently pass it over to the hands of a Healer who walked sandy roads caring for the destitute and desperate. A sense of security she had not known since she was a little child ran through her veins like a refreshing stream of water putting out the destruction of fire.

Slowly Ali looked around and the dimness of dusk was quickly deepening the moonless shadows that seemed to seep through the countryside. She hadn't realised how the time had passed. She shivered and stood up. It didn't seem to matter any more if she saw him. She felt stronger, braver, more resilient. She had a choice – she could say no. She had that right... and she would exercise it. Ali picked her way carefully over the rocks towards the track back to town. There was a silence in the night now. Only an occasional bird called into the night, crying, mournfully hooting for their mates who had disappeared in the flames – stirring for a restless night prowl.

She saw the lantern bobbing on the track towards her. She froze... she was out here, all alone. It swung in a bold manner... determined and quick. It came towards the corner swiftly. She struggled off the track in the dark and hunched in behind the blackened trunk of a tree holding her breath in silent caution.

"Ali? Ali...." It was Lloyd. She breathed in relief. It was a foe she knew... loved. In a way it would be easier if she considered him a weak willed man. Why couldn't he be like the clichéd picture of clergy who simpered around on the fringes of life with a bible as their only defence? It is not hard to reject a despicable man.

She stood up. "I'm here Jake." She was hardly aware she had dropped the "pastor" – a designation of friendship.

'Oh Ali! Thank God! Are you okay? Please forgive me! If you had come to harm…" He stopped and checked himself. "Are you okay?" he repeated quietly. He sounded tired, strained.

"Yes, I'm fine."

"Then why? Out here… on the darkest evening of the calendar-month? You have been gone such a long time! I've been checking in all day… surely…" Again he stopped. He suppressed a deep sigh and waited.

"I'm fine. I was thinking about some things…"

"Em told me you might be here. She didn't want to betray your confidence, but she was getting worried. We both were…"

"I'm fine." Her words sounded like an inarticulate parrot to her own ears, repeating herself over and over.

"I am relieved… and I am glad you are alright…" He searched the darkness to catch the light in her eyes, but the evening had darkened too quickly… and it would be disrespectful to lift the lantern into her face. He could only surmise what she might be thinking. Perhaps it was better this way. "Ali… I waited… I needed to talk to you some." It was urgent… something that could not be postponed anymore. What was not right, needed to be righted, because time and life and opportunities were so short… so transitory. This crisis had shown him that.

Ali thought about the things she had wanted to say… the things that had flooded her soul. If anyone would understand it should be a Pastor… but she held back. What if he despised her understanding of God? What if he was angry with her for pulling the pin on his very effective plan?

"Ali… I wanted to say I am sorry… really sorry. I fear I have not been fair to you. I beg your forgiveness. Wait… hear me out please. It was wrong to expect so much of your acquaintance – commitment without commitment. It does not work in God's eyes like that." A catch caught in his throat as he struggled with the words. "Please… I would like you to keep the ring if you wish… a thank you… but I release you from what I had hoped it might represent. It was wrong. No one should ask that. It was not fair. I'm truly sorry."

She blinked in the darkness… relief and disappointment stung her tear stained eyes at the same time. "Lloyd, please I would rather you took the ring…" She handed it over in the dark, willing her fingers to unlatch their grip. How tempting to save this trophy of friendship. When she discovered the truth of Jimmy's unfaithfulness, his ring had stung in a toxic band. Here she treasured this friendship yet at the same time resented its looseness. It was kind of apt it was a couple of sizes too large. She needed closeness to be binding, good times and sad times… a reflection of life in the form of promises that would encompass all their lives… not just outings. In handing it over, she willed the dream to the hands of her Father. It was His now.

Softly he spoke. "I understand…" And he turned the lantern around. "Please allow me one more excursion… so I can walk you back."

"Thanks Lloyd. I'm sorry the plan did not work for long…"

"I'm sorry it lasted as long as it did. It was something that should never have started." They turned and walked in silence back to the shop, and Ali tasted the finality of his statement as more salt on the tip of her tongue.

Pastor Jake felt blank… like the slate of his emotions had been wiped off. He was too tired to feel. Just now their plan seemed so trivial. Immature… when a whole community had just gone through what they had… fighting for its existence. He was sure there was more tragedy to come. "Emmaline's beside herself. She has seen Mrs Lawson. Nat still isn't back."

51.

A figure emerged from the smoke, taut lines of exhaustion etching the drawing of a profound truth into his face. Even in the smudges of soot and grime over his brow and face, his eyes humbly smarting not just from the smoke. He was oblivious to it, except that he knew something had been birthed in his spirit. He had been through a purifying furnace that was hotter than the raging fires he had fought so furiously for the last seventy-two hours. If anyone was to ask more of him, he was barely able to raise his eyes, or speak. Yet he knew that his life was a gift. He could not deny God's hand in this.

He stumbled around the burnt out smouldering shell that had been his home. He had no tears for the history and the lost years that had been consumed in one violent fire-ball. His mother worried him most. How would she fair? He sat down on the stone step that had lead onto the verandah. The charred trunk of the wilga tree standing like the marker of a grave. He used to step so confidently here. Now it was positioned like a stone alter in the middle of the burnt out rubble and ashes. He half raised a smile as he thought of a sermon Jake had preached once about being living sacrifices. He had never felt so dead, and yet his spirit was experiencing new life, a vitality he had never known was possible. And the wonder of that thought pressed through the exhaustion into his spirit.

He sat for an unknown period of time… considering how he should face his mother. Nat felt no urgency. He was procrastinating – an indulgence he rarely allowed. Here time stood still. How could he let his Mum know that her life had been burnt to ash? All her tangible memories were gone – there was nothing left to hold them. He looked at the jumble of embers and burnt rubble and thought how this had been just five days ago. Then his heritage had been intact... even if it had been a tense, strained wholeness. This dry summer had held a predictable foreboding from the start. He had always known this destruction was on the cards... and he had dreaded its possibility, but now he was looking at the result. In a way, the anticipation of the disaster was worse than its reality. Now it was done, and the insane impossibility of fighting it was over.

A movement caught his eye and he stared amazed as Pepper tottered towards him. A whine escaped the straggling form. Nat stood and scooped it up. His tail was singed and his paws burnt. "I can't believe it! How could anything survive this?" Even in his exhaustion, he marvelled at the tenacity of nature. It was almost at the same time that he realised that there was something of that same tenacity in his own soul... and his mother's. Survival. "Citygirl was right. We are the same... you and me..." he muttered into Pepper's mottled ear. He half chuckled as he sat back on the ground in the ashes. "More than our good looks and compliant natures – hey Pepper? We're survivors..."

He leant back against the stone step as Pepper snuggled in against his scorched shirt. He closed his eyes. The thought stayed with him. Citygirl. What a blessing there was no Citygirl in his life, no girl at all. It was not that he didn't want it, but it will take years to get himself back to a place where he could reasonably provide a home. It amazed him. He was acutely aware of an ache in his chest when he thought of her, yet he could not bring himself to resent the way things were between them. It was better for her to be spared the trauma his Mum would endure. At least the Bathrobe was a well-padded one, and Citygirl would be provided for. It was not everything – but it was one thing.

Emmaline walked along the track towards the smouldering ruins of the Lawson homestead. Heat radiated off the blackened landscape and smoke spiralled from smouldering fallen logs that refused to go out. Gathering clouds darkened the smoke hazed sky. She stepped slowly, dreading the truth of what she would find. He would fight until it killed him. She knew it. His mother knew it… and they could wait no longer. Uncle Alf and other men were still out in the paddocks, sorting through the smouldering remains in an impotent effort to salvage one last vestige of control. Slowly they were returning home. Counting the cost would go on for months.

Em stumbled. She could do this. It was the least she could do, a penance for her peculiar brand of stubbornness. She shuddered as she remembered the clang of the school bell raising the alarm. She had been holding Richard's arm walking away from the Church. He was in the middle of a very pretty speech about the void that her going from ELLIOT HOUSE had left in the social set… and in his heart. He was just getting to the significant part – Emmaline knew exactly where it was going, and she was somewhat annoyed he was beating around the bush. Still it was what etiquette demanded and he finally presented a ring. She almost laughed that she had been so fickle about such details.

When the bell tolled its urgent warning and call for assistance, Richard froze. Then he swore. Em almost expected that the line on his grim mouth would adamantly insist that she leave with him. Right then. But all he did was raise his hand in frustration, and exclaim nothing was going to plan, because lately... nothing ever did. As if this fire was all about him. Then he gathered himself and benignly shrugged and observed that he would be best utilised at the hospital.

"Richard – surely you are going to help?"

His eyes looked trapped, like a dingo hounded into a fence. "Emmaline – this is helping. Someone has to do the background work. It is just as important. I'm not one to push to the front."

"Front? What we need is help out there on the fire front."

"Out there? That's impossible – these things should be handled by the experienced. I have no proficiency in such."

"Experience? Who has experience with a disaster like this? This is not something one can practise. It's not like playing the piano... or tennis!"

"Come Emmaline – it is best I utilise my strengths where I have experience. Don't get all high and mighty. It is possible I will walk away and not come back."

She stared at the ring on her finger before she understood that he truly believed such an ultimatum would make a difference. And he was right: it certainly did. She would not wait for him to do the walking. She turned back to the schoolyard. Surely there was something she could do.

"Emmaline! Don't walk away. Don't do it. Your Grandmother will be displeased. She will…"

"Grandmother? What Richard? What will she do? Grandmother Edith never sent me a civil word – by letter or in person. You are not here on her behalf… because if you are, your proposal is a fraud."

"Come Emmaline… let's not argue. We are civilized and respectable adul…"

"No Richard. Let's fight. Let's get ugly! You brought Grandmother into this… as if her approval is somehow more important to you than I am. You're not marrying her!"

He paled under her barrage. It was not the kind of social tact he expected from the heiress of ELLIOT HOUSE. "Lady Edith is your only family. You must know she is important to me…"

"Actually, I do have family here. And I can't believe for a moment that you've suddenly developed a warm and affectionate regard for each other. You are useful to each other… although Heaven knows how!" She turned away again and then stopped suddenly. "Oh. I get it."

She stopped, looking towards a town activated by panic. It was like she stepped out of time and everything slowed down. Every doubt cast in her mind flashed with clarity. She heard her words echoing across her bush breakfast with Nat. She could no longer defend him. She turned back and took the ring off her finger.

"Emmaline! You know we are suited to each other... you have said so – many times!"

"Grandmother sent you to draw me back. I am the loose cannon in her highly controlled life. If you succeed...she approves... she reinstates my status in her will. I inherit... you inherit... and you have protected a healthy allowance to live out your life! I am quite incidental to the plan!" Em turned and looked him square in the face as she pressed the ring back into his hand.

His features twisted away under her scrutiny. "I need to go and help now, just as you said."

"You will help fight the fires?" Perhaps she had misjudged him.

"I meant at the hospital... where I am useful."

She closed her eyes in embarrassment. "Nat was right." She didn't mind that he was. Nat would go fight for other people's places... and Richard's only plan was evacuating to the hospital. She felt sick to her stomach.

With each step down the track towards Nat's place, Em knew he had continued to fight... and now she had to know how it ended. During those unending days of fight, they had no idea who would win. Nat could be losing everything in this uncontrollable battle. She heard more than one volunteer down a coffee at the Barbershop and report Richard was found asleep in the linen store. When would someone fight for her like Nat, and not for a cut in an inheritance?

Josie, like the rest of the congregation, never made it home after church. Em had helped Ali set up a first aid station bandaging less severe burns and handing out water canteens.

On her breaks she went to the hospital to get supplies and speak with Josie and others. There was a desperate need to bury the agony in her spirit with busyness. Men had come in burnt... or burnt-out in exhaustion, but Nat was not one of them. Workers rotated through the kitchen at the hospital to go back and fight the fire. Nat was never seen. Em quietly told Josie of her intentions to find out. Josie's hollow eyes just nodded gratefully. She said nothing. She could lose a house... but a son? Someone she loved... again? Of surviving that she was not so confident.

Em came upon the silent ghost of a shell that a few days ago was the Lawson homestead. The hush was loud – engulfing everything in the enormity of its void. It was as if death hung its hat on the gate. Tears welled in her eyes. How could so much be lost so quickly? Strong men, strong houses... gone. It was like war, only there was no enemy to focus one's hate upon. Everything was destroyed.

She forced herself to walk around the site. Her step faulted as she trod on debris and her eyes fell on his slumped figure against the stone steps. "Oh no!" she whispered in hollow fear. She stumbled down beside his figure – still warm from the fire he had fought so determinedly. "Nat... Oh God! You weren't supposed to die." Nat's consciousness roused from his exhausted sleep. The privacy of this grief opened a fissure to strong feelings that she hardly knew lay dormant. Sobs racked her small frame. "I knew... I... I knew you would never give in. You stubborn, stubborn man!" Anger gushed out in hot, distressed tears.

Nat held his breath and listened in amazement to the honesty of her anger. He slowly opened his eyes, but not far... years as a proficient squinter holding him in good stead. Stubborn Citygirl. Not so tidy now. They were two of a kind. He wanted to reach out and calm her, but he hesitated. He was under a spell. Any movement might break the magic. He didn't want it to disappear... not yet. Such moments are fragile.

"Oh Nat. These days... not knowing... it was the hardest thing. It... I hoped... that we could... be... we could... the idea that... Oh! I wanted so much to try again." She was late... too late! She flung herself across his chest in deep despair. Pepper squalled out in protest. "Pepper? He rescued you? Again? Ohh...."

The incoherent confession, her out pouring of tears that tracked gullies through the soot on his skin, stunned him into a further reverent silence.

"God... how am I going to tell Josie? This will kill her. She'll never make it."

"We... we could just not mention it then..." His hoarse voice crackled from dryness and grit. His eyes – red from heat, smoke irritation and dust, opened slowly. He stirred and sat up.

She jumped back, shock pounding through her chest. Surely, she was hallucinating from distress.

A quiet smile played around his lips, dry and cracked, reflecting the sadness in his eyes. "Good to see you Citygirl..."

"Nat?" She stared, barely able to comprehend. Without conscious thought she handed him the canteen from around her shoulder.

He took a drink and cradled his hand and poured a little into it for Pepper to have a drink. He lapped thirstily. "Perhaps you don't recognise me," he said huskily. "Nat Lawson. We went riding a couple of weeks ago… to check the dams…" He looked at her steadily. How he wanted to start over. "Welcome to my place," he said grimly, with a tired gallant sweep of his hand.

Em sat in the ash-covered ground. The vastness of her relief falling over her in trembling waves, tears streaming down her cheeks. "Oh Nat – I'm so sorry."

He shrugged a little. He was too.

Silence.

He stirred again and stared at her, mesmerised by the evidence of her agony. The things that she said… at least, alluded to… he needed to know. "Citygirl… you came here?"

It was a question she could hardly answer. More tears choked at her dry throat. Josie was spared. She was spared. The farm had not been. She didn't know how to express that without sounding trite. "I – we… we had not heard anything. Your mother… she looked like she was going to die if she didn't know one way or the other… I couldn't stand it any longer."

"Is she okay?"

Em nodded. "She will be." He was alive. It was almost more than what they dared to hope for.

"Mal?"

She nodded. "Exhausted… a few burns. Nothing major."

"Alf and the others?"

She nodded. They were alive. Their house and dairy survived, many of the cattle hadn't. As they went around news of their neighbours, they were wounded and bruised. But alive.

"You here just for family then?"

Tears clung to her lashes, now dusted with ash. She knew what he meant. How could he not know the torment of these last days? She shook her head mutely. "I needed to know too."

"Where is the Bathrobe?"

She stared at him in apprehension. The smoke, the heat... dehydration... it had affected his mind. She offered him another drink. "Oh Nat, everything is gone. I'm so sorry..."

He smiled at her troubled eyes as he realised she thought he was delirious. "Everything? Gone? The Bathrobe... Millard... Pritchard... he is gone too?"

"Richard? Oh, *that* bathrobe!" Her mind floated in relief back to that morning on the verandah. It seemed like three life-times ago. She could not suppress the laugh gurgling in her throat.

"Is he really gone?"

"He left as soon as the roads were opened."

"There – see some good can come of a disaster. I'm assuming you won't be Mrs Prichard Somerville any time soon."

"Ever."

"Are you okay with that?" He searched her eyes for regret, or remorse... or sorrow.

She held his gaze evenly. "Yes... I'm okay with it. You can even say 'I told you so.'"

He relaxed and leant back against the step, and smiled. She noticed that he made no effort to reproach her lack of judgement. He paused and turned towards her, his hair falling across his face. He ran a tired hand through his hair and pushed it out of his smarting eyes. "Citygirl... I might need a haircut..."

"Oh Nat." She scrambled back to his side. She had never seen this man so vulnerable. She stroked Pepper as he arched his back and rubbed against Nat's hand.

He turned his head towards her. "I heard what you said... earlier."

"I was distraught... incoherent... I thought..."

"You thought I was dead... and that made being honest okay. Well... I'm thinkin' honesty is good whether I'm dead or alive..." Boldness took hold of him. "I'm very much alive and I'm thinkin' perhaps you regretted how we found ourselves together... always uncivil and uncaring."

"Oh Nat... these last days... I wanted to undo so much. To never have the opportunity to leave on good terms... that thought was unbearable. I'm so sorry."

"I felt..." She started to pull away, and he held her wrist – gently, wincing as he made an effort to sit up. "I felt those things too."

She looked down at his hand, raw burns peeling the skin on his forearms, blistered and weeping. "Nat – your arms!"

He ignored her. He held her hand lightly, gently. "Citygirl. It will take a while to get back on my feet. But I will. I will! If you could wait..."

She stared at his face, lines of exhaustion etched around his jaw, battle weary from his ordeal. He was asking permission to fight for her. It touched the very core of her soul. "Nat – I can. I am not going anywhere." Em knew in her heart that he would work like a Trojan to make that time as short as possible, so he could make a proper proposal… secure and worthy of her assent.

He closed his eyes and nodded. How could he lose everything and suddenly feel he had gained more than he ever dreamed possible?

The irony of her situation seemed unexpectedly ridiculous. "Two declarations in a week… and I thought I might never interest a man!"

He looked wounded. "Oh Citygirl, I'm sorry – I didn't speak properly… I don't have a good way with…" Suddenly he did want to be chivalrous, worthy of her refined ways.

She lifted his hand in hers and gently studied his wounds. "Oh, Nat Lawson you are mistaken! Richard may have command of a respectable vocabulary, but when fine words didn't work, he simpered out of town with his tail between his legs. It doesn't matter what words you use because I cannot fault your heart. I never would have believed anyone could be as gallant. I am honoured."

Just then, it was as if the whole world stood still. The cloud-darkened sky broke through with sunrays… as rain, gentle fine rain… misted like gold onto their skin. The dry earth and ash puffing up dust into little round balls as droplet after droplet fell. He turned his face to the sky as he witnessed the life-giving miracle.   "Citygirl… my beautiful, stubborn Citygirl… don't you ever change your mind on that."

Part 3

The Preacher's Lass

"Dear Malachi,

    Children are a heritage of the LORD. My son... nothing I could write seems adequate. I feel overwhelmed with a sense of blessing from the hand of God. He has created eternity in my home, and I have the privilege to hold you in my arms. Of all the things that I do... the work that consumes my days in providing for our family... nothing lasts... another workday, another contract, and another case. Season after season and the ground lays fallow if we don't persistently till the soil for the coming season. All work cycles around... but you son, you are eternal. You are a work that will last.

    I pray that God will capture your heart early... that you will be a man who will fight for what is right... that you will stand against the things that are unjust. The bible is full of men who specialised in fighting... but Caleb... he was a man who knew how to take new ground... to stand against the tide and fight. He was a person who was not daunted by giants... and even when a generation balked and fainted, he walked into the inheritance of God because his heart did not fade.

How God? How can I instil such values into the heart of one so young? How can I transpose what stirs me, into my own flesh and blood? I guess by following the example of Caleb also... standing against the giants and declaring to the untaken territory, that it belongs to the Kingdom of God first, and for our family second. Malachi, my son... we have a lasting heritage to build.

~ your devoted father, always"

52.

Josephine Lawson sat at the kitchen table, sipping a cup of tea and counting out the board-and-lodging takings by the light of her lamp. She instinctively looked over at the mantelpiece to check the time and sighed. That was something else that was gone. That clock had been a wedding present, measuring the hours and the minutes of their life together. It had also ticked away the hours of pain and the work that Matt's death had brought. It was not right that the clock was not there, helping her count the moments. It had been a constant in her life: that ritual Matt had performed, turning the winder at night before he retired. Somehow, doing that one activity was the key that gave structure to Josie's day, during those senseless, meaningless months, years, decades after his death.

Josie put aside the money and took up a list of things that she had written out for Malachi to attend to. He had not come home this late for over a week, but it surprised her none. The bushfire had changed so much for them. The homestead was burnt to the ground. Some of the out buildings were saved, but only a couple. They were starting again. From scratch. It had taken a while for the shock to set in and the enormity of what it all meant to really hit home.

To start with she was so sure that having her eldest son alive would be enough. She had been so exhilarated Nat survived the fire-storm that ripped through their farm. She knew that to live through the loss of Nat would be akin to surviving the death of her dear husband all over again. Not everyone in the district came through this disaster without losing a loved one. But even so, that does not prepare you for the reality of the day-by-day struggle of ongoing survival. Or the strain. She was older now... less resilient... she didn't have youth on her side.

Then there was Emmaline. That young lady came through this ordeal with a connection to Nat that was like breathing air to him. She was a snorkel that kept him going, helping him focus on what was needed through the trauma. He was so fixed on getting the farm working again, to be able to support a family. There was so much about Nat that reminded Josie of his father, during those early years. The pioneer years, she called them. But as Josie sat at the kitchen table silently counting rent, she knew that she had lost her pioneering spirit. Her eldest son was moving on without her. His life energy was being poured into Emmaline Farrington, a spoiled brat of a girl from the city. Exclusion hurt.

In desperation, after the fire, she took the house in town and let the rooms to pay for the rent. Funny, the kinds of things that present as challenges: something as basic as bed-linen was one thing. Josie went on a borrowing mission from those who had survived the fire. Sheets and pillowcases, starched and ironed... and well patched on Mrs Wallace's treadle sewing machine, was the best she could do. Slowly she was making headway, and able to buy new sets of linen to replace the borrowed ones. She ordered two sets at a time: a new set to return to the borrower and one for the house. Almost by default she had a boarding house that was the town's only real alternative to hotel lodging.

Pastor Jake was the first to take a room. He had relinquished the manse to a family who had lost their home in the bush fire, and taken a room at the Creek Hotel. It was not hard to make the move out of the raucous, smoky, musty pub. Mr Tolbert was a teacher who was also not keen to stay in the noisy rooms above the bar. When the last of what Malachi called the 'refugee families' were finally resettled in their own homes, life at the boarding house acquired a type of routine. Most of the other boarders now were a rag-tag assortment of short-termers – businessmen passing through, and travellers needing respite from the road. Wattle Creek was a layover stop for the coach on the western service where the train did not run. Josie quickly made a name for her respectable boarding house.

She stared at the list in her hand: fix the tap on the rain water tank and the door knob on Mr Tolbert's bedroom; nail the boards on the side verandah; adjust the lamp in the hall; swing the gate properly; find another clothes prop for the clothes line. These things were just general maintenance. The house was not in good order when they took the rental, but it had plenty of rooms. The things that needed attention urgently were fixed when they moved in. Jamison was the landlord, but his interest in attending to upkeep and repairs was as limited as his reputation for generosity. He insisted that for the rent that she was paying, the maintenance had to be Josie's own responsibility. She knew that if she was to present the boarding house as a fair alternative to the hotel, it followed that she needed to be true to her word and provide just that.

Her youngest son Malachi, had joined her in town to help at the boarding house. He was only a baby when they moved to the farm, and had never shown any inclination for town, but it didn't take him long to appreciate the number of attractive benefits it provided. He took a social liking to two-up and cards with his mates. It had been a slippery slope to being a regular at the pub and getting a reputation for being a tough competitor in boxing fights. He was one for taking winnings with his fists so that he had more to present at the card table later on in the evening.

Josie sighed and put the list back on the sideboard. It didn't seem likely that Malachi would get to these things tomorrow either. When he was this late, he slept away the next day, and emerged in the evening to go out again. She shook her head. She didn't know what to do about it. Matt would have known; only this time she pulled herself up short.

It would be twenty years next June… that year had been the wettest, coldest winter they had known. The chilling fingers of death made it even colder and bleaker. But after two decades, surely it was time to let the clock stop ticking. Perhaps this was what the burning of the clock symbolised. Her existence had irrevocably turned a corner and now she had to admit that it would never be satisfying again. What it really meant was that it was going from bleak to bad to worse. Nat had moved on. Toby had moved on. Malachi had lost his way… and she, she could hardly blame him for that. She had never found her way back from that terrible day in June when Tom Redding came riding breathlessly up the road.

Josie picked up her cup and hurled it against the empty mantle piece. There was no clock to stabilize her day, no portrait of her husband to comfort her with his photographic gaze. She was angry: a silent, violent rage that stirred her trembling frame. Her home - the home that she and Matt had built together, was destroyed, burnt to ash. The memories... those precious things she would remember at unexpected times as she worked around their house, were gone. The memories had been demolished in a fire-ball that left nothing to salvage. She would have nothing now to prompt her to remember the gentle amazed look Matt gave her when she told him she was pregnant with Nat. They had been standing by their marble topped wash-stand in their bedroom. That moment had given birth to Matt's determined resolution to go farming for his son's sake, to build a heritage worthy of a Lawson. Or what about the memory of the first time he lifted tiny Malachi in his arms over their cane bassinette: their third son, when Matt announced he had finalised the deal on the farm, or seeing Matt prop Toby in his lap, reading to him in his old leather armchair. How could God do this to her? Was it not enough that He took Matthew? Was there no end to the blows that God would inflict? Year after year?

53.

Mal lifted his glass and set it down when he remembered it was already drained. He quickly ordered another by signalling the bar-tender. He carelessly looked around the room through the smoky haze that hung over their secluded corner. It was a privilege – this corner, for regulars and invitees. It was the mark of a man with cards to be included in this small round table of gambling knights. Mal glanced at his hand of cards. It wasn't too bad. His evening had been plush so his confidence was high. Confidence is one thing, however he was shocked when the others pulled out a rule that his inexperience hadn't come across. He could hardly argue with a whole table of veterans. Then it happened again… and again. With less drinks he may have walked away. With less chips, he may have cautiously committed himself. In his warm, relaxed, confident recklessness… he did neither. He got cleaned up, and then kept going, determined to retrieve a skeleton of honour… and he continued to spiral down in a whirlpool of desperateness.

Finally, they closed the table. Mal stumbled out into the street. It was a mild enough night, but you could tell the chill of the changing season was on its way. An occasional lamp flickered down the street. No… that was lightening on the horizon as an approaching storm rumbled in the distance. Too far away to be a concern, even if he had registered the weather. He could not believe his luck. He could not believe the bad plays he had made. He could not believe the others had played fair and square.

He staggered towards the boarding house. For once he almost wished he could go home, to the farm, to his old room or lay on the weathered chaise lounge on the verandah… watching the stars. Home. There was no such thing anymore. His mother's house was filled with strangers, invading the space that was rightfully his. He pushed unsteadily at the gate and tried to open it. His mother should get a decent house. Even the gate jammed because it didn't swing straight. He shrugged and stumbled on up the street. No bother. He would go where he could open the gate, or where there was no gate. He could watch stars there… anywhere.

He found himself by the creek. Wattle trees swaying along the ridge in the night breeze. The charred trunks were covered in new yellow-green foliage. He could smell it. The rain had worked its miracle by touching the world with new life. But it hadn't touched his heart. There was no new start for him. As young as he was, he felt he had reached the pinnacle of his success, then crashed and burnt it in the very same hour. In the shadows of the night, he could see the dark scars of the fire that had burnt his known world into a cinder box. He dozed fitfully, not drunk enough to sleep out the night in oblivion and not sober enough to make a move. The stars blinked and hid themselves behind clouds. He could not watch stars from here either. Nothing; nothing… was right.

The rumbling of thunder disturbed him. Large drops of rain splattered his face. He rolled over and reached up to pull his hat over his face. His felt hat was gone, dropped somewhere on his unsteady walk along the street. He moved under a tree to shelter from the rain, as the world shook from a violent crack of thunder. A lifetime of bush craft ingrained in him forced him to a safer place. The irony of seeking refuge now, when he so carelessly despised his life before, had no impact on him. He struggled to his feet and made his way to the railway bridge by the light of dazzling lightening strikes. It would be more protected there. He huddled in under the framework of the bridge, sitting in the dust, as the thunder clapped and roared. Large drops of rain gathered momentum and then it bucketed down.

He crouched in the dark, chilled by the rain. There was nothing to do but to sit this out. The night shadows thickened like a winter soup as the rain pelted against the bridge, broken only by flashes of white lightening. He moved over to avoid a gush of water running through the slatted framework of the bridge above him. He could hear the sound of the creek starting to run above the driving rain and grumble of thunder. He shifted up closer to the large wooden pylons. His arm touched a body, cold and clammy from the wet. Mal was sluggish from cold and a flattened ego. He never expected that his occupation of the bridge shelter was a territorial invasion. The bridge-dweller lashed out, thumping his face, splitting his lip, catching him by surprise punching him against his cheek, and then winding him breathless. Instinctively Mal hit back. His reactions as a boxer in make-shift street fighting rings kicked in and he hit hard. He struck again, blindly, seeing only by reflex through the dark. The defender of the wet weather refuge went limp; he had knocked him out.

By the glow of lightening flashes he went over to the gushing stream of water and washed his face and lip, struggling

478

for breath, trying to clear his head. He went back to check his opponent. It was unlikely, but there could be money to ease the desperateness of his situation. His debts were not to be sneezed at. He turned over the heavy coat and he felt along the pockets…waiting for a flash of lightening to light his crime. A burst of brilliant white, lit up the hair matted by rain. He almost resisted. An anonymous victim would take the sting out of committing a felony that his mother and brothers would despise. But what did he care? He had already stooped lower than he ever imagined possible. Perhaps if he knew who he was, he could make it up to him when times turned around. He was totally unaware that by this one single act, he was committing himself to the belief of a better future. He roughly pushed aside the dishevelled, dirty hair. Light flashed over the face. He swore in shock and recoiled. It was… he was… she was… a woman. Her body covered in a heavy man's overcoat and limp from his blows.

Any man – of any race or creed, would not have generated this reaction in him. A woman? Oh, dear God! How worse could this day go? Had he killed her? Mal stirred to action. He splashed water on her face and she whimpered, but otherwise stayed unresponsive. He leant down and felt for breath. It was faint but regular. The rain steadied. He had to do something. His mother. Mum would know what to do. He hoisted her up, her frame a dead weight in his arms. He stumbled out, disorientated in the dark, losing his footing in the slippery mud. Then he remembered: the train tracks. Staggering in the rain, he climbed up onto the ridge and followed the tracks back into town. Struggling to keep his balance along the uneven sleepers he carried the matted haired woman in the saturated overcoat, back to town.

By the time he stumbled into the familiar streets, muddy stormwater still gushed along washed out gutters. The downpour had passed and only a light drizzle flicked against his face. He kicked the gate with his boot, forcing it open. He struggled around to the back porch and banged on the door. He knew it would be unlocked, but the doorknob was high. His body ached, his arms numb from carrying their burden, but that hardly compared to the burden on his conscience. He could hear his mother stirring inside. He called out. The door rattled and Pastor Jake stood in his night-robe staring into the dimness with a lamp.

"Mal! Man – what is this? Quick, inside… what happened?"

Mal stumbled forward forcing him to take her as he collapsed shivering on the floor. Pastor Jake stared in shock as he buckled under her weight juggling the lamp still in his hand. He lifted her, and in the shadows carried her to the living room calling for help, as he laid her on the lounge. "Josie! Wake up! Josie!" he called urgently. He turned up the lamp on the table beside her, and gently pushed back her hair. The bruises on her face told a story.

"Mal – no time to quit man – go get Doctor Wallace!" He stayed crumpled on the floor, mud and water pooling where he fell. Pastor Jake firmly gave him no leniency. "Mal – we need the doctor. Go man. Now!" Through the haze Mal registered his penance was incomplete. He struggled to his feet and turned to shuffle outside. Pastor Jake stared. He was not sure his message would get there. "Here; you stay with her. Wake your mother. Get some towels. Boil some water. I will fetch the Doctor." And he fled outside in his slippers and night-gown, running breathlessly to the doctor's residence through the muddy streets and back again.

Doctor Wallace snapped his bag shut. "Who is she Josie? She's not one of the local girls."

Josie shrugged. It was a mystery all round. One thing she could guarantee: if there was trouble to be found, Malachi would find it like a pup finds its mother. "What's the problem with her?" Somehow she wanted to disregard Malachi's confession. If he wasn't responsible, that would absolve her of any obligation of having to try and fix it.

"Josie I would like you to consider letting her stay here. She has spoken some, but she is malnourished; she has feeble blood. Some of your stews could possibly be the best remedy for her."

"She'll be better off in the hospital. You should organise for her to go there."

"I could. Yes." He paused. "But she is not sick... just weak. I feel another woman around her would be more benefit than patients."

Josie shook her head. Both the nurses were women… wouldn't that suffice? There was no way she was ready to be a byway house for down and out charity cases. It wasn't her way, and it certainly didn't pay the bills. "I only have two rooms left and I need them to be paying. We know nothing about this girl... and who she might be connected with."

Doctor Wallace looked at the girl in the bed. One glance at her sunken eyes and haggard, exhausted expression told him there were circumstances surrounding her being here. He wasn't sending this lass to the hospital ward. If Mrs Lawson could not help he would approach his wife. He felt irrationally determined about it. "Mrs Lawson, I understand your need to be discerning about who takes your rooms. This admirable trait is one of the reasons I ask you to reconsider. This young woman needs a reliable person around her just now. We have no idea where her family is." He quietly lowered his voice. "Your rates are reasonable. I'd be willing to cover the costs until we find out more about her circumstances. Even a short-term boarder may compensate a vacant room. Although," he paused significantly, "I would consider it necessary that you told no-one about these arrangements. We must respect the girls' privacy."

Josie blinked. She felt shamed that the Doctor would consider her not charitable, but she had a business to run and a farm to rebuild. However, a paying room, that changed a lot. She blinked. "What needs to be done for her Doctor?"

He smiled encouragingly. "Just help her as she needs. She is weak, but not an invalid. Plenty of your farmhouse broths would undeniably support her cause."

That brought up another problem. "But Doctor, the vege garden isn't going well yet. I've enough to make for normal meals, but my broths... I wouldn't have nearly enough for both." For someone who always had a regimented supply of fresh produce, it was not an easy thing to admit.

"Would you be offended if my Louise brought down some things from her garden for the lass? We have stuff going to waste since it is just the two of us."

Josie blinked. A nervous habit she acquired when she felt backed into a corner. She knew Mrs Wallace would never let her produce go to waste. Yet Josie could think of no good reason to refuse. She didn't want to sound selfish and inhospitable. How annoying. She nodded. "The veges might help."

Doctor Wallace grinned. "Mrs Lawson, your circumspect hospitality is to be commended. Louise's carrots are second to none. I trust the blessing you give, will be returned to you multiplied."

Josie could not smile over his acclamation. The whole situation just reeked of unpleasantness. She should not jeopardise her regular board. What would Pastor Jake think, her taking in a rag-a-muffin stranger like that? Once Josie would have thumbed the opinions of others; now-a-days she did not have that liberty. She had bills to pay and commitments to keep, and it was dependent on the good will and estimation of those around her.

Pastor Jake came out early, stepping gingerly around the squeaky board in the hallway. He jumped when Josie met him at the door. "Uh, oh... Good morning Josie," he said properly.

"Pastor Jake. Good morning. Going for your walk? Did you sleep well?"

"Well actually. I hardly slept a wink. Much to think about from our late night visitor. How is she? Awake yet?"

"Dr Wallace was very hopeful that she will be up and about soon."

"Poor thing. She looked quite dispossessed. I wonder what she is going to do."

Josie took a breath. Now. This was her opening. "Her family is no doubt worried…"

Jake nodded soberly, even though he didn't think so at all. Women who reside under bridges probably do not have relatives pining to know their whereabouts. The likelihood of locating her family, if she didn't volunteer the information, was as probable as flying to the moon.

Josie took a deep breath and tried to keep the disgust out of her voice. He was after all, in a sensitive frame of mind. "The Doctor said he wanted her to stay here, until we found out more of her circumstances… and…"

Jake broke out into a grin. "Mrs Lawson you are generous indeed. Please… allow me to contribute to her board. It would be the least I could do."

Josie raised her eyebrows. Normally she would have been up front and declined, but things were no longer normal. Her other room was still vacant, and there were a myriad of things to fix. Besides, she was sworn to keep the Doctor's contribution confidential. It would help her get on top of things, having board for one room plus some. "Pastor Jake, that is very generous…"

"Hardly at all Josie. What you have done is very commendable…"

He left for his walk, a hymn whistling on his lips as he walked down the street, muddy from the overnight rain.

She went back inside. Suddenly having this charity case under her roof, did not seem such a shameful act. The teacher emerged looking like a barn-duck desperate for a morning splash in the dam. "Good morning Mr Tolbert. I trust you weren't disturbed last night. There was a bit of a commotion."

"You said it!" he said gruffly. He had slept very poorly.

Josie didn't particularly like Mr Tolbert. Unfortunately for Mr Tolbert, anyone who had the audacity to replace Mr Hewitt when he retired from his position at the school-house automatically carried a black mark against his name. Mr Hewitt had mentored and tutored her children through the tumultuous years of their fatherless schooling. She was certain that any man, and in particular – this man, who replaced Mr Hewitt would not be equipped to deal with the realities of normal life. How could he possibly help the younger generation traverse the vast seas of learning?

"Last night was like grand central station," said Mr Tolbert who had no interest in perpetuating superficial courtesies today. "If it is going to be like this, I would have done better to keep the room at the hotel."

Josie quickly tried to think of a way to smooth over his antagonism. It would not do to have him go back to the hotel disgruntled. Stories get around. "There was an emergency: we had to get Doctor Wallace. We would do the same for any of our guests, Mr Tolbert. In a crisis it's the least we should do."

He grunted as he poured his cup of morning tea. "The knob on my door hasn't been fixed. *That's* the least you should do." His head was thumping, and he had a busy day ahead of him. The students were always more restless when his head throbbed.

"I have made arrangements for that to be attended to as soon as possible Mr Tolbert."

"It appears these fly-by-nighters have more priority than regular guests."

"She will only be staying with us for a *while*," Josie said with emphasis. She paused as she realised that she still didn't know the mystery of the woman's identity. "She is not well at the moment so I will not disturb her with introductions until she sees the Doctor."

Mr Tolbert pursed his lips. Well, as long as she wasn't a noisy guest. Perhaps if he went to the school early he could write up the lessons on the chalk-board and keep the lid on the chatter before they get wound up. He took his leave without a word.

Josie stared after him. He paid his rent on time; and if there had been any doubt about that, she would have had no conscience in generating a hullabaloo just to get rid of him. She didn't need the aggravation.

54.

It was ridiculous that one person in an overcoat could upset her equilibrium so. Josie took in some oatmeal porridge for breakfast. "Good morning. It is late but we thought you might like to lie in this morning. Did you sleep?"

The young woman stared fearfully out from under the covers, her bruised face and black eye giving her the look of a wounded possum. Josie placed the tray down on the end of the bed. "I brought you some breakfast," Josie said when she did not respond. Josie waited. What could she say? Nothing relevant came to mind. She could hardly demand to know why she was lying in her freshly washed sheets covered in a mud layered overcoat, with matted hair that looked like a crow had constructed its random nest of sticks on her scalp. Josie turned to go and then stopped. "Oh. We didn't introduce ourselves properly last night. My name is Josephine – or rather, Josie... Josie Lawson. What is your name?"

The girl continued to stare. Without shifting her gaze, tears streamed down her face. She answered faintly, "My name is Laura… Lawrence."

"Laura. Oh." It seemed impossible that the owner of such a benign name could cause her so much anxiety… apart from the obvious dispossessed alone-in-the-storm situation … or the being slogged-by-her-son scenario.

"Okay. Well Laura, eat up your breakfast. I'll bring in the water for your bath. Use the clean night gown so I can wash the sheets and your coat..." She spoke with clipped detachment.

Laura clutched at the collar of her coat. Her voice was weak. "No thank you. I'm fine."

Josie stared. "No? What do you mean 'No'?"

"I won't have breakfast. Thank you. No bath, no clothes. I will not be staying. I have family... I will be going there."

"Well that's a given! But first things first..." Josie resented the imposition of this girl, but now that she was refusing her offer of assistance, she felt put out. If the girl had family, they should know. "A bath will freshen you up. I'll send a note to let them know when they can come by for you."

"No thank you. No need. I will go to them."

"Where do they live?" She wasn't a local; she may not realise a Wattle Creek address could be anywhere within a circumference of fifty miles. She could hardly walk if that was the case.

"Home." Fresh tears.

She was being as vague as a moonbeam on a stormy night. "*When* will you be going then?"

Laura jolted... as if she suddenly realised her plan required action. She moved, clutching the big coat around her neck. "Now. I will go now..." She awkwardly wriggled to the side of the bed and put her feet out of the bed. Dried mud crumbled to the floor. Josie cringed in disgust. This would never do. She wanted so much to hold open the door just to make sure she made it outside. Laura struggled to release herself from the tangle of sheets... and as she did, it was like someone cut the strings that held her upright. She swayed and tottered, falling limply… collapsing in a heap on the bed.

Josie grabbed at her, holding her head as she rolled over and was sick. "Oh great…" murmured Josie. There was nothing for it now. The girl was having a bath even if she had to personally undress her and hold her in the water like a rebellious housedog. The sooner her relatives showed up… the better.

Pastor Jake kept to his morning routine. He walked down to the creek and sat on a rock and prayed as he watched the sun rise and play on the ripples in the creek. In his mind he walked around the pews in the church and asked God to protect and bless each family. There was one place that he left to last, one face that he lingered over. Ali: Alice Dampier. Doe eyed and serious; bubbly and effervescent… efficient and creative. Every mood was imprinted on his mind. He shook it loose. He should not dwell there. She had rejected his friendship. She wanted to be independent… wounded from a miserable engagement gone wrong. But he couldn't leave it alone and now he was battling with his own humanity. All he wanted was to declare his devotion. Not good. Not good at all. A pastor should protect the wounded; promote God's healing… not push in. He should not override God's plan for her life out of his own selfish desires.

All his intentions to stay unfettered emotionally so he could pastor and mentor and support these people now seemed foolishly ambitious in light of his obvious weakness. So, he prayed then for himself, for his integrity, for strength to have the courage to stay out of her way, to respect the space she requested. He held the Russian puzzle ring in his pocket, making and unmaking the puzzle blind. He did it automatically, a habit as he prayed for God's blessing in all of her endeavours. They had laughed about this ring – how it symbolised their friendship, how it might fall apart like the links in the ring. But there was nothing funny about it now. Jake interlocked the rings back together; willing their friendship back together. "Oh God. This is not what I had in mind. Not at all." And he meant both the emotional attraction, and his willing it to be legitimately established.

Then, aside from this, there was the nameless mysterious visitor who had been thrust into his arms in the early hours of the morning. It had shocked his senses as he opened the door still sluggish from sleep. This was a new diversion. A wholesome one, one that was altruistic in the purest sense of the term. As far as he knew, this young woman had nothing, no connections, no influence. She held no attraction, and yet was deserving of all the support, he – as a shepherd, could give to such a wounded lamb. But there was a greater benefit that drew his attention. This was a diversion that would keep his mind occupied with things other than Ali, for no other reason than this was her specific request. He knew he needed to oblige her in this, even when his mind and his heart didn't want to go anywhere else.

Josie quickly went and retrieved the metal bathtub and a pile of clean towels, thin from years of use. She stoked the fire and put on a large boiler of water to heat. Josie positioned combs and washcloths, and a water jug for washing her hair. She folded a fresh set of clothes on a stool. Finally, she filled the tub using a bucket to tote water. There wasn't any fine perfumed soap; that was the plight of starting again. There was only laundry soap for personal ablutions so she grated some into the warm water, stirring up suds. You just do what you have to do. She wished she had soft genteel soaps she could pamper herself with. In all her pragmatic habits, this was the one vestige of the past that was very dear to her. She regularly made up skin lotion from oils, herbs and spices for her own use. It was a crude mix, because some of the usual ingredients were far outside her budget. She poured a little of her favourite lavender mixture from the jar into the water.

Then with squared shoulders, bracing herself as she went to put her hand into a hornet's nest. Josie approached the bed with firm determination. She carefully peeled off the sheets, soiled with mud and vomit. Rolling Laura over, she undid the buttons of her large overcoat. Laura's neck and face were flushed from being overdressed. Slowly Josie rolled her back and peeled off the jacket, like pulling the heavy canvas off a covered dray.

Then, just as Josie released her other arm, Laura came to life. She turned and grabbed the coat from her hands, clutching and yelling, "Go away, stay away. You can't take my things! This is my coat, mine! Leave me alone, go away! Leave me alone!"

But Josie had made up her mind. This fiery little thing was sick and half starved. There was no way that she was going to be staying in her boarding house for another second, in that coat, with that smell. She yanked it free and tossed it on the floor. "You are having a bath – no person in my care is going back to their family, smelling like a long drop. You've been sick. You need a bath... and that is that. *And* we will do it now."

"No! I won't! You can't make me! I won't. I won't! I won't!"

Josie had branded calves and man-handled livestock. She had mothered three headstrong men from boyhood. A young woman with a childish fixation on a coat like a three-year-old, was not beyond her ability. "I guess I disagree Miss Lawrence. The tub it is." She pulled off her pinafore and tossed it with her heavy woollen overcoat, followed by her blouse and skirt.

"No!" She snatched up the sheets in modest shame. She began to whimper... "Leave me alone... please... stop..."

Josie had long been sun-dried by the down-to-earth concerns of life. She had no sympathy for this infantile display of inhibited bashfulness. "Oh, please child. You cannot be serious. I'm a woman with as much skin as yourself." She firmly offered her a towel and tried to extract the sheet from her clutches. "Come now. You will be wanting to see your family soon. There is no need for..." Josie's sentence hung in the air as the sheet fell away. The towels, thin and worn, did little to hide her abdomen, showing the first swollen signs of motherhood, made obvious by her emaciated frame.

Laura froze, shamed and humiliated. She closed her eyes and tears rolled down her bruised cheeks. She didn't know what to do. She didn't want anyone else to know. It was too hard... too awful. That's why she needed to come to Wattle Creek. That's why she needed to leave this house.

Josie stared at the girl in disbelief. How stupid she had been? Of course, Dr Wallace had alluded to this by saying that this girl needed to have a woman with her. But Josie didn't want her boarding house to be known as a by-way for adulterers and fornicators. She would never hear the end of this from Mrs Hollis. And what about Pastor Jake! Oh my goodness. He was contributing to her board! Josie said goodbye to that extra board straightaway. The girl couldn't stay. She had enough problems of her own without being loaded with the problems of the promiscuous. Besides, she could genuinely tell Dr Wallace the girl refused to stay. Josie would take her anywhere she needed. Anything... to get her to go. Josie urgently needed Laura to be ready when her family came to collect her... if such a family existed. Suddenly she doubted that very much.

"Well then, I've been a mother myself. Even in drought, it has been my rule to look after myself, because the facts are no one else is going to do it for you. You cope with things much better if you get enough sleep, eat as well as you can and feel clean. It keeps a sense of balance – looking after the basics."

Laura did not move. Josie had no idea what to do... and was not even sure if she had even heard her. "Okay... we will break it down even further. I'm going to sit you in that there tub and you're going to get wet all over. *All over*, you hear?

And wash your hair. There's soap there. I'm going to take the linen and soiled things out to the copper, so I can do the laundry. While I am gone you need to put on the clean change of clothes on that stool. I know they will swim on you – but you need something until your clothes are dry."

Laura stared some more, unblinking through her puffy eye. Finally, she murmured, "Will it drown?"

"Drown? You won't drown if you keep your head above water..."

"Not me... the... the..." She could not even say it.

"Oh. The baby?" Even to Josie's ears it sounded insensitive. Still... apples were apples. No point calling a granny-smith some exotic tropical fruit. She didn't believe it helped in the long run. More tears. For Josie, the doubts the girl harboured were not ridiculous, just tragic. Where was her mother? A boarding house lady shouldn't have to respond to something like this. That was what a mother should do.

"It'll be fine." At least that's how she thought of it. Not a person, not a life... an "it". This was not like the pregnancies she shared with Matthew... planned, longed-for, precious. "I had baths a plenty before my boys were born..."

Then, without explanation she felt a prompt in her memory. It was the first time it had happened since the farmhouse had burnt to the ground. She thought of the gentle touch of Matt's large, strong hand on her abdomen... softly feeling the wonder of their creation move... independently, alive, separate... growing, nurtured.

The memory made Josie falter. This girl would have no one to share these moments with: no special delivery for a long

494

awaited wicker crib; no one to massage away her tired aches as the time grew close. Just hiding and shame. Josie was no beacon-bearer of grace and tolerance, but at that moment she could not feel great about this girl being alone. There was nothing good about having to fight solo, in ignorance about what was happening to her. Josie turned away in the light of the revelation and did the only thing she knew how to do. She went to work.

She shuffled Laura aside to the chair and removed the remaining linen. She stripped the pillowcases and the mat from the floor, bundling it all up in the sheet like a big pudding. She left, shutting the door firmly behind her, but she left it unlocked just in case she felt the need to run. It would simplify things if she were gone.

She took her bundle outside to the laundry and sat on a stool for a long time. This was not her problem. This girl said she had her own family to look after her and her baby. Suddenly she was assaulted by the wonder of new life: it was a baby... a person. She shook her head. No, it was just a bump. Why was she getting emotional over something that didn't even exist? She placed her hand over the place where Matthew had touched her pregnancy so long ago. She knew he would approve of this. For him... for Matthew, she would do what she could.

55.

Mal stirred on his bunk. When they moved into the boarding house, he had insisted that he be given the sleep-out. He wanted to come and go without feeling his mother tracking his movements. If he came in early in the morning or left late at night, he didn't want to see that look in her eyes – that disappointment of not measuring up. He wasn't like Toby: his brother was just a couple of years his senior and a century more mature. Toby – the intellectual, the loner. Toby hated getting his hands dirty and hated working like a man. Mal could never see how Toby could seriously belong to this family. He was too out by himself. Alone. But then, at the moment, he felt more alone than Toby ever seemed to be.

He wasn't like Nat either – his eldest brother would order him around like a farm hand. He learnt to stand up to Nat early. They had countless fights in the stockyards, coming in for smoko with a split lip and bruised egos. Nat was not his father. He didn't want him to be his boss. They had learnt an uneasy partnership and mostly it worked... as long as he did it Nat's way. At least he could thank Nat that he had learnt how to fight. There was a quick buck now to be made by being a back street champion. He didn't want to spend his time playing Nat's tune. Nat didn't have rhythm, not like his mates.

Mates. His neighbour, Fred Dampier, was the one mate who could keep in time with Mal's rhythm. They grew up wandering over paddocks with rabbit traps and rifles. They could shoot anything that moved and didn't have to worry about grown-ups getting in their face. Their only boundary was to go as far as you could ride and still get back for dinner, because, let's face it; Mum's tucker was better and easier than having to get it yourself. Fred knew how to laugh and they had cooked up some classic pranks together, egging each other on to greater feats of daring and practical jokes. Until Janie. Fred got it in his head that this bubbly, demanding, fine-looking girl was worth more of his attention than his mate. Mal couldn't, for the life of him, understand that. Girls were girls… but mates were mates. Fred's lack of loyalty to this basic code was a betrayal of the greatest kind. It just wasn't the same after that. So, in the end, to leave the farm behind was not such a sacrifice; well, it had been drained of its heart anyway. Mal found other mates who could spin a good yarn, play a fair hand, share a drink and a laugh.

This new life was a tumultuous ride of highs and dips. But the dips never lasted and there were always the winnings from another fight that would bring up the tally of debts to zero. Fighting fair was Mal's quick-fix. What blew him away was that not all people played by the rules. Last night was evidence of that. He started to suspect a serious deviation from the rules when he lost most of his accumulated winnings in one fowl swoop. It happened so fast that it was only later that he felt he was being set up. With another drink under his belt he acknowledged it could have been a bad hand, but from there it went down the gurgler like he had never experienced before. Goal posts were being moved; variations of house rules were flung around in circles until he was dizzy from the motion. There was no way he could kick a goal, or land a solid punch from all the ducking and weaving. The next drink he took for fortification made his head spin. The rest of the night was a nightmare.

Mal groaned again and rolled over. His head ached, his body ached, and his feet ached. He felt like he had been hit by a goods train. Train... train-tracks... He reached up and touched his face, wincing as he felt the puffy, swollen flesh. He struggled to sit up. Perhaps it wasn't a nightmare. He shook his head, thick from morning syndrome. His throat was dry, and his eyes remained unfocused and stinging. He wasn't showing his face around town until this was healed. If it ever got out that a girl slugged him, his street fighting challenges would hardly hold water any more. And he needed a fight, a big challenge – to cover last night. He groaned and rubbed his forehead. Mud caked his hair; his chin was rough and unshaven. He felt like refuse a cat dragged in. He struggled to his feet and took a moment to steady his stance.

He went through the living room out to the laundry. He passed a woman sitting looking out the window. Her hair was damp, her posture lifeless: another uninteresting border. How could his mother stand it?

Josie glanced up over the steam of the copper as Malachi made his way down the stairs to the back laundry. "Has everyone forgotten how to bathe in this place? Go and wash Malachi, or I will stick you in this copper and boil that mud off your shins."

"Mum – last night... the girl. Is she alright?"

"If you mean, did you knock some sense into her? No, I don't suspect you did. Did she knock any sense into you? I doubt that too."

"Oh, come on Ma… no girl ever…"

"Malachi – your face tells its own story. Now – I'm not saying you meant to… but I'm thinking that you're going to have to be real nice to this girl, given what you did to her."

"I brought her back here didn't I? I probably saved her life."

"Yes probably."

"Then what's the problem? What's to be nice about?"

Josie paused. Last night gave her the hope for her son she had long been looking for. She didn't want to blow it by saying the wrong thing. How do you ever know what's the 'wrong thing' or the 'right thing', for that matter? "The problem is… I think she may be lost…"

"Lost? As opposed to homeless?"

"Take your pick… the end result is the same. She will be staying with us for a while."

"How can she be lost when we know where she is?"

"We can't locate her family. She had some details written down… but the piece of paper turned to mush in the rain. She has only sketchy details of who she's looking for. It's not enough to go on. There's no one in the area by the description she gives… even among those who might have left the district. She does not know how current the information is either."

"So… what's to be done then, that we haven't already covered?" Malachi felt vindicated. His part was played.

Josie shook her head. Steamy strands of hair clung to her forehead. "Pastor Jake has tried to help too... and that brings another problem. I fear she has fixated on him. She's hardly spoken, but every word she says has been a question about him..." Mal looked away and smiled. Throwing someone at you at three o'clock in the morning could apparently leave lasting impressions. His mother prodded the sheets in the hot water with a broom handle and continued. "It's not the sort of situation that the Pastor needs to bother himself about ... so I want you to help out some."

"Ma – it ain't my problem. Besides, that's what Ministers of Religion do... look after homeless types."

Josie jabbed the linen, releasing a bubble, submerging them again. "Cods-waddle it's not your problem. You slogged the girl senseless and then brought her here for care. So, care we will. *We*: not me... not Pastor Jake... not Dr Wallace... but *we*. You made it your responsibility. And I'm mighty proud that you did what you did Malachi. You could have easily left her..."

"Hell... I never even thought I could've left her and not got involved."

"Well that's a mercy! Otherwise some unidentified girl would have been found dead in a few days... and you would have murder on your conscience and the Law on your tail. That's not something Laura needs to know mind you."

"Laura? She has a name..." For some reason the revelation was a surprise. It was like looking at her face by the glow of a lightening storm. Slowly the anonymous namelessness was being replaced by identity... a person.

"Malachi... you are involved: like it or not. Now the first thing is to see to the list of things that need fixing around here. We don't want the regular guests being put out by the extra boarder."

"That's got nothing to do with them. You can't make it related just because it suits you. They've got their rooms. It's none of their business who else we let rooms to."

"If they make it their business and walk... it's their business. And ours. We will do what we can to keep things smooth – that's all."

"This whole thing is unfair. She belted me in the dark. I can't be sentenced for reflexes."

"This isn't a sentence. It's life."

"Life sentence. Fair dinkum... I'd rather be ordered around by Nat. Trying to keep this lot happy is like pacifying a bunch of nursery school babies... the way you wipe their snotty noses for them all the time." But he said nothing more. He turned around and went back inside. He collected the list of chores from the mantelpiece where he knew it would be sitting. He would start at the top of the list. If nothing else, his Ma was methodical; there was a predictability about her that was just as oppressive as Nat's strong-arm tactics. When he was a kid he found that comforting, never having to guess. But well, now he was a man ...

Josie went back to the copper and dragged the linen from the water. "As if you'd have a clue, Malachi Fredrick Lawson, about wiping up after nursery kids. Runny noses would be the least of your worries."

Pastor Jake opened the door, and stood there momentarily as he took in Laura's sallow complexion staring out the window. He cleared his throat and walked over to where she was sitting. "Excuse me Miss Laura. I have made some more enquiries…" She half turned towards him, saying nothing. He cleared his throat again. "There does not seem to be any recollection of a family in the area by the name of Lawrence. It just isn't a name that is from The Creek district. Mrs Hollis remembers there may have been an old-timer prospector over Mallee Hill way, but she said he died nearly ten years ago. He didn't have any family that she knows of… or who we could ask. I'm sorry… perhaps you misunderstood your information."

"Mallee Hill? Where is that?"

"Well, it's west of here… the next town along. Not big… a little smaller than here."

"Do they have a Church?"

"Yes, as a matter of fact they do. A Catholic Church and a little Salvation Army outpost. Nothing else."

"The old-timer… did he go to church?"

"Well, I didn't ask about his religious affiliations. You seem mighty concerned about your relatives' Christian loyalties Miss Laura. That is admirable. As the local pastor, can I ask about your own spiritual standing? Where would you normally worship?"

Laura turned away. "I don't have a problem with God much. Just with some of the people who worship him."

Jake stared at the gaunt lines around her face reflected in the glass. He could hardly blame her for what he saw there.

She went back over her list of points. "I didn't misunderstand: the name was Lawrence; he wasn't a local; moved here from a bigger town east; was involved in the Union Church – and you just said Mallee Hill doesn't have a Union Church; been in the Wattle Creek area for a long time… about twenty years."

"Well, we can keep asking around. Someone may have heard something. I certainly don't know everyone around the district yet." He paused then as a new thought flashed through his mind. "It wouldn't have been Lawson would it? I mean… that would be ironic… ending up here with Mrs Lawson. From what I understand, Matthew Lawson came here from the city…" Laura turned and looked at him intently. Her focus spurred him to continue… fitting puzzle pieces together that had been piled in a random jumble – surprised as he felt them slide into place. "Mr Lawson was very involved in the Union Church – an elder I understand… just like Josie's oldest son, Nathaniel, is now. Their family has been around Wattle Creek twenty or so years. I remember that because Josie told me that Malachi was a babe in arms when they came to the district to take up farming. It kinda fits: Lawrence… Lawson… Could it be?"

He sat down in a daze. Was it possible? Had the hand of God brought this young lass to the very home of her estranged family? Like the leading of Abraham's servant to the home of his brother's Nahor's relatives, providing the way so that Abraham's son Isaac would have comfort and love after the death of his mother Sarah, in the form of beautiful Rebekah? Nothing about God surprised Jake: nothing and everything. God was the same yesterday, today and tomorrow.

56.

"Slut! You cannot come here and say these things! You vile, horrible, malicious... Get out! Now! Out!!" Josie picked up a chipped jug that was sitting on the wash stand and flung it at the door. It shattered into a million pieces. "Don't you ever, *ever*... show your face here again! I tell you I will not be responsible for your safety if you do. Get out!" Her frame trembled with rage that could not be contained. Tears of fury ran down her cheeks as she gasped for breath. To think that she had washed this girl's clothes and held her head in sympathy while she vomited! How she wished she had drowned her in it!

Laura edged out the door. Her pale face drawn, her eyes filled with anguish. She had so wanted to believe this would make a difference. But it didn't. Nothing changed. It was always the same. She left silently... quietly... invisible... like a vacant wisp of smoke on the wind. Nothing.

Mal came in after going out to the farm on a mission to salvage some hinges for the garden gate. "Hey Ma, Nat's started on the..." He stopped and starred at Josie on her hands and knees, viciously scrubbing the floor in the vacant room. The bed was stripped down to the iron frame; the windows were bare of their curtains. "Ma – where's the girl... Laura?"

She turned and spat the venom of a taipan, raring up and flanging out her collar in a seething rage. "Don't you ever speak that name in this house again or I will disown you and personally send you to hell!"

Mal stood stunned. Never in all his twenty-three years had he ever heard his mother – the battler, the fighter, the defender, the controlled, the guarded… ever speak such bitterness. The gall dripped from her tongue without apology. Her eyes burned through him. The little boy in him wanted to run and hide under the bed. The adult in him… nah…. the street-fighter in him, stood his ground. Dancing around, working a strategy… to find the opponent's angle… to calculate where the next strike would come from.

"The floorboards look kinda clean enough Ma…"

"It will never be clean enough… after… after…"

"So, she's gone. Never thought we'd agree on anything so soon Ma…"

She said nothing. And returned to her scrubbing.

"So, I take it she found her family…"

That did it. In a single move Josie jumped to her feet and hurled the scrubbing brush at his head. He ducked as she picked up the bucket and pitched the sudsy water all over him. He stood there dripping; and slowly, deliberately, he wiped the soap from his face as he made another evaluation. Then he turned and left, without saying a word.

Malachi took a calculated guess and headed for the creek. He found her sitting under the railway bridge gently rocking backwards and forwards, as if lost in some autistic daze. "I brought you some milk and fresh bread. Better drink it now though… before it heats up and goes lumpy." He put it down beside her and stepped back. He did not know what act of violence could have spun his Mum out so completely. Perhaps the episode that cost him that split lip was not just a once off. Perhaps she was pathologically violent. Laura stopped rocking. He looked at her face. There were no tears... no remorse in her eyes, just reflections of echoes - scared and abandoned.

She stared at the bottle for a while. Finally, she picked it up and drank. She grimaced. It was already warm. For some reason she wasn't afraid of this man. Perhaps it was because she saw the bruise darkening on his cheek and the cut on his lips scabbing over and knew she had managed it once; she could do it again if needs be. But she didn't think it would be needed. Josie had told her of the journey in the rain along the train-tracks. Even when her head ached from his punches, there was a comfort in the idea that he had struggled through the storm to bring her to safety. Few men had done that for her. She had come this way to find such a man...

"Can I ask what you did to Mum? She was completely freaked out when I got back to the house."

She looked at the bread. She felt bloated from the milk. It sat like vinegar in her stomach. How could she tell this stranger, even if he had carried her, the implications of what she had discovered? "Your mother doesn't want me to come back."

"Yeah, she gave me a couple of hints to that effect too. But my question is *why?*"

"She hates me."

"Hmm. Another astute observation. What did you do?"

"Nothing."

"Don't buy it. She was ready to kill you... and me..."

"You? Why?"

"That's what I want to know. You must have done something."

She had. She was not sure she was prepared for the anger again. It was not safe. Still, she was moving on tomorrow. No one would believe her anyway. Pastor Jake was right. It fitted too well to be a co-incidence, but he hadn't known why she had this urgency to locate family. "I am her step-daughter."

Malachi's eyes flew wide open. He swore in shock. His mind spun around and did a flip. He could barely speak above a whisper. "What do you mean?" He shook his head like someone was holding him under water. "How?"

"Your father... is my father... the same..."

"No way! He's a saint! He would never!"

She knew it. She felt cruel... that she had to be the evidence of the man's fallibility. She looked at Malachi's dark unruly hair and tried to match her own features. She favoured her mother. Many people said so... but what else did they have to compare her with?

Mal stared at her and a smile leaked into his eyes. "Whoa. That's weird. I've been told my whole life that my father was the next thing to Jesus Christ. He never did anything wrong. He always had the answers... even when he was dead. This is unbelievable... I'm looking at evidence that he might have been human." He burst out laughing. "Might explain my rebellion after all."

Now it was Laura's turn to stare at him in shock. "You aren't angry?"

"Why – it ain't your fault."

She stared at him. Unexpectedly tears streamed unstoppable from her eyes. Was he right? Was she innocent of this man's infidelity? Her head said that of course she was not to blame. Her heart had longed for this father, yet it was not so easily vindicated. Mal's flippant response gently lifted a burden, like a block and tackle, from the pit of her stomach.

"But you knew him... how your father was... and yet he wasn't like that at all..."

"Oh, you mean... I've been lied to, all my life? Believe me, that's a relief."

Laura hardly knew how to respond. She was so prepared for a volcano that the trickle of laughter sounded sacrilege, out of place. It rose in his throat, and then, like a pipe bursting from pressure, hysterical gasps gushed from his lips. He sat down beside her gasping for air, abandoning himself to the frenzied hilarity. She watched him silently, waiting for it to pass.

"Oh hoot. Saint Matthew Lawson falls from his pedestal. The base has cracked wide open. No wonder Mum wants to kill you... revenge for murdering her marriage and slaughtering her lucky charm. He was her Saint Christopher and she wasn't even Catholic."

"You should be sad for her – not happy."

"Well, it's obvious she never really knew him... and still she inflicted him on us. It wasn't right. It's come back to bite her. And I bet all she can think of is about protecting his marred reputation – when he did it to himself. *Dad this... your Father that...* I've had that every day for twenty years! I'm completely over it."

"He was a good man. My mother said so."

"What? *Your* mother said so! And what right has she to say that?" He looked at her frame, and her eyes. "You must be close to the same age as me. That means your 'good' father had a wife with two kids and a third on the way... and a mistress to boot. Even I think there is betrayal in that."

"My mother said he tried to look for us. But when he could not locate her, he moved to Wattle Creek. When Mum found out he had been searching, she did some investigations herself. She decided not to tell him about us because of the destruction it would cause his life. She stayed away on purpose – to protect him. He never knew I existed."

"He didn't know? But if your mother knew where he was, she must have known he was killed. Why would she protect a dead man?"

"Same reason your mother does now. She loved him."

"So why now? What has changed now?"

Tears welled up in Laura's eyes. "Mum's sick... really sick. I thought it would be one thing I could do for her... to find him... and let him know. I thought it might help her get better... or at the very least, I wanted them to be able to say goodbye..." The words choked in her throat as the tears fell on to her old brown woollen coat. "She never told me he died. I didn't know. I failed... so badly."

"He's been dead for twenty years. That's hardly your fault."

"Perhaps she didn't know... or maybe she forgot... when she got sick. Some nights I would lie in bed and I could hear her whispering his name. It was like she was delirious with happiness. She was improving so much. I really believed we would be united... a family... for a while. She started talking about him... all the things that they did together. I've been gone so long; I don't know even how Mum is. What if she died all-alone... without me.... without anyone? I should not have come. But I had to try. I should not have come..."

"Did you tell her what you were doing? Where you were going?"

She shook her head. "She would never have let me come."

"Well that's a surprise... young woman travelling alone... to nowhere... to a man that doesn't exist."

Laura burst in to fresh tears. "Don't say it. I know I should not have come. Oh – how I know it. I have failed... I have let her down... so badly..."

He smiled in a detached sort of way. He wasn't even sure why he had come here himself, except to say that he wasn't going to waste a trip through a thunderstorm in the middle of the night to have her lost now. Mal shrugged. "Well, I guess you found out. That is something."

"Do you remember him?"

"Dad? Na. I remember his photo though. It hung above the clock over the mantle-piece, at the farmhouse. Ma says Nat got his determination, Toby got his brains and I am most like him in looks. Think it's the nose. Still, never did feel grand about the fact his one inheritance to me was a big snooter."

Laura closed her eyes, imprinting his face in her mind. It made her feel sad. It was how she imagined a normal family to be, comfortable with ordinary things like hair and noses and smelly feet. She would never know about that, but at least she did know something. She had seen his wife, his son. Even if it wasn't the happy ending she had dreamed about as a little girl, now she knew. She wanted the pain to go away, and now it might. Yeah she knew part of it, and the rest she would never know. But her mother... Perhaps she still believed that he had been alive all these years, loving her silently; confined by a life he could not escape.

The hush around Laura and Mal drifted on the water like a leaf, swirling on the current, as random private thoughts consumed the air space between them. Mal had nowhere to be. He was comfortable in the lethargy of warm afternoon and he stretched himself out.

"So..." Malachi finally said with a lazy smile. "Last time I was here, you slogged me a beauty."

"Last time you were here it was in the middle of the night... and you smelt like a brewery!"

He chuckled. He wasn't really that keen to remember his self-imposed social grounding was due to scars inflicted by a girl... or that he had knocked her out in a most ungenerous manner. "Okay – I shouldn't have brought that up."

"Nup... pretty sure it's not the most gallant thing you've ever done – knocking your sister out ... even though you did carry me to the doctor."

Malachi sat straight up. "Whoa. Not good. What did you just say?"

"You knocked me out... even though you took..."

"No no. The other thing..."

"It wasn't gallant..."

He shook his head violently. "Oh no. No, no, no. You're not doing that to me. No way."

Laura closed her eyes. So, it was all right for his mother to have her life ripped apart, but he wasn't willing to own her either. Typical. "Look. I've been told variations along the way as well. My mother never said he had a family. Perhaps she didn't want to know... and just ignored what was in her face. She believed in his integrity as much as your mother. Perhaps he was sorry he had ever been with my mother... and disowned their relationship... or maybe he wanted it to go away without having to tell her. Perhaps that is why he never tried to find me. He didn't want me to be me. There are other people caught in this deception you know. Not just you... and your family. I never had the chance to find out... to really know who I am."

Mal turned away, his voice off hand. "Who cares anyway? Seriously... it's twenty years ago. You're you. I'm me... but I'm not your brother."

"Who cares? I care! How can you know what it is like not to know who you are all your life? You've stared at your father's portrait until you were sick of it. I have longed to, until I was sick. Big difference Malachi. Big difference. So, don't go telling me it makes no difference!"

"It doesn't make us brother and sister."

"Doesn't it? My understanding is that the same father makes us half-brother and sister. How can that *not* be, just because I wasn't intended or wanted or convenient... because it throws out every concept of yourself you've ever had?"

"It wasn't part of the deal."

"What deal? There was no deal Mal. It just is." The sun streamed through the slatted gaps of the railway bridge. The mid afternoon warmth soaked her tired body, and she leant back against a bank of sand, and closed her eyes, exhausted. She was so tired...

Mal stood up and paced backwards and forwards along the creek. This was so unfair. To carry her through the driving rain made him feel like a hero; to bring her supplies before she left town... made him feel kind-hearted... and yeah, a little defiant towards his mother. But to be her brother? For some reason that felt like the day his farm cat had kittens in the shed... responsible. He was not ready or willing to be responsible just yet. It wasn't part of the deal. And the weirdest thing was... he knew his mother would not applaud this newfound sense of conscientiousness. But he couldn't help it. In fact, it probably added fuel to the fire. He couldn't blame his mother for forcing this on him, like a list sitting on the mantel-shelf. The fact that she would despise him for it, made it more convincing. It was there... and he couldn't ignore it.

"Oh..." He groaned like his insides were burning as he continued to pace. He had a choice... and every fibre in his body was fighting between the easy thing; versus the approved thing; versus the responsible thing. The easy thing won. When Laura opened her eyes, Mal was gone.

57

"… Unidentified girl found dead… Suspect accused of murder… Life sentence… Not involved! No deal! But you are involved… Brother and sister… There is no sentence… It's just life… Life sentence… That makes us brother and sister… It just is…"

Malachi jolted awake on his bunk, lathered in sweat. His tongue was furry and dry. He struggled up and went to the washstand to pour a drink of water. The eerie grey light of the moon shone through the gauzy curtains that blew about in the night breeze. He took off his undershirt and threw it in the corner. He leant over the basin and felt like throwing up, his back shiny from perspiration. He was not getting involved. She should go back to her mother. This was not his problem. He never asked for a sister. It was ridiculous for him to be like this.

He poured himself another drink of water. He wanted to choose the path of least pain. He had assumed that path was walking away. But that stupid girl and her romantic fantasizing about his father… her father… had made it impossible for him to resume normal. Just now, did he really have a choice? He stared at the moonlight making ghostly shadowy patterns on the wall from the curtain. He was sure there was no choice. He would have to go and make sure she was okay. It was just a matter of putting her on a train so she could return safely to her mother at least. Great. He had the enthusiasm of one condemned to the gallows. But he consoled himself that at least with gallows, life expectancy is short. Minimal pain.

He pulled on his boots and shirt, and grabbed his hat from the peg behind the door. He threw together some supplies in a blanket and took the canvas water bag from the nail behind the pantry door. He was tired, and he had no intention of walking… even to the bridge, lugging this stuff. He went into the stables and saddled his horse. He would at least be comfortable no matter how short the distance. He had no sense of time as he rode out toward the railway bridge.

He tethered his horse by the creek and made his way toward the cover of the bridge. Now his senses were tuned, his eyes catching every shadow and movement. A Mopoke flew past and he stilled. What if someone else had stumbled across her possie? Would she sleep with a waddie close to her side? Laura had only split his lip last time. She would be capable of a great deal of harm armed with something more formidable in her hand. Or would it be used against her?

He could hardly say what he expected. Cautiously he waited in the shadows as his night vision scanned every dark form for signs. "Laura?" No response. No movement. He moved more boldly. The place felt empty, abandoned. In frustration he rampaged around, calling her name. Would she have gone so soon?

Finally, he sat, subdued and wrapped himself in the blanket intended for her… and he resigned himself to wait for dawn. There was no thought that he could crawl back to his own bed now. As the moon sank low and the pre-dawn streaks of light paled the east sky, Mal stirred. He boiled the billy and made a cup of tea. Now quiet and focused and clear, he looked for signs that marked the direction of her travel. He could easily make up any distance on horseback. He looked about in dismay as he saw that his impulsive stomping during the night had eradicated any evidence of Laura's exit. It could not be helped. He scanned the parameters of the bridge and looked for signs along the creek. It was not that difficult after all. She dragged her boots heavily. She was headed out of town along the railway track. Surely she was not thinking of walking back home?

He swung into the saddle and followed her steps in the rising morning light. He dismounted and followed where she had gone into the scrub for a break. At another place, he saw where she had laid and rested a while under the low shade of a wattle tree. He was brought up in the bush and spent years trailing the paddocks, but he was well aware he was no tracker. It was surprisingly easy to trace her movements, and imagined her journey as he followed her heavy steps. He wondered how far she could have gone, but he noticed the distances between where she rested became shorter and shorter. Perhaps it had been getting towards nightfall... and she was tiring more.

It was at that next resting place that he noticed something that brought a frown to his forehead. A dark red stain on the leaf litter where she had sat. Was she injured? Had she been attacked? And then almost by relief he realised it was a womanly matter. He was aware of these feminine concerns – their monthly cycles, but his information had been gleaned mostly by osmosis rather than accurate education. His primary understanding was that men were not to interfere. Period. Non-negotiable.

He was reluctant to show himself when he came to where she stopped to sleep during the night. He tethered his horse and sat quietly. She lay like stone – immobile from exhaustion, her woollen coat drawn tucked high under her chine, her small cloth bag serving as her pillow. As he sat sentry, his eyes honed in on detail. She stirred and he could see the stains on her skirt where the coat parted and she moved her legs restlessly as she was rising out of her heavy sleep. She had covered some territory. Dr Wallace had said she needed rest and Mal knew the few days at her mother's house would hardly count as sufficient. In the end, inactivity drove him to make a small fire to boil some water for a cup of tea. He was breaking sticks across his knee, and adding them to the fire, when he glanced over and saw her staring at him... unafraid... unmoved.

"Mornin'. Want a cuppa tea for breakfast?" He tried to make it sound as normal as he could. As if she would have expected him to trail her movements through the night to serve breakfast tea by the railway track, under the shade of eucalypt gums and Banksia trees. "Don't have much food, but I can do toast."

He poured the drink into a mug, and placed it on a rock near her feet, stepping back cautiously, like she was contagious. She noticed it immediately. He despised her still. Then why had he come?

She reached for the cup and stopped, her hand suspended partway. She gasped, her face pale and beading with perspiration. A groan escaped her throat, deep and heavy. It seemed to settle and she reached for the mug again, anxious to drink. But as she drew her legs up and brought it to her lips, pain grabbed her once more, like a strong man twisting her arm behind her back in a paralysing grip. She dropped the mug of tea in the dirt, tears streaming down her face. "Is it evil to want this to go away... to be finished?" she asked, gasping for breath.

He stared at her – like she was a foreign thing. He had heard some women had a hard time during their monthly...thing... but he had never expected violence like this. "I guess not..." He shook his head in bewilderment. It was beyond his comprehension. How could ladies celebrate womanhood in such routine agony?

Again, she was silenced by pain... and he could no longer contain his reserve. "Oh Laura. Please... can I help? Do all women go through this?" He went to retrieve the cup but she grabbed his arm and held it. He reached out holding her shoulders, supporting her. And she pressed against him, timid and afraid.

Now he lifted the canvas bag to her lips and she licked the moisture around her mouth. Finally, he asked. "How long does it last?"

"What?"

"Well, the monthly... you know... womanly..." He looked away. He was traversing very personal, sacred ground. But he didn't have a clue. Was he looking at hours... days... weeks, of this? His mother never spoke of it. He scanned his memory and nothing hinted to this secret path of suffering.

"Monthly? Oh." She touched her skirt... her petticoat folded between her legs. This would be the test of family. She knew real families were torn apart by such things. It might be too much for such a tenuous, fragile, embryonic family... such as theirs. "Mal, I haven't had a Woman's Monthly… for two months now."

He didn't get it. Was it a conspiracy? Did they make this whole thing up for sympathy? "So you don't have monthlies every month… it is only a ruse?"

"No. Every month… on the month."

"But you said two months? Are you sick? But you are having one now… right? That is a good thing? Isn't it?" The questions seem to disturb her and she gripped his hand again.

"I'm glad they're back… I wasn't expecting any for nine months." Tears welled in her eyes. In one way she was grateful that she had helped her mother with nursery maid care. She knew the basics, she knew a bit about what was happening. But it is never the same when it is your abdomen that is stretching, and your body that is suddenly acting in so many unfamiliar ways that you hardly recognise it anymore. She wanted her mother…

"Nine months? But that's… Oh." The implications of the statement froze him. The strain in his larynx was deep and tremulous as he asked, "You're pregnant?" His mind went into a spin. "How could that happen? Are you a mistress to someone… like your mother was to my father?"

She pulled away in disgust. "What… do you think this is like farming? A family business handed down from generation to generation?"

"I don't know what to think! I find out you're my sister… because of that… that type of circumstance. And now I find out your pregnant… like your mother… without a husband. Unless you do have a husband… or someone else's…

519

and if you do... where is he?" He didn't want that. He wanted her to be above that... his sister. An immaculate conception, a virgin birth would be good about now.

The pain gripped again. Tears gathered and fell. Would she ever stop crying? "There is no husband... my own or anyone else's."

"What then?" His eyes focused unseeing on the smouldering coals in the small fire. He swallowed hard. He didn't want to hear it. His mouth grim, the muscles working tight along his jaw-line.

"I needed to come to Wattle Creek like I said. I stopped one night in a little hotel. This... he... I only remember his teeth, grinning at me... snarling at me. He hit me and I must have been knocked unconscious when I fell. I don't remember anything but the pain. I thought it was happening again... that night under the bridge. But your Mum told me you saved my life... that you carried me back to town... in your arms." She paused. She hadn't considered it was not true. It felt true. But she had never verified it. "Is that true?"

He sat stiff as a plank, as if he believed that by moving he would break something. "In all fairness I did slug you... but it was dark... and you hit me first and I couldn't see. I thought you were just an ordinary bum. And I was going to toss your pockets for money... but that was all... 'til I saw you were a girl... and then I panicked – and that's when I took you home. But... Oh no! I never touched you. Not like that. Goodness me. You're my sister!" The confession tumbled out... unhindered and frightened. He could not judge because of his own reprehensible dealings, his own shame.

Laura closed her eyes. Mal had no idea how her heart relaxed in hearing his honest confession. She spoke softly to contain her relief. "At the hotel, I was really hurt... I couldn't go anywhere... but I couldn't afford staying in the room for weeks and weeks. This lady, Mrs Witherslow... she looked after me... until I was better. I would've stayed longer, but then I told her more about the attack... well... I thought she would understand. I didn't know she'd kicked me out. She said I was an ungrateful sinner... that I could be the bearer of the Devil's child. That's when I realised I hadn't had any... you know... no monthly... for a long time... and that it might not be just because I was hurt. I remembered how my mother had looked after a couple of girls in trouble. I guess she knew what it was like to be alone. I had nowhere to go... but I couldn't go home without finding what I came for. Coming to Wattle Creek has taken a long time. Nothing has worked out. Nothing at all...

"Oh Mal – I am so relieved I'm bleeding again... that means there is no baby. You said that it wasn't my fault what my father did... or my mother. When you said *that*, I felt I should not be angry even if I had a baby. Perhaps the fault is mine... and I must live with that. But it is not a tiny baby's fault for the wickedness this man did to me. God will help me forgive. I know that in my head, but at the same time... it is a relief that it is over... and I won't have to carry it or nurse it... and not worry how I am going to feed it... because no one gives the likes of me a position... Not now. Not ever."

Laura sipped more water. Mal looked fearfully at her face, pale and drawn. "I have to take you to the Doc. You gotta be taken care of..."

"No," she said. "I'm not going back to the doctor."

"Well I'm thinking it might not be up to you.

"I never asked to be here! You gotta believe I never did anything… it wasn't my fault. It wasn't!" She burst into tears. "It wasn't my fault…"

"I never said you wanted it to happen. No not that. I just meant we have to keep fighting… even if you don't want to. You are not a coward Laura. You have Lawson blood."

"And look where it got me! I have nowhere to go. I'm stuck on a railway track between Wattle Creek and nowhere." Literally and emotionally. An overwhelming aloneness swirled around her. She felt faint. It was not worth fighting. There was nothing left to fight for. Her epic journey to find her father had concluded in the most dreadfully pointless way. Why did she ever think it would be worth the bother? She echoed her fate, "I have nowhere to go…"

"Just now, the only place we gotta go is to get you help. I don't want to spend the rest of my life not being able to sleep, because I didn't try everything." He almost shuddered as he remembered the sleepless, tormented night where his mind refused to ignore the very things he demanded it to ignore. It wasn't fair… that he had to be tortured by some innate sense of family. "You didn't get here by avoiding questions… but asking them… facing them head on."

Malachi stamped out the fire and buried it in dirt. "Laura – I'm taking you back to town. It is a fair way and we need to get going." She struggled to her feet. The cramping had eased some. He shook his head as she took some steps towards the railroad, "You ain't going to *walk* there. You'll get on the horse and I'm walking…" He padded out the saddle with the blanket not designed for side-saddle travel, and hoisted her into it awkwardly. "We'll take it slowly… just let me know when you need a break. We can't go to Mum's… so I'm taking you straight to the Doc. We'll just see what he says and then make a plan from there. Somehow we'll get you back to your Mum's place so you can see her."

For the first time Laura's heart was touched by his consideration. But she would not surrender to his kindness, because eventually he will leave… again. However now, just now, he was an angel sent from heaven. A solitary tear fell as she looked away, hiding her embarrassment. "Thank you," she said.

They travelled slowly. The sun rose quickly and they seemed to make little progress. Mal stopped frequently under the shade of sparse gums. The fragrance of eucalypt hazed in the high noon sun. He helped her down, and laid the blanket out for her to lie down for a while. He pressed the canvas bag to her lips. This was not good. She was not holding up. Strange. He remembered something Pastor Jake had said. *God is our very help in trouble. He wants us to call on him. Not just in crisis… But if it takes a crisis… God will take what He can; He wants our attention that much.* "Oh God, I'm reluctant to ask… but can You help out a little? What do I do?" He looked at Laura lying exhausted on the blanket. He didn't know how long to let her rest. She could not ride anymore. He set to, making a pole stretcher out of saplings, lashing the blanket together and running the poles through a primitive harness made of rope and stirrup straps. Dragging this behind his horse would be a rough ride, but at least she could lie down.

Once again, he was all alone, responsible and confused… and holding a mother guinea pig, ready to have babies in the rain. That guinea pig disgusted Nat. His brother didn't see the sense in things that couldn't be sold or eaten, or didn't make a buck. But regardless of the lack of value his brother had for that life, Malachi had stayed up all night and fought. The funny thing was he had sold those baby guinea pigs in the schoolyard and bought his Mum a nice bar of lavender soap for her birthday that year. She had been so pleased.

58.

Pastor Jake walked along the creek pacing backward and forth. It had been a long time since he felt this agitated... and he couldn't account for it. He stopped and sighed. "God, there is something... and I don't know what it is. Holy Spirit – you know all things... and I feel you want me to pray for someone." He stopped, confused and restless. There was nothing for it. He had to go with it. "Heavenly Father, I ask that you would protect this person. I believe You know who they are, and what is going on with them. Hedge them about with your protection. Please, I place their safety in your hands; hold back those things that would come to steal and destroy life, success and peace. Intervene, Lord Jesus, on their behalf. Keep them safe..." Over and over – backwards and forwards he paced. He sat and then stood... unable to settle. He continued to pray... words and thoughts tumbling over each other until finally he sat and was able to rest. The crisis was over.

He closed his eyes and quietly thanked God in faith for the safety He had just provided. He felt weird and a little disappointed that God wasn't a gossip. It would be kinda neat to know the details of the battle he had raised a sword against, towards the war-front. Still, God was God. If He felt he needed to know - he would. If not, he could live with that. He looked up and started. Ali was coming down the track, the evening sun spilling over her shoulders onto her fair hair. It took his breath away.

Jake quickly closed his eyes and turned back towards the creek. How could he go from interceding through the promptings of the Holy Spirit one moment, to wanting to take this woman in his arms and hold her until he grew old, in the very next? It wasn't the way Pastors were supposed to think... or feel. He didn't know where to look. If he pretended he was meditating, she might go away and not disturb him. Then he wouldn't have to talk to her. But he wanted to. He desperately wanted to know how she was fairing. He sat still, frozen like an ice sculpture, holding his breath, listening for her step.

She was humming softly; her step light and even. He heard her stop and mutter uncertainly, "Oh my... Pastor Jake... I have disturbed you... I'm sorry..."

Now she had spoken, he had to respond. He calmly opened his eyes, his heart raced uncontrollably. "Ali! This is a surprise - to see you here. Is everything alright?" He grimaced at his clumsiness. Of course, she was all right. He heard her humming and at harmony with the world just three seconds earlier.

"Yes... I believe so..." she faulted, almost as if she doubted it. "I like to go for a walk sometimes after I close up the shop... to clear my head. It has been a long week. It is a lovely afternoon... don't you agree?"

Yes. She is lovely. He nodded. "I needed a spot to pray. It seemed too pleasant an afternoon to stay inside my room."

"You come here often? Oh, I'm sorry I didn't know. I won't..."

"No, no... not routinely. Not in the afternoon anyway. I'm normally a morning walker..."

"Oh."

"How is your family? Your mother and father well?"

"Yes – the good season has taken the pressure off a little. Dad is getting back on top of things. Mum is well."

"Oh." This was ridiculous. How stilted was their conversation?

Suddenly Ali remembered something. "I just came past Doc Wallace's house. Malachi was carrying a woman inside. He didn't see me, but she looked hurt. There was blood on her clothes. I hope she's okay."

"Malachi? Was it Laura? Slight... light brown hair..." His eyes burned with a sudden interest, clouding with concern.

"Laura?" Ali looked at him keenly. Why would he be so very anxious? "Could have been... Do you know her?"

He remembered Josie's distress the morning Laura had left. It didn't take a genius to add up the sum of what had transpired. There would be no happy ending here. He felt embarrassed by his naivety. "Laura was a border at the house. She was hurt when she came in, but I understood from Mrs Lawson that she left when she was well enough to travel. Perhaps Malachi went looking for her..."

"Why would he go looking for her?"

Jake shrugged. He didn't know for sure. He wished he hadn't said anything. He didn't want to speculate... rumours were rife as it was. He didn't need to fuel this fire. "Please Ali. I'm not sure who would know her. It's probably best if you don't mention this to anyone. Most think she has left the district."

Now Ali was really curious. "Is she a friend of yours... this Laura person?"

"We talked some. There was barely time for friendship – she was quite unwell... and then she left."

Ali turned away. She had thought her own vulnerability, her wounded history was not robust enough for a pastor. But with the sonar of a woman, she detected that his interest in this girl was genuine... personal. Was it more than a pastoral concern? She was acutely aware that Laura's helplessness had not caused him to recoil. So, if it wasn't Ali's frailty that created a barrier in her relationship with Pastor Jake... it must be something more fundamental... something about herself that was essentially unattractive to him. She probably wasn't pretty enough... or spiritual enough. Yes, that was most likely it.

Fair enough. She had declared many times her desire was to be independent. But with new determination, she was not going down this track again and again. If she couldn't have the man that she had fallen for, inadvertently, unintentionally, she would travel that independent road for the rest of her natural life. She turned away, grieved. How many times did the dream have to die? She had given this over to God on so many occasions. Yet every time she saw him, it loomed larger than ever. Well – she wasn't going to run away. No. This district had to learn to accommodate both of them. She knew he walked this section of creek, now she would keep away.

"Ali? Are you okay?"

"Yes, I'm fine. I was just thinking of that poor girl. In comparison, I have little to complain about. A busy week at the shop is a blessing."

"Oh, Ali. How succinctly you put things in perspective. You have a compassionate heart." One more point in her favour. Was there nothing he could fault her on? "I will drop by the Doctor's and see what I can find out… to put your mind at ease."

Her mind or his? "Malachi will no doubt appreciate the support. He looked very distressed." She smiled like an angel, then turned and walked away.

Jake watched her walk down the track. He hoped against hope that Mal hadn't slugged this girl again, and then in the aftermath of remorse brought her back to be treated. But he was well aware that upsetting news can cause people to act brutally… and if his mother was anything to go by… this was one household that was very upset.

59.

Doc Wallace walked out to the sitting room where Mal perched on the edge of the lounge, distractedly twisting a leather strap in his hands. He was conscious that his dusty clothes would grime up the upholstery if he sat back comfortably. Doctor Wallace waved to Mal when he anxiously stood as he entered. "Malachi… please sit down." He struggled to remain seated… every muscle tense and tight. He couldn't even ask how she was.

Doc Wallace seemed to understand. He poured himself a cup of coffee from the tray that his wife had set on the occasional table between them. He waved at the spare cup. "Do you want one?" Mal nodded distractedly. Perhaps the Doc was not worried. That was a good sign. "Tell me Malachi… what do you know of her circumstances?"

"Not much. I know she's got a bun in the oven… just early. She told me some bastard attacked and had a go at her on her way here to Wattle Creek. She left her mother … to look for her father, and she doesn't know if her mother's still alive because she was sick when she left home. And she said it was best if the... the baby died…" Even Malachi was surprised at how he relayed the few facts he knew so dispassionately as if he had known her a lifetime.

"So… did she trace the father?"

"She was looking for *her* father… not the kid's father."

"Oh. Any luck?"

"Nope. He died when I was three. She is my half-sister."

Doctor Wallace could honestly say he was not often surprised, but even he had to set down his coffee mug and gather his thoughts before he spoke. "She told you, that your father... *Matthew Lawson,* is her father?"

"Yeah."

"But what could she possibly have to gain from such an accus..." He quickly corrected himself, "...claim?"

"Nothing Doc. That's just it. There's no fortune, no inheritance, no title... nothing. She made no effort to claim anything. She's just looking for her father."

"Who has she told?"

"The details fit... it can't be a coincidence. Good old Dad... You're going to try and protect him too, aren't you?"

"It is not about that... but ensuring what's said is true. If it is not accurate, I'm not convinced it's helpful spreading such information around."

"How is it not *helpful* if Laura finally has the truth about who she is? She has spent her whole life not knowing. If this *helps* her... then that is *helpful* enough." Mal felt protective.

Doc Wallace did not disagree. He quietly asked. "Does your Mother know her suspicions?"

"I think Mum's the only person she's told... well, except for me. And it sent her into a major meltdown. That's when Mum threw her out of the boarding house." Mal gulped at his coffee. Then he told how he looked for Laura during the night... where he found her the next morning... "Has the baby... well, has it died?"

Doc Wallace nodded. "I listened for a heart-beat, but then... sometimes they are elusive... this early."

Mal stood to his feet, ready to leave. "Doc? Please don't tell Mum she's here. If Mum knows I bought her back... she'll go ballistic... really. I think she would do Laura harm. Me too, for that matter."

As he shook Dr Wallace's hand his eyes locked on Pastor Jake's face as he was being ushered into the room by Sarah, who announced with raised eyebrows, "Pastor Jake Sir. He has come to see the convalescing patient."

Mal stared. How had he found out about Laura? Mal had been watchful as he led the horse in the back way, and then cradling Laura in his arms he went to the Doctor's place. He knew he should have used the cover of darkness to shroud his movements but his concern for Laura became so intense it was over-riding all else. He could have sworn no one noticed, and life in Wattle Creek just went on. He clenched his fist in frustration. He had been so careful, yet he had messed up.

Josie was infuriated! Nothing she did or said seemed to penetrate Mal's hardness. She could feel him icing over and the stones in her own heart were getting colder and colder from his lack of response. At least that girl had gone. Impostor! Evil mischief weaver! Josie didn't know what she was capable of. The rage she felt frightened her. It was like she was clinging onto a flimsy branch on the side of a cliff, and Malachi was slipping further and further away. He was falling away... she couldn't reach him.

Proximity had no bearing on his absence. During the day he attended to chores now. Yet come nightfall he would leave. She didn't need to ask where. Josie had investigated enough in the past to know she didn't want details. It wasn't bliss, but the ignorance made it manageable. Courtesy between them was becoming harder and harder to manufacture.

Oh, that Matthew would come and sort out his son. On one of those days when Malachi was just a baby, her active toddlers drove her to distraction, and she had sent them outside to play in the yard. They had let the hens out of the chook-coop and a dingo had come in and taken one. She was in the middle of making jam and spotted the boys tracking across the paddocks to rescue their hen. She had gone after them in panic. They returned to the awful stench of burnt fruit and sugar, a ruined pot and charred stove. Only a trail of feathers across the yard marked where the remaining chooks had been. One of the working dogs was wounded from fighting the wild dogs.

That faithful dog never recovered. When Matthew came in late that evening everything was in chaos. Malachi was in his crib screaming, and that night he developed a dangerous fever. *"You're out in the paddocks all day. The boys need their father Matt! This is not what we planned... I don't want them growing up without you."* Matt had no heart to argue with her as he looked at the lines of stress etched into her heart. After that Nat, as young as he was, always went with Matthew. Josie sighed. Malachi needed his father now... and still Matthew hadn't come in from the back paddock. For twenty years he hadn't come.

Now Josie felt a new anger... not at death; not at an imperfect world that had caused her suffering; not at Sam Kane who refused to step up to the plate for her boys in Matthew's absence; not at the farm and its interminable work; or even her own weakness that caused her to be so tired she could not even cry herself to sleep at night. She was angry with Matthew. How dare he die!

Malachi stayed out of his mother's way. He fell into a listless routine where he went to visit the Doctor's house every evening. He was never allowed to see Laura unchaperoned, or stay long. Once or twice he wandered over to the Pub afterwards and hung around for a while, but left pretty quickly when pressure started to bear on him to come good for his debts. Promises and reassurances would only delay the inevitable a little while longer. He needed a fight... with a lucrative pouch attached.

He went out to see Nat, but Emmaline was there, and they were none too fussed about having a little brother interrupting their dream-building and strategising. They had locked themselves into a bubble the size of the farm. In better times, Mal may have asked them to buy out his share, and got rid of his burden that way. It wasn't going to happen now. He knew it.

On his way back to town, he pulled into Dampier's farm. Mrs Dampier came out to the gate when he rode up. "Malachi! It has been such a long time... come in – I was just getting some lunch ready." She chatted as she made sandwiches. "Alf will be in shortly. Wouldn't you know, I've some leftover apricot pie. Don't suppose you'd like a piece?

You'd be doing Alf a favour to get it out of his way… he's not needing it. Did you know that Fred and Janie have gone away for a bit… with their little one? They're finding it hard, but they'll get there."

Mal eyed the pie. His mouth started watering and he pulled up his plate. He'd told Fred that being married wasn't a bed of roses; that it'd tie him down. But none of that mattered to Fred. He was bewitched by the beautiful Janie and lost all his good senses. Mal didn't think that the real Fred would ever come back.

They heard Alf banging his boots on the boot-jack near the back stairs. He sat at the table as Alma set down his lunch. "So Mal, how's it going Lad? Nat's doing a fine job getting things back on track. How's your Ma?"

There was no need to respond in detail as the questions flowed. Mal just nodded and shrugged. "The boarding house is getting on… a couple of regulars, some extras."

Alf stirred his tea after he finished his meal. "Fred's away… would you be open to giving me a hand down at the yards? Need a lift with some posts." Mal didn't mind. It was not like he had much to do. He hadn't put in a full day since he moved into town.

They lifted and wired; dug and positioned; compacted and stayed the posts. Alf never said much, and didn't expect dialogue… and in the freedom of the silence of log trimming, crow-bar and shovel work… snippets of Mal's heart was shared. Alf just nodded and said significant things like, "Hold this while I grab the strainers…" or, "There are some matters that you gotta ride out like a wild brumby… and it'll do its darnedest to buck you off. Some other things – you just find a gentle hand will turn them around so they will be as easy as a saddle pony…" or, "It ain't easy but you're doin' good. Keep at it son." To the passer-by he could have been talking fences and horses. But Mal knew.

When he finally mounted his horse to leave, he nodded and said quietly, "Uncle Alf… thanks."

He shrugged… and said simply. "I needed a hand doing the yards. Drop by again anytime. You are as much family to me as Fred and Ali. Bless you son." Mal quickly turned his horse down the road and kicked up a dust storm back into town.

Sometimes it is in the mundane things that the turmoil of life is clarified. Mal's visit with Alf proved just that. Laura was part of his life: unsought and unwanted… but that didn't make it any less true. Destiny had turned up the cards and revealed her existence. Alf didn't know the details… but Mal felt he couldn't have summed up finding his sister any better. He could buck and fight and kick and scream, but he knew, his heart would not let him forget about her, and it would torment him for the rest of his life if he didn't do it right. Just now, as ever, Mal's purpose was to be disrupted as little as possible. A life-time of nightmares left to layer down scars on scars, terrified him more than choosing to acknowledge this thing. So, acknowledge it he would. And when she was ready to go public with it, he would be right there beside her.

60.

Doctor Wallace went in to see Laura. He had been very militant about restricted visitor time. She was to rest. Jake stood quietly in the corner of the living room, looking out the window. His hands were pushed deep into his pockets. Mal paced back and forth impatient to see her. They both turned when the Doctor returned. "She said that she would like to see Malachi... alone." Finally.

Mal bounded to the door and paused looking at her washed out face against the white of Mrs Wallace's linen. "Hi Sis..." he said almost shyly. He was determined to own her, to go against the tide of reaction that he knew would come if the town found out.... *when* they found out. He was actually looking forward to that day, and the chaos it would cause everyone's neat and tidy preconceptions. It had even taken the Doc's breath away.

She grinned at him tiredly. "You don't have to call me that, you know."

"Why? You ashamed of me?" he flashed back mischievously.

"Of course not... I thought it might have been the other way round..."

He cocked his head on the side and considered her. "You look a little rested. Hey, I brought you something..." He pulled out of his pocket a little wooden box. "You can't tell anyone..." he said in a conspiring whisper. Her eyes widened, absorbing the mystery. "Here… and it goes with this…" he said as he placed a folded piece of paper on the bedspread.

He nodded encouragingly. She quietly slid open the lid of the tiny wooden box and gasped as she saw six little lady beetles captured on rose petals inside. She gasped in amazement as two buzzed their way out of their prison towards the window. "It is an old Gaelic blessing. They say lady-bugs carry the spirit of contentment and security. They are small and fragile… but I know they'll suck the life out of any aphid that gets in their way!"

Laura unfolded the note and quietly read the words. She laughed. "Really? They look so benign and cute."

"So, do you… but there is more vicious self-preservation in you than anyone is likely to admit. So, you keep sucking away at your aphids. Don't let them push in on your rose petals. Okay?"

"Okay." She grinned, but it quickly faded. "Oh Mal, I'm not sure what happens now. Where do I go from here?"

Malachi picked up an escaped bug and went to the window and let it out. "You're not the only one who feels trapped against their will. We'll make a plan once we find out what's going on. Did you know the blessing only works if you let the lady-bugs fly away, fly away home?"

She shook her head. "I bet you made that up!"

"No, it is actually true… the whole nursery rhyme is about being safe:

Lady bug, lady bug ~ fly away home,
Your house is on fire, your children all gone…
All except one and that's little Ann.

For she crept under the frying pan."

Laura smiled. "The rhyme adds a touch of authenticity... even if it is a tragedy about incinerated lady-bugs. You could be a lawyer. You can make a case stick on the flimsiest of evidence. Or a politician... you'd be good at that too... or a card shark. Oh – you already are." She relaxed with a smile. "So, this is my frying pan: The Doc says I have to rest. Has he told you anything?" When Malachi shook his head she continued, "I don't mind you knowing stuff... as long as it stays with you. Don't go telling all of Wattle Creek."

"Tight as a safe..."

"Doctor Wallace said he... the... he..." she swallowed. She didn't want to say it. Speaking it out would make it tangible, solid, confirmed, protected. Her throat constricted around a lump that stuck at the base of her tongue. She tried to swallow the emotion. It was better off the way things were: gone... left behind... finished. She tried again. "He wanted to wait to see if... if the..." She couldn't say it.

He shrugged, unconcerned. "Fine. We wait then."

She blinked. She got that. He was offering support... togetherness. She wasn't going to have to wait alone. Why would he want to do this? Wasn't she the evidence that things were not what they seemed, for the last 20 years? What if he left... would that be worse than if he never offered to stay? She didn't know what to think. Wasn't he embracing the family thing just a little too easily? She looked away... her mind a myriad of questions and doubts. "You're sure about that?" she asked.

He was comfortable as he looked at her with a disarming smile. "Yes, I could not be more certain about anything. On my Lady-bird's honour. They tell on you, if people don't keep their word. You know that don't you?" And he placed the open box, and the rest of the lady-bugs, out onto the window ledge.

"Well... I have at least four witnesses." Suddenly Laura sobered. "Malachi, I don't get it... why are you helping me? You don't even know me..."

"What's not to get? It's simple... four lady-bugs will gossip my darkest secrets if I don't... or it could be that blood is thicker than water." And he looked into her eyes and nodded. "You're okay Laura Lawrence... welcome to the family."

"It amazes me that you can say that. Your Mother was totally different."

"Well, little sister, I look at it like this. I have an older brother – who I have fought with all my life... and he specialised in treating me more like hired-help, than family... worse sometimes, I reckon. My other brother is as close to me as an alien from space and left town to study books of all things – he's an academic. Mum always insists family is the important thing... but in reality, I didn't see a lot of benefit from it. I've done my bit and helped them out. So here... I'm thinking... here will be something in this for me: someone who is family that I can *like* at the same time... someone who needs me instead of using me."

She smiled tiredly. She could hardly say she was displeased.

Mal cleared his throat and grimaced. "Oh, I better give up my place. Pastor Jake wants to say hello. You may not remember him... he's a border at Mum's place."

Laura's smile faded and she struggled to sit up. "No," she whispered urgently. "He'll tell her. She can't know I'm here."

"Yeah, I agree... not such a good idea... better that you rest," he said. What did he know about this religious man... really? What if he got it into his goody-two-shoes pastor's head that it was best for everyone that the truth be exposed? Even Mal, in all his desire to allow the facts about his gold-plated father come to light, knew that the damage just now, would not be to the dead... but to the living. "Well, he already knows you're here... I'll make sure he understands he tells no one... until you're ready. Okay?"

She was reassured by his determinedness. "Okay then... I'll see him." Pastor Jake was ushered into her room.

He stood at the end of her bed, uncertain what to say. "Miss Lawrence... I wanted to offer you my prayers and support while you are recuperating."

She shrugged and looked away. What can you say to such a declaration? This was very awkward.

"You won't be returning to Mrs Lawson's Lodge soon?"

"No." She didn't elaborate. "As soon as Doctor Wallace says I can travel again... I will be going."

"Oh – you will be leaving Wattle Creek? Is there nothing that can be done to change your mind?"

She stared at him confused. "I have nothing here. It was a mistake to come."

"I understand it has been a very lonely place for you. I hope that will change. May I visit you again?"

"I want no one to know. Please... Mrs Wallace says I may stay here until I am ready to go. That is enough."

Doctor Wallace came to the door. "The patient needs rest Pastor."

"Of course." Pastor Jake nodded and turned to go. As he stood in the door, he remembered. "Oh... I have a confession to make. Someone else does know you're here. Ali... Alice Dampier. She saw Mal carry you inside when you came back. She was the one who told me of your return. Well... she didn't know it was you of course, but I surmised it might be the case."

Malachi stared. Ali had known all this time? Who else knew? Mal didn't consider Ali working at a barbershop would be a silent ally. He hoped a Pastor would not prove to be a poor partner to have in trouble either. How do you judge these things?

Doctor Wallace spoke to them in the hallway as they prepared to leave. "Do you think Ali would consider visiting Miss Lawrence? Since she already knows of her being here... a gentle-lady visitor would certainly be of benefit." Malachi gathered that the Doctor thought her active alliance may forestall an ignorant slip of the tongue.

Pastor Jake nodded approvingly. What he liked most about the plan was that it gave him a legitimate reason to talk to Ali. Co-conspirators... in assisting a needy soul. Already he could see bridges being rebuilt in their friendship. "I'll ask her…" he said, and he hoped he didn't sound too eager.

61.

Ali felt her scissors and emery board in her bag as she swung open the gate. It was bizarre that Pastor Jake was so anxious that she visit Mal's waif. She had seen more of him in this last week, than all of last month. It was becoming quite disconcerting, except that he seemed so relaxed, and besides, they appeared to be business calls only. But she was at a loss to know how she should explain her visit to the Doctor's house… especially when he had insisted that no one should know of this girl's whereabouts. She could hardly claim that her coming to visit was based on ignorance. Still, Ali reasoned, his suggestion of a hairstyle or a manicure was a simple enough decoy, and the idea tantalised her growing curiosity.

She knocked at the door and waited for their housemaid, Sarah, to answer. She looked over the garden with a smile. She rather liked Mrs Wallace's alternate style cottage garden. It was free… no boundaries… practical and unruly at the same time; creative and unconventional… and very unexpected. It was fresh. *Good on her*, congratulated Ali privately to herself. Sarah ushered her inside, to where Mrs Wallace was sitting.

"Good afternoon Mrs Wallace. Pastor Jake said that the Doctor suggested I call on your houseguest. I wondered if I may…" Her voice trailed off, uncertain. What sort of respectable people invites themselves to tea? Well… perhaps technically she didn't… but she certainly was not here at Laura's pleasure.

She sat quietly in the sitting room, basking in the afternoon sun, while Sarah went to prepare Miss Lawrence for her lady visitor. Finally, Ali was ushered into her bedroom. Laura sat sallow and tired in the bed. She warily nodded to her guest. Ali shifted uncomfortably. "Good afternoon Miss Lawrence," she said formally. "I've come to visit." Silence bounced in her ears.

"Please excuse me. The Doctor has insisted on bed rest. Probably just as well. I don't have much energy."

"I wanted to bring you something. I was thinking about my mother's Melting Moments biscuits... but you already have the best cook in the district at your service. Sarah's talent in the kitchen is legendary. And Mrs Wallace's flowers are unrivalled. So, I wondered if I might offer you a manicure." She laughed awkwardly... "Selfish of me really... I thought it might make it easier to visit, given that we don't know each other. Pastor Jake has been asking me to come and call on you for ages." Again, her laughter tinkled uncomfortably. "He's a veritable nag."

"Pastor Jake wanted you to come? Why?"

Ali shrugged. She didn't know... who could fathom the man's reasoning? "Perhaps he felt Mrs Wallace was lonely and having me visit would help ease her pain." Her smile faded as she looked over and saw Laura's face blanch even more at her comment. Perhaps the girl had no sense of humour. "Oh no. I'm sorry Miss Lawrence... I didn't mean to imply that you would not be company enough. Not at all." Grief. This visit was going from awkward to uncomfortable to death-by-embarrassment. How could she leave quickly and harmlessly before she committed another faux pas? Her instincts were correct; she was not the right person to visit at all. She needed to get out of there quickly without making a scene.

Laura's face relaxed some. It was good to have someone who was not going to put on airs around her. "Please, have some of Sarah's apple cake. It is a favourite of mine. Perhaps we can have your Melting Moments next time."

Next time? Ali was not sure she could handle *this* time. She looked at her. Laura's white face highlighted the dark shadows that lingered under her eyes. "Are you getting better? I do trust my neighbour is not giving you too much trouble."

"Who? Neighbour?"

"Malachi. His family have the farm next to ours out on the Mallee Hill Road. He spent a lot of time with my kid brother growing up, so that at one stage it was hard to work out where the neighbour stopped and the brother bit started. His whole family is like an extension to ours."

Laura closed her eyes. She was so tired. How could one family have so much… and her lot, be so meagre? Where was the justice in that? Still, Ali could strategically map who's who in the Lawson terrain for her. "I know what you mean… Mal is like a brother to me too… and I haven't known him that long at all."

"Is that because he slugged you like a street fighter?"

"Hmmm… so you heard about that?"

Ali studied the crumbs around the slice of tea-cake on her plate. "Yeah… it was a pretty juicy topic that week… not much happens in small places. You get used to it…" Maybe… Ali was less and less enthralled with small town discussion trails.

It felt like a perpetual wash-day, with the private and most personal things being aired to the whole of Wattle Creek. She felt there were private items that were strung out on that community clothes-line that no one should ever have to see.

"Tell me about Mal's street fighting…"

"Not much to say really. I've never watched a fight. If you listen to what people say, I think he's won most back-street titles. Nat – that's his older brother… reckons he's good because of his personal coaching…"

"Nat… the bully…" she murmured quietly.

Ali heard her, but didn't comment for a while. She took up Laura's hand and massaged cream into her skin. She brought out her scissors and emery boards and gently started shaping her nails. "Nat probably seems tough but he's the responsible one. He's always looked out for me… and I love him dearly. But I tell you… just sometimes, I wish he would do something radical and wild. He is so full of responsible bones. When Emmaline, that's my cousin… came out to visit for a while, she started working with me at the Barber shop. Well, you know how these things go… she's engaged to him now. They're just getting the farm back on its feet before they get married. The fire nearly wiped them off the map. Nat's stubborn to a fault… but I think that is a family thing. Toby's the same. I guess Mal is too."

Laura took another sip of tea and stared at her cup. It started to rattle against the saucer and she put it aside. If Malachi was her brother… then Nat was too… and his intellectual counterpart… Toby.

Chit-chat was easy for Ali once she warmed up... and she rambled on as Laura asked and prompted questions about the family... their background...their father... how did Malachi respond to this and that. "Scary thing is that Toby married my best friend. It is like I have a match-making aura... without even wanting to. You'd better be careful, because if you come within fifty feet of my zone... you could end up being married to a Lawson!"

Laura laughed at that. She wasn't going to make the mistake of telling anyone what she knew again. Instead she asked more questions about Mal. Always... it came back to Mal. When Ali thought about it she didn't know that much about Malachi. Sure, when they were kids, Fred and Mal ganged up on her. She was the rich actress that the bushrangers were ambushing; the unlikely maiden that had to be rescued, banished to tall towers at the top of rambling Wilga trees. Mal had kinda grown up in the shadows of her peripheral vision. She never had a need to focus on him. He was her other kid-brother, and like most sisters, she found him really annoying most of her childhood. She had forgotten to outgrow it.

Mal signalled to Pastor Jake. Normal comments about the weather died on his lips as he restlessly cleared his throat. "Just wondering if you're still visiting Laura," he asked in a strained voice.

"Miss Lawrence?" Jake's eyebrows knitted together, curiously studying Mal's blood shot eyes.

"Yeah."

"Well yes, I have been to see her a couple of times. She seems a little brighter. Doctor Wallace is insisting on bed rest, but I would have thought that she'd be up and about a bit more now. She doesn't look frail."

"She ain't putting it on Pastor."

"Oh no, I didn't mean that at all…"

"Then what did you mean?"

"It just seems a long time since she's been up and…"

"She needs rest."

"Oh well, it is kind of Mrs Wallace to let her stay." He couldn't get over his disappointment that Mrs Lawson had turned her back on a needy soul. It was apparent she rejected Laura. And if his summations were true and they were family… perhaps she was a long lost black sheep. It might be because her unknown background could sully the good reputation of the boarding house. Still, it was unnecessarily harsh to push her aside.

Malachi looked at him intently, and convinced himself the man had no idea about the extent of Laura's quest… or the state of her condition. Apparently his mother had not enlightened Pastor Jake as to Laura's suspicions and why she was here. Well, that was hardly unexpected. But this ignorance made him dangerous. He did not know the importance of keeping the little he knew quiet.

"Pastor Jake?"

"Yes Malachi?"

"About Laura being in town… she doesn't exist… she was never here."

Jake's head went back as if someone had belted him across the cheek. "How can you be so cold-hearted Malachi? She *does* exist. Why would you want her to disappear like she is somehow insignificant?"

Mal reach over and grabbed his collar, his street-fighter stance coming to the fore. "Just tell me that you've said nothing to no-one."

Now Pastor Jake's head shot up. No one had ever challenged his integrity before. It was like throwing acid in his eyes. "I have not divulged the confidences of Laura or yourself. I gave my word on that."

Mal's voice cracked some, his fists tense. "I'm wanting you to promise you will tell nobody. *Nobody...* especially my mother."

Suddenly Jake understood. Malachi didn't despise this girl. Oh, how blind he had been. He quietly reached up and removed Mal's hands from his shirt. "Don't lose your grip Mal. You're being very melodramatic... not at all like a Lawson. Sure, love can be a difficult..."

Mal nearly decked him. He screwed up his face and turned away quickly. How could he suggest such a thing? "Oh, Pastor that is sick. I'm not in love with her."

"We often deny what is close to us. She's an attractive girl. I don't know her well, but it seems to me that she has every capacity for..."

"Stop it! Just stop it. I can't love her. I don't. I am her brother." It was out before he realised it.

Everything in Jake's mind froze. He couldn't comprehend what he meant. "Brother? What do you mean?"

"She was looking for her father. That's why she came here. My father, Saint Matthew – yes, the very same... had a mistress and fathered a daughter... before we moved to Wattle Creek. I have a sister."

"Laura is your *sister*? When she was looking for her family... she was looking for... her *father*? Not *extended* family... not cousins... uncles... aunts..." Jake sat down heavily. "The Doctor knows this?" Mal nodded. "And your mother?"

"Yep. That's it. So, you can't let on that Laura is back. Mum will exterminate her... and I don't mean by emotional freeze."

For the first time in a long time, Jake felt like swearing. How could he stuff it up so magnificently? So much for his super-spiritual Abraham parallel; so much for his uncompromising condemnation of Mrs Lawson's inhospitable response. Things fell hard into place. "No wonder. But if she is family... in whatever capacity... surely..."

It was as if Mal could read the direction he was thinking. "Pastor... my mother has only one passion... and it ain't God. That passion was... and still is... my Dad. And in case you haven't got it yet... this is not happy news, because it has sullied the idea of who my father was. Mum will protect an assault on his name and his character. She'll kill for him I have no doubt. But even if you don't think so... personally, I'm not inclined to test that theory. For her own sake... and Laura's... Mum mustn't know she is back in town." Mal sat down on his haunches. Finally, he understood. He was protecting his mother as much as his sister. It was a family matter... divided loyalties... on both sides... both strong. And he was caught in the middle, playing a tenuous game of balance, like walking a tight-rope over a very deep ravine.

62.

Laura fidgeted listlessly with the chenille bedspread. She felt so tired. She was glad the Doctor had laid down the law about staying in bed. She would not have managed to get up even if she wanted to. Her arms and legs felt like they were filled with lead. She couldn't understand why she was not getting better. Perhaps she had the same disease her mother had – whatever that was. The fear that she would never see her mother again gnawed at her mind.

Mrs Wallace came in after Sarah had cleaned away the breakfast dishes. "Laura, my dear... Doctor Wallace wants to talk with you this morning. He asked me to stay with you when he does. Would that be all right? He's back now..."

Laura's eyes clouded. This was serious. Perhaps he had found the reason why her health was not robust... a terminal condition. She could hardly ever be ready for that news but she could not hide. She nodded her consent. She needed to know.

Dr Wallace came and sat by her bed. He smiled as he took her hand and quietly asked after her health. "How are you feeling Laura?"

"Tired... bone tired... that was how my mother described her sickness..."

"Are your symptoms getting any better?" he asked, almost distractedly... like he knew the answer but was getting around to the point by taking verbal detours.

"The tiredness seems to be there all the time. I have a constant upset tummy. It had abated for a time, but now it seems to be back with a vengeance at the most unexpected times. I can't concentrate… I feel peculiar…" She could have gone on… and on… "Doctor… do you know what is wrong with me?"

"Yes Laura. I believe I do…" He paused and looked over to his wife who came and sat on the bed next to her.

She looked at them fearfully. "It is bad isn't it? I am dying… like my mother. I…"

"No child, no. Not at all. You are healthy and strong. Nothing else could account for you getting through what you have and still be…"

"Healthy and strong? I'm not dying?" A familiar fear started to stir in the pit of her stomach again and she didn't want to give it a name. "That's not true. I don't feel healthy at all."

"You know that after the attack it was possible that you could…" Laura ripped her hand from his gentle touch. He quietly, persistently continued. "Laura, you knew that you could be with child… pregnant?"

"No! It died! It's over… there is another reason why I am not well… I have a sickness! I can take an elixir for it! I'm going to get better."

Patiently he let her struggle with the fear. "All the things you are experiencing are about being pregnant… becoming a mother. You need to rest because of what you have been through, but other than that… the baby is well."

"But all the bleeding… a baby doesn't survive that much bleeding. Mum would tell girls that it was God's choice… that it proved their innocence. I'm innocent! The baby should've died. It *did* die. I have a tumour!"

Doctor Wallace cringed. Only the miscarriage of a pregnancy was proof of innocence? What nonsense theology. What guilt to carry for another's crime. He paused. He was waiting for the storm to abate, but he waited in vain. "Laura… dear…"

"I didn't deserve this. You said it was unlikely. You said it was over… gone! I am innocent! I didn't ask for this. I didn't want it to happen to me! God knows this is true!" Then another horror filled her mind. The hope she had nurtured was smashed. She was banished from the love of her own mother again, this time forever. "I have brought shame on my mother! She doesn't deserve this. I don't deserve this! It wasn't my fault! It has to be gone. I will never see her again."

"I don't know your mother… but it sounds to me that you love her very much. That is a great example now you have a baby of your own to think of."

"A baby! I don't know anything about babies." Her voice caught and heaved, and she thought she would be sick. "You… you could make it die. Or…" hope sprung to her eyes, "… if I just get up and did what I usually do… and if I started bleeding again… I would be just leaving it to God… then I won't have to…"

"I'm afraid I can't endorse foolishness just because you feel it will give divine endorsement to your predicament. I am a doctor."

All she could think was that some nameless monster with a heinous smile had forced himself on her… in her. How could she love someone... an equally nameless someone... whose origins were in such grotesque, frightening violence? Would this baby... who was growing inside her, turn out the same? Would it impact his life in some insidious, cruel way that he would never understand, or have no control over? She looked down at the clean, soft sheets and felt the irony of the cold, soiled hardness that smeared over her emotions. "It would be better if it went away... and that was the end of the matter. It wasn't my decision then... why should it be now. It is outside my control. It will die... I *want* it to die. See, I am not like my mother at all!"

Mal sat at the bar and took another drink. There were so many wrongs his father was responsible for. He knew the neglect of an absent father; but that was nothing compared to what his father had imposed on Laura by refusing to acknowledge her right to be called his daughter! He was a Lawson. The pride in which he had always been obliged to carry that name was tainted. But what could he do about that now? He had a choice. To do nothing... or to do something. "I guess," he thought, "I can still do the honourable thing."

He needed to get active; not passively wait out vindication like Laura wanted. Problems generally didn't fix themselves. He remembered Nat standing over him in the machinery-shed. "You broke the plough... and unless you get your hands dirty and fix it... it'll stay broke. Problems don't fix themselves." Malachi watched Laura spiral down into a morass of confused anger. This was not a problem of his own making, but he could not stand by and make no effort. It may not make amends for his father's unspeakable crime, but there was something he could do. He needed to talk to Laura about it.

He got up from the stool, when a man stopped him. "Hey Lawson – heard you were after a fight. Got a challenger for ya." Mal knew this man, and his lip curled as he looked at his smooth vest-coat covering his coarse language and coarse motives. Still, he did need a fight, and he had quietly put out the word. He would do what he had to do.

He nodded. "When?"

"Now."

"Now? You're kidding right?"

"Mal – you ain't the best deal anymore. Besides, you skipped out last time..."

"Sounds like you're stuck, to be asking me at all. My stake is worth more – because you don't have a fight without me."

"You know it don't work like that. I've put your name up, but we can't go changing the stakes – there's a whole code this goes by... it ain't my call." He considered Mal's defiant stare. "Still, if it is going to sway you some, I'll see what I can do."

Mal considered him. As if he would. Malachi's mouth was pressed in a grim line; his eyes burning with a cold fire. He felt anger rising up from the pit of his stomach, building a pressure inside him. What a bag of slime! Fancy making out there was honour in this back-alley wager. More disgust piled on top of his loathing. Rage burnt the inside of his nostrils. He was angry at Laura's fate. He was angry at the monster who did this to her. He was angry with his father for not being who he was supposed to be. He was angry with Nat – for being a boss instead of a brother and a mate. He was angry with Toby – for getting off so lightly just because he was brainy. He was angry with his mother – for loving a failure of a man and continuing to do so. He was angry with God – because He could've done something about all of this, but didn't. He was angry with himself because he couldn't stay detached and unconcerned. Oh boy. He wanted to hit something… and hit it hard. "I'm in," he said curtly. He followed the man out the back pulling off his shirt and rolling his shoulders as he went.

Laura was asleep. Malachi sat by her bed looking at her face, pale and soft on the pillow. He felt a little better, beat up, but the tension was released. For now.

She stirred quietly, her lashes fluttering against the light as she focussed on his frame slouched in the chair by the window. Suddenly she sat up. "Mal – what happened? You look like a horse kicked you!"

He pulled his chair closer. "Mornin' to you too. The horse don't look so good either." He wasn't too perturbed. Skin heals. And he was back on top of the street ladder. Someone on the sideline had made a comment about him being slugged by a girl, and he walloped him for his remarks, just for free. After that there was a more respectful appreciation of his round of wins, by those laying bets on the side. He grinned a little lopsidedly. "They ran out of challengers. The money will pay out the credit-tickets I have. And I have some left over."

Laura shook her head. It was hard to accept the acquisition of these wounds was voluntary. She made no effort to put on a brave face. The whole of idea of subjecting yourself to a fight for entertainment or even income was not natural. "You sound pleased with yourself..." She frowned, unsure what to do. She reached out and dabbed her handkerchief to his cheek.

He winced, and pulled away. "I've been thinking..." Mal pointed to her abdomen. "We've gotta give him the best shot. That little fella is my nephew, remember."

Laura blinked. No, she hadn't remembered that. Did everyone have a claim on her and this baby now? Was her life no longer her own? Oh, come on. Wasn't Malachi the one who left her at the bridge without even a goodbye? When it gets uncomfortable next time he will go again... but that time, she will be left holding a baby. That was the injustice of it. "Why would you want to be uncle to this thing... when I don't even want to be his mother?"

He could think it... he could even fight it... but he didn't like hearing her say it. "Hush Laura – don't let the Pastor hear you talk that way..."

"It's all right for him and the Doctor to be so high and mighty about all this. It's not their life."

"They're good people Laura... they really are..." She grunted. Was he turning against her too? The whole world was on a mission to ruin her life.

"Why? It is the truth – you know it. Where is the God of love Pastor Jake talks up? I don't see it at all."

"Oh Laura… You know I'd kill to have the chance to rip that monster's throat out… but we don't know who he is. It's like fighting a ghost. We can only deal with what we have access to. That's all."

"Why am I being punished for something I don't even know about?"

He didn't understand these things. The only response that worked well for him was getting in a boxing-ring and swinging like an orang-utan. He didn't have any answers. "I want to help, that's all I know. No matter how I look at it, I am not sorry that you are here. Maybe I can…"

"Oh Mal… I…" Laura sighed. What could he do to help? This was beyond help. What if she died? Then there would be no problem. It would have to go away.

"Shhh. It's okay. I'm here. I want to do something…"

Malachi was the one good thing in all this greyness. That was something for which she was grateful. She felt sad she had missed growing up with him, but thankful they had finally connected. "Thanks Mal… you're a great friend. But I'm not sure there is anything you can do."

Mal blinked. Was it true? Had he gone from stranger to brother to friend? He smiled through the bruise on his lip. He hadn't even realised it. It cemented his urgency to do what he could. His plan was specific. "I want to find your mother… to let her know you're okay. So, I can tell her why you haven't come home."

"Mum?"

"If she… well, you said that you didn't let her know where you went and why. She'll be out of her mind for you."

Her eyes clouded. "Mum? Would you do that? Go there?"

"I want you to write a letter that I can give her…" He didn't say what else he hoped for. That might not happen.

Tears spilt onto the covers. How torturous was this confinement. "She won't understand. What if she hates me?"

"I figure we have to give her the best possible chance to understand."

"And you're doing this for the baby?"

"No. I'm doing it for you. What is best for you will be best for him. You're his mother."

She pointed to her womb in disgust. "I'm sorry that I don't love him. I don't even want to. Should I lie about that too?"

He shrugged. It seemed to be another question that was beyond his comprehension. For the first time he could remember he desired reconciliation on the ledger, a balance that made sense to his head and his emotions and his spirit. He resolved to talk to Pastor Jake about it sometime.

Ali came every Tuesday and Friday to visit. To start with she set herself specific little tasks to set about doing, but after a while, hair, nails, clothes, pedicures and facial massages were less central to her visits as their friendship grew. This time Ali propped Laura up in the sun-room, her slippers off, massaging her favourite rose perfumed lotion into her feet.

"Ali I love your visits. You are always here for me." The first time she said it, Ali was overwhelmed. Now she wondered if somehow Laura was trying to lock her in, and make her feel guilty if she didn't come. Ali dismissed it.

"Have you heard from Malachi yet?"

"No – I don't expect he'll write..." she said distractedly. "Ali, I'm think'n I should leave. I cannot remain anonymous forever. The whole town will eventually find out I am here. Then they will work out *why* I am here... then they will cause a whole stack of trouble for the Doctor and Mrs Wallace."

"Doc and Mrs Wallace would have factored that in when they asked you to stay."

She grunted. It hardly seemed possible that people would sit down to a round table, before doing something like this. Surely, they would have just done it; and lived to regret it. That was the way of it.

Ali gently massaged her feet. "I don't think you should do anything until Malachi gets back."

"But what if he doesn't come back... I'm going to look pretty stupid looking over the horizon if he has decided I was too hard to bother with."

"Don't think so Laura. I know this family. They are as loyal as. Just wait okay. You'll know about your Mum then as well."

Laura grunted again.

Ali was sure Laura didn't understood them like she did. "Oh come on Laura, for me then. And Pastor Jake... he feels the same way..." Ali ducked her head down and tried to cover the heat rising in her cheeks. They shared a secret, and how precious their conspiring moments were.

Laura saw her blushing response, but pursed her lips and said nothing. She could hardly deal with the agony of trying to explain how she felt, much less acknowledge anyone else's emotions were tied up in this tangled mess that was her life. Did no one think about her in this? They might enjoy the intrigue, or think of her mother, or the baby... but her? She was an incubator with nothing to offer.

63.

Mal wandered along the wharf and stood looking at the sea for a very long time. He had dreamt of holidays at the beach when he was a kid, but the scene before him smacked of a reality that was nothing like a child's romantic sea-side daydream. There was the rank smell of fish and the loud noise of industry drowning out any sound of the ocean. He looked again at the address on the paper and approached a fishmonger for directions. He pointed along a back street and up the hill. It was not far.

The lion-head door knocker – aged and rusted from the salt air, did not work. Mal stood on the low step of the drab cottage, his hand suspended as he went to knock on the peeling paint of the door. Was he was doing the right thing? He turned around and almost left. He reminded himself again of Laura... dear Laura... displaced and alone. He didn't want to confirm her worst fears but as he looked around, he had a grim feeling that her mother was not here. Had she left or died or was so frail that she didn't know up from down?

He checked the address again. He couldn't think of any reason not to proceed. Hadn't he come all this way? There was nothing for it. He knocked at the door. Silence answered. He shuddered as he realised the cruel paradox that all his doubts might be realised. He knocked again more firmly... and again.

He turned back down the cracked path. As his hand opened the squeaking gate he looked back at the small cottage, tidy in its state of poverty. This was where Laura grew up. This was where she dreamed of finding her father and lived with her mother. It was evident to Mal he was too late. Her mother was long gone. The cottage had an aura of hardship about it, but it was not neglected like the neighbouring derelict shacks; it was not what you would expect as the home of a very sick woman, an invalid living or dying alone.

His mind struggled to formulate direction – he had come without a contingency plan. A plain grey-haired lady walked slowly towards him. He stopped her, removing his hat. "Excuse me Ma'am... I was wondering if you know the whereabouts of a Linnet Lawrence? I believe she used to live in that cottage."

She was stooped and tired, and she looked at him, eyeing the yellowing bruises on his face. "And who might be wanting to know?"

"Me," he answered simply. He folded his hat in his hands.

"And you are?"

Hope jumped into his eyes. Perhaps his woman could help. "Excuse my boldness Ma'am. My name is Malachi Lawson. I am a friend of her daughter.... Laura."

The woman reached out and grabbed him, no longer fearful of his rough appearance. "Oh, glory be! Laura! Is she alright?"

"You know this woman... where I can find her?"

"Come Mr Lawson... come inside. We need to talk." She grasped his elbow and guided him back up the street and into Laura's old home. She sat him in a clean, but worn, faded lounge and sat opposite in an equally old club-lounge chair. "My name is Linnet," she said.

Pastor Jake pulled a chair close to the bed, wiping his palms restlessly on his trousers. "Laura I have thought a great deal about your situation. I find myself burdened by your predicament in a way that is unprecedented in my experience. I see your tears and I have searched my heart for a solution. I think I have one if you would hear it out."

Laura stared into a painting on the wall. Malachi was gone so long. She felt so alone. Would he come back this time? She willed him to come back… soon… as if her wanting it could draw him like a magnet. She sighed. He was not a force like gravity. He was his own person… he had to choose to come back. The risk this involved scared her. There were no guarantees, and the note that she crushed in her hands under the covers did nothing to allay her fear. He had scrawled a note to say he had arrived. The postmark was Inlet Bay.

"Laura? Can I tell you what I have to offer?"

Everything inside her screamed for time, time. Just a little more time. Yet the clock was relentless: ticking away the moments, as her abdomen continued to swell involuntarily. She needed solutions. Reluctantly she drew her eyes back to Pastor Jake sitting on the chair beside her, waiting. Finally, she nodded and went back to staring at the painting on the wall. It was a child's painting of a little fishing boat tied at a wharf. Was Malachi standing on the wharf at home? Did he like the sea?

Could he hear the gulls, and the thumping of fish baskets and the lapping of the water against the wooden pylons?

Pastor Jake cleared his throat like he did before he got up to deliver a sermon. "Well then… I have never done this before. Laura… will you marry me?" Laura continued to stare passed him. "Laura? Did you hear what I said? I'm giving you an offer of marriage."

Instantly her eyes snapped back to him. "Marry you? Why?" If he was expecting exclaims of wondrous delight he was sorely disappointed.

"Well, like I have already said. Your baby will be born without a name or a father. If I marry you before…"

Tears welled up in her eyes. She clutched her abdomen carefully. It should mean so much that this man would place value on a baby, her baby with a nameless, unspeakable background. But she didn't get it. Why would he give up his whole life for her? It was preposterous, even magnificent in its intent, but the tears that stung her lids were not from gratitude.

Malachi sat in the chair and stared at the woman sitting in front of him. "You are Linnet Lawrence?"

"Yes, my name is Linnet. I am Laura's mother. Although our surname is…" Her voice faded. He knew where Laura was.

Now he was here he could hardly believe it was so simple. Perhaps Pastor Jake was right: there was a Lord who managed the universe in detail. "Thank God. Laura will be relieved you are okay. She was very worried about your health Mrs Lawrence."

She frowned then. "She was worried? But she ran away…"

"Oh no… Mrs Lawrence… Miss…" He stopped confused. He didn't know how to address her.

"Just call me Linnet."

He mumbled an apology. "Linnet." He shook his head. "I came because Laura was desperate to know how you were. The Doctor won't let her travel."

"Doctor? What is wrong?" So, there was a reason for her silence. Tears of relief spilled onto her sleeve. Laura was alive! There were so many questions it hardly seemed possible to stay silent before another question reared up demanding an answer.

"Linnet… there is no nice way to say this. Laura… she is… well, pregnant."

"You're the father? Are you married like respectable…" But she knew even as she asked, that Laura was not married.

Married? Respectable? If he were the child's father… would he marry her? Or would he be a case of 'like father – like son'. He held up his hand as if to ward off her verbal blows. "No! No… My interest is as family! I am her brother…"

"Brother? Are you insane? How can you be her brother? I have never…"

His lips twisted at the obvious observation. "Half-sibling." So, she didn't know either. The web of deceptions tangle far, he thought cynically.

A look of deep betrayal flickered across her eyes, and her face went pale. "You're lying. How can you say such a thing?"

"Are you denying that Laura's father spent many years at Wattle Creek?"

"No – I cannot."

"You cannot be ignorant of the fact that he had a wife and family there. I am the third son."

Her hand started to shake. "Wife? Family? You're lying! He never married. He didn't!" Mal didn't need to say anything. His very existence was screaming louder than words. Finally, her gasping calmed. When she spoke it was barely a whisper. "You're mother… is she still alive?"

"Mum? She's fine… and yes they were married."

Her voice squeaked in a violent tremolo. "Your names are not even the same…"

He shrugged. What could he say? A name change to cover a shameful past. He could bet his last penny that was not an original strategy. The more he heard about his father's reprehensible behaviour, the more shame he felt. "I'm sorry to be the bearer of bad tidings. But I'm the evidence he was no saint." He almost wanted to say that they were madly in love… that his mother totally believed that he only ever had eyes for her. No doubt Linnet would say the same. It seemed unnecessary. "Laura was on a mission… to find her father. That is why she left… to find him… and to bring him back to you."

"But she was too late. He was long gone…"

"Well, we both know that… it was an idiotic plan from the start. But she didn't know. She thought it might help you… if she was able to do that while you were unwell. She is determined and relentless."

Linnet's mind was spinning from the news that he bore. Could Mal really know her daughter after all? "I should have told her, but I couldn't. I never gave her specific details… deliberately… I always tried to protect h… her."

"She must have felt she had enough to work on… pieces of a puzzle she was determined to solve. Like I said, Laura is tenacious…" Malachi looked sceptically at the woman before him. What was so attractive to his father? Twenty years surely had not been kind.

Linnet measured the young man before her. Was he really his son too? The battered bruises on his face giving him a brutal, coarse look. How could he be part of her life, in this totally disconnected way? "Laura's not married, is she?" she said again. It was a statement, rather than a question. "If you're not the father to the child… do you know who is?"

"I'm sorry Mrs… Linnet… Laura doesn't even know."

More tears spilt on her sleeves. It was a raid on her personal world; the things that she had constructed in safety around her were being torched to the ground. "Oh Laura… how could you not even know who the father is? Even I could accept an unbridled love. I understand the grace of God in honest weakness… but to slide down into debauchery? Intentional wantonness?" She needed to know the worst of the worst. She would not spare herself anything. The sins of her mother... her father... visited on the next generation. "Was she... she working as... a...?" She gagged and was almost sick.

"Laura? No! No... This is not her fault... please Mrs Lawrence. Please believe me. Laura is not the prodigal you imagine. She is no whore! It was not like that at all."

"Then how? How could this happen?"

How? He could no more answer that than grow wings and fly. "She was attacked, but she wasn't able to identify him. Why don't you believe her? She is your daughter!"

"Laura I could believe. You... that is different. I don't know you. You turn up here, with nothing but a story about my daughter and her father. How do I even know that you are for real? This is ludicrous!"

Malachi shrugged. "I'm here ain't I?" To him that was enough. As if he would make all the effort to fabricate this story to a penniless spinster who was his father's mistress. He needed it less than she did.

"Then what do you want? If you want to sell me your silence... forget it. It is worth nothing now. I have lived the secret too long. If you want money because you're the father... you cannot seriously think my circumstances are worth anything."

"I told you I'm *not* the father and I don't want your two-bit money! What's more, so you have no doubt, I don't give a fig about you and my hypocrite father!"

"Then what? What can you possibly want by coming here?"

"For Laura! She needs her mother..."

Tears rolled down her face.

"I want you to come back to Wattle Creek. Laura has no one… and it won't be long before the baby comes. She is not allowed to travel."

"You are out of your mind. How can I…" She stopped.

Mal stood up. His jaw worked back and forth. It was daft. Laura didn't need her at all. They could work it out by themselves. He should never have come. He'd been away too long. "Forgive me. I forgot to give you this." He handed her Laura's letter. "I'll come back on Saturday to get your answer. I leave for Wattle Creek on Monday. I have enough for two tickets, but I need to get back – with or without you."

She wouldn't take the letter so he put it down on the table. She heard his wordless accusation that she was failing as a mother; that she was not demonstrating the care that she ought. Her Laura. How could it be that when one dream comes true, it lives only to dash another to the rocks like a sea eagle's prey?

Laura stared out the window. Nausea stinging the back of her throat with gall. He could not be serious. He didn't love her. That is not the picture of marriage she hoped for, even to a good man.

"But Laura, I couldn't make such an offer without love. Be reassured – real love is the only motive here."

"Love? You sound like you're delivering groceries to the cook's store."

"Romance is not the only qualifier for marriage. It is about commitment and faithfulness. That is more enduring. Many marriages work well without infatuation. Better perhaps."

"So, you don't deny it? It is almost insulting. I can't. It's not right."

"What is insulting is your circumstance... inflicted on you, and your baby... outside your control."

"It doesn't seem right. You don't even want to pretend. That's what I don't understand."

"A marriage is legitimate when people promise before God to look out for each other. You have no one else to do this. This is my offer... to look out for you."

"I have Malachi. He looks out for me. He's my brother. What you offer is no better."

Pastor Jake blinked. She had a point. Why couldn't her brother be her protector? They were already family by birth... by blood. Could it be that such ties were indeed thicker than water? Did it have to be a husband? Pastor Jake knew in his heart that God designed marriage for couples to stick it out. The harsh reality was, Malachi was not known for his stability and consistency. She could be left high and dry again... abandoned in a society that regarded such circumstances as leprosy. "I thought having a legitimate name for your child would be important."

"It is. But he has a name. It is Lawson. That is legitimate enough."

"You don't want to get married then?" He didn't look all that disappointed... much like a boy might be if he wanted to try out a kite and it was not a windy day. Nothing hinted that her refusal would ruin his life. Laura tried to believe that he didn't sound almost hopeful as he said it.

"Sure, I want to get married, but not to someone who feels sorry for me. It is humiliating that the best I can hope for is being a sympathy bride."

"I don't feel sorry for you Laura... I feel angry. I want to right this travesty. I thought this was a way it could be done." Was he just getting carried away with his hyperactive sense of obligation to fix this injustice; that he could only see this one solution? Were there better options in God's economy? He had thought that this was God's idea.

"I just didn't expect to marry someone because I made him feel angry... or sorry."

"Oh Laura... not you. Your situation... I have tried to explain that."

"But your heart is not in it Pastor. It is written all over your face."

"I have no idea what you mean."

"Ali." She said it softly and distinctly. She stared at him carefully. It was a test.

He physically jolted. "That is ridiculous. What are you suggesting?"

Yes. Just as she thought. He failed. Miserably. "Oh, what do you think I mean? You try so hard to be indifferent when you are together... but you can't stand being around her because..."

"Stop. That is enough. I take it that you are refusing me?" He tried to sound pastoral... but now he was the one who felt humiliated. There is no honour in being exposed, caught out. He had never been improper with Ali. Never. She didn't even know.

"I'll think about your idea," she said tentatively. Perhaps it was the best course of action after all. She did not have enough options to dismiss it completely out of hand. But it had to be the best decision to make. She wasn't going to say yes... just because he had asked.

64.

Malachi returned late on Saturday afternoon. He left it as long as he could. He wanted to believe that Linnet would come back with him, but when he looked at her face, and saw the swollen eyes and rubbed face, he knew that she would not.

"Why? I cannot understand how a mother would not travel to the ends of the earth for her daughter? What am I going to tell her?"

"Tell her nothing. Tell her that you did not find me."

"Why? You're no damned better than our good-for-nothing father! You cannot expect me to tell her that! One look and she'll figure out her mother is ashamed of her."

"No! I'm not ashamed... of her. But... of me... I cannot expose her to who I really am. I tried..."

"Mrs Lawrence! How can you say that? This is not about you!"

"Malachi, stop calling me that. I told you Lawrence is not our name."

"Well of course I know that. How could it be? But Laura said her surname was Lawrence. Some habits die hard that's all."

She looked away not wanting to confront his accusing stare. She knew where he got the name Lawrence. How could he know what she went through? "Our family name is Torrens. She was wrong to..."

"Wrong? That's rich! It makes no difference to me what her name is, or was, or should be. She is who she is. She was just trying to find out *who* that is."

"You must understand I have agonised over what the right thing to do was. I wanted her to know her father... but I could never do it. It would have destroyed him."

"Noble no doubt, but now your daughter has destroyed her life, chasing your dream. Doesn't that rouse in you the slightest sympathy?"

"Oh, she has my sympathy..." Her puffy eyes spilt more tears.

"Well, I am none too convinced it is enough." He turned and walked to the door. He dumped an envelope on the table as he passed. "That has the Doctor's address in it. They are the *good* people who have been trying to clean up your mess."

He left to go back to the wharf. The dingy little pub where he was staying did not offer comfort, but he could have a drink and fuel his anger. He wouldn't hesitate to put up a brawl tonight either. He might even start it if no one was willing to pay, and give a freebie to those who wanted spectator sport.

Malachi's head thumped and he had dragged himself down the stairs to the vile fish-laden air of the wharf. It was nauseating, but it beat the rank urine taint that seeped from the mattress in his closed room. The window wouldn't open. This day would have to be the culmination of his childhood sea-side dream holiday. He had a day to kill before he made his way back to the station tomorrow. The sun shone off the shallow lapping waves of low tide washing sea-weed like a careless washer-woman. He watched a grey gull bob and buoy on the waves around the weed and then walk up onto the shaly sand. Another bird effortlessly floated up on the breeze and hovered above a huddle of gulls squabbling over a decomposing fish head. Their persistent cry was echoed by a preacher down further who was standing on his box calling for the lost to come home. *Stupid*, thought Malachi, *the very point of being lost, is that you don't know where you are.*

He looked distractedly at the rest of the mid-morning traffic. For a Sunday... it seemed busy. The open-air meeting was finally breaking up and the preacher carried his soap-box now filled with books and tambourines back along the wharf. A few of those with him strung out, going their separate ways. One man counselled a drunk who was propped up against the wall. Mal recognised the repentant reveller from last night. He had put up a fight. Disinterested, he looked back out over the ocean. There was a boat or two bobbing on the waves further out. How restless they seemed; how easily they could be set adrift. Where would they end up if they followed the mercy of random currents and purposeless trade-winds? Most likely, they'd end up nowhere special: shipwrecked.

"Well hello. Malachi Lawson. What are you doing here?"

Mal jumped. He didn't know anyone in Inlet Bay. He scanned his jumbled memory of last night and spun around stammering his embarrassment at being recognised. He felt like a kid caught smoking and drinking scotch under the railway bridge again. That had happened once or twice.

Mal stared at the face that belonged to the voice, covering his eyes from the glare with his hand. "Reverend Bernard? How unexpected."

"Malachi, what brings you to Inlet Bay? It is a long way from Wattle Creek."

"Family business."

"Oh…"

"And you Reverend? I didn't expect you to minister among fishmongers and boat-builders. Like you say… Inlet Bay is a long way from farmers and dairy cows."

"Oh, not that far… they are much like the people at The Creek. Quite genuine. Christ was equally comfortable by the sea, among fishermen… as farmers and trades-people." And he blushed… a purple sort of stain rising from his collar up to the top of his balding head. "I am not preaching here… officially. I work at the fish market – doing accounts during the week. But Sundays I help out… along the wharf… the open-air meeting."

"So, did you come from here?" For some reason, Mal found it hard to picture him splashed with the sea spray on a fishing trawler.

"No… I was originally from further down… the inner city."

"Family here then? You had a sister who was sick when you left The Creek?"

"Hmm." He chewed his lip and mumbled something quite incoherent.

"Oh, I'm sorry... My condolences..." The man was obviously very upset.

Bernard shrugged and twisted away. He didn't say anything. He looked out to the horizon and then suddenly turned back. The expression on his face was unexpected. It was one of being torn – torn between doing the easy thing and the right thing. Malachi knew that look. It was a dilemma he was familiar with.

"Actually, it was not my sister who was sick... but a very dear friend."

Malachi stared at him. What did it matter to him about his family lies? Nothing was ever what it seemed. But when he cast his eyes down under the scrutiny of the younger man, and mumbled some more, Mal suddenly jumped to his feet. "Unbelievable! This is no coincidence. Linnet Lawrence...Torrens. She wouldn't be this 'sister' of yours, would she?"

"No...no you are right, she isn't my sister. I felt that if others supposed she was my sister... 'sister in Christ', it would cause less misunderstanding." Again he mumbled something. It sounded a bit like "be sure your sins will find you out..."

"But it was Linnet who was sick wasn't it? You left Wattle Creek to look after Linnet Torrens?" When he would not deny it, Malachi swore. "You came from the city... you were involved in the Union Church!" He stared at Bernard, guilt and embarrassment tearing away the polished priestly composure Mal always remembered and took for granted. Perhaps it was the absence of stiff, black ministerial robes that seemed to give him a limp appearance.

"Yes, but that is history now. When I got back Linnet was very sick. I looked after her until she recovered. It has been a slow recuperation… still she tires easily." Suddenly it occurred to him. "How do you know Linnet?"

Mal evaded a direct answer. "We met the other day…" The revelation staggered him. He took a deep breath trying to settle the rapid pulsating in his head. "Say Reverend, would you like a cup of coffee? A familiar face is doing me good."

Laura walked around Mrs Wallace's garden once. There was a cool breeze and she sat quietly in the mottled shade underneath the jacaranda tree. It was the first time that she had been out in a very long time. The sun seemed unnaturally bright in the pure air. Mrs Wallace smiled out from underneath her sun hat as she selectively pruned the faded blooms from a climbing rose. Her Chinese gardener wordlessly pruned her hedges and weeded along the borders of the path. There was a quiet unity of purpose in their labour.

Sarah came out and whispered something to Mrs Wallace who just smiled and continued on snipping. It seemed to Laura that nothing was hurried in Mrs Wallace's world. Yet it was not like she didn't accomplish anything. There was not a pie in Wattle Creek that didn't have the fingers of Louise Wallace in there, helping out. Sarah emerged again, showing Pastor Jake to where Mrs Wallace presided over the rose trellis. He bowed formally and asked permission to speak with their charge. There was a ceremony about his visit that was foreign to Laura.

Pastor Jake presented Laura with a bouquet of flowers and then quietly retreated and sat nearby on a separate chair. He made no effort to make conversation, as if the lazy morning sun offered all the company he desired. Laura glanced his way occasionally wondering if there was some particular thing she should say. She could think of nothing clever... or even mildly engaging. She decided to let it be. This was his idea. What if she said something inappropriate... or offended him? This man had asked her to marry him, yet he was a completely unknown quantity. She distractedly studied the pretty selection of flowers. And then she saw, emerging deep from the throat of a lily-bloom, a little orange lady-beetle, the black patterns reproducing the markings of a harlequin along his back. She watched fascinated, as it climbed in and out and around the throat of the flower... and finally he lifted up his little shell wings and flew away. She smiled, remembering Malachi's little comments. It was as if she could really feel the ancient blessing rest on her. Who else but Mal would think of bringing bugs to visit a bed-ridden patient? It was perfect in every way. Bugs remained and perpetuated long after cut flowers faded, she thought, looking at the arrangement in her hand. Every girl likes flowers... or they should, she was sure. But for her, bugs were more interesting.

Finally, Pastor Jake got up to leave. He hadn't seemed bothered by their lack of conversation. "Laura, my dear..." She jolted uncomfortably at the familiarity of his address. "Laura. I am reluctant to press you for an answer... but it follows that if we are to be married before the birth of your baby, then preparations should be made... in a timely manner." She stared

582

at him vacantly. "Can I impose upon you to consider my offer and tell me what you would like to do? I won't press you for an answer now... but I can certainly come back tomorrow."

Laura shook her head as she watched him go. He was not going to press her for an answer, but he wanted it by tomorrow? How so? It hardly seemed right to go along with it just because it was infinitely more convenient to do that, than to do nothing. She wished with all her might that Mal would come home. She could discuss it with him. He would know. For all his street fighting bravado, Mal had shown remarkable intuition. Perhaps it was the family connection they shared.

Then suddenly, as if on cue... a lady-bug circled and spun in and landed on her flowers. A blessing! Malachi had given his blessing without even being here. She called out, "Pastor Jake! Pastor Jake?"

He spun around and looked at her as she said, "Yes! I will!"

He came back to her and knelt on the grass, taking her hands in his. "Laura! You are going to marry me?"

"Yes. I will. A baby needs a father... and you seem to want to do that."

He smiled, almost wistfully. "You and your baby will be safe with me," he said sincerely.

65.

Mal and Reverend Bernard went down to the wharf and found a grimy little café. They sat opposite each other in a booth where the hard wooden seats had been carved with the initials of many passing customers. As soon as Malachi ordered a pot of coffee, their little corner stall became a confessional.

"We decided to marry as soon as Linnet's health allowed... nearly four months ago now. She is my wife. But it would appear that there are many things that have been against us. Perhaps there has been too many years... too much pain... the hardest of all was when Laura disappeared."

"Laura!" Unexplainably Malachi felt a lump in his Adam's apple that he could not swallow.

Bernard looked at him quickly. "You know Laura, don't you? That is why you are here. Is she safe?"

He nodded. "She came to Wattle Creek. I met her there," he said. Then he added, "She was looking for her father."

Bernard looked stunned. "But I was already here." She had gone looking for him... and he was right here!

"*You* are her father? How could Laura not have met you if you were caring for her mother for so long?"

"Oh, we know each other... it's over two years since I resigned and left Wattle Creek. While Linnet was unwell I came and nursed her. I did maintenance around the house. Linnet has taken a long time to recover. We agreed to say I was her cousin. It didn't seem wise to load this history on Laura at the same time her mother was so critically ill. Linnet thought it best. She wrote a letter in case something happened but I never needed to give it to her because Linnet was getting better... all be it slowly."

"So, Laura knew you, but didn't *know* you were the one she was looking for!"

"Our plan was to break it to her gently. As Linnet got stronger, she started to talk to Laura about the years when we met... what had happened back then... how we had fallen in love – the mistakes we made. But she never identified that person as me. Then one day when Linnet woke up, Laura was gone. We knew she had left voluntarily – because she had carefully taken things... and enough money for a ticket and some food. We couldn't trace her... she took a train to the city... that is as far as we got. Her trail went cold very quickly. But she hadn't taken much, so we expected her home very soon. But she never came... we have not heard from her since."

"...and you were here all along. Why didn't you say something?" Suddenly Malachi reeled to the side like something hit him. "I'm not her brother!"

"Brother? Why would you think you are her brother?"

"She was looking for her family. She knew some specific things, like her father had come to The Creek district from the city about 20 years ago... and he had been involved in the church. She kept giving the name Lawrence... but that was all. It seemed no other family matched the profile... except ours. Lawrence – Lawson. It wasn't a big stretch. We were convinced that Dad was her father... that made me her brother."

"Matthew Lawson... an adulterer? Are you out of your mind?"

"Apparently."

Bernard closed his eyes and sat down the coffee cup. One crime... one little lie... and the implications were going on and on and on. "I was not a minister of religion when I met Linnet. I was not even a Follower. I knew as much about Jesus Christ as the average homing pigeon. Yet we were wildly in love... and poor as church mice. I thought that phrase had the feel of romance about it. I decided to apply to the church to become a minister... that way we would have a regular, if meagre living. They sent me away to training... and it was there I met someone completely unexpected."

"There is *another* woman?" Malachi shook his head. This narrative was blowing every concept out of the water he had about this middle-aged, portly, balding, celibate minister. He loved a woman... (as if that wasn't extreme enough for all his childhood memories of the Reverend). Perhaps more than one woman, it seemed. He looked at him sideways. Was he some sort of incognito loving machine?

"No – it wasn't a woman... it was Jesus Christ. I had been to church a few times... not regularly, mind you... but enough to think that religion was a safe, predictable, secure place. The Jesus I met was somewhat different to those ideas. I wrote to Linnet to tell her that I had had a revolutionary experience... but she never wrote back. I thought that she despised my choice. I knew I was not the first to endure rejection for the name of Christ. During the first year of my studies, I searched for her with the intention of formalising our marriage... but the house where we lived was vacant... the forwarding address was empty also. She had just disappeared. I understand now that she had gone into a private confinement, a place for unwed mothers. I even advertised... but in the end I had to accept that she had rejected my choice. I never even knew she was pregnant.

"I had made a decision that Christ would be my life... regardless of Linnet's dismissal of my revelation. So, I applied to a few churches. Wattle Creek was the first, and it seemed good to make a break from everything that reminded me of her. I immersed myself in more studies because that was the only thing that would help me not to think about her. Theology became my second romance. I never married, because in my heart, I believed the only thing that didn't formalise what we had... was that we never had a ring."

"Later, I discovered Linnet only received my letters after Laura was born, telling her about my posting to The Creek. It was post-marked many times... even by a small Post Office on the South coast. It was then she made investigations and found I was settled. She followed my career during my years at Wattle Creek. All this I never knew... until she was very ill and she sent me a letter. She was not certain she would come through that crisis and she wanted Laura to know the truth of her only living relative. That is when I came here. Until now I had presumed that Laura had discovered I was her father and found the whole concept repugnant... and that is why she left."

"Laura's dreamt all her life of finding her father. If you had told her up front...even if it was not as she imagined... surely the truth would outweigh the fantasy."

"Can you imagine how angry I was when I learned I had a daughter and had never been included in her life? She was my baby! Laura has grown into an enchanting young woman. She still doesn't know how saddened I am by what we missed out on."

"Reverend... she doesn't know anything! Laura has no idea about you. She thinks that *my* father is *her* father. We constructed a very believable scenario with the information we had. It is flawed... but convincing none the less. Right now she is sitting at Doc Wallace's house thinking that Matthew Lawson betrayed his wife, and abandoned his mistress when he found out she was pregnant. And the best plan he could come up with was to leave the city and go to the country to be a farmer. I believed it too."

"Every day I pray that God will keep Laura safe wherever she is."

"Well, just so you know... your God hasn't done a very great job of that. She was attacked after leaving here. She's pregnant from rape. She's been mugged (Mal omitted that he was the perpetrator of this crime)... and tossed out of accommodation twice that I know of. She's nearly died from a miscarriage... and even that didn't succeed so now she is facing a destitute life as an ostracized unwed mother. Yep... doesn't look like God has been doing too well on the score of keeping her safe. Failed miserably, I'd say."

Tears pooled in his puffy eyes. Quietly, like a liturgy he said, "God is not neglectful or vindictive. It breaks my heart that my Laura is so hurt by the choices I made. But overlay all that with the Father's plan for her life. It will win out... if she aligns her will with His – it has to prevail. I must believe that with every fibre in my body… or my whole life is a lie."

"Well if that's His idea a *good* plan, it sure as anything scares me witless should there be another one that isn't so good. This isn't right! Laura has had far more than a fair share."

"Malachi, there is no "fair share". The tragedy is that it won't ever be fair… while the devil has open reign."

"Like we have a choice then. The world's damned and we are with it."

"But that is the miracle. We are not damned if we choose to. We can choose *not* to be part of the destruction. It is a "yes–no" choice. Just because it is simplistic, it does not mean it is simple… because it certainly is not easy! It is riddled with conflict and strife… but our choices actually depend on this conflicted reality."

"How so?"

"If there is no choice – and no boundary line to define it, how can we choose right? How can we demonstrate loyalty to God – our creator, without the opportunity to make a wrong choice… or a right one?"

Malachi stared out the window at the sea-water, foaming and tumbling over itself in its hurry to reach the shore. Waves swirled against the beach like the emotions swimming around in his head. "You gotta be kidding! How can you say such things? You haven't got a credible bone in your little black suit and tie. You abandoned a pregnant woman and then her child… who is now facing a similar fate."

Mal never expected him to buck, or to shout, or be outraged. After-all he had listened to his monotone preaching every Sunday since he could remember. He genuinely thought the man was incapable of passion, but he was hoping for a reaction of sorts. Anything, that might indicate he had been knocked off his formal self-righteous perch.

Bernard lifted his gaze from the muddy coffee grounds lining the bottom of his cup. His eyes were misted and humbled, and there were the shadows of deep sorrow there. "I guess, you could not be more correct. And yet, in another way you couldn't be further from the truth, than if you thought you could fly into the sun and not be burnt."

"What do you mean?"

"Simply this. I always thought my standing as a Follower of Christ, was dependant on my ability to live the life I talked. I did that the best I could. I tried to make amends for my wrongs when I became aware of them. But this time, I have failed… in the beginning… and in the middle… and at the end. And it all highlights one thing: I am human… I have stuffed up. In that you are right. My personal reputation is shot."

He stopped. Malachi shrugged. He was a little surprised he would agree – but he knew he was right. Bernard took a deep breath and continued. "But I have hope… not in me… but in God's grace. God knows that I sincerely want to do better… and He assures me my credibility is as His child… and not on my blameless performance, or even in giving a pretty good rendition. It is entirely dependent on Jesus cleansing my past and opening the way for me to dialogue with Him. With my sin forgiven God is able to talk with me, even in my failure… and I must be willing to talk back to Him and to tell him I am sorry... ask for wisdom and strength to do better:

590

dialogue with God. It will continue to work like that until I've got nothing shameful left to come to Him about. We both know that isn't going to happen until I get to Glory... because I will have many more failures to endure while I draw breath. It is the way life is."

"What a cop out. You can't just get away with murder by this 'Jesus will wash away my sin' clause."

"Jesus told his disciples to forgive seventy times seven. Do you suppose He would give a mandate that He himself was unwilling to lead by example? I know His grace does not make sense; it is not logical... that is what makes it Grace."

Mal understood "sin" – anything that wasn't the perfect option, which tainted everything he touched. Mal also understood the concept of "paying for sin" as well – *do the crime and pay the time*, whether that be in money, or in the slammer, or just trying to fix up the mess afterwards.... and guilt. There was always guilt. Mal reckoned *that* was the most killing of all... because even if you could pretend it wasn't there, it would gnaw your insides out like a parasite... unseen, painful and deadly... nightmares.

Mal stared at his mug. He could deal with the physical consequences of things going wrong but could he be free from these internal consequences of guilt, failure... shame, simply by bringing it to God? Is that what it meant... that stuff about Jesus taking our burdens and washing away sin? A lifetime of teaching in church suddenly aligned. The story of Jesus dying on the cross made sense: it was not an unforeseen tragedy; or a miserable failure; or half-hearted compromise... but a balancing of the ledger. Reverend Bernard was saying that the guilt could be lifted. Not because the crime didn't happen, and not because the price was reduced to a manageable level like a market catalogue sale... but because God was willing to pay the full price... on the cross.

"You know Malachi. I taught these things all the time at Wattle Creek... but it is just now that I have really had to live by them. My very sanity depends on it. It has become a matter of life and death for me."

Mal said nothing, but he understood. Suddenly he wanted to get away... he needed to think. There were some things he needed to dialogue with God about.

66.

Ali stood by the window, her face pale, her eyes flashing lightening, before they clouded over in a dark storm. "He what?"

"He asked me to marry him."

"Pastor Jake?"

"Yes, I said that. He said he wanted to… well, he wanted to right the wrong that had been done. It made him angry…"

"He's marrying you because he is mad?" Ali could contain herself no longer. "Well, he's certainly that!" and she fled from the house in a rage.

The news in Wattle Creek spread like a grass-fire. The pastor was marrying an unwed girl in trouble. No one knew who she was, or why she had come to Wattle Creek. It was a scandal. There was no doubt they made up the story about the girl being saved from a destitute future, to protect the Reverend. You could tell by looking at them it was not the first time they had been together. It was just as everyone expected: Mrs Lawson was more a Madam of a bordello than the proprietor of a respectable lodging house. No wonder the pastor was not interested in any of the local girls… the child was undoubtedly his… and on… and on… and on.

Mrs Lawson was furious. "Pastor… I have no idea how you can lift your head in this town, but there is no way anyone who looks at that girl is going to be keeping a room in my house. I'll give you the courtesy of sundown, but you are to be out of the house no later. Don't be coming back." He had no choice but to pack up and go back to the pub's noisy little room above the stairs.

When Jake came into the barbershop, Ali deftly took over from Emmaline. "I'll be handling this one," she said in a quiet, icy tone. As his haircut progressed Jake could feel her rage. Of all the people in Wattle Creek, this shocked him the most. He didn't expect Ali to stand by in self-righteousness. She knew Laura's story... her isolation and her pain. She was her friend. It was a blow. He had been depending on her support – quiet and constant, to see him through this. It was bitter to realise that even Ali would let him down. How different people are when the tide of society is against them.

Doctor Wallace took a walk with Pastor Jake down by the creek. He had very little to say, and Jake appreciated that finally he had found one who would offer quiet support. Sure, Jake hadn't expected everyone to understand, but the intense violence of mistrust and the all-inclusive judgement, was like a mob stoning, pummelling the life out of him. The Doctor quietly communicated that the congregation had requested he stand down. Jake stopped walking, trying to comprehend. "Surely you told them it is not my baby."

"True. I did."

"Then why? I really felt that this was an act of grace – of communicating God's love in a tangible way to someone who has been battered by life more than I can even imagine. I honestly felt that this was something that Christ was asking of me." He shrugged. He was not so sure any more. "Perhaps not... perhaps it was just an altruistic deed on my part. But regardless of that… why would they judge me in this? Why is it so incompatible with the office of Pastor?"

Doctor Wallace quietly shook his head. "I have given my summation of the situation. Most of the arguments go toward *the appearance of being blameless*. They say that they cannot know, and they need to be sure that the Pastor of the church is walking in integrity."

"But what about Mrs Lawson? She knows the truth."

"Josie has said nothing."

"Of course." He sighed. "So, they really believe I am responsible?"

"It is the general opinion. Laura refuses to say anything. *You* refuse to defend yourself."

"Laura is only silent because I particularly asked her not to engage in arguments and justifications. I could not see that it was helpful. Perhaps I was wrong. This is a shock. I didn't see my time here being cut short. I'm not finished with what I set out to do. I really believed that I would know when it was time to move on. Perhaps it is time… but it sure doesn't feel like it. It wasn't supposed to be this way. Not this way."

His heart was grieved. Not only because people could not see who he was, or who Laura was… but by the reality that the very things that he wanted to do here were being terminated. And it felt like death. All the seeds, all of the dreams and hopes and plans that God had sown in his heart, were falling on the road side, being picked off by birds, and being choked out by circumstances. But there was a more practical blow. How could he support a wife?

"And you Doctor? Have you changed your mind?"

"Jake, I know you would have only done what you thought was right at the time."

"There is a *'but'* in the way you say that Doctor."

He nodded. "But… perhaps it was not the wisest solution. We have all been showing support to Laura in many ways. I am concerned that you are throwing your eligibility away, when your heart is not in it."

"There you are wrong Doc. My heart is in this one hundred percent. That is the truth. Romance is not the only love. Eros versus Agape. I told God I wanted to operate more in Agape love – selfless, sacrificial, healing, generous love. That is when He asked this of me. I can hardly pray a prayer of that calibre and then deny its answer."

The Doctor shook his head. It was irrational and he was yet to be convinced that God operated in the irrational. "You have a remarkable way of looking at things Lloyd Jacobson. Even Jesus understood betrayal in the face of generosity. Please forgive our blindness and our Pharisaical stance."

Jake scowled involuntarily. Forgiveness is so all encompassing. It is easy to throw verbal assent around when the issues are not so impacting. His character was smeared, his motives questioned, his livelihood stolen, bereft of his friends. The Doctor reached out and put his hand on his shoulder. "You must forgive Jake – or the good you desire will be snatched away. But if you do, God will continue to use you to provide love to his people, regardless of your office within the Church."

He knew he was right, but at the core of his being, it hardly seemed enough. He wanted his position back. With a pang of insight he realised he had minimised the privilege of doing what he had been doing. "Oh Doc, I thought the announcement would be the hardest thing. But I was wrong. Walking it out is going to take more than I ever imagined the cost to be. Will you pray with me?" Doctor Wallace nodded grimly and they knelt together by the Creek, their hands gripped in violent submission to the will of God. "Heavenly Father I feel this is my Gethsemane. I need your courage to walk this road. I walk where I am misread, misjudged, mistreated. Yet I know it is nothing that Jesus did not do Himself. Help me to be faithful to You. Help me to follow Your walk selflessly. You are mighty and worthy of honour. Oh God forgive me if I have brought shame on Your name. But please... in spite of me, bring healing to Laura. Bring healing to your Church. They are your people and I know you love them more than I can. And yes Father, like the good Doctor says... I do forgive them. Your will, not mine... be done."

As they stood to their feet, Jake reached out and grabbed his hand in a firm handshake. Doctor Wallace pulled him in to a warm embrace. "God bless you son," he said with a lump in this throat. Jake blinked back the emotion that he felt... raw uncensored feelings. With God they would work out a way. He had given Laura his word. There was nothing for it now... but moving on with the plan.

Malachi and Bernard walked slowly up the narrow street to the house. They could hear the bellowing of fish-wives and the drunken abuses of sailors as they passed by the doors on the thin-walled cottages. "Do you think you can get her to come back to Wattle Creek with me?"

"I'm not sure Linnet would consider her health strong enough yet. We will see." Besides that – this last week, it was as if a dam wall was being erected against all the connection they had ever made. Linnet said she wasn't feeling well again. Perhaps her fragile body was failing.

"You understand that it is not for myself that I'm wanting this. Just for Laura. She needs her family... more now than when her mother was sick. You should come too."

"We will do what we can. Still, Laura has you..."

Mal snorted. "I no longer qualify remember? I am not family anymore."

"Well, that is your door then, isn't it?"

Mal blinked hard. He had been thinking of his loss... a sister that didn't exist. Suddenly the whole landscape released, like opening window shutters on a clear Autumn morning. He was not her brother!

Bernard smiled at the look dawning on his face. "You have my blessing," he said evenly, "...as her father."

The relief he felt was heady, and he almost considered feeling guilty about that, but no matter how hard he tried, from that point on, Malachi could not be disappointed.

They sat down while Linnet gathered some tea things. She glared at the two sitting on the lounge sharing some father-son moment. How dare they sit there like there was nothing amiss? She banged a cup on the tray and the handle broke off in her hand. She banged another. This time the whole cup broke... and another – the lip smashed. She lifted up the saucers and shattered them on the floor. How dare he! Tears came... tears held back in fear and silent suffering. Instantly Bernard was there. "Hush my dear, hush. Laura is safe... it is okay. We will go to her."

"Laura," she sobbed. "Laura? How can I face my daughter when the man I married has a family waiting for him back there as well? How can I lift the shame of that? For twenty years Mr Bernard! *Twenty* years I only thought of you... and the only thing that kept me going was that I believed you were holding on to what we had as well. Ha! The deception is exposed! You had not waited for me at all like you said. You selfish, self-righteous, hypocrite! All you needed to do was to stay away. Why did you come? What is more...I never guessed! How could I be so blind? You sit in there with your son – the very evidence of your unfaithfulness and you expect me to embrace him with open arms. How can I? How? Don't stand there as if you cannot comprehend what I say! Do you want to go back so that you can see her? That other woman? You're married. Our marriage is a polygamous lie! There is nothing you can say for yourself Laurie Bernard!"

Bernard stood stock-still – the violence of her accusations washing over him as he realised the confusion had exploded into a monstrous thing out of all proportion to reality. He had no idea his wife had been carrying this burden around so stoically. Her frozen remoteness now made sense. Then another thought shot through him: her expectation was unrealistic – that she presumed that he would wait for her, she demanded it like a ghost … even when he had no idea there was anything to be waiting for. To him, a marriage under these circumstances would not seem unreasonable. And yet he had waited… and the relief that he felt over the silent, lonely years was extreme. He said nothing for a long time.

Linnet groaned. "So, there is nothing that you have to say? Nothing?" Bernard went to take his wife in his arms, but she shook him off like a hideous thing caught in a spider web.

"Depends if you want to hear what we have to say," he said quietly.

Linnet looked up. The lack of remorse in his eyes was another knife in her chest. Was he so callused that he seriously did not consider anything to be amiss here? She had heard of people like this. Cult leaders who twisted the fulfilment of their whims out of women like a lemon… until all they left were twisted, dried up, bitter shells of people. Was her plight beyond repair? Why did she so desperately want him to reassure her? Why couldn't he tell her it was all a big mistake?

He looked over at Malachi who stood quietly by the door. Mal indicated the latch, and silently mouthed the words, *Will I leave?* Bernard shook his head.

"Tell her Malachi…" he said quietly.

Malachi raised his eyebrows and shrugged. "It would be better coming from you." There were shades of Laura coming through.

Bernard sat down and waited. He was not sure that Linnet would hear anything he had to say. Finally, she perched on the other end of the sofa. "I will give you one opportunity to defend your behaviour. You will not stay here anymore, whether you were married to her or not."

"Linnet, be reasonable. You can't throw me out before you have heard what was even..."

"Reasonable? There is nothing reasonable about being shown for a fool."

"I was never married! There was not even a relationship. Nothing. On my word! Laura went to Wattle Creek to look for her father. In relaying our history you referred to me as Mr Laurance, so that was the surname she was looking for – Lawrence." He looked to Mal for support of his story.

Mal sighed. Suddenly he didn't want to be so involved. "Lawrence is not a name around Wattle Creek district – so when that came to a dead end, she tried to fit together bits she understood from the story. She knew her father left the city and he was involved in the Union Church. My father was an elder in the church, and we had moved to The Creek not long after Reverend Bernard arrived to take up the pastorate. The name Lawson seemed a close enough fit of the evidence for someone desperate to find her roots. I believed it too – it seemed too close to be a coincidence, which meant she must be my half-sister. But it turns out she's not. My father's name is Matthew Lawson." Mal shrugged. He could not explain it any better. "Reverend Bernard just never figured in what we had constructed. All in all – it is a case of mistaken identity."

Bernard looked at his wife who was staring solidly at the faded lounge that she was sitting on. She said nothing, so he continued... quietly. "Malachi is not my son. I was never married before I came back here to ask you to be my wife.

Laura is still at The Creek fully believing that her father is Matthew Lawson – Malachi's father. Matt was killed a few years after I went there… in fact I conducted the funeral. He was a man respected in many ways." He paused. He could not be sure how much Linnet was absorbing. "Did you hear me Linnet? I have never been married. I have no children… other than Laura. But she still doesn't know that. I want us to go to her as soon as we can... on the train."

Linnet sighed, tears of fear spilling from her eyes. "It barely sounds plausible… that story is more fantastic than the accusation that you have been living with that other woman all these years. What is the truth?"

"It is simple – we go back to Wattle Creek. It is a tight knit community… everyone knows everything about everyone. They know how I lived all those years. *That* I could hide from you – but not from them. Not in a million years."

67.

Laura sat outside in Mrs Wallace's garden. Her abdomen swelling so her clothes no longer fitted. Why wasn't this condition one that could be hidden? It was embarrassing. Mrs Wallace had Sarah sew some new dresses. Laura fingered the soft fabrics, warm and shimmering in the sun. She had expected the dresses to be made out of cheaper, hardwearing fabrics. But no, Mrs Wallace insisted that dresses for ladies in confinement should be comfortable and becoming, because it was the easiest thing to feel uncomfortable and unbecoming.

Laura had never spent so much on clothes. It didn't feel right. Why would Mrs Wallace spend money on her? She could never repay what these outfits were worth. She sighed. She owed them so much. They had never once suggested board and lodging. It wasn't as if having her there did not cost, and more than just food and washing linen. There was a social price. People openly accused the Wallace's of entertaining iniquity and endorsing immorality. The Doctor was furious when he found his horse lame, which he said had been no accident. Then someone took to Mrs Wallace's garden with a hoe and reeked havoc on her precious plants. Yet the Wallace's did not blame her. Still they were kind to her, and they spoke of God having a purpose for her and her child.

A tear fell on her dress, the water bleeding into the weave of the fabric. Did everyone she touch have to go through pain? Why would God allow such awful things to happen? Where is the plan in that? She had expected a reaction to her engagement to Pastor Jake... well, no longer Pastor... just Jake. But she had thought it would be a kind of reluctant acceptance of her and her baby. She had wanted her son to have a name, a father. When an esteemed community figure came begging for the job, it was an opportunity for her child. It had seemed immoral to pass that opportunity up. But in the end, the result was she dragged him down to be a social outcast too.

"Oh God... it is not fair! This is not part of the plan you had for me. If there was a plan... it is destroyed!"

Joseph took Mary to be his wife... when she was an outcast. Her life was different to what she expected, but it had a plan.

Are you saying that you meant this to happen?

I meant for Lloyd to show you My love. Just as Joseph did. Just as Jesus did.

But he doesn't love me! He is just giving my baby a name.

Greater love hath no man than this: that a man lay down his life for his friends.

Greater love... greater love: the words lingered in her mind... *greater love.* A love that would give up everything for another. Love that would give up their own wishes... their own ambitions... their own romance... for another. That is what Jake had done: he was giving up his own romance for her. That is what Joseph did... he gave Another's Child a name. That is what Jesus did... he gave up His life... His heaven... for this life. To demonstrate a greater love... to his friends... and his enemies.

Love. A greater love. A love greater than trauma, a love greater than being abandoned; love greater than taking. A greater love that gives.

Laura sat in the sun soaking and bathing in the inner warmth that filled her and washed her clean, as the revelation washed over her. Tears came, falling on her pregnant body, washing away the shame and the humiliation. She was loved... her baby was not the product of hate... but grace. An instrument to show her love. And as if he heard, the baby moved and bounced in the understanding that he was loved too.

God, I am sorry. Please forgive me...

I forgive you.

God I have attacked You...

Can you forgive your attacker?

God I forgive him. God I have abandoned You...

Can you forgive your father?

God I forgive him. God I have hated You... without understanding who You are.

Can you forgive those who hate you without even knowing you or your circumstances?

God I forgive them.

And with that came release. Released to be free... and to love her baby... in the face of trauma and abandonment and hate.

"Nat, I came out here... to ask for a job."

Nat jammed the crowbar into the dirt, pulled up his hat and wiped his face on his sleeve, as he considered the man before him. "Sure I got plenty of work… not a lot of cash flow for an extra hand though. You know how it is since the fire."

Jake pursed his lips. He wasn't too keen on begging. "Well, at this stage, I can't afford my board at the pub. I'm just after a stop-meet – board and keep, until I can find something."

"You're at the pub?"

"Yeah – your mother… and I… thought it was best that I give up my room at the boarding house."

"Uh-huh…" He considered him carefully… and quickly gauged the lay of the land, but didn't pursue it. He was as stunned as the next guy, by the man's engagement. He had his own thoughts about it, and had wondered what was behind it. "Well, we can slap up another bunk – might have to be in the shed though. Only got my one room donger till the house is built. If you're okay with that, I could do with a hand."

Jake thrust his hand into his. "Thanks Nat, I appreciate it. I'll get my stuff… which isn't a lot… not surprisingly."

When Emmaline heard that he had engaged Jake's help, she was agitated. "Nat – I'm not so sure this is a good plan. You know what everyone thinks about this, including your mother."

"Mum had the girl in her house, and was looking after her for a while. That's where they met. It could be he really has feelings for her."

"That's not what I meant." He raised his eyebrows waiting for her clarification. She took a deep breath. "Okay – I don't know. It's just that Ali is really upset… and she was very good friends with him and Laura. She must know something… it doesn't feel right."

"Ali?"

Em nodded. "He has always come in to get his hair trimmed. He's the regular that Ali taught me basic trims on. But she won't allow me near him anymore. Last time he actually asked that I do his hair, but she refused to let me. It's just getting worse. I could swear that she was going to slaughter him with that razor. I'm not sure she is even safe. She cut him. No wonder he confided he's not coming back."

"She cut him?"

"I don't think it was on purpose… but Nat… she was absolutely livid. I had no idea what to do."

"Did she say anything?"

Emmaline shrugged bewildered. "Nothing."

"Well, sounds like he needs sanctuary – between my mother throwing him out onto the street… and your cousin taking to him with a machete…"

Emmaline put her arms around his neck. "Maybe we should not get involved. This whole thing is … awkward."

"Awkward and me get along fine. I gave the man my word. We've been good mates and he's in a bit of a spot…"

"A spot of his own making – by all accounts."

"Doesn't make it less of a spot, whether we take everyone's account on it or not."

"He might have lost his mind… for a *pastor*. The whole thing is not good."

"Oh, come on Em – It's not the first time a man couldn't…" He stopped as she cringed in disgust. "Look, I've spoken with him. He seemed okay… a little subdued perhaps... but given what's happened you'd hardly expect him to be frolicking with laughter."

"What about Mal?"

"What about him?"

"Well, I don't think he's going to be too impressed to come back to find out she's engaged to Jake."

"What's Mal got to do with it? He doesn't have a shine for her, does he? You don't think it's *his* kid?"

"Well... I don't know. He's been different... and when you look back... it's only since she's been here in Wattle Creek."

"Goodness – your imagination is something else. It could be... gee... I don't know... that he's growing up?"

"You don't need to use your sarcasm on me Nathaniel Lawson. I've said my bit... and I'll leave it at that. But you could do me the courtesy of respecting my point of view."

He grunted. Emmaline acquired a particular tone when she was unimpressed. "Em... I do mind your point of view. I just kinda think the stories you're hearing could be clouding your good sense. It's just gossip Em. We don't deal in that." He quickly backed down when he saw her eyes flash. "Still, maybe with Jake around we'll get to understand a bit more."

Emmaline softened. "Nat – caught you! You're as curious as any about what is going on here."

He shrugged and wiped his hands on his trousers. "I can't deny it. Smoko is over..." and he stood up and went back to dressing timber logs and stacking them to the side.

Jake didn't have much to pack up. He borrowed Wallace's buggy to move his few boxes out to the Lawson farm first thing on the weekend. He went in to visit with Laura before he left. He watched her sitting in the garden in a soft blue dress... her light brown hair shimmering in the mottled shade of the trees where she sat. She looked up when he walked across to meet her. There was something different... a softness. Was it the blooming of motherhood? Protectiveness swelled within his chest. "God I can make this work... with Your help, because you have asked it of me."

"Good morning pretty Lady... you look a picture sitting here in the garden. The perfect place for a confinement I would think."

Laura smiled. Perfect would be in the arms of a man – who romanced her as well as sacrificed for her. She tried to give it up... but it niggled her. A safe home was good... the offer generous, but she wanted the completed picture. Not just for her, but for her son... so that he could see his mother and his father being *in* love as well as tolerant and kind. She knew too well, there were worse things in a household, but the rainbow begged her forward. Was it unreasonably selfish? Was she being impossibly naïve? Was it just an illusion? She had to admit – probably yes, to all three. But she wanted to pursue it... to allow the possibility to exist.

Although Jake never said a word of it, Laura knew his passion had already been given to another. The thing that amazed her most was she felt no jealousy. She didn't even resent that this man, whom she believed would follow through and keep his word, was not able to grant her more. He had honestly offered what he could, but it left her feeling sad. It could have been a fairy tale had it been both ways – with both dimensions of affection between them. *God, help me to be gentle... to love him as he has loved me. Help me later, down the years... if the dream does not come to be... please, help me not to resent this moment and become bitter in regret... because I let go of the security option.*

She almost thought she imagined it... but a sweet pulsating in her spirit confirmed to her that what she was about to do was right. It felt like a test... a measure that she could use to trust God with her future... and not the man who stood before her.

Jake sat down quietly and looked at her, fascinated by her shape. It was beautiful; it bore life. Responsibility stabbed him again. "Laura, you know the church has let me go. I don't have a trade. I have spoken with Mr Tolbert at the school, but he does not have any teaching positions at the moment. Until I find a job, I am going to work with Nat Lawson, to help him on his farm. He still has a lot of building to finish before he and Emmaline are to be married... and he wants it done by Christmas."

She jolted as he spoke the name Lawson. Every time she heard it, it affected her. That is why she was doing this – so it would be different for her children. Jake saw her reaction and was concerned. "I will be living out there, but I will come and visit when I can. Laura, I want you to know that I will do everything I can to give you a good home. It may take longer now, but I am committed to this."

Her lips were pressed together thoughtfully. "I know. You will make a good husband. Jake..." She paused and quietly raised her eyes to him. "Jake… I want to let you know that I have forgiven my attacker. The pain in my heart… it is less now."

"Oh Laura… how brave you are." He wanted to say more… but felt unworthy. He had not walked in her shoes. He had no right to sound like a pastor now. Somehow, he had to become a breadwinner… a protector… and… his mind baulked at the rest. He would go down that road when he got to it.

"Brave?" She laughed. "That's the last thing I feel."

"But it is true. To let go of the past is a difficult thing." That he could say with great sincerity. It *was* difficult.

"Jake, I have something to say… and I'm scared… but I need to tell you this…" She swallowed hard.

He looked at her concerned and gently he reached to hold her hand. "I'm listening… when you are ready," he said gently, trying to reassure her of his care.

"Jake, I've decided not to marry you." She took the modest ring that he had given her and placed it back in his hand.

He reeled backwards staring at what she presented to him. He didn't know what to say – what to think. What was wrong with him? Would no woman ever accept a ring of his? He was trying hard not to be relieved. He had figured there was not much left that could wound him. Wattle Creek had pretty much taken the scoop on how to emotionally pulverise someone. But he felt like she had slogged the wind out of him. "Laura… I… I really believed that this was what God wanted me…us, to do. Will you reconsider?"

"Jake, I am so grateful. I have never known such generosity... but this is my choice too."

"But you said yes. I don't know what to say..."

"I'm sorry. I have talked with Mrs Wallace, and I have thought about it a lot. This is what I want."

"Why would Mrs Wallace pressure you? You don't have to do this. Perhaps you need to reconsider... think about it for a while. We will not do anything official until you are sure."

"Mrs Wallace didn't pressure me. She helped me to see my own reservations. I am sure."

"Even so... say nothing. Next week we will make it official. I want you to be certain. Please promise me you will give it a week." He returned the ring to her hand.

Laura nodded and slipped it back on her finger, but she knew in a week or a month, it would not change.

Jake stared at the ring that sat on her finger, but now it symbolised nothing. Had he been unkind... ill-mannered? Had he not given her enough space? Would God look on this as a failure? "Oh Laura... what did I do wrong?"

"Jake – nothing... nothing at all. I feel that with God in my life... there is another way, and I want to try it."

"But what are you going to do?"

"I'll stay here for a while with Mrs Wallace... until I can go back home to my mother."

"That's it? I..." He was floored. He hadn't really wanted this... so why did it hurt?

There were tears in her eyes as she took his hands and she kissed his fingers in a caress of goodbye. "Thank you, Jake for showing me a greater love."

68.

All the way out to Lawson's farm Jake went over and around what had just transpired. "Oh God, I didn't even want to do this… yet you asked. I tried so hard not to be the reluctant groom. Should I have been less frank, less honest? Yet I couldn't say what was not. Perhaps I should have tried harder. Maybe this was Your intention Lord… but if I wasn't going to marry her, why did I have to go through all of this? I have lost my job, my ministry. I've no income… my reputation is on the rocks; the town has lost any respect they may have had for me… perhaps even for You. Oh God… I seem to have got it so wrong. I tried to trust and honour You… but nothing has gone right. My one consolation was that I could say I had obeyed you… that we could build a marriage on that… but now, even that is shot."

Perhaps he had not even heard correctly. Had he gone off like a loose cannon, shooting off his mouth before his head and his heart were engaged? He wasn't sure anymore. At the time… it had seemed clear… but now, when it all came to naught… with nothing to show for it but a very long list of things that had gone awry, the clarity fogged over. Even for Laura, he wasn't good enough.

Did you act to be the heroic groom, or to emerge unscathed? Was your obedience pure?

Perhaps that was it. Perhaps his motives were screwed up. There was no question in Jake's mind about God's integrity. Of course, He is the infallible, the immutable, the all powerful, but Jake's humanity… oh, that was vulnerable to error. "God – how do I tell? Search me, O God, and know my heart: try me, and know my thoughts: see if there be any wicked way in me, and lead me in the way everlasting…" The horse plodded on, rhythmically rocking through the waves of confusion, remorse, trust and surrender. "Oh Lord, I did what I thought was my best. If it wasn't enough – I'm sorry. If my motives were twisted, contaminated by my selfish agendas, forgive me. Help me this day, to hear you more clearly, and follow you more obediently… without reluctance or fear, knowing that your plan is good."

In praying that prayer he turned a corner in his journey. He left behind the scenic vista of preaching and ministry and pastoral care. Now he was walking through a gateway to a new scene, a solitary life, of manual labour, and scraping out a living from the soil that was cursed from the Fall of Adam. By the time he turned into Lawson's gate, his heart was realigned and settled. He could continue. He would. Different was not bad… just different. It might take a little getting used to, that's all.

Nat pointed to the shed. "You're lodging is in The Hotel Grande," he said good-naturedly. He opened the heavy wooden door, and showed Jake a cleared out corner down the back. Nat had strung up hessian as a divider. A crude wooden bunk – more like a camp stretcher made from roughly hewn timber and wheat bags, slung together in a crude sort of hammock, had been put in there. A couple of wooden packing cases, which served as a table for the little kero lamp stood back to back. As Jake looked at the sparse accommodation, he thought of the Shunamite woman's hospitality towards the prophet Elisha. The room this woman built for the prophet had a bed and a table with a lamp also. Jake smiled. It was illustrious company he was keeping. No one could despise such quarters, in the light of that. He did think he might be borrowing the company of Nat's cat Pepper, when he saw mice running comfortably along the tackle and ploughs, and other salvaged burnt out bits and pieces of farming gear.

He unloaded his boxes and went back up to Nat's hut. "I'm taking Doc's cart back into town now. I'll be back in a couple of hours."

"Can you cook?"

Jake blinked. "What?"

"Food – the usual grub… can you cook it?"

Cooking was something he avoided. He had a couple of bad experiences, but nothing was beneath him now. Jake raised his hat to his employer. "I'm sure I could learn with a few pointers."

"Well, be back before sun-down and we'll get you those pointers."

Jake nodded. With the skills of a mess cook – he could join a droving outfit … or get a job at a shearing shed. Suddenly this different life had all sorts of possibilities. "Back before dark then."

When he rode up later that afternoon, he took the saddle off his horse and was rubbing him down when he heard a polite "Ahem," behind him. He flinched as if he had been caught with his thoughts plastered all over a billboard. He wondered if he looked as discarded as he felt.

"Oh Emmaline. Good afternoon."

"Nat wanted us to give you some cooking tips, so if you come up to the hut when you're finished... we'll get started."

Jake leaned over the back of his horse and grinned. "No worries Ma'am. At your service." It will be good to start doing something productive.

Emmaline look bemused and she smiled graciously. "See you soon then."

Jake was anxious not to delay the afternoon routine. He quickly washed up in the barrel by the well, and was heading towards the hut when he stopped dead. He heard the sound of laughter. Even though he could not see, he knew that musical tone. He forced himself to step forward. Ali was laughing and messing around with a ladle, her blonde hair falling over her shoulders as she danced about the rough bush kitchen. As she turned, her laughter died on her lips.

Jake stared back. Surely this was a joke. What was Nat up to? Was he going to suggest he take cooking lessons from Ali?

Emmaline ignored the tension that shot between them. "Hi Jake... we thought we would start with the fire. I'm not much of a camp cook, so I asked for help..."

"What's he doing here?" Ali made no attempt to hide her hostility.

"He's working with Nat for a while," said Emmaline quietly.

Jake averted his eyes. This was not good. He had to survive a week... a whole week! Perhaps Laura would change her mind after all. Perhaps she would say yes. For some reason, it was suddenly very important that Laura confirm herself as his fiancé – so that he would be committed and taken… and this would *never* be an issue… ever again.

"Emmaline – I need to see you inside. Now." Jake looked away as Ali grabbed Emmaline by the sleeve and pushed her inside the hut. Its thin walls did nothing to muffle her tense accusations. "What is going on? You know there is no way I would have come out here to help you knowing it was *him*. He is working with Nat now? Why wouldn't you tell me he was the new workman?"

"Ali – you said yourself that you wouldn't have come. I need your help – really. I can't cook… sure I do a bit in your Mum's kitchen, but out here with nothing but a campfire I haven't a clue… it will give me a chance to learn as well. It will help Nat so much having someone who can do the meals."

"You could've asked my mother."

"Ali…"

"No! You know how I feel. This is totally unfair."

"Well, just think of it as a hair cut at the barber shop – you won't let me near him."

"Em – there is a world of difference."

"Why?"

"That is my shop. He's going to be working here. That's different."

"You're still in charge. He is here to learn…that's all. Please – for Nat's sake."

"You've set me up."

"Ali… how could I know that you would not want to see him? He was your exclusive charge every time he came to the barbershop. This is just another place."

She could not deny it. "Don't make out you're doing me a favour…" She stomped out and banged the door behind her. She brushed past him barking as she went, "Set the fire. We need coals for dinner. We have stew on the menu tonight."

The train hissed steam as it pulled into the station. The guard blew his whistle and a few passengers alighted, trailing along the station platform. Malachi carried their cabin baggage while Bernard held Linnet's arm, supporting her carefully. The trip had drained her reserves. Mal spoke with the stationmaster who hailed a porter to fetch a cab. A spritely silver haired lady stopped them as they made their way to where it pulled up. "Reverend Bernard? Praise be… you've came back! Oh, the Lord provides in mysterious ways. It's sad times we see. The first time I laid eyes on that young whipper-snipper I knew he lacked the maturity to truly do the job. The young ones are so flighty, undisciplined, passionate."

Bernard gave her a firm smile and removed his hat. "You are looking well Mrs Hollis. Yes, the Lord's ways are unfathomable indeed. It is good to be home." Home. He hadn't expected the waves of nostalgia that assailed him as he set foot on the platform. Everywhere he looked it felt so familiar.

He helped Linnet climb wearily up into the buggy, as Mal stashed their luggage, strapping it on the back. "We'll go to Mum's boarding house Jack…" Mal said as he climbed up beside the driver. The driver leaned forward and carelessly flicked the reigns. Mal looked at Ol' Jack, agelessly carved in stone and asked conversationally, "So Jack. What's been happening?"

The old driver shook his leathery head. He was perplexed. "The place has gone turned on its head, Mal-me-boy. It ain't like it used to be, when we knew where we were, and what was what."

Mal chuckled. "The Creek doesn't change that much… ever. You're getting old, that's all."

"Old, it may be. Ain't ever seen the like of that business with the Pastor though. It is a terrible thing…"

Mal nodded absently. He had so much to tell Laura.

Jack hunched forward on his knees. "Never heard of a Pastor be'n sacked before. Rightly so… gone got himself a girl pregnant. But guess you knew that hey? Bringing the Reverend back."

Mal glanced at him sideways, his ears pricked. "Pastor Jake? Really?" It seemed the most unlikely situation. So, he wasn't a saint either. All these good men… falling from their pedestal. Suddenly Mal realised his father was innocent. Matthew Lawson had faithfully put his family first. Mal's anger had grasped at his alleged infidelity with both hands. He wanted him to be guilty. *Sorry Pa. I'll try and match the way you lived… but with a touch of realism. No halo.* Mal straightened in his seat. "So, who's the girl? Someone in the Church?"

"Na – some lass from out of town. He's marrying her, but it don't fix it none in my mind."

"Marrying her? Are you sure?" Mal shrugged. Maybe Jack was right... things had been changing dramatically.

"The Doc's Missus has been looking after the lass. Why they'd be getting involved in the whole unsavoury business, doesn't make sense to me."

Mal's mind went into a spin. Laura? Surely not! Oh, this was wrong! "Married?"

"Not yet, but it's a patched up affair if ever you saw one. It just don't ring true."

"Ain't that the truth!" Mal had to see her. Now. "Jack – take me to Doc Wallace's place. Straight away."

Jack raised his eyebrows slowly. More evidence the world had gone berserk. "Once people knew where they wanted to go... and went there." He turned the horse up the street. Bernard leaned forward from the back, a query in his eyes.

"Got to see her Bernard. Now."

"But Linnet needs rest. She's nigh to collapse."

"Jack will drop you straight off at Mum's. I just gotta..."

69.

Jake raised his eyebrows as he set to work chopping the wood. This was going to be one long afternoon. He duly gathered the kindling and wood, then set the fire – the way Nat had showed him on a few of his previous pastoral visits. It seemed such a long time ago. He felt the contrast between then and now. They were poles apart. He was hardly practiced enough to be proficient. It took more than a couple of attempts before he had the fire going. He looked over his shoulder at Ali, trying to gauge if she was softening any. She stood by the hessian draped lean-to with a look of severe determination on her face. She was not going to make this easy. His best strategy would be to learn quickly. Finally he banked the fire with larger logs for plenty of coals.

He stood up and wiped his hands on his moleskins. "And now?" Where was Emmaline? She at least helped buffer the tension. Hadn't she wanted to learn camp-cooking? Ali was driving him nuts.

Ali picked up a large wooden handled butcher's knife. "While the fire's burning down, we get the food ready. That way when the coals are right we can throw it on." She brandished the knife recklessly. Jake eyed it cautiously. "Here – chop the meat and veges." She threw a slab of salted beef onto the table, scattering a collection of potatoes, turnips, carrots, pumpkin and onions into the dust. Jake patiently picked them up and wiped them off. He diced the meat, and Ali indicated that it all went in the cast-iron camp oven. He added the vegetables chunk by chunk. "You'll need to peel the onions," she said. He knew that. The whole set-up was primitive. "A little water. I add sage when I have it… or oregano is okay." She tossed in a sprig of both from a couple of pots she had brought from her Mum's garden. "That's it. Not exactly a precise art," she said patronisingly.

Jake held his tongue. Simple, for the simpleton. Education wasn't Ali's calling, that's for sure. He was sure she could make the best of men seem stupid, but he felt he would rather play with a taipan, than ask her to clarify anything. Get bitten by one of those snakes, and at least you're dead within minutes. This was going to be a slow paralysing, tortuous death… and it would most likely take all week. It wasn't looking good.

Ali took off her apron. Jake paused. Surely, she wasn't going to leave now? "Ali – what about the fire? How do I set the camp-oven? Come on!"

She looked at him exasperated, as if the average toddler would know what to do. "Yes. Well you know… dig a hole, cover it with coals." She didn't elaborate.

"Well? Help me out. You'd get no points for tuition if someone was paying you to do this."

"And who says they are not? No one in their right mind would suffer this for free!"

He ignored that. "How deep? How many shovel-fulls? How long? Just stick to the facts."

She pursed her lips in a thin line. "I don't know… you just do it. Plonk it in the hole. Use enough coals to have a thin layer on the bottom, sides and over the lid. Two hours… should do it." She watched him struggle with it. When he queried if it was right, she shrugged. It wasn't perfect but it would do. She picked up her apron, wiped her hands, tossed it aside and walked away. She was wiping her hands of him.

Jake rolled his eyes. He had no idea why she should despise him so. It made no sense to him. He wanted to let it go... but he couldn't. "Ali!" He ran after her, and she kept walking. "Ali... will you stop? Now." She ignored him. "Ali!" He caught up with her and spun her around.

Her eyes flashing in the evening light, her voice cold like ice.

"Jake... I have nothing to say to you."

"Well that is the world's greatest lie. You've got plenty to say and I want to hear it."

"You're kidding right? You don't listen to anything I've got to say about anything."

"Ali – don't be daft. You've lost your mind. I regard your opinion over anyone else. Please... what have I done?"

She stared at him. Could he honestly not know? Did he really have no idea? Was she so, so, *so* unattractive that nothing stirred him? Was he completely immune to her as a woman? She couldn't stand the thought. "Forget it. You're thicker than the cross beam in Nat's shed."

"What? You're not making sense."

"I guess you're perfectly right," she said in disgust. "No judgment at all." She moved forward, but he stepped in front of her.

"That's not good enough. This is about me marrying Laura isn't it?" She was Laura's friend too. Why would she be so displeased with him?

"Bravo. The man has a sixth sense."

"Laura told me she explained it to you. You can hardly believe all the rumours that it's my baby. Ali – you wouldn't buy into that gossip would you?"

She screwed up her nose. "Your baby? If it was, that might make it the slightest bit reasonable."

"Why? She has no one... no one at all Ali. It is what I could do... her baby needs a father... a name... honour. In the face of such an atrocity, no one is there to offer it to her. I thought you would understand and support me in this. I was counting on it."

"There is no way, Lloyd Jacobson, that I would support you marrying..." She stopped suddenly and fled.

Jake stood shaking his head. Was she having another breakdown? He checked his pocket watch and went back to the fire. He waited as the sun dipped behind the horizon, and then lifted the oven out of the coals and called Nat to dinner.

Malachi stepped inside and wondered how he would start. Could she really have given her heart to a man so soon, so easily? He felt sick to the stomach. Sarah took his coat. "Miss Laura is on the back patio," she said quietly.

He stepped out onto the brick paved portico. Potted plants created a soft border around the perimeter of the stone chairs that made up part of the low wall. Laura turned as she heard his step. She let out a squeal of delight! "Malachi! You're back. Oh, it is so good to see you! It has seemed like forever." She flung her arms around him and he stiffened involuntarily. She was engaged to another man. She thought of him only as her brother. He tried not to react, but it was like asking an egg not to cook when simmering in boiling water. The physics of nature cannot be denied.

She held him. "Oh, I have missed you. I am so glad you are back."

He could feel her swollen belly against his... and the baby kicked. Mal held his breath for a moment, amazed by the lingering sensation of the movement. Finally, he held her at arms length. "Well, look at you... someone should tell you: Motherhood agrees with the damsel."

She blushed. How good it was to see him. "Tell me... did you...?" She left the question hanging.

Mal nodded, his heart breaking. How different he had thought this would be. "Your mother has come to Wattle Creek with me..."

"Mal! Really? Oh, thank you! I must go to her now..." and she went to grab her coat. Mal held her arm.

"Laura, she is exhausted... she needs to rest. You will see her when she has recovered from the trip."

"Is she well? Has it been too much for her?"

"I'm sure she'll be okay with some rest. She recovered from her previous illness. You need to take it easy too." He couldn't help himself. He felt protective. He didn't want her over excited.

She laughed at him. "You sound almost..." she shrugged. She was amazed the difference him being here made. She felt safe. She had a family – she didn't need to create one. God had already provided before she had asked. "You've changed since your time away. I didn't realise my mother would have this effect on you. I should have sent you ages ago."

He smiled at her exuberance, and almost felt reluctant to raise the subject but he needed to know the facts. "So... I heard there is a little controversy surrounding a particular woman and the local Pastor..."

She nodded coyly and smiled, drinking in the sight of him. How did her mother react? Did she freak out like Mrs Lawson?

"What's the story? I was told it was about you and Pastor Jake."

"He asked me to marry him."

So, it was true. She seemed so unmoved. She just stood there grinning at him. "And you said...."

"I wasn't sure to start with. I said yes... but..." Immediately she remembered her promise to say nothing until next weekend. Why did she ever agree? She knew what she wanted.

He grabbed her hand and stared at the ring on her finger. "That's great isn't it? You don't even know the guy. Why would he make such a proposal?"

"Actually, I know exactly why he made the proposal. You sound as if it is the most offensive thing to be married to me. I didn't expect this from my brother!"

"Don't hold back any secrets from family then. What was so incredibly urgent that you needed to get engaged the minute I am out of your sight?"

Laura stared at him. He was taking the family thing too far. "He said that... forget it. I don't have to explain his actions, or mine to you. He has been very supportive."

"That is obvious, isn't it?"

"He didn't have to Mal. We are going to announce the date on Saturday." She said it to sting him. If she accepted Jake, they might announce the date. She stared at him defiantly. "The Church has shut him out, now he's got no income and nowhere to live... you're mother refuses to have him at her place as well... because of me. Well – he never said that... but I know that's the case. He's had an awful time... and it's all because he chose to identify with me. No one understands."

"I can certainly get in that line. I don't understand it either. Do you love him?"

"No... well, yes... but not like that."

"Well you should – if you're going to marry him!"

"Mal – that's not fair. He's given up so much."

"And that makes it right?"

"It's not a bad place to start." Suddenly Laura was defending the very things that she had questioned herself. She didn't like his possessive accusations.

"But is it enough?" He wanted her to say no. He wanted her to say she desired more... he wanted to offer it... but she turned her back.

Laura walked out into the garden. She had to get space between her and her brother. She had enough pressure without him adding to it.

Mal followed her out onto the lawn. He stopped behind her. "My Dad isn't your father. Your mother wanted to explain it to you, but I thought you should know," he said, and then he turned and walked away.

Laura spun around but he had already gone. Matthew Lawson was not her father? Then who? Was she back where she started? Was this uneasy truce she had made with herself just an illusion? Was this knowledge her security... a history and identity she had grasped with both hands because knowing something, no matter how marred, was better than nothing? Had she fooled herself into thinking that God was enough? Was He really?

She sat on the grass, weak from the uncertainty that assailed her and was suddenly transported back to a little girl who would lie in her bunk at night and wish with all her might that Daddy would come and tuck her in. She cried and cried... and when she was spent, she lay on the lawn and looked up into the cloudless evening sky. No one should have to live without a Daddy... not her... not her little baby. No one. Perhaps she should say *Yes* to Jake after all.

70.

Dr Wallace came out as the long afternoon shadows started to fade in the evening light. "Laura? Are you okay? You've been out here a long time..."

She didn't want to move. She didn't want to go anywhere or do anything. "I'm okay."

He looked at her swollen eyes and tear-stained face... "Are you sure? There is a visitor to see you, but if you don't feel up to it..."

"No. I'm fine." She didn't feel fine. She didn't want to entertain visitors. The sour taste left in her mouth from Mal's visit lingered. How quickly it had turned from something so sweet.

"Come in out of the night air then. There's a dampness about it." He reached out his hand and helped her up. He took her arm and they went inside. In the sitting room sat a tall familiar face. He stood up as soon as they entered.

"Uncle Bernie! Mal didn't tell me you were here. How is Mum? Mal said she hadn't travelled so well." She went over and gave him a warm hug, and Dr Wallace excused himself. Laura realised again she did have family – good family... even if it didn't have the appearances of what she expected a family to look like.

"Your mother is tired... but otherwise fine. Her health has improved greatly. Laura..." He tried not to look at her abdomen. She looked so much like Linnet... twenty years earlier. This is how she would have looked... carrying his child... his daughter. "Laura... I've something to tell you. Your mother had wanted to tell you but she asked me to come to you straight away..."

"It's okay – Mal told me. Matthew Lawson is not my father. I just don't understand why Mum won't say *who* it is. I've asked so many times. Is it so shameful to be my father?"

A pained look came over Bernard's round face. "Oh, Laura dear. No. Never! It is an honour. You have to remember she was very sick... she is very protective."

Her frustration did not want to hear why. Her mother hadn't always been sick. Laura shook her head and she sat down wearily. Would she ever understand why her life was like this?

"Mal came back to the boarding house after he saw you, and given your reaction to his news we thought it best to delay it no longer. Last time we tried to strategise and break this to you gently – you left in search of your father before you knew the whole story. We don't want you leaving again without hearing this from one of us."

Laura sighed. Uncle Bernie was very good at rambling. It didn't matter. Her fabricated world was a fantasy. Perhaps it was better she would never find out the reality. Reality was so disappointing. Just like Malachi. He disappointed her.

Bernard looked at her concerned. "About a month after you left, your mother had a turn for the worse. She was so worried about you I thought she would not recover. But she did... slowly she came to terms with her life... and what she considered her failures. She eventually was well enough for us to go ahead with our plans..."

He faulted. He felt so afraid. He had a level of acceptance as a beloved uncle... but as her father? He nearly gave in and left, but he had promised Linnet... he promised himself. He struggled to continue. "Laura... those plans were... that... as soon as your mother was strong enough that we... we would be married. Laura, that's what we did – as soon as we could make the arrangements. We are married."

Laura leaned back in her chair. "Marr- married? Uncle Bernie... is that even legal? Isn't that...?" She shivered. This was not good. Surely God would condemn such a marriage.

Bernard quickly continued to reassure her of the validity of such a union. "Laura, it is fine... because... and this is what I need to tell you: I am not your uncle... nor your mother's cousin... I..." He didn't want to live without the whole truth, but he didn't want to lose what he had. He ploughed ahead... praying for courage to bolster his fading heart. "Oh Laura... I am so sorry. I never knew your mother was pregnant. I left where we were living in the city to go to the Seminary... and then she disappeared. When I couldn't find her... I took the first job that was offered to me... that was the call to Wattle Creek. I came here as their Reverend, and I worked here until your mother contacted me nearly two years ago. It was just as Linnet expected – if this news came out, it would be impossible for me to stay in the ministry. That is why I resigned immediately... that is why she was protecting me all these years."

She stared at him. "You? You're Mr Lawrence? How could I not know it was you?"

He looked out into the dark shadows of the past. "She used the name Mr Lawrence because... well, you know my name is Laurie... Laurance Bernard. Your own name, Laura Bernice, is your mother's tribute to our relationship as well."

"Why didn't *you* tell me?"

"We were worried about you coping with your mother's sickness... and this as well. We should have told you straight away... I know that now, but then, with so many pressures, we thought it best. Your mother wanted to give you some background. She thought that it would help you understand..."

"Understand? That I had to grow up without my father? How can I ever understand that?"

"Oh Laura. The number of times I have wished we could do it differently... but we can't undo our mistakes. We can only try and make amends. Please, forgive me..."

Laura sat mute. The anger at knowing the truth welled up and threatened to overwhelm her. Having it so close to her for all that time and being unaware... locked out in a conspiracy between the two people who should be there to protect and care for her. How could they? "I know you want me to be happy about this. I know you want me to understand. But I am sorry, I don't. I am not sure I ever will." She stood to her feet. "Tell Mum I cannot come and see her tomorrow." Then she left and went to her room.

Laurie Bernard leaned forward and put his head in his hands and wept. For the lost years, the lost opportunity to be family, the lost daughter he was deprived of when it counted... and now, when he thought he had found her, she was walking out of his life again. This time of her own choice. He wished he had said nothing.

Unbelievable bad luck. Ali was there the next afternoon to teach a different meal. "Why did you come back when my company is so repulsive to you? We can survive on stew," he said.

She looked up at him from where she sat tending the fire. He really did have no idea about this. "I am not some masochist. I was not kidding when I said I would not do this voluntarily. Nat offered to pay for this service by giving me some meat. It saves me having to buy it. Em is looking after the shop for the rest of the week. Even barbers need to take extra work if the opportunity presents itself."

Her spite and directness hurt. Would she seriously only be in his company if there was some pay off? How could they be mortal enemies? When did that happen? He retreated to the counsel of his best friend. *"God, please help me. I don't understand how this happened. I love her! And she hates me. Please help me reconcile with her. I cannot marry Laura without her blessing."* But for once his Friend was silent; and it frustrated him more that he wasn't given a solution, or absolved of his responsibility to right whatever wrong was committed.

He swallowed his pride, and cleared his throat. "Ali, I am sorry for any offence I may have committed…"

She grunted. "I doubt that sincerely."

Now that annoyed him. How dare she judge his motives! "You have no right to say that! Why do you assume my motives toward you are not sincere?"

She just sighed, and dumped some brushed potatoes in front of him. "Scrub the dirt off these…"

He dunked each one as instructed. It wouldn't make any difference if he made a meal fit for a king, it would still taste like mud – just like the water that washed the potatoes. Tension made the air he breathed rank in his nostrils. He was acutely aware that once he would have considered it a privilege to be tutored by Alice Dampier.

Then she pointed to a large blue warty pumpkin. "That's next."

He picked it up and placed it on the table. He took the large knife and lifted it high and stabbed it through with unexpected violence. "I'm not doing another thing until we sort this out. I can't stand it. I need to know what's going on."

Ali stopped and folded her arms. Once she might have been moved by such a display. "I'm paid to instruct… it is your responsibility to learn. Cut it into pieces about the size of a small potato," she said smoothly.

"This has got nothing to do with cooking and you know it. I want to sort this out now."

"And why all of a sudden do you get what you want?"

"Ali! Stop it. Just stop it. Down tools. We are going for a walk."

"Nat will not…"

"Rot. Leave Nat to me. Come now." He went over to take off her apron, but she swung out of his reach.

"Jake, I am not going for a walk with you. I am here for one reason only. I am obliged to do nothing else."

"Fine. We'll do it here. I don't mind. Exactly what are you trying to teach me?"

She looked at the stabbed pumpkin. "Roast pumpkin," she said firmly, picking up her own parring knife.

He lifted up his knife and sliced through the tough skin with force. "Is this the way to cut things up? You are quite the perfect coach, good as you are at cutting remarks." He hacked away with the action of a woodchopper, thrusting the blade through the tough woody skin of the vegetable.

"Well look at you – you're doing fine. Stab away. If you turn it over, you can stab it in the back. You have your own established history there." She lifted up the paring knife and threw it hard. It embedded in the wooden beam behind the bench.

He paused, lifting the knife in his hand high like a machete. "I have never stabbed you in the back!" And he brought the blade down hard splitting the piece in two. "You…" He stopped. He felt like a two-year-old, having a tantrum. He took a deep breath. "Ali. I don't understand what I've done."

"Sure! I cannot believe you have no idea." And I'm not going to confess to you my inner most feelings on *this* matter, she added to herself most emphatically.

"Please Ali… I'm dying here."

"No more than I am."

"You certainly don't look like a woman waning." He slashed at the pumpkin again in frustration. "Ali, the

636

independent…" Stab. "Ali the capable." Hack "Ali who needs no one!" Slash "You are not being fair!" Chips of blue pumpkin skin flew onto the ground.

She stared at the chopping board and the mutilated pieces of yellow pumpkin being placed to one side. Is that how he saw her? Of all the things he could have said, this unsettled her. Independent? Capable? Not Ali the air-head, or Ali the flighty, or Ali – the pathologically co-dependent? She faulted. The rhythm of her attack disrupted. "I'm not being fair? I thought that is what you wanted," she said faintly. She turned away and started to sort through the few remaining wilted carrots in the vege box.

He heard her muffled comment as if it had been blared through a mega-phone. She thought independence is what he wanted? Is what he wanted important to her after all? He plunged the knife through the pumpkin, into the chopping board and hunkered down beside her in the dust. "Ali, why would you think…" He couldn't even frame the question properly. He looked at her hunched shoulders striving so hard for control, sorting through carrots as if her life depended on it. "Ali?"

"No Jake, I am not putting myself through this anymore. You do what you can." She stepped around him, picked off her apron and flung it down.

It was as if his eyes were opened, and suddenly he saw a transparent heart that ached to have him understand her vulnerability. He was shocked, and instinctively went to respond. Oh Ali! For so long this had been his greatest hope. He cringed at his own blindness.

She saw him go towards her and then hesitate. She turned away and walked unsteadily from the lean-to. She leaned heavily on a tree scarred by the marks of the fire that ravaged the farm, her heart beating wildly. Jake went after her and stood on the other side of the tree, out of sight and just out of reach. He didn't trust his feelings. Especially now he had to be careful. He felt her tearful, wordless declaration and he wanted to soothe away all the things that he had put her through. "Oh Ali… I didn't know. I thought I understood you… but I didn't know." His hand shook violently as he wiped his forehead. How could that happen?

Ali moved so her eyes were able to lock in on him, anguish filling up all the spaces by the things he didn't say. Why wouldn't he respond? She waited for him to say something, anything, but he didn't. He couldn't without betraying everything he had devoted to God through his commitment to Laura. He was not yet released.

Ali closed her eyes in pain. Things could not get much worse. She knew without a doubt that he understood perfectly what her heart and mind felt. Now that he had an explanation he most likely despised her weakness. Hadn't she said she didn't want to be attached; that she wanted to stay independent? He obviously scorned her lack of commitment to those things she had spoken so strongly about. Finally, she forced her feet to move. "Well, at least that is out of the way. We had better put this camp oven in the ground or dinner won't be ready when we are." She turned away, tears streaming down her face, unseen.

Jake wordlessly went through the motions. Again coals were shovelled around the oven, and he silently filled up the billy for tea. He could not speak... not even the common courtesies. All he wanted to tell Ali was the relief and joy and agony he felt; that his heart was bound by the very same pain. But how could he say such a thing when it was he who had extracted an unwilling promise from Laura for another week... 'til Saturday. Then Laura would give her final decision. But what if she changed her mind? It was a trap of his own devising and the spring was tight, ready to trip at the slightest movement. Helpless and alone, when he lay on his bunk that night; he could not sleep, his thoughts consumed by Ali.

71.

Linnet stood by the door, drinking in the sight of her daughter, alive, well… and blooming in motherhood. Her heart leapt with relief. She could not be absolutely certain she was okay until she saw Laura sitting in the garden, her hat shading her face, as she quietly read a book.

Linnet nervously chewed her lip. *God, what if she will not see me?"* She hadn't wanted Laura to see her faded and sick and weak again. Almost on cue, Laura looked up and saw her mother. "Mum!" she started to her feet, her heart pounding.

"Laura!" They clung to each other for such a long time, hardly moving for fear the other might fade and disappear.

"Oh, my baby. How I have missed you," she whispered into her hair. A cramp crept up into Laura's leg, forcing her to hop away as she tried to stretch out the muscle around the awkwardness of her shape.

"Here darling… sit and let me massage it out." Linnet's slight fingers, thin from sickness, gently kneaded the muscles and she felt the tension knot release. She smiled indulgently. "Malachi tells me I am going to be a grandmother," she said as if there was no visible cue for her to make such an assumption on her own.

Laura frowned. He hadn't come back. He was not her brother, and he felt he had no further part to play. She had to admit: it was probably true, but it didn't lessen the pain. Without warning she felt tears sting her eyes. "Oh Mum, what am I going to do?"

"Sweetheart, hush. We're here now. We will make a plan. There is no need to be anxious. You can adopt the baby if you wish."

Laura started at the suggestion. Her mother was completely and totally a hundred miles away from what she was actually meaning. But it was complex, and the energy to explain it was too much. She let it ride and nestled back into her shoulder – a favourite position from when she was little. *Malachi Lawson, we were going to make a plan. Where are you now when I need you?*

They sat together, saying nothing for a long time. Eventually Laura went to speak just as Linnet started to say "Darling, I…" They both stopped and laughed, linking little fingers in a wishing game from her childhood. "You first Sweetheart."

Laura almost went to protest, but her mother insisted. Laura held her baby shape. "How do I describe it? I… have felt that everything has been ripped away… and now, gradually… except for one thing… I feel it is being gathered back together."

"One thing is missing? What is that?"

"I dream of a husband…"

"But you are engaged to the Pastor. Is this not what you want?"

"Jake is a good man. Even when the church stood him down, he did not renege. He would be a great father. God has provided the impossible…"

"Believe me, you will also have a husband. Why are you hesitating?"

"Mum... I told him 'No'. But he insisted I give it a week, so that I don't make a hasty decision; to have time to think about what is best. Perhaps he was right. Perhaps I will accept."

Linnet looked away. Would her daughter's young years also be robbed of a man who loved her? *Oh God, please – not my daughter too. Spare her that loneliness... the agony of being alone.*

"Laura darling, please... consider. You have a great offer of marriage. Being alone... even with the best of intentions is a hard road to travel when you have a young baby... and a little child... and decisions to make... and nights to nurse fevers. It is hard to try and create a family and have no one to share that purpose with. Companionship may not sound very glamorous, but dear, from someone who walked this other road... the alternative it is not the easiest journey to travel... alone."

"Why is the alternative always being alone? What if someone can love me for me? Not for my pregnancy, not my baby ... or my tragedy. Why is it so bad that I want more?"

Linnet stared at her daughter and she saw shades of her own idealistic stance so many years ago. "Laura, I see in yourself a reflection of how I was when I was your age: strong... stubborn... intense. I sacrificed my own desires for what I thought was right and best. But the truth is, years of hard reality tempers the best intentioned high-flying principles."

"You know Mum, I don't want to say that I resent what you did. I get it – in a way... but I have thought so hard since Uncle Bernie... well, Bernie, came over the other night. It is exactly this that makes me want to shoot higher. I know I don't want this baby to grow up without a father… this is my dilemma. But more than that… I want to live with a husband who is in-love with me… not just make do. If I intentionally move now – of my own choosing, I eliminate the possibility – the hope of that forever. You had that… and I lost my father… but you still had the man you love. Mum, if I marry Jake… I will lose that part of being a wife, for the price of a father. Jake is a good man. He has offered more than I can ever repay him for, and I will appreciate that forever. But is that the price of a marriage? I'm not sure… It might be enough, but I don't want to do it until I am sure."

"Perhaps in time this will come as well. Arranged marriages have had less to work with. This is not a bad thing."

"I know that. I know it. But…" She shrugged. How could she explain the longing in the pit of her stomach? It was not logical, it was not sensible… it was not even fair on the man who offered her everything in his hand so selflessly. "God has promised to be the father to the fatherless. He was for me… Perhaps that is enough for now. I am not brave enough to eliminate the hope of more from the canvas of my future forever just yet. I hope Jake does not hate me for it."

Malachi tried to stay away with his head… but his heart would not let him. He felt bound by something that was stronger than genetics. He had fought so hard against Laura being his sister and now he understood why. He felt his throat constrict when he thought of their last parting. It was a miserable business. He could not consider giving it up, because something within

643

compelled him to fight. He stared at his unshaven reflection in the mirror above the washstand. He hadn't slept. He looked like refuse.

Malachi had always won his fights by going in hard and never relenting. Only once did he come undone; by a weaker fighter who fought with his head. Until that fight, brawn had always been enough. After that encounter he had silently studied his opponents, and became smart *and* relentless: a combination that left him undefeated. He knew he could go professional with some real coaching. How was he fighting this time? What winning manoeuvre would ensure victory in this ring? There had to be something more than weaving and ducking and fancy footwork that would make Laura, the celebrity looking on in the box-stand, take notice of the players in the spot-light. The true winner would be the one she presented the medallion of her heart to.

Posh and twaddle. He splashed cold water over his face. Had he completely lost his marbles? He wished he could just drag Pastor Jake into the back alley and knock him out cold. That would be quick and painless, but he knew he was fighting a more sophisticated game. Would any woman be sufficiently taken with a street fighter when they already had a respectable offer? What would Laura need when she had her baby to raise? What did *she* want? He stared at his reflection again, then grabbed his razor and slashed it back and forwards on the leather strap that hung behind his door. What would it take to be a father as well? He had no role model to lean on. As he thought despairingly about the odds, it was as if a firm hand rested on his shoulder. *You have me.*

He leant forward on the washstand and closed his eyes. *God – I've got precious little time and no money. This is hardly a tempting offer.* He lifted his gaze and challenged the man staring back at him in the mirror. He wasn't going down without a fight and he was willing to wage war with his wits more than his fists if that's what was needed. Within seconds he finished his shave and decisively changed his shirt. He went out and delivered an envelope to the hand of Sarah. "Please give this to Miss Laura," he said when she answered his knock on the door. She raised her brow and nodded without a smile. Next he went for a walk… to the blacksmith, the saddlery and then across the street to the cobbler.

72.

Dr Wallace came to the boarding house and knocked on the door. Josie answered the door with a reserved nod. "Did someone call you? I didn't know anyone was ill."

"I've come to see Reverend Bernard. Could you let him know I am here to speak with him?"

Josie quietly moved aside to let him in. Doctor Wallace sat in the Lounge, his head nodding respectfully in prayer. "*Your will be done on Earth as it is in Heaven...*" He stood when he entered the room. "Reverend thank you for seeing me. Did you want to take a walk?" They went outside into the back yard. There was none of the carefully manicured gardens of Louise's gardens, but it offered some fresh air. "Reverend, the Congregation has asked that I talk to you on a delicate matter."

This was only a matter of time. Bernard took a deep breath and braced himself. It pained his heart that he had hurt those he had spent so many years trying to reach and touch. Doctor Wallace looked to the ground, as if he was willing it to rise up and swallow him. "They are asking that you consider letting them reinstate your call to Wattle Creek."

Bernard looked stunned. Surely, he had heard incorrectly. "Sorry Doctor? What is it they want?"

"They want you to come back as our Minister."

"But what about Jake... Lloyd? He will be my son-in-law."

"They feel that they cannot hold the sins of the son against the father."

"But it was I who resigned. Surely you understand that it was because I am not blameless in this matter. Linnet and I discussed this before we came. It is our decision not to hide or deny what has happened or the circumstances behind Laura's birth. Pastor Jake is covering a great deal in grace by marrying Laura. I sincerely cannot endorse the idea that marrying her is a sin. Surely the extremes of these views are incompatible with holding the office."

The Doctor felt relieved. He hadn't expected the balance of reservation for such an offer. Perhaps he was the right man for the job after all. "Are you rejecting their invitation?"

Bernard sighed. He had a wife to consider. She may not want to move to Wattle Creek. They had already assumed that Laura and Jake would move away from here after the baby was born. "I... I don't know. I need time to consider... and pray."

Laura looked up when the door opened and the envelope was delivered on a tray. All morning she had gone over and over the visit with her mother. She was no closer to understanding what she should do. *God, I'm in a place where I don't know what is right or best or even proper... please help me!*

Laura asked who delivered the letter. Sarah hardly paused as she responded with downcast eyes, "He didn't say..." is all she said.

This was an unexpected diversion, and it was a relief not having to think about her problem at least for the moment. She tore open the paper, and sat amazed as rose petals spilt on to her bed cover and a little lady beetle crawled out from under his blanket of petals and flew to its freedom. A flicker of hope shot through Laura, as she searched through the petals for a note, or an acknowledgement... but there was nothing. Slowly she crushed the petals between her fingers absorbing the last of their lingering fragrance. *Please God, please... You know what is best.*

Ali stood watching Nat as he pegged out the foundations for the house. The start of construction had finally arrived. It was a shame that Em was not here for this moment. They had worked so hard on this together. "So, you and the Pastor sort it out yet? Em said you were like two cats in a bag the other day."

"Nat... I cannot stay. I wanted to let you know."

He looked at her, trying to read what was behind her distress. Sure, it was inconvenient, but that aside, he hated to see her upset. "Has Jake done something? I'll knock his lights out if there's been anything inappropriate. Damn it – the man's engaged. I thought he would be safe."

Ali sighed. Jake would never be safe for her anymore. She could no longer pretend. *God, this is a nightmare beyond my imagining. Please help me.* "Nat I'm sorry. Don't blame him. It is me. You can tell Em that the Shop is hers. I'm going..."

"Going? For good?" Ali nodded. "Hang on girl... leaving everything? You gotta think before you take such drastic measures. What can be so desperate?" He looked at her face and immediately swore in amazement. "You've gone and got bitten again."

Nat was Nat, and her eyes welled. "I tried not to. I tried… but it has happened. Now he knows. I thought that perhaps he didn't love her, but I was wrong. He's going ahead and marrying her. I cannot stay here. I cannot. I'm sorry Nat."

Nat took her and put his strong arms around her. "Oh Ali, I wouldn't have asked you to come if I knew the extent of it." He held her for a long time, desiring to protect her again from the hardness of life. To be eluded twice of reciprocated devotion, with the best of intentions, seemed incredibly unfair. Finally, she settled, drawing on his strength. "Don't worry about the shop. We'll work it out. Em and I… we'll do whatever you need." Finally, she stood back, and straightened in determination. Nat watched at her in admiration. She had grown so strong. "Hmm. Then I take it the man can't cook?" he said.

Ali gave him a wistful smile. "He needs a wife, and unless you like stew, you need a cook."

He looked at her keenly again. "Are you sure that he's in the clear? I can go and sort this out."

Ali dried her eyes, slowly dabbing their moisture. "I tried to think if he provoked me. He didn't Nat. He couldn't. I know he wouldn't, not intentionally. I think he was in shock when he realised. Perhaps I shouldn't have let him see; but I guess I wanted to be sure."

"And now…"

"Wattle Creek isn't big enough. It is time for me to seek a larger horizon."

The next envelope was delivered just on sunset. Sarah raised her eyebrow again and took it inside. Laura looked at the tray and recoiled. Did he feel he needed to retract his wordless message of contrition? Did he mean to clarify it, to say that it was not what she thought or what she had hoped?

Sarah stood patiently. "You won't know deary… until you open it."

Laura reached out to take the note, and Sarah carefully wiped the tray over with a cloth from her apron pocket delaying her exit to satisfy her curiosity. Laura looked to Sarah for guidance. "Really? Should I open it now?"

The older lady nodded. Laura slowly ran a finger along the paper. Again, there was no message: just a little lady-bug that clung to the paper…and a strange token that she held in her fingers, rolling it backwards and forwards in a thoughtful manner. What ever did it mean?

Josie came in with cups of tea to the living room where the Reverend sat with his wife. "Please Josie, take a moment to have tea with us. You are always busy looking after your boarders."

Josie looked irritated. If Laura's story was true this woman had known Matthew. With a kind of morbid fascination she had tried to find out more, but always there was little opportunity to ask questions failing an out-and-out interrogation. That was not the only reason she hadn't demanded they leave. The reality was that they would be gone shortly anyway. With the Pastor no longer taking a regular room, it seemed practical to let them stay just a couple of nights. It was a moral compromise that was heinous to her, but expedient, if she was to meet her rent by the end of the week.

Josie put down the tray and sat impatiently, looking at her work roughened hands. So much had changed since Reverend Bernard had left. How could he be involved with such a tramp as this? He had seemed such a moral man. But then appearances were deceiving. The couple sat sipping their tea and offered some courteous social chit-chat. Josie barely responded. She was focused on Linnet and her connection with Matthew. "Do you know anyone here in Wattle Creek?" she asked Linnet eventually, trying to sound detached and polite, glaring into the teapot to check the level of water and the quality of tea-leaves.

Linnet sipped her tea. "No, not really – just Bernard… and well, Malachi now of course. Your son is a fine young man."

"Yes, he is. Of my three sons he most favours his father in looks." Josie looked at her keenly. There was no reaction.

Linnet considered her cup before she spoke. "When Malachi came to us about Laura, there was a terrible misunderstanding. I thought Laurie was Mal's father. As you can imagine – I was very angry. I didn't… couldn't… speak for days. I felt betrayed by a very old deception."

"Why would you think someone other than my husband was Mal's father?"

"It's hard to explain. Malachi believed his father was Laura's father also... so to me, because I knew that Laurie was..." Linnet reached over and held Bernard's hand.

Josie interrupted, trying not to sound shocked or relieved. "You Reverend? You are Laura's father?" Josie felt she should have been horrified by the immorality this news implied, but her emotions seared her thoughts, burning everything else away. Matthew had been true to his declarations of devotion. He was straight as a die. She knew that. She always knew that.

Linnet put down her teacup. "Yes, before we were married, and before he was involved in the Church. We were young and I was barely mature enough to confront the reality of everything that meant. We have made some terrible mistakes. But we have made an uneasy acceptance of these things." She reached forward and picked up her cup again, taking a moment before she continued. "Then all of a sudden Malachi's assertion turned everything upside down. All I could see was the knowledge that, if what he said was true, it meant that Bernard had a mistress – or worse... another wife... during his time in Wattle Creek... while working with the church. And I had not found out until after we were married ourselves. It was all very twisted... and very confusing. Suddenly I was living with a stranger and married to someone I did not know. But then, when one is angry, it is hard to see what actually is."

Josie stared at the woman sitting on her lounge, sipping her tea. Suddenly she was no longer the enemy, but an ally... someone who had walked the same confusing agony as herself. The pointlessness to her pain, based on falsehood and half-truth, however misguided and unintentional, flared her anger up again. Josie's knuckles started to turn white and trembled as she held her cup. "Then you may understand how I felt when I was told that my Matthew was Laura's father. I tell myself I didn't believe it, but there must have been some doubt in my mind. Perhaps I was angry that I doubted. I wanted to kill someone." Josie expected that her earnest confession would be judged with horror or at the very least, some serious 'tut-tutting'. Linnet nodded and sipped her tea as if Josie had just noted the sun sets in the west. It sounded like a normal everyday reality.

Bernard looked at this woman with whom he had walked side by side for many lonely years … and for all their togetherness, there was never a connecting. "You have been angry for a very long time Josie. Then something happens that allows all the emotion to blast its way through. Your reaction may not have been just about Matthew's fidelity, or Laura's probing questions. It could be related to all the times you were grieved… for your loss, and being left unprepared, and him not being there for the boys. Is this possible?"

"But I love Matthew. How could I be angry with *him*? It was not his fault… it's not like he wanted all this…"

"Of course not… but doesn't that make it harder to explain and accept? It seems wrong… and unreasonable… and unfair when you love him so much. How could it be that you should feel this way? It seems so wrong that you push it down and not recognise it… or discuss it… and so the pressure builds…"

Just then a kookaburra burst into a hilarious cackle, laughing his song in a mockery of the things that Josie felt.

653

"See," Josie said, "that bird thinks this is foolishness... and I would agree."

"It is no joke Josie. If you don't deal with this, perhaps next time something will snap... beyond your control. Even if it never gets to that, you will never regain the peace you had when you were married."

Josie gasped and stared at him in disbelief. What right did he have to say something like that? But Bernard continued gently. "You forget Josie. I was there. I saw how you were back then. You have always thought your joy and your peace were connected only to Matthew. But it wasn't... it was the way you related to God in those days. Matthew was a beautiful part of your life, but he wasn't the source of it. I'm not sure you understand that..."

Again the kookaburra burst out laughing, mocking the seriousness of the moment. Bernard listened to it for a moment. "Listen to that kookaburra... it is a bird known for its joy. But I have always been fascinated by the knowledge that this bird, in all its laughter, devours snakes - poisonous deadly reptiles, for food. It feeds on them. But there is one rule that it must obey if it is to retain its joy. It *must* let go of the snake and drop it to the rocks. Only this will kill its potential danger, and allow the kookaburra to laugh. If it doesn't let go of the snake at the right time, it can whip up and bite it. Hanging onto it will destroy it. Anger is your snake Josie. If the Kookaburra holds onto the very thing that it was meant to let go of – it becomes the instrument of its death. If it lets it go... its power to harm is broken and it can be used to make it stronger."

Josie quickly stood to her feet. "I have work to do. I cannot sit and listen to this foolishness all morning." And she left clanging the teacups on the tray all the way to the kitchen.

Every day, another envelope arrived. Each time her heart jumped, as she tore open the seal to find what was inside. It was always something small and unusual... accompanied by a lady-bug. By Friday night, Laura laid out the strange collection on the small occasional table in her room. Laura stared at her bizarre assortment as she readied herself for bed. She wished she could be certain what the cryptic messages meant. Never once did he deliver them to her in person. Never once were they signed, except by a lady-bug. Only Malachi knew of this special motif of their friendship. She was mesmerized by the intrigue.

Suddenly she had cold feet. The future you can see is much safer than a table full of strange symbols. She hadn't been able to tell her mother of these odd collectables, and Sarah nodded sagely as if she understood it all very well, and then murmured about the lack of bench space and the extra dusting that they were causing. Slowly Laura climbed into bed. Tomorrow was Saturday. Tomorrow, she gave away her future... into the hands of God.

73.

Laura woke on dawn, her heart beating wildly. She got out of bed, gathered her treasures into a pouch, and picked up her shawl. She penned two notes and left them on her pillow and slipped into her boots.

Jake arrived at nine o'clock precisely. One week. That is what he had asked of her. Mrs Wallace answered the door, and offered him quiet solitude to read the letter. He knew then Laura had not changed her mind. He sat down weakly and Mrs Wallace sadly shook her head as she watched him reverently slip to his knees, the open letter trembling in his hand. She closed the door quietly to allow him space to mourn in private.

How long he stayed there searching his heart he could not say. He doggedly denied it the satisfaction it screamed for... to scramble to find Ali. *"Oh God. This is not going to look good, but I have to let her know. Please God. Don't close this door now... please... don't let it be too late..."* He could only pour out his heart to his Friend, asking for a reprieve, to at least leave with the opportunity to bare his heart to her with the truth. Jake was not sure how long he knelt there, restrained by the realisation he may have missed by a fraction of a moment, the opportunity to satisfy his desperate desire. The silence of his refuge closeted him in. He didn't register the comings and goings of the busy Doctor's home. He did not hear Malachi arriving at the house. It was only later that Jake realised with guilt, he had not thought of Laura at all.

When Sarah opened the door to Malachi she looked surprised. He was clean-shaven, his jacket brushed and his boots polished. Mal held in his arms an enormous bunch of wild daisies. "I want to deliver this one in person, if I may impose?" he said, bowing slightly.

"Miss Laura left you this..." Sarah said quietly, slipping him the note. "Mrs Wallace doesn't know about this one..." she whispered as she firmly closed the door in his face.

Malachi turned away stunned. Why wasn't he allowed to see her? He had to admit he was treading a very tenuous line, recklessly courting one already engaged, but his rationale was he had the smallest window while she wasn't yet married. He walked down the street out to the edge of town. He went off the road and sat down on a log, the flowers falling beside his shoes as he tore open the envelope. A little lady-bug tracked over the simple note. *"Meet you there. You know where."*

His face relaxed and he smiled as he put his finger in the path of the little bug. It climbed onto his nail, and he brought it up to his face peering at it closely. At least she would see him. At least now he could try and communicate more clearly than his last petulant outburst. He tucked the lady-bug back into the envelope. "Patience little mate... you can have your freedom later. We have somewhere to be!" And with that he grabbed the scattered daisies, now looking just a little drab and he bolted.

As he came towards the railway bridge, he hesitated for a split second. What if she wasn't here? What if he didn't know where they were to meet? He inhaled deeply and plunged around the corner breathless from his hurry. He burst in on her solitude, and Laura looked up smiling.

"I knew you would come…"

He dropped the flowers at her feet, his heart in his mouth. "I was hoping I had it right."

"The messages I received were more cryptic than that…"

"How did you go? Did you understand them all?" He felt again the risk of the gamble… the thrill of the card table fading in comparison of seeing her here, waiting for him.

Laura stood up and moved back into the shadows of the bridge. Laid out on her shawl was each little token. "No, not really… but I understood the lady-beetles. Each little bug spoke that blessing you once told me. I could wait for the rest."

He took her hands and turned her around. "Laura, I am not kidding here. I want you to know that I will not share my affections with a priest. I am not your brother. You have to choose."

She looked at him. "I already have," she said softly. "That is why I came. I couldn't face his disappointment."

"You've already told him?"

She shook her head, and turned away, embarrassed by her weakness. "I chickened out. Last time I told him, he talked me into another week. What if he insisted again, and I gave in? So, I wrote him. I didn't trust myself."

"You told him a week ago? Before we came back? But you said…" She held up her left hand and shrugged. The ring on her finger had been placed firmly in the envelope with her note. He stared mesmerised by what he saw, her fingers bare and un-pledged.

"He wanted another week. After all he had offered me, I thought it was only fair. But I knew, before you came back."

"What did you know, about him or about me?"

"Only him…"

"But you didn't tell me!"

"I wanted to, but I promised him a week. How could I tell you?" It almost felt like they were arguing over the colour of the sky – something that happened outside her control. She turned away. Perhaps she was wrong. Would they always argue?

"Laura, please… I'm sorry. I felt trapped. When I finally found out what I wanted all along, it seemed it was snatched away from me. I know why I fought so hard against the knowledge that… well, I didn't want us to be brother and sister."

She turned back to him, the tears in her eyes now welling up for a different reason. She went to the shawl and picked up the first little gift and handed it to him. He held it between his fingers: a hand-forged iron nail. He swallowed hard before he spoke, his voice hoarse from emotion. "Nails hold things together. My heart is nailed to yours, and I want to start building a life with you. That will take many nails… like this one… made by the blacksmith in the forge… the fire of experience. Apprentices make the nails. They might not be great at this when they start, but with practice they get better… straighter… stronger."

He reached down and replaced it on the shawl. Then he picked up a small leather heart-shaped pouch lashed together with fine leather lace through holes punched around the edge.

"There are two hearts… separate, and now tied together… to make one heart… but a heart that can hold things." He put it back beside the nail.

Next he picked up a tiny horse-shoe token, made from a cobbler's tack. "A little horseshoe… traditionally for luck… but I don't think Christians can talk about luck because God doesn't deal in chance. But he does deal in blessings, and it is the shape of the letter "u" … so for me, this is about how *you* are a blessing to me."

He laid it beside the heart and then picked up a pile of small sized playing-cards taped together in an awkward way. One twist and they stood together in a little card house. "A house… made of cards. My history is not great… I don't have a lot of good things to be proud of… but they've made me who I am. I will not gamble again, that is my pledge to you. I will put my energy into providing a house." He stood it next in line and then picked up the final symbol. There were three little gum-nuts. The two large gumnuts had little faces chiselled into the wood with simple lines, making little gumnut dolls, and with them was a little carved baby-size gumnut. "But a house without a family is just collapsible cards, so more than just having a house Laura … I want to build a home."

He lifted the roof of the card house and placed the gumnut family inside. "See…" He pointed to the first three tokens, lying side by side: the hand forged nail; the small leather heart-shaped pouch; and the tiny horse-shoe token. "See, together they say *I* ♥ *U*. Laura, I do love you and…" he pointed to the little house…" I want us to be a family together."

Finally, he picked up the little heart-shaped pouch again... and gave it to her. She took it gently, the symbolism of what he had shared stunning her into silence. She opened up the little pouch and cried out in amazement. "This wasn't here before. It wasn't!"

Inside was an orange lady-bug and a tiny band of twisted wire, and she lifted it out carefully, as he slipped it gently on her finger. "This is my ring to you... until I can buy a real one... if this is what you want..." he added quickly. He didn't want to be presumptuous; but he had a conviction – it was a family of permanency he was working towards. Although it seemed he had nothing, he had everything he needed to start: God, ingenuity, strength and a willing heart to work hard for his love.

"Oh Malachi... I want to..."

At her words he took her in his arms and kissed her... and it wasn't a peck on the cheek of brotherly affection.

74.

Jake pushed open the door to the Barber shop and the bored little bell tinkled. "Be with you shortly," called Ali from the back area of the shop. She was hurrying to clean up – after the final customer for the day. A chapter in her life was closing. Jake flipped over the 'Open for Custom' sign and locked the latch. He pulled down the little blinds that covered the glass panels in the door. He sat on the waiting bench and picked up a newspaper to hide his fear. He didn't know what to say. He didn't have any idea how to begin. He prayed she would not shut him down before he began; however that might be.

"I was just about ready to close up for the day. Is there something that..." She couldn't see the face behind the newspaper but she knew exactly who it was. He didn't move. "I don't think it is a good idea that you are here. You should go," said Ali quietly.

He lowered the paper and folded it carefully and placed it on the bench. "There was a time when you begged me to come in for a hair-cut."

She looked warily at him, as she would a snake, wondering which way he would go. She wanted to slug him with a shovel.

"You even offered to do those trims for free... just to have me here."

Ali looked strategically for an escape, or something to defend herself with.

"But I always paid. I never took advantage of you Ali. Then or now. There was a reason for that."

Ali backed up and bumped into the barber chair, and inadvertently ended up sitting in it. She sat there ill at ease, trying hard to make the move look intentional.

"It is the same reason that I ended our rather flawed arrangement of convenience..."

Someone rattled the door and knocked on the glass. Ali did not move, paralysed by his quiet voice that went on relentlessly.

"I ended that... because I saw very clearly I was in the wrong. I said I wanted to be unattached, and I thought most sincerely that was the truth. But I met someone who changed my mind. I had the convenience of being in company, without the liberty to make a more lasting commitment. We had said that if we met someone, we would stop that arrangement. Of that I was guilty."

She had no idea he had known Laura way back then. Why didn't he mention her before?

"So, you see my dilemma. I am in love... silently in love... and I wait for a sign that this other person may be open to hearing the truth of my position. Gently... gently... I tell myself. I don't want to scare her off. I go about my business. I see her everyday... I preach every Sunday... waiting. I get my haircut. Still there is no sign that anything has changed. It is like a comfortable torture. A reality I live with. It goes on and on for so long I think it is dead... a lost hope."

He swallowed and avoided her eyes. He couldn't look. He had no idea if she is getting this or not. He continued before he lost momentum.

"Then along comes Laura. She is the epitome of what my ministry represents. She is traumatised, wounded, alone, carrying the scars of her history around in her body. She so desperately needs healing, and I have no solutions. Nothing I can do or say or offer her, impacts her world. My words… all that I hold out to her, like bread to a starving person… she rejects… even though I know this is her gateway to healing… her gateway to God. She just needed to allow herself to accept the bread. But she couldn't. I was praying for her one day and praying for myself – that I would be less obsessed with my one precious lost hope, and more focused on being what I had desired to be in the beginning: an instrument of restoration and peace and healing and hope…" He choked, and gruffly cleared his throat.

God… screamed Ali in her mind, *tell me it's true. Tell me Laura wasn't the reason he stopped the arrangement.* He stole a look towards the barber's chair where she sat like an ice-sculpture. For someone he spent so long watching and analysing, he felt he should have more luck reading her thoughts. He ploughed on doggedly, refusing to quit until he was finished.

"I believe God asked me to marry her. I don't understand that, but I know that today Laura returned that ring. She has chosen not to be my wife. And somewhere between those two places, she has found God and her healing has begun." There – he said it. He sat still, waiting for a response… anything. He remembered how a week ago, a similar declaration had elicited no response from him, for reasons that Ali could not possibly know existed.

Finally, he stood up. The polished wood on the floor seemed like glass that would crack any moment under the weight of his burden. "Ali, I have waited so long to tell you that I didn't want a relationship of convenience because I want to be your husband. I thought that I had been chosen to take a different road and I believed my hope… my selfish, earnest hope… would never come to pass. But last week, for the first time, I saw that perhaps you… no, I saw definitely, most clearly, into your heart and I don't know how I was so blind to what you allowed me to see. How could I not see that before? Last week, I did not have the liberty to let you know my sentiments, but now I have that freedom and I cannot wait another second. I know a lot can happen in a week, but please Ali… I'm dying here…"

"Welcome to my world," she whispered softly.

He cringed at the pain that sawed back and forth between them.

"Have things changed so much from last week?"

"A lot has changed. I've decided to leave Wattle Creek…"

"Leave? Why would you go?"

"To see you married to another woman would be too hard to bear."

"But I have told you... Laura made that decision. We will not be marrying."

He stuffed his hand in his pocket and pulled out the little puzzle ring. Ali's ring. She stared at it, almost in panic. "Why couldn't *you* choose me?"

"I chose you long ago. The rest… like I said… I didn't feel that was my choice." He walked over the glass, treading softly and knelt in front of the barber's chair, his emotion reflecting in the mirror of her eyes. "Ali… all this feels so very inadequate. I wish I could explain it better. You must know I never pretended to let Laura think I had the measure of romantic affection one would normally expect from a husband. I couldn't lie. She even knew why it was so, even though I tried to guard my emotions well…"

"But still you would have gone through with it?"

Suddenly Jake stopped, an idea dawning on him, shedding light on what had been a confused, dark night of his soul. "Perhaps this was my Isaac. Abraham was asked to sacrifice the thing dearest to him… his son Isaac. But at the critical moment God provided a way out. He needed to know that Abraham would have gone through with it. Oh Ali. You are the thing dearest to me; and I see that God has released me… but perhaps he needed to see first I would follow through if He asked me to."

She looked at him cautiously, her heart pounding in her throat, as if she was not sure that his declaration was real. "Well, that could explain why I have felt bound up, laid out and tied to a stake for a burning. For the record, this has been the hardest week of my life. I don't want to leave Wattle Creek."

"Then don't leave; because if you do, I will follow you to the ends of the earth."

"I don't want to give up my barber shop."

"Stay... you don't have to give up the shop."

"I don't want you to marry anyone else."

"Ali, there is only one way to be sure: you marry me."

"Just this morning you were officially engaged to someone else. Can you do that?"

"I can if you are willing. Officially – I agree it does not look good. And I confess... it may not be easy. My reputation is marred; my livelihood is dubious. I cannot even cook. It seems I have nothing worthy to offer you."

Ali reached down and held his face in her hands as he knelt there. "Lloyd Charles William Herbert Jacobson, you came to The Creek with no reputation, and a terrible haircut. We worked on those then and we can work together at whatever comes our way from here. I can teach you to cook, and you have offered me your devotion, which is worth so much..." She paused for a moment as her voice faded with emotion and she swallowed. "Yes, I will marry you."

He rested his forehead on her knee in a brief moment of relief. Finally... finally... "Oh Ali... may I give you back your ring? It was always yours. Remember we talked about our friendship being bound together with God as the third band, always linking us together? I want this to be the pattern for our marriage as well." He gently slipped it over her finger.

She caressed it affectionately. "I love this ring: everything about it is perfect – it cannot be any other way. It was the hardest thing for me to relinquish this. I so desperately wanted to keep it."

Jake shook his head. He had been so convinced it was a sign of her indifference. "Why… why didn't you? I wanted you to have it."

"Perhaps I had an Isaac too, and this ring represented that. My one disappointment was that it was loose, not binding and firm, as a commitment-ring should be. The first thing I will do is have it resized."

"It is a commitment ring now… binding, for every part of life, not just for social convenience. I want to buy another ring too, one worthy of you Ali. I will…"

She smiled and gently leaned back in the chair, looking up at him as he stood to his feet. "Lloyd Jacobson… you need a haircut. No fiancé of mine will go about town looking like a vagrant."

"Please be gentle. My last visit to a barber has left me a little nervous. I was cut. And I think you should know, my beloved is a barber of great repute and she will not tolerate scruffy, shoddy workmanship."

How she loved the sound of that: "my beloved". She moved then, and lowered him in the chair. She ran her fingers through his hair, her touch slowing and lingering over the fall of his part. "Oh Jake, I have done your hair countless times, and it never felt like this…"

He was spellbound by her touch. "I would have to agree…"

She closed her eyes, unwilling to pick up the blade to start. Tears fell freely and he swivelled in the seat to hold her. "Ali, my dearest, I am so sorry. I wish it hadn't been like that. I wish you did not have to go through the waiting for this."

"Perhaps it is the more precious because I see now how valuable it is… and how fragile. Oh Lloyd, we must, we *must* fight to protect this… always."

"Ali, I have seen you in action. I know you can hold your own. I promise you here, now, I know that there will be times when we will fight and disagree... but for every argument, it will be first covered in my respect and my love for you."

"If I know that you love me, and you want the best for me, then we can work on the rest. Please, I beg your patience. I have been working so hard at being independent; it has become a habit..." She wiped her eyes and smiled gently, turning the chair back so she could comb his hair once more. "Once we clean you up, there are cooking lessons to complete…"

"Not sure about the cooking. My last experience was pretty dreadful also… too many knives flying around for my liking."

"But Nat needs you to do it. It is part of your job."

"It is true. Just now I would prefer a different job, one that does not involve knives."

"Oh. That would be disappointing…"

"Why? You want a cook for your husband?"

"I want you as my husband; not what you do. But the thing is… Em is going out to the farm when she is married. Our business has grown and it needs two barbers, and I was thinking Wattle Creek would need a new barber. But it could not work if the candidate was adverse to blades."

Jake reached up and quietly held her hand as she combed his hair. "Ali? Are you asking me to work for you?"

She shook her head, their eyes connecting in the reflection of the mirror. "Oh no. I'm asking you to work *with* me. Jake..."

"Ali? Is this what you would like? Side by side?" He stared at her in the mirror. It was perfect. His pastoring days were not over.

She nodded, and smiled a little mischievously. "And I could keep an eye on my husband, in case he feels led to save some other poor destitute from a life on the streets."

"Lack of trust is not a great way to start a partnership, much less a marriage."

"Jake, believe me I wouldn't let you lose on my customers, if I did not trust you,"

He smiled, and stretched out full in the chair. "As long as *you* always do my hair..."

75.

The Church's one foundation
Is Jesus Christ her Lord:
She is His new creation
By water and the word;
From heaven He came and sought her
To be His holy bride;
With His own blood He bought her,
And for her life He died.

The congregation shuffled their hymnals and as the last verse finished, books were snapped shut and they sat down. Laura sat with her mother, the words of the hymn sinking deep into her spirit. New insights would burst into her understanding at unexpected times. The revelations would make her heart pound in anticipation. *Lord God! You are my foundation! It is Your work in my life... each life... that will build up Your Church. How amazing... that You see this motley crew as your bride. You declare your love for her... just as Malachi declares his love for me.* As she thought it, she turned her head just slightly... and caught his eye. He was unable to look anywhere else.

Everyone craned their necks to watch Reverend Bernard walk to the front. The shuffling ceased. "Brothers and Sisters in Christ..." Reverend Bernard cleared his throat nervously. Things rarely stay the same, but how tempting to pretend that his extended absence was a version of long service leave and just revert to the comfortable way things had been.

"I have been away for a long time. And it is good to be back. But you will find some things changed with me. That is why I wrote the letter describing all that has happened. It was essential that you understood what you were getting, in inviting me to return to this position."

Doctor Wallace had read the letter at the Congregational meeting. It had been received with a stunned sort of silence, until Phil Pollock stood firmly to his feet. "It is my understanding that there is none of us hasn't got something in our past that we ain't perfectly proud of. That is what the grace of God is. The man has done what he could to set it right. I see no reason not to go ahead. He's being up front with what happened."

"This time..." said someone from the back. "He told us he was resigning because he was going to nurse his dying sister."

"So, you think it would have made us more understanding if he had said he was going to nurse the mother of his daughter, whom he hadn't known existed... to a woman who wasn't his wife?"

"Well what about the fact this daughter is pregnant and not married? That ain't good. If a man can't control his own children..."

"I ain't goin' to dispute the girl's story. Hasn't she been through enough?"

"Why can't Jake come back? It's not his kid... and the Reverend confirms he was only marrying her to give it a name. Besides, I heard that Laura-girl called it off."

Doctor Wallace looked at the polished timber floor. Everything they said was true. How is it that we can't turn back the clock? Their demand for Jake's resignation was emotional and premature. In the end, they accepted his resignation, and offered the position to Reverend Bernard, knowing that the two would work together, depending on the level of ongoing care Linnet would need.

Reverend Bernard looked at the faces of the congregation. He could hardly explain the changes that had been forged into his heart in the time he was gone. "The last two years has been like an enforced separation from family... and even though I was reunited with my own family whom I thought was lost to me for this lifetime, I missed this... I missed you." His hand swept over the faces of the church.

"But now..." He stood before this group of unlikely friends, and called them family. How tragic: he spent so many years feeling isolated and alone when he had family with him all the while, waiting to be acknowledged. His voice wavered with unfamiliar emotion. "But now, God in His grace has restored to me a double portion: my family within my family. I confess to you, that I wondered if it was correct and proper, that someone responsible for so much heartache even had the right to presume to take up such a position again."

A ripple of uneasiness flickered through the church. It was unexpected Reverend Bernard would be willing to say outright what had been bandied around behind the closed doors of a congregational meeting. Would he leave, now, after all this?

"But three things reassured me that this privilege was not out of reach. It was this hymn that spoke these things to me, and that is why I chose to sing it this morning.

"The first is that, sin is sin... even if unintentional, and without malicious motivation. And God is still God... even for the intentional and the malicious things that we do. *'With His own blood He bought her, And for her life He died'*. Christ died for my sin... and my failure. Whether I meant to or not, does not even come into the equation.

"The second thing is that God is in the business of re-creation, not just restoring old furniture, giving a repair-job. He is about doing a new thing. I am *'His new creation - by water and the word'*. My past is not just buried and hidden out of sight... but it is being transformed... changed from the very essence of my core.

"Lastly... God is actively searching for his family so it can be restored and complete. *'From heaven He came and sought her; To be His holy bride'*. God is not content to let things ride out as they are. He is a groom, wooing his bride – jealous of her unfaithfulness, and tender in supporting her through pain and labour. I didn't actively seek this position; but God was, on my behalf. You voted, when I didn't even apply. How like God: to open doors we thought were closed forever. It comes down to one thing...

The Church's one foundation
Is Jesus Christ her Lord:

"This is not about me – Laurance Bernard. Nor is it about my wife, Linnet and our years of separation. Nor is it about our daughter Laura, conceived and conceiving out of wedlock. Or whether she has a marriage to protect her own child's violent beginnings. As far as a minister of the Gospel of

Christ goes, that is a pretty grim rap sheet. Thank goodness each of us is being transformed, wooed by the eternal groom through our pain. He loves his Bride enough to die for her."

He spoke quietly and firmly. He calmly took a seat behind the altar, but no one for a moment assumed he was finished. Somehow they understood, even though he had always been a learned man, now he was speaking out of his heart, and it gave a genuine authority to what he was saying.

"No one is exempt from such extravagant grace. I am included; you are included; our family is included; this church is included; all of Wattle Creek is included. I have met with Pastor Jake, and we are keen to work together, because this is our commission... our privilege... and our obsession: to help build such a community on that foundation of grace! It is a place to build friendships... a place to raise families... and a place to connect with our Father God. We honour your invitation to join you in this venture."

76.

There was a firm knock at the door. Josie opened the door and quickly showed the gentleman into the living room, closing the door against the wind. She jammed the long sand filled sausage along the bottom of the step to block the draught blowing through as she latched the door firmly. The fire burnt low in the hearth, and he gravitated towards the fading warmth. It was a miserably cold day and his suit coat had tell-tale signs of dust and grime around the collar, a sure indication he had come in by coach. "You are fortunate sir; I have a room available for tonight. How long would you be looking to stay?"

"I'm here on business, but I expect to be on the next coach out of town."

She nodded, mentally working through the things that needed to be done: clean towel, fresh water, an additional meal... the list automatically played in her head. She opened her register and asked him to sign against the date. He handed over his lodging and paused. She looked at him impatiently. She needed to start the extra chores now.

"Mrs Lawson. I am here on business..."

"Yes, yes, so you said. There is a lamp on your desk. You are welcome to work there."

He cleared his throat uncomfortably. "I would like to make an appointment with you... on this matter of business. My client has..."

She looked suspiciously at the cut of his suit. "Me? Whatever are you talking about? You are a lawyer?"

He nodded soberly. "I represent..."

Josie's face screwed up with tension, and her eyebrows knitted together anxiously. "You want an appointment with me? You are in Wattle Creek to call on me Mr..." She checked the register, "Mr Hanley?" she whispered. She looked at him, an unspoken question hanging between them. Fear started to spread its wings over her. He wished he had said nothing until the morning. He could see that she was agitated now she realised who he was. When he nodded, she quickly added, "Then I would like my son to be present. Malachi is of age."

"I just wanted to make a time..."

"Of course. Tomorrow. Ten o'clock..." The last thing she wanted to do was accommodate some lawyer coming to sue her out of some dark history. Why was it that every patron that came to board had something to needle her sense of security? Why couldn't she just put up a sign that said a waver of all liabilities, past and present, was required to be signed in blood before lodging could be offered?

"Mrs Lawson, thank you for understanding. It has been a long day. No one is trying to sue you." She jolted as she realised he had read her mind. He smiled, reassuring her, "It is a very common assumption. I'm sure you appreciate lawyers have a very low satisfaction-index when it comes to visiting."

She looked at him curiously then. She suspected he was making sport of her position. She cleared her throat. "Tomorrow then. Dinner tonight will be served at seven if you would like to join us. Of course – given you have been traveling, I can put something light on a tray for you to have in your room." She was hoping he'd opt for the room suggestion, so that she didn't have to sit through a meal with him at the table.

He offered a tired smile again. "No, I would be delighted to join you in the dining room. I feel like I have been eating off my lap for a week."

Josie nodded curtly. "And... breakfast is at six." He picked up his bag, and followed her to his room.

The next day he disappeared after breakfast and at exactly ten o'clock emerged from his room with a smart leather case. "Mrs Lawson, is there somewhere we can talk privately?"

She nodded and opened the door to the dining room. Malachi was sitting at the table reading the local newspaper. He rose and shook the man's hand. "Mr Hanley. Mum tells me you have requested a meeting."

He sat down very officially – his thinning hair slicked to the side. "Mrs Lawson, Mr Lawson..."

"Sir – you're old enough to be my father. Just call me Malachi."

"Ma'am. My client is... Matthew Lawson, your late husband."

Josie gasped and covered her mouth with her hand. She started to shake as her face went pale. "Take it easy Mum... let's just hear what the man has got to say. My father died twenty years ago," he said looking at Mr Hanley.

"Yes, may he rest in peace. Mr Lawson engaged our services just prior to moving here to Wattle Creek. He gave some very clear instructions, and it is now my incumbent duty to follow those through."

"This is ridiculous. Twenty years!"

"I must apologise Madam, our instructions were to make this visit after your youngest son..." he looked significantly in Malachi's direction, "Malachi's twenty-first birthday. Mr Lawson clearly stated that these directions were to be carried out, even if he was no longer living. I have to say, at the time of Malachi's birthday, two years ago, my brother passed away and there were a number of matters during that period which he handled that were overlooked. It is my endeavour to attend to these things now, on his behalf."

Josie stared straight ahead. Malachi put his hand on her arm, as Mr Hanley opened up his leather case. "His instructions were clear and simple. He has a number of bonds and stocks for your sons, and yourself... and a letter for each of you. These were sealed and were not to be opened until this time. I have taken the liberty of valuing the bonds and stocks. They are a tidy amount. Given the time-frame, they have done well... without exception."

Josie took the envelopes and signed for them. "Couldn't you just have mailed them?"

Mr Hanley nodded. "Yes... but given the nature of bequests and requests after the death of a loved one, my preference is to handle these things in person. It seems more in keeping with the wishes of the client."

Josie nodded. "You are right to assume that this is no easier than then when his last will and testament was read. Why now?"

"Mr Lawson... senior, was a friend of my brother... and I can only assume that they had discussed this in detail and that Matthew respected his ability to handle such matters." He paused and waited a moment. "Mrs Lawson... that is all. Thank you for your time. Please contact me if you have any further concerns regarding this. I am booked on the coach that returns the day after tomorrow – so I am at your leisure until then." He stood respectfully and turned to leave.

Malachi stood. "Hang on a minute. Am I correct in assuming this service was paid for by my father?" Mr Hanley nodded. "We owe you nothing?" Malachi clarified. Again, he nodded. "Then why are you here?"

Mr Hanley looked quite unperturbed by the challenge. "You are correct. Mr Lawson paid for the transaction. It is only right his instructions should be delivered in the sentiment intended."

"Well then, I'd like to see the original inventory of the stocks and bonds." Malachi stood by the table and thoughtfully folded his newspaper and put it to one side. Josie stared at him; the action caused waves of melancholy to crash over her. The mannerism was like looking at Matthew twenty years ago. "You see I have a problem. The problem is this: a lawyer has travelled for three days, on a twenty-year-old account; even though we were none the wiser of it. He'll get nothing for his efforts because my father already paid for the service two decades ago. Now even for the average ethical businessman that appears overly altruistic. Sir, the inventory?"

He coughed a little, looking carefully into Malachi's face. "Hmmm. The original details of the stocks and bonds?" He hesitated. "You must understand..."

"The thing I understand is that its omission is pretty unprofessional given you have been so meticulous about following his instructions in everything else... *with* the spirit intended. It appears that I would not be unreasonable in assuming some of these stocks and bonds may have been *lost* in transit. Because I am absolutely confident such an original list was submitted."

"Embezzlement is a serious crime sir. What is the basis of such an accusation?" Mr Hanley almost looked amused by the allegation.

Malachi looked at the man with contempt. "I have lived with the way my father did things for twenty-three years. You get to know the system behind it. I suggest you produce the inventory because, I repeat, I know on my father's grave such a register exists."

Mr Hanley pulled out the chair and sat back down at the table. "You think like a lawyer Malachi Lawson. If you ever want to explore such a position I am looking to engage an intern..."

"And what makes you presume I would work for someone who steals from widows and orphans? Goes to *character*, your Honour."

Mr Hanley's eyes held an amused glint. He placed his leather case on the table and opened it. He pulled out a file and extracted two yellowed sheets of paper that he pushed across the table towards Malachi. "I believe this is what you are looking for. This file is for your perusal also. Excuse me Ma'am. I will go and make a cup of tea. Then I might have a look around town."

Josie said nothing. It was bleak outside, hardly the weather for sightseeing, but she was too relieved to see him leave to protest. She sat with her back straight and her heart bent and beaten. She held in her hand three *envelopes addressed to her sons*. She handed them to Malachi. "Please see that your brothers get their envelopes... in person." She silently rose and disappeared into her room like an apparition. That was how she felt: drained of body, substance, life. It was too much. She couldn't go on. Josie sat in the severe tall backed chair in her private room. She leant heavily on the little desk beside her as she stared at the envelope. It had her name written across the front in his hand-writing. "Oh Matthew – why now?" These bonds could have relieved such burden all those years ago. If she had known about them eighteen months ago, they could have pooled them to restore the farm and take advantage of the rains. Even six months ago! A swarm of "what-ifs" buzzed about her head.

A sickly queasiness swam around her stomach as she swallowed some acidy reflux. She hardly knew how to confront this evidence. Was it, Matthew's provision or his neglect? A Kookaburra laughed, late and cold in the morning mist. The words of Reverend Bernard rang in her ears. "Anger is your snake Josie. You need to let it go, before it poisons you."

Finally... she weakly broke the seal. The familiar handwriting sprang from the page. How could she so easily forget the way he wrote? It took a long time to muster the courage to read:

"My dearest Josie,

I can hardly image how life will have matured and developed when we are reading this letter. Forgive my dramatics. This mini time-capsule to give a check on all the ambitions, and goals and dreams we have for our family. We have flown these dreams around like the brightly painted kites I fly in the spare block down the street with Nathaniel and his neighbourhood mates. They are grand ideals that have pushed us to move on, to start a new style of life. Plans that are colourful and bold; plans that need lots of string and a fair toss of wind to fly...

Yet I fear that in the grind of daily life, we might look back and see nothing like our youthful hopes have materialised. Or we may look back and be able to confidently agree, regardless how things look, we have chosen to stay and fight. We have persevered and battled those things that came against us to destroy our family, and prevailed. With God's grace this is what I pray for.

During the first week of each of our boy's lives, during those busy, tired, magical days when they were so tiny they could rest on my forearm, softly smelling of their mother's milk, I wrote each a letter. It is a prayer: a statement of a father's prophetic hope for his sons. These letters are enclosed for them to read now that they are men. I want them to see the things I saw then as I prayed over them. These hopes are birthed in the spiritual and I pray that God would take what he sees in their potential and grow that seed to a harvest. Only the Father sees how many apples are in the apple-seed.

And for you my beloved... my soul mate... my love. Life is a mystery, forged like wrought iron in a blacksmith's coals. The intricate patterns can be fine, like lace, under the hand of the master's anvil and hammer, or chunky and cumbersome when we kick against the goads. I cannot presume to know where and how we will be, when we read this letter twenty-one years from now, but I know that God is faithful. He restores... delivers... protects... provides.

Just now it is hard to imagine ever having to struggle to be proud of our boys. Yet this is our mandate: to love regardless of the choices they make, regardless of the tone of their hearts or the style of friendships they will choose. God give us grace for those things, when kissing grazed knees is no longer the greatest pain they bear.

So, Josie, here is to a sweet future. Whether the weather has been fair and fine, or bitterly cold... or blistering hot... I pray that together we will be sweet, that our attitude and character will be like music that will make our Heavenly Father's heart sing with pride.

God bless you my darling... abundantly, totally, more than we can hope or imagine...

Your devoted husband always...
~ Matthew

When Josie finally stirred, she found herself kneeling by the chair, her face drenched with tears, the letter crumpled in her clenched hand. *"Oh God... I have worshiped a god other than You. I have looked to Matt for the love and security that he knew only comes from You. Forgive me Lord... forgive my unwillingness to let him go... and the anger it festered. I hardly know how to let it go... how to live without it. Please help me. Hanging on is killing me... I know it... but I have forgotten how to drop it to the rocks. Is it possible to restore in me a sweet spirit when bitterness has been my byword for so long? God, please... I beg you... restore to me the dreams of my husband. Matt prayed for the girls the boys would marry and all I have considered is that they will steal my sons away. Help me to embrace them as I know he would have. You have brought them into my life... just as I have come into theirs. Help me..."*

She stayed by the chair as the chilled air seeped in under the door and crept along the timbered floor. When she finally rose, stiff from the cold, new warmth had started to grow in her heart; a quiet, unobtrusive glow, of a dream restored to life, and the flavour of it was as sweet as sugar.

77.

Malachi sat at the table staring at the papers before him. He had gone through the file line by line. He had matched each entry, and accounted for all the stocks and bonds. Nothing was out of place. It was as tidy and sorted as everything else Matthew Lawson had done. But there was one piece of paper that froze his mind. It was a letter confirming the payout from a partnership: Simons, Hanley and Lawson. The name matched the typed letterhead on some of the other documents. Simons, Hanley and *Lawson*? His father was a *partner* of a lawyer's firm? Not just an office worker turned illegitimate farmer? How could he know so much about the ways and character of a man, and not know that he had chosen to leave such a profession? It explained so much: how he had money to move and buy up a farm; his attention to detail, like this visit from the past. He didn't remember ever asking, but he had built a picture in his mind that they had lived, if not in destitution, at least very modestly in the city: grimy, cold and overpopulated. The assertion that farming was a choice – he had never considered that perhaps it really was embracing a genuine heart-felt opportunity. He had always assumed it was the lesser evil of two poor options. Did he have to leave? Had he been caught doing something wrong? Why would he make such a dramatic change?

Then Malachi read his father's personal letter. On the very threshold of becoming a father himself, he had in his hand a transparent communication, parent to child, father to son.

The words reflected his desire, not just to have a house but a home, a lasting heritage. Of all the things he knew about his father, this he understood: the desire to build a legacy that would span the confines of mortality.

It also screamed a lot of questions. There was a knock on the door, disrupting his musing and Mr Hanley came in. "So, Malachi, have you had an opportunity to audit the documents?"

He nodded. "Yes, everything is in order."

"You looked disappointed. Are you shocked?"

"A little. It would be simpler if you were a snake. This letter... Simons, Hanley and Lawson... who are they?"

"The firm. Hanley was my brother... who died recently, as I mentioned. Lawson is your father of course. Simons offered me the partnership a few years after your father left. So, it was Simons, Hanley and Hanley for a while."

Malachi shook his head and shrugged. "I didn't know... or I had forgotten, that my father was a lawyer. I think of him as just an office worker... accountant's clerk maybe..."

Hanley raised his eyebrows some. "I understand he was good, but it didn't always sit well with him. Some things are just law. Our office handles a lot of the mundane. He got restless..."

"You said your brother was the friend through whom my father made this arrangement?" Hanley nodded. "Did you know my father? Did he *have* to leave? Was it something that was recommended due to... ahh... circumstances?"

"I didn't know him well. I was a junior intern working under the supervision of Fredrick. My brother is... was fifteen

687

years my senior. In the end – yes, your father had to leave because Simons was ready to kill him for bailing out." He chuckled... "Your father was liked and respected. There was nothing untoward in his exit that I am aware of. You resemble him Malachi. I was quite serious in my offer..." He put his card on the table and pushed it towards him.

"Your brother was Fredrick?" Malachi mused. "My middle name is Fredrick." He coughed and stood to his feet and reached forward in a handshake. It was an offer with the means to provide a home... to start a new life... to make choices... to fight in a different ring. It had appeal. "Thank you for your time Mr Hanley. I will seriously consider your proposal. Perhaps choice cuts both ways..."

Banging at the door interrupted Mr Hanley's response. Sarah bundled into the room flustered. "Malachi. Mal... your wife... Laura... Sister Tyler... the midwife has called for you... the baby is on the way..."

Mal leapt to his feet, the chair crashing behind him as he bolted for the door. He stopped suddenly and paused. He returned and grabbed the card from the table. "Mr Hanley excuse me," he said pumping the man's hand, calling as he left. "Sarah, go and get Doctor Wallace... and the Reverend. Laura's father is about to meet his grandson!"

He ran down the street. Laura had been restless this morning when he had told her of his mother's meeting with the lawyer, but he had put it down to her strained relationship with his mother. It had not even entered his head it might be time... or that he would be gone so long. When he arrived, Sister Tyler had already taken dominion of their little home and it had the feel of a military camp. There was water boiling on the stove and clean linen stacked on the sideboard. She had flannel wraps in the warming tray under the stove and the bassinette stood empty beside the fire as well.

Malachi tried to push past into the bedroom, as he heard Laura's muffled groans, but was firmly and severely blocked by Sister Tyler's bulk. "Mrs Wallace and I have this all in hand young man. Don't think for a moment you can bully your way in here. This is women's business. You sit there and have a cup of tea, or I'll send you straight back to your mother's house. Do you understand?"

He nodded mutely. Arrogant, pompous, conceited, self-opinionated woman! Laura needed him too! He clenched and unclenched his fist. Why was his reflex to want to solve a problem by slugging someone? Dr Wallace came and sat by him at the table and poured himself a cup of tea. He put a gentle restraining hand on his arm. "Sister Tyler is the best midwife I've come across. She knows what Laura needs."

He thumped the table when he heard more muffled cries come from the bedroom. "Shouldn't you be in there Doc?"

"No... she is doing well. Nothing is going wrong. Believe me I prefer not to attend any births. That would mean they all go well. 'Well' does not mean easy... unfortunately. It is not an easy business..."

The vigil continued. Reverend Bernard came and made a pot of coffee. Malachi went out and cut up some fire wood for the wood-box... and then kept going until the whole wood pile was split, just so he didn't have to listen to Laura through

689

the thin walls. As evening closed in, Jake came with Nathaniel and sat with him on the porch oblivious to the icy cold that ripped through their coats, watching the hurricane lantern swing in the wind. When they could stand it no longer, they went back inside and thawed out by the stove.

Around two o'clock in the morning, Sister Tyler called Dr Wallace. Malachi jolted from his doze on the lounge, Nat restraining him as fear jumped into his eyes. Sarah shuffled to and fro, fetching wraps and clean water and fresh linen. Then the tiny cry of a newborn broke through the night air... and when Sister Tyler emerged after what seemed an eternity with the bundled package of new life, Malachi thought his heart would stop. Doctor Wallace stood behind her. "Congratulations Malachi, you are a father. A healthy daughter."

"Daughter?" A girl? Why had they always assumed the baby was a boy? "Laura? Is she okay?"

"She is doing magnificently. Here son, sit down and meet your baby girl."

He sat weakly and took her in his arms, gazing into the tiny face, wrinkled and puckered from all the cares of her short harrowing life. He smiled... amazed, and stood up and walked past them into the room where Laura lay asleep. She stirred as he bent down and kissed her, holding their daughter between them. "Beautiful lady, we have a daughter, Anne Grace Lawson."

She smiled through her exhaustion, resting back on the pillow. "Lady bug, lady bug ~ fly away home... All except one and that's little Anne..."

Malachi stared at the baby in his arms, pride swelling in his chest as he thought of both his girls. "So starts the next generation of Lawsons. *Together we have a lasting heritage to build.* By the Grace of God, I trust we do as well for Anne. You know Laura, I think I have a letter to write..."

The End